To Stu Fi

Years of Faithful Service —

NIGHT RIVER

Wow!
Hopefully This is A
Book —

Mac

HUGH MACMULLAN III

Contents

CHESTER ISLAND
CHAPTER ONE

I was having a perfect evening. Then I heard the yelling and saw the lights.

Perfect – everything I'd hoped for and needed for four years – the slap of benign waves on the hull, the sigh of shrouds in the breeze and the gentle rocking. I watched two ospreys work the shallows, saw herons commuting back to their nests for the night and maybe saw a bald eagle. Perfect.

In the thickening dusk, my sailboat lay at anchor east of Chester Island away from the thunder of the Philadelphia Airport and out of the Delaware River's shipping channel. Leaning against the mast, I watched the sun set to starboard, over the Island – fizzing its treetops, reflecting off the River's muddy waters and back-lighting the City of Chester.

One wristwatch, the black plastic Timex, read 6:59 p.m.; the other, a Suunto 10X Wrist Top GPS/watch reminded me it was 3:59 a.m. in Kandahar. Sergeant Johnson had given me the Suunto the week before, my next-to-last day in-country. "At least part of me will get out of here," said Johnson. "Return it to me if I get stateside, Lieutenant. Keep it safe."

I smiled at the memory, and considered how my world had flipped – gone from foot-patrolling bomb-laced streets, using the need to set an example and dark humor to offset the fear every sane Marine experienced – to sleeping out, alone, overnight on a dark river, anchored safely, with my boat, my dog, my favorite single malt and my thoughts.

The sailboat, *Larke*, was a diminutive black-hulled beauty, a Victoria 18. I'd bought it when I was eighteen; and I laughed at folks who thought it was too small for the river. Hell, I'd taken it through the C & D Canal and half-way down the Chesapeake and downriver to the edge of the Atlantic Ocean. She was bulletproof – made in the early days of fiberglass boats, when everything was overbuilt. I love her.

I also love my dog. Smokey is an eight year-old black Lab; and she is quiet, obedient and very bright. Her dog equivalent I.Q. is about 190. She's smarter than some people I know. My Pops said Smokey needed no training – she came from the kennel in South Dakota, in a crate, by air freight, seven weeks old, weaned, already knowing everything a dog needed to know.

I'm the only person I know who fishes seriously from a sailboat. The shrouds, stays, mast and boom get in the way of casting, the boat can't travel faster than five knots, and it has no live-well or fish-finder. But the very challenge of fishing from *Larke* somehow makes it more worthwhile; and I love to anchor, place two rods in improvised rod holders and bottom fish for channel catfish. I read, nap and look up at the rod tips every so often – and think about things. In Iraq and Afghanistan, if I had trouble falling asleep, I'd imagine how I might land an eighty pound striper from *Larke*, anchored in the River, alone and at night.

Before the commotion, I'd been thinking about the life I'd led for four years and the life I might lead for the next fifty or so. I'd paid for my Wharton degree with an NROTC scholarship, taken the Marine Corps option, and done the Quantico, Camp Lejeune, Iraq, Afghanistan thing. I made Captain the day I was discharged. The Marine Corps, in the form of my Company Commander, told me they'd miss me. I knew I'd miss the Corps right back, believed I was better off for the experience, was in great shape, was only a little worn out from the stress of it all, and had made friends I'd stay in touch with forever. I was not tempted to be a lifer.

I was one week away from beginning the job I'd gone to Wharton to obtain: an analyst's position at Howell & Barrett, Philadelphia's flourishing boutique investment banking firm. Barrett himself, then a sixty-three year old former Marine, had hired me four years prior. When he'd heard of my pending four year commitment, he'd stood, reached out for my hand and said: "Semper Fi. You're hired."

He'd told me he'd be happy to wait for me, that I'd be worth more to him in four years, and that four years would come around sooner than I thought. He'd laughed at my name, Ryan O'Brien, and said my parents had a sense of humor. I told him I was named after a favorite uncle and was only half Irish; and I accepted the position immediately. I was to have my own small office, share an administrative assistant, the very best technology support, and have free access to a nearby health club. The job had a future. I had a future. Plus, no landmines were going to blow my balls off on the way to work.

Flashlights and yelling in the dark on Chester Island seemed impossible – the Island was empty. The tiny satellite image of the Island on Johnson's Suunto displayed nothing but brown grass, a few stands of trees and areas of mud. The Island's elevation was listed as four feet. Its shape was that of a deep-bellied triangle – a deltoid – aimed north-west. I decided to have one last patrol before joining the corporate world, one more for "L" Company, 3rd Battalion, 6th Marines. I told myself this was not a restless need for action, but action to preempt a restless need for action. Maybe the single malt with the huge, smoke and peat finish knew what I meant. One more foot patrol, before I started the rest of my life.

• • •

Anchor aweigh – and on the outgoing tide, *Larke* drifted toward the Island. I anchored again, careful not to rattle the chain rode. We were in three feet of water, thirty yards from the southeast side of the Island and away from the lights and noise. I eased over the side, barefoot, into the water, into shin-deep muck, sandals tucked in my shorts. Smokey whined. Either she wanted to come with me or she didn't want me to go. I considered her feelings, how I'd left her with Pops off and on for most of four years, and called her over into the water with me.

I tried to recall the name of the Sergeant who'd said: "take your time. Stay away from the easy going. Never go the same way twice." I knew he'd said it on Guadalcanal and that I'd come up with his name eventually. Meantime, although it was easy to take my time in the river muck, it certainly was not easy going – at least for me. On the other hand, Smokey paddled along effortlessly beside me, looking up at me from time to time. I got the message, and abandoned walking, launching myself forward in an awkward breaststroke.

Near the Island, the bottom turned sandy; and when we reached the shore, there was a two-foot strip of beach. I put my sandals on, Smokey shook herself and we edged to our right into marsh grass. There was no moon yet. Johnson's magic wristwatch informed me that it would rise at 8:21 p.m. and be 74% visible. There was a breeze from the southwest. We couldn't see the flashlights from our position, and the yelling had stopped. I crept forward, Smokey walked slowly, snuffing at the air; and I used the Suunto's compass and GPS features to navigate us into a stand of trees.

We lay there quietly, listening, getting used to the dark. I recalled parts of a poem by Emily Dickinson – something about "when light is put away . . ." and "something in the sight adjusts itself to Midnight . . . ." It seemed to fit. Smokey's eyes and a trace of her graying muzzle became visible. She sniffed the breeze. There were no mosquitoes; and I assumed there was nothing much warm-blooded on the Island to feed them. There were crickets. A barred owl called, sounding a little like a dog. Smokey paid it zero attention, but seemed to be intrigued by the smell of something. She stood and stretched her nose forward; and I figured we'd head in that direction – but we'd take our time.

We groped, scrabbled and crawled, stopped often and stayed away from any easy going. I went hardcore Recon and rubbed mud on my face, hands and legs. The Island had its quota of blackberries; and their thorns plucked at my T-shirt. Smokey seemed to be enjoying herself – Recon Dog. I felt a little foolish, guessing that the end of the game might be a teenage beer bash. In that case, I'd simply return to *Larke* by a different route.

I'd been to a Basic Reconnaissance Course for two months at Camp Pendleton, near San Diego, but it was mostly theory, doctrine and concepts involving squad size recon aimed at specific targets. This was a one-man, one-dog recon for fun and ennui preemption – but if it was worth doing, it was worth doing right, and so I put all the skills I'd learned about movement, noise and route choice into the effort. We snaked our way in the general direction of the center of the Island, where I thought the flashlights were. I mostly crawled, with an occasional roll. Smokey walked beside me, sitting when I stopped to rest. We were very careful and very slow. It took us twenty-five minutes to cover fifty yards. I thought we were very good.

"You're very good," said a voice. "Now stand up and put your hands behind your head. Take two steps towards me."

Definitely not teenage drinkers, I thought. I stood, put one hand on Smokey's head and whispered, "stay." I took two steps forward and stopped, hands behind my head.

"You don't look familiar," said the voice. "Who are you?"

I figured that how I acted and what I said next was important. Keep me from being arrested. Or shot. This whole thing was weird. I decided to try so sow some confusion, offer some ambiguity. "Same team, different guy. How'd I do? When'd you make me?"

A figure stepped forward, one confident step, in camouflage, with a rifle pointed at me. First, I checked out his gear. The rifle was an M4 carbine with a noise suppressor. Civilians were not supposed to have this weapon. Hanging from his neck, the man had night vision goggles – image enhancers. Civilians did not need this piece of gear. I didn't think they had a thermal imaging feature, and supposed Smokey was safe as long as she was quiet and stayed put.

"We had you for over ten minutes," he said. "Nice moves. Recent military?"

Next I checked him out, kept talking. "Just out. Back from Afghanistan. A week."

Hmm. White. About my size, but soft. Incipient love handles. Camo pants, black shirt, do-rag. Tattoos up and down his arms. Not military. Certainly not Al-Qaeda – I'd be dead already. Who the fuck was this guy? Where were the others mentioned, the "we". What were they doing here?

I talked some more. "Got bored – you know. Signed up for this gig. Cool. Mostly did all Urban Recon in-country – you know. The slam-bang, hit the door type of stuff. Thought I'd give something quiet a try – you know. See if I'm as good as I thought I was." I noticed the M4 stayed pointed in my general direction.

Maybe he was stupid, slow, challenged in some useful way. "Where's the rest of the crew?"

Dumb enough to answer, anyway. "They went to check out a small boat, it showed up on the radar." He pointed to a mobile radar unit – a portable perimeter surveillance unit. Most important, he lowered the rifle. "How about some I.D."

Radar. Holy shit. Radar! The need for speed in the human central nervous system is not hard to understand. Thinking fast is a genetic adaptation directly connected to staying alive – avoiding the predator, killing your enemy. The panicky digital superhighway of the quarter of a million miles of axons in my brain chose this moment to go on autopilot – to bypass thinking and go right to talking. After it finished talking, I hoped it would think of something really clever to do.

"Sure," I said, taking one step towards him. "But I gotta tell you, your team is losing some points for the flashlights and noise. Who was responsible for that?"

"Shit – that's all on Marvin. Dumb fuck. We bin out here four times now. Nothin' ever happens. He gets bored. Fools around. Playing ghosts and stuff. You know?"

"Yeah," I said, "I heard he's on the brink. May have to be replaced. Lemme think about what to say in my debriefing. I won't lay it on you – you know. In fact, you'll get points for nailing me." I lowered my hands, raised my right wrist and lit up the Suunto, and started talking into it – like it was a recording device.

"It's 19:47 hours. This is Unit Two. I've been made after twenty-two minutes of creepy-crawly on Chester Island. Unit One still unobserved. Guard alert and professional. More at in-person debriefing." I unstrapped the Suunto and handed it to Oscar. "Talk into this," I said. "It's the latest gizmo. Tell 'em your name first."

He leaned the rifle against his leg, butt first on the ground and reached for the wristwatch – a little intimidated to be talking into it. "Where do I talk into? What am I supposed to say?"

"Right there," I said. "Start with your name."

"This is Max," he said.

BAM! I sucker-punched Max with a roundhouse right to the point of his chin, he sank to his knees and toppled over. I grabbed the rifle, used the butt to crush the goggles around his neck, his shoelaces to tie up his hands and feet and his do-rag to gag him. He was still out when I toppled the radar unit, smashed what looked like the expensive business end of it and took off, the rifle slung over my right shoulder. "Here Smokey," I whispered. "Good girl."

"Never go the same way twice." Now I remembered who said it. Gunny Sergeant Charles C. Arndt.

DOG GONE
CHAPTER TWO

The Island was dark; and we were moving fast. After thirty yards running, two falls and the loss of one sandal, I slowed to a walk. Lights from the Commodore Barry Bridge behind us, from the casino and racetrack across the river to my left and from the intermittent airplanes taking off from Philly International reminded me I was not in Afghanistan. Smokey appreciated the slowdown – she was not built for speed.

In situations like this, I had been trained to consider options, weigh them, and quickly decide which one had the best chance of success. The problem was, I didn't really know what success was – not going off on one last idiotic patrol would require a time machine; and I could only think of one acceptable option: getting Smokey, *Larke* and Ryan and his single malt impaired axons back to my boat club undetected. Then I could calmly think about the whole affair and decide what to do. If there was anything to do. Maybe I'd just forget about it all, stay away from this part of the River for awhile, and start thinking about a quiet, uneventful future at Howell & Barrett.

I decided to walk quietly to the two-foot ring of sand that made up the Island's beach, then jog to a spot near *Larke*. If no one was around – the rest of whoever was with Max (he'd mentioned a "Marvin") – we'd wade out to the boat, I'd haul eighty pounds of wet dog aboard and we'd make our getaway. We'd sail, use just the mainsail; and not start the noisy 4HP outboard auxiliary. A man, a dog, a plan.

Excellent hypothesis, lousy luck. There was no jogging. Trees leaned across the beach at random intervals and piles of water-logged driftwood slowed us further. I'd learned that the roots of a toppled tree were called "rootstocks", and that they remained in place long after the tree rotted away. I'd seen a few small ones in the pine woods at Camp Lejeune. Nothing like them existed in Afghanistan, of course, since anything flammable there was collected and burned for fuel. I'd never seen a rootstock as large as the one that loomed before us – fifteen feet tall and as wide – with gnarled, twisted roots spiraling out from its center, beckoning. It blocked the beach, extended out into the lowering tide and back into a tangle of vine-covered deadfall. The moon chose this moment to peek over the horizon, so I knew it was 8:21 p.m. It was going to be bright once it popped off the edge of the New Jersey trees on the mainland.

Smokey stopped, sniffing. I sensed she was about to growl and placed one hand over her muzzle. "Shh. Good girl," I whispered. I felt the bristling hairs on her neck, and figured something or someone was on the other side of the rootstock – between us and *Larke*.

I've acted on some really stupid ideas in my life, but most of those accomplishments resulted in calamities that hurt no one but me. I'd made sure that my platoon was well away from the napalm and gasoline-soaked brush pile before I'd exploded it, producing second-degree burns on most of my back and resulting in much head-shaking and lecturing from my C.O.; and sleeping in my Senior year in college, forgetting about a Monday Seminar – the day I was due to present – required lots of extra effort just to graduate, but affected no one else in the seminar; and falling in love with a girl in high school who was about to move a thousand miles away certainly hurt no one but me and my letter-writing fingers – cramped up from the necessity of asserting my love for her (she insisted that e-mails and texting wouldn't cut it) through marginally-legible, fountain-penned twice-a-week letters. This time, though, I really screwed up.

I decided that it was likely that someone was behind the rootstock, laying in ambush for me. Since I needed to get around the rootstock and off the Island to *Larke*, I decided to try to flush out the ambusher by heaving a hunk of driftwood out into the River, to my left – to see what developed. If nothing happened, I reasoned, it was likely that no one was really waiting for me. Maybe I'd throw more than one chunk of driftwood – over the rootstock, or into the tangle off to my right. At any rate, I grabbed a likely chunk of driftwood, cocked my right arm and let go – heaving it out into the River. Splash. Worst idea I'd ever had.

Smokey, fully endowed with the genetic mandate to retrieve, retrieve, retrieve, splashed noisily into the River, focused only on bringing back the driftwood to her idiot master. She chuffed out toward the stick. I heard the unique sound of three silenced rifle shots on semi-automatic: phut – phut – phut. Smokey swam on, oblivious to everything but the need to get the stick, the stick, the stick.

"It's a dog! It's just a dog! Don't shoot my dog! She's just a dog! Stop shooting! I give up if that's what you want." I stood up, prepared to walk around the rootstock with my hands up.

Phut, phut, phut, phut, phut – a short burst of automatic fire caused a brief churning of the River around Smokey; and she stopped swimming and floated, motionless.

"You bastards! That was my dog! You killed my dog! You fuckers! I was going to come talk to you. I was going to give up – surrender – or whatever you weirdos call it. You fuckers – now I'm going to kill you! You're dead! Dead!"

Ryan the high school football player would have charged around the rootstock, oblivious – down the field under the kickoff, insane with toxic teenage mix of adrenaline, testosterone and the exigent needs of team – coaches, girlfriend, parents and kid brothers watching. Ironically, the ". . . do you want to live forever . . . ." mentality – part of a likely quote by Sergeant Dan Daly, USMC two-time World War I Medal of Honor recipient – had been trained out of me by the very organization that glorified Daly. The Corps did not now want Marines dying, going one-on-one with an enemy having an endless supply of under-equipped suicidal whack jobs. If I was going to get even for Smokey's shooting, I was going to have to be at least a little bit smart about it.

"Here I come." I sprayed a short burst of automatic fire at the left edge of the rootstock. I squirreled to my right, into the tangles. I lay still. Quiet. Let them worry for a few minutes – think about what they'd done. I listened. I heard a whisper.

"Why'd you shoot, Marvin?" said a high-pitched voice. "It was a dog."

"Why not?" said a deeper voice – careless, not whispering at all. "What's the point of having these guns if we don't shoot 'em. Like you said – it was only a dog."

Then he yelled, to me: "bring it on pal. I'll do you just like your dumb dog."

I was quiet, thinking Smokey was smarter than Marvin. Had been – past tense. She was dead, damn it. Don't take the bait, I thought.

"Stop it. Don't talk." said the first voice. "That guy sounds really pissed. In fact, don't even whisper. That way he can't tell where we are."

"I'm not gonna talk. I'm leavin' you here to guard the beach. I'm goin' back to base. Gonna talk to Max. See what's up with him. Gonna check in with Bama. Stay here."

"No! You bastard. You did this! You deal with Mister Pissed-Off. You shot the dog. You stay here and you guard the beach. Bama's doing something to the boat anyway."

"Bye-bye," said Marvin. I heard him crash off through the brush – away from the river. I saw the bright circle of light from his flashlight bounce randomly over bushes, grass and trees.

• • •

I lay on my back, adding up what little I knew: 1 – the bastard who shot Smokey was leaving, heading back where he'd find Max; 2 – the bastard's name was Marvin, and that it was pronounced "Mar-*vin*," emphasis on the second syllable; 3 – Marvin was careless, noisy and using a flashlight; 4 – Marvin was an idiot, Max was none-too-bright, and the person on the other side of the rootstock seemed rational, but terrified; 5 – there must be others involved with this, others with smarts, with training and with some understanding of whatever it was that was going on out here on this lonesome, empty Island in the middle of seven million people; 6 – that person's name was likely "'Bama", short for "Alabama"; and, 7 – 'Bama was in the process of doing something to *Larke.*

Shit. An hour ago I'd been having a perfect evening – content with my boat and my dog – pondering the significance of a gift from a friend still in Afghanistan. Now *Larke* was in the hands of someone named 'Bama, Smokey was dead, and the Suunto lay on the ground next to Max, where I'd forgotten it. To undo some of this I'd need to kill Marvin, retrieve the Suunto and figure out what to do about 'Bama. Beating Marvin back to where Max lay bound and gagged was my first step.

"Stay here," I commanded the night air. "Keep your eye on that rootstock. If anyone shows their face, shoot 'em. I'll watch this side."

I moved ten feet or so to my left, directly behind the rootstock. I stage-whispered, in a near-falsetto, "yeah Sarge. No problem." I fired two rounds – one left, one right, and took off, quietly retreating back down the beach the way I'd come. I thought there was at least a possibility that the panicky person behind the rootstock would think there were two of us.

If I've been somewhere once, I'm very good at getting there again. Understand, I'm not all that great at finding something for the first time, especially at night. Night orienteering and compass marches in the featureless pine woods of Camp Lejeune always left me confused – often finding myself at the same wrong place several times. But if I'd been somewhere once, I could find it again, quickly and with confidence.

At Basic School, a Major Davis, instructing on night movement and location, once told me that I was potentially outstanding at night navigation; and he went on to talk about confidence, overcoming neural responses to lack of light, and navigation by subliminal use of something he'd called absentials – places and things that were not there. He'd offered me the opinion that I was utilizing first-tier absentials by remembering what wasn't there as I navigated to a place I'd been before; and that if I could learn to advance to using second-tier absentials, I'd be able to find just about anything, anywhere, anytime. I made the mistake of asking if there were third-tier absentials, and he'd gone on to bewilder me with mention of dark matter, the cosmos and the critical need for humankind to understand it someday. He baffled us, but we knew he could silently and unerringly find his way around in the dark. He was a Basic School legend, someone we talked about for years after graduation. I'd wished I'd had half of his skills in

Afghanistan; and I wished he was with me on Chester Island.

But I needed only to get back to the place where I'd tied up Max and ruined his night vision goggles, tipped over the radar and misplaced Johnson's Suunto. I thought of it as "headquarters". As long as I got to HQ before Marvin, Max was still tied up and 'Bama was not yet back from buggering *Larke*, things would work out. I honestly did not know exactly what I'd planned for Marvin. My first thought, while still enraged over the act, had been to disarm him, tell him why he was going to die and then to kill him – or shoot him in the balls – or something similar. Two minutes into my hike back to Max, I knew I wasn't killing anyone; but I was still pissed enough to do something awful to Marvin.

I got back to HQ with ample time to spare. I don't know if I used absentials to navigate, but by then, the moon was high enough overhead to help with visibility. I crept up on Max, now awake and struggling with the shoelaces that I'd used to tie up his hands and feet. 'Bama was nowhere in sight, and the beam from Marvin's careless flashlight was still dancing – now about fifty meters away. I walked up to Max, knelt down and signaled for him to be quiet, pointed his own weapon at him and whispered: "I'm removing your gag. Don't talk. Do you understand?"

Max nodded his head – yes.

"Listen up," I said. "This is all a mistake. I'm going to let you go in a couple of minutes. But I'll shoot you if you don't do exactly as I say. Understand?"

Max nodded – yes.

"When Marvin comes nearby, he'll probably call out to you – ask you if everything is alright. Answer 'yes'. Understand?"

Max nodded yes again; and I moved off a little ways, pointing the rifle at Max as I backed away.

Marvin and his magic flashlight stopped about 20 meters out. Sure enough, Marvin called out to Max: "Yo Max. It's Marvin. Everything cool?"

Max answered exactly as I'd told him to, with a simple "yes."

Marvin waltzed into HQ, dumbfounded to find Max on the ground. "What you doin'?" he said. Max said nothing.

"He's lying there tied up, you idiot," I said. "This is Max's rifle I'm holding here, it's an M4 and it's pointed at your back. Drop your weapon. Now!"

I admit that I was not prepared. I'd assumed that Marvin would do what I would do – drop the weapon and turn around. I'd assumed he'd do the predictable thing – the rational thing. Nope. Not Marvin. I should have planned for something unusual, something less than reasonable from Marvin. After all he'd shot a dog for the fun of it, talked loudly in a situation that called for quiet, left his post at the rootstock and walked carelessly with a lit flashlight back to HQ.

Marvin did three things. First he said: "here's the gun." OK – I'd expected that.

Next Marvin used two hands to throw the M4 high into the air, over his head, towards me. I did not expect that.

Finally, Marvin disappeared. While I watched the arc of his flying rifle, concerned that it might be headed in my direction, he vanished, running so fast as to be out of sight as close to instantly as I'd ever seen.

"You'll never catch him," said Max. "He's the fastest person I've ever seen. Plus you've scared him off. Hell, 'cept that he can't swim, we'd probably never see him again."

I felt a little sorry for Max. He'd done what I'd asked him to. Marvin's disappearance was my failure, not his. "I'm sorry I hit you. I wish none of this happened. I'd like to find some way to let you go," I said, "but I can't figure out how I can do that and still get off this Island. Any ideas?"

"Wait for 'Bama," said Max. "He's in charge."

"In charge of what, exactly?"

"You've fucked up a government operation," said Max. "We're

private contractors – we work for Homeland Security."

HOMELAND INSECURITY
CHAPTER THREE

I sat down, cross-legged, close enough to Max to whisper – facing him, the M4 on my lap. Homeland Security. What the crap had I done? Could these guys really be doing something important – something that I'd screwed up? I tried to think clearly about everything that had happened, but I was exhausted. The adrenaline rush was gone; and I sat there, mud-covered and tired.

"What exactly are you doing for Homeland Security?" I said.

"I honestly don't know," said Max. "I know this. I'll be screamed at and fired when 'Bama comes back and finds me tied up and Marvin's weapon lying there in the mud. I almost don't mind the firing, but I hate the yelling around. Why not at least untie me?"

I thought about it and decided it wouldn't hurt to release Max. I had his weapon. I worked my penknife out of my shorts pocket, leaned over and cut the shoelaces from Max's wrists. He rubbed the feeling back into his hands and untied his feet.

"Thanks," he said. "I still owe you for the sucker punch."

"Maybe some other time," I said. "Not tonight. I'm beat. Tell me at least a little about what you do here – even if you don't know why you're doing it. Start with how many of you there are here tonight?"

"I can't tell you much," said Max, "'cause I don't know much. There are four of us here tonight – plus the boat operator makes five. You met two of us. Everything else is above my pay grade. Let 'Bama explain it."

I realized I wasn't going to get much information from Max; and I decided I was probably too tired to make sense of it anyway. My vague plan was to stay awake, listen to 'Bama when he got back, apologize for whatever mess I'd made, and ask for help in finding Smokey's body. Then I'd take *Larke* back to the boat club and try to forgive myself for getting the best dog I'd ever know killed. I hoped she'd died instantly – never knowing what hit her. I hoped she'd died happy, swimming after a stick thrown by her idiot master – not that I thought of myself as her "master" anyway. We owned each other. That's the way it'd been.

"Mind if I smoke?" said Max, patting his shirt pocket.

"No. Go ahead."

"Want one?"

"No thanks, I'm too tired to do anything but sit here and feel sorry for myself," I said.

So I'd joined the CivDiv – mentally and physically. It didn't feel good. It didn't feel right. I sat there thinking that I shouldn't be so tired, that I should have a plan, that I should be considering contingencies. I was ashamed of myself. I was sitting around for someone named 'Bama to show up and fix everything. I was acting like a middle-aged, out-of-shape civilian.

• • •

I thought some more. I missed the Corps. If I were still part of an Infantry Company, I'd have a structure, a hierarchy, a place from which to think about what had happened. People would be depending on me; and I'd be relying on them. Instead of sitting around, waiting for something to happen, I'd be sitting here improvising, considering some useful Marine Corps acronym or mnemonic device, while a squad was out on perimeter, alert and watchful. I'd probably rely on the old standard: "SMEAC". It required a consideration of the "situation", a summary of the "mission", a plan of "execution", a review of "administration", and method of "command/signal". My C.O. would be expecting me to recommend some plan of action. I wouldn't be tired – or at least I wouldn't dare show it to anyone.

The situation was obvious. I'd gotten myself into a jam involving Homeland Security subcontractors, terrorists or gun-toting crazies out for a weird good time. It was unknowable exactly who these people were and what they were doing. My dog was dead and my boat was likely damaged; and I was mud-covered and tired on a barren island in the Delaware River – at night. That was the situation.

My mission was to undo as much of this as possible. I'd execute the undoing by passively awaiting 'Bama's arrival, or by doing something myself. That was at least an active thought and worth considering. I supposed the administration of whatever plan resulted would be up to me or 'Bama, depending on my decision regarding the mission's execution; and the command and signal part of subsequent events would be fluid. Come to think of it, these guys must have some ability to communicate.

"Do you have communications with 'Bama?" I said.

"I did, before you broke the fuckin' thing. It was a very expensive piece of my night-vision goggles. 'Bama's probably been calling me. He'll think I've been asleep. Come to think of it, I have been asleep. Thanks to you I'm screwed."

'Bama had probably tried to communicate with Max – and gotten no answer. 'Bama was probably on his way back to Max right now, worried that he couldn't reach him by radio. 'Bama was probably not an idiot. 'Bama was probably being cautious about his approach. 'Bama could be close by, hidden by brush and tall grass.

I thought some more about my options: passively wait for 'Bama, explain everything to him as best I could and hope for the best; or, get myself off the Island somehow and try to figure out what had happened later. The finest officer I'd ever known had been my first Company Commander – a six foot-five Captain. He'd been smart, experienced and dedicated. He'd even had a sense of humor. He'd told me once that every once in awhile, a military situation had to be dealt with by pure instinct; that no training, no experience, no classroom, no books, no mnemonic devices – nothing – would work except instinct. He'd towered over me and smiled when he told me he thought my instincts were pretty good, and to trust them. He'd died in a helicopter crash, well after he'd been promoted out of our Company, but his words were still with me; and I decided to listen to them. My instinct told me to get the hell out of there, immediately.

"I'm going to take a leak," I said to Max. "Stay right here. I'll be right back."

I removed the magazine from Marvin's abandoned M4, placed the weapon back on the ground and retreated off into the high grass. "Stay put," I said to Max. "This may take a few minutes. I've gotta drain the main vein."

I moved quietly towards the northwest side of the Island – the Pennsylvania side. I was about fifty yards from Max when I realized I'd forgotten the Suunto. I turned back to get the watch Johnson had entrusted to me, when I heard yelling. I couldn't make out the words, but someone sounded really pissed off. I assumed it was 'Bama and that he and Max would soon be looking for me. I turned around again, and reached the River's edge in eighty yards or so, waded out to waist deep water, dropped the M4 and the extra magazine and started swimming towards the lights of Chester.

· · ·

As soon as I was in the water and swimming – using a quiet breaststroke I believed I could maintain indefinitely – I sorted through what I'd always called "keep-alive" thoughts. The muddy Delaware River was about three-quarters of a mile wide at this point. It had an outgoing tide moving along at about three knots. There was little traffic on the river and it would all be in the channel. Running lights would warn me of anything headed my way. The water was temperate, and I didn't think hypothermia would be a factor. I could do this.

'Bama and Max would probably look for me on the Island first; and that would give me enough time to get reasonably far away from them. Next, they'd use the boat, probably in widening circles. The current was much stronger than I was. I was probably swimming along at not much more than one knot. The current was three times that fast. So when I reached the other side of the river, I'd be three miles downriver – past the Commodore Barry Bridge, and somewhere on the west side of the City of Chester. The City of Chester would not be a friendly place for a wet, barefoot white boy with a crew cut, dressed in shorts and a T-shirt. I'd probably arrive at about 11:00 p.m. It was Friday night.

I swam on. It was dark behind me, but the moon was bright, and I worried that 'Bama and Max might see me on the surface of the quiet water. After about twenty minutes, just as I reached the New Jersey edge of the channel, I stopped swimming and turned around. There was still no sign of a boat; and there were no running lights headed towards me from either direction. The Bridge loomed off to my left – a concrete and steel colossus. I knew that when I was swept under it I would feel a little helpless. I'd been under it before, in *Larke*, and eddying currents formed by abutments had rocked us. We'd felt ambiguous magic there, and wondered if our presence was appropriate. At least when I got the other side of it, I would no longer be visible from the Island.

When I reached the other side of the channel, and was about to go under the Bridge, I looked behind me again. Sure enough, there was a boat running back and forth along the Island, in a widening gyre. I couldn't hear a motor and figured it was an electric one – built for quiet and not for speed. I was carried under the Bridge then; and I stopped swimming and simply treaded water until I was in the clear on the other side. I heard the hum of tires above me; and I wondered what motorists would think if they knew someone was in the water below them.

I'd been forty minutes in the water at that point, and I figured I had about another twenty to go. I was feeling very tired and wishing I'd been a Navy Seal instead of a Marine Corps grunt. Those guys could swim the River twice while I was doing one lap. I thought of how it always seemed that when doing something exhausting, I could always manage to just finish. I knew it was all mental, but I thought of the hardest things I'd ever had to do, and I realized that, although this might be right up there with the most dangerous, it was not the most difficult. I occupied my thoughts with other experiences of exhaustion; and I tried to recollect which of them had been the hardest.

While stationed at Lejeune, I'd been selected by my Battalion Commander to represent our Battalion in the JFK 50 mile run; and I'd finished it – respectably, in the pack and exhausted. I remember being passed by lots of women; and I remembered thinking that I might be able to go another mile or two, but if they told me I'd get a million dollars to turn around and return to the start, I'd just laugh at them and head for food, beer and a shower.

I sorted through other Marine Corps moments of exhaustion; and I realized that, although they were cool to talk about, none of them had equaled the exhaustion that went with high school football camp one day in August of my senior year. It had been unseasonably hot, but we were in full pads and running windsprints after a long afternoon practice. I'd been an end, desperately trying to be a starter after two years of warming the bench while I grew a little.

I was not particularly fast, but when the coach signaled that the first two linemen to finish the next sprint could be done for the day, I gave it my best. I finished back in the pack, while two speedsters, one of whom had sandbagged the previous sprints, trotted off the field. We ran three more of the damn things; and I never was able to run fast enough to miss a windsprint. After the coach ended the practice for the team, everyone but Ryan O'Brien ran off the field – to hit the swimming pool before chow. I crouched down on a muddy knee, got up, walked about ten steps, took a knee and repeated the process until I got to the platform tent I'd shared with seven other guys. The tent was empty; and they were all swimming. I collapsed on my cot and fell asleep in my pads. I've never been that tired since.

And so I got myself across the Delaware River that night by recalling other moments of exhaustion, not by thinking about 'Bama or Max or what I was going to do next. I talked to myself a little, the usual: "come on, Ryan, you can do it, and Ryan, you asshole, what have you done to yourself this time." But talking to myself hadn't really been necessary. I'd somehow known I'd finish the swim ever since high school football camp.

I looked for a place to get myself ashore. It seemed that most of the shoreline was taken up with old wharves, rotting pilings and bulkheads too high to climb. Further to my left was an area of dark, and I swam to it and found a way ashore in what appeared to be a little park – maybe it was a wildlife sanctuary. At any rate, I mucked ashore into woods, knowing I was surrounded by a small, dangerous city.

BAREFOOTIN'
CHAPTER FOUR

Placing one bare foot after another, I edged into scrubby woods away from the muck of the shore, shivering a little and wishing that I had something on my feet. I wished I had a lot of other things too – a steaming hot thermos of very sweet coffee, dry clothes, a jacket, my wallet, cellphone and car keys – but most of all I wished for shoes. I picked my way deliberately through the litter of leaves, sticks, rocks and trash; and I wished for shoes.

I let my weary Ryan imagination wander where it would; and found it wishing I could sit down, dunk my muddy feet in a warn tub of scented water, abracadabra up a long-haired princess to kneel down in a velvet gown and wash and dry them for me – and then help me pull on some old warm wool hiking socks, while her hair spilled down in front of her face and she looked up and smiled as she pulled back her hair so she could attend to my feet – and she'd ask me what kind of shoes I wanted and, although I'd settle for anything, I did the cool thing, and told her to chose for me; and she'd thought a bit, smiled again, did that thing with her hair, twice (once over each ear) and settled on my old, broken-in

Salomon XA Pro 3D ULTRA Trail Running Shoes which I'd left in my closet in my new apartment; and as soon as they were on my feet, she tightened the Quicklace system with a single competent pull on each shoe and tucked the laces into the tongue, stood, placed a hand on my head, fondly, and vanished.

"Ouch! Shit! Fuck!" I stepped on something hard and sharp. It was a small rock about the size of the rocks used between railroad ties; and that's because that's what it was: railroad ballast, the crushed rock used to level railroad track; and that's because I was creeping up on a train yard – a vast, multi-tracked train yard full of boxcars, piles of rock and ties and all the equipment that went with a been-here-for-a-hundred-years train yard. If Sanford and Son had operated a train yard, it'd have been this one. I paused at the edge of the woods, scanning the yard for signs of life. A small animal ran across the tracks in front of me, as if to say: "here's how you do it, Ryan – you dumb fuck."

Humankind's most important advancement was not the invention the wheel, or the development of the internet. Nor was it the taming of fire or wind. It was the invention of the shoe. Whoever the genius was that first thought to put something on his or her feet before leaving the cave one morning was getting my vote as the smartest human ever. Screw Einstein. To hell with Goethe. Fuck Michelangelo. I didn't need them, I needed Trainyardopithicus Chestercityus to invent me something, anything, to get me across the god damn crushed rock ballast ahead – two hundred yards of it.

I picked up a branch from a nearby tree and broke it into a five-foot piece to lean on and started out across the yard. The moon made for bright going; and I couldn't decide if that was good or bad.On every step, my feet encountered a rock or two. I shuffled. I tried to glide. I moved rocks with my toes. I leaned heavily on my stick. I winced. I swore quietly. I made it to the first tracks. Standing on the cold steel rail was a balm to my bruised feet. In the direction I was headed there were ten or twelve more tracks, each with unavoidable crushed rock ballast. So it was decided for me – walk along the rail, use the staff for balance, don't fall off.

• • •

By the light of the moon, I made my way East along the train tracks. I was thankful that the stick I was using for balance was a nice weight and length. I thought of it as a staff and wished it had magic powers – to light my way, to transport me to my car, to smite enemies and to protect me from whatever else might happen this strange night. The train tracks converged from the dozens within the train yard to six, then four and, finally, two. I assumed that these were the major rail lines that ran east all the way to Philadelphia, past Essington, where my boat club and car were located.

I walked out of the train yard on the left-hand track, balancing my staff in the middle like a tight-rope walker. Off to my right were factories and warehouses, often protected by razor-wire fences; and off to my left seemed to be occasional small groups of houses. Finally, I reached a street, Clayton Street, which dead-ended at the tracks. Tired of the balancing act and the dark, I turned left onto Clayton Street and headed for a well-lit street that turned out to be either Rosa Parks Highway or 2nd Street, depending on which signs were to be believed. I turned right on the street, walked two blocks and discovered that I was also on Route PA291, a road that would eventually take me to within a mile of my car.

I decided to walk on the right side of the street – the factory-warehouse side. The other side of the street was comprised of vacant lots, intermittent groupings of old houses and darkened churches. After six blocks, I saw a dilapidated, one-story taproom, "Albert's", with a blinking red neon Miller High Life sign in a dirty window. There were no cars outside and I wasn't sure the bar was really open. I continued along 2nd Street. I saw no people walking anywhere and only an occasional car, usually headed in the opposite direction. I decided that hitchhiking would be a failure – not only was there little traffic, but my bare feet and wet shorts and T-shirt made for little curbside appeal. According to my wristwatch, it was 11:21 p.m. I guessed that I was about seven miles from my car, that I was walking no faster than two miles per hour, and that I would reach my car by about 3 a.m. By then my feet would be raw.

The Commodore Barry Bridge loomed overhead again; and I would walk under it, headed in the opposite direction I'd swum. Near the Bridge and across the street I noticed an old wood-frame house with a wrap-around front porch; a house that had apparently been converted into a church, since a white, unblinking neon light in a bay window said "Jesus Christ is Lord." I hobbled across the street, climbed the steps and knocked on the door with one end of my staff. Then I stood back from the door, since I didn't want my appearance to frighten whoever might answer. There was no need for my concern on that account.

"Jameson, come look. We got a Pilgrim on our porch."

The speaker of these words was a middle-aged black woman who'd opened the door. She was almost my height, wearing a black dress and holding a handbag. She was unperturbed by the appearance of a shoeless, wet, white guy with a big stick banging on her door late at night. I got the impression that she had just been leaving when I knocked. "Come in," she said. "Leave your staff on the porch. I'm Sister Alberta." She stepped aside while she held the door open for me.

I stepped into the small foyer. It was dimly lit, but off to my left was a much larger room, empty of people, but bright with lights and lined with rows of wooden folding chairs. At the front was an altar of sorts – a table covered with a white linen cloth supporting a vertical wooden cross with a crucified Jesus on it. It might have been my exhaustion, or the cumulative effect of the strange events of the evening, but the room really did feel like a sanctuary to me, and perhaps a little sacred.

"Jameson, come here. You gotta see this. What's your name young man?"

"Ryan," I said.

"No," said Sister Alberta, "your whole name. Your Christian name. You are a Christian. Am I correct?"

"My name is Ryan O'Brien," I said, "and I suppose I am."

"You suppose you are what," said Sister Alberta, "Ryan O'Brien?"

"I suppose I am a Christian," I said. Now the words seemed to come out of me in a rush. "I've been baptized and gone to church some. Not much for awhile. I've been in Afghanistan. There aren't any churches there. Right now I'm really tired. I swam across the River and walked here from the train yard down the way. Before that, guys with guns were shooting at me and one of them shot and killed my dog. I don't really know what's going on. I'm very tired. May I rest here awhile?"

"You may, my son," said the slender man who'd quietly walked into the room. "I'm Reverend Jameson Jones." He placed a hand on my shoulder. He was considerably shorter than Sister Alberta. He was modestly dressed – gray trousers and sweater vest over a blue long-sleeved shirt – with nice shoes. Although he was short and slender, he had a surprisingly deep voice. I supposed it was an effective preaching voice. He steered me into an adjoining room and into a comfortable old armchair. "Where are your shoes and the rest of your clothes, Mister O'Brien? And what's this about gunfire and swimming the River?"

I told him a short version of everything that had happened. Sister Alberta had disappeared into the back of the house and returned with some hot coffee and a blanket. She'd laced the coffee with whiskey, Jameson, I imagined, and with lots of cream and sugar – just the way I liked it. Even the short version of the adventures of Ryan O'Brien that night took awhile, but neither Reverend Jones nor Sister Alberta interrupted me. I couldn't talk for a minute or so after I told them about Smokey, and how I'd gotten her killed by foolishly throwing a stick into the River at the wrong time. I concluded by telling them I had to get back to my car, go home, get some sleep and figure everything out in the morning. Then I pulled my feet up under the blanket and fell asleep.

PILGRIM
CHAPTER FIVE

It was morning when I awakened. I was on a couch, in pajamas. I could hear singing in the adjacent room – the room with the wooden folding chairs and the altar. I lay on my back, pulled the blanket up to my chin and listened to the singing. It was a subdued a cappella gospel song, being sung by children, whose high, pure voices were twined around each other in harmony. They were singing rounds, repeating some of the lines several times and playing with the melody effortlessly. They made mistakes, though, and giggled when they did. Mistakes, giggling and all, I thought it was the just about the sweetest singing I'd ever heard.

The words to the verse were something about being sanctified and holy, not being moved and being like a tree planted by the water. The words "I shall not be moved" were repeated often.

When they stopped singing, one of the children giggled loudly; and another shushed him. "Don't wake the Pilgrim," she whispered. Then I laughed out loud and five or six heads peeked in the doorway.

"It's OK," I said. "It's time for me to get up anyway. You all sing really well."

The kids clustered around my couch. "Are you really a Pilgrim?" one asked. "We saw your staff outside."

"We heard you swum the River," said another. "Is that true?"

"We heard you don't have shoes," said a third.

Just then Sister Alberta sailed into the room. She was carrying my shorts and T-shirt, washed, dried and neatly folded. "No more questions, children. Let Mister O'Brien get up and get dressed." She handed me my clothes and shoed the kids out of the room like chickens in a barnyard. "Knock on the kitchen door when you're dressed," she said, pointing her chin at the door she'd used to enter. Then she closed the door to the sanctuary and returned to the kitchen.

I did not really feel dressed after I put on shorts and my T-shirt; but I knocked on the swinging door to the kitchen and Sister Alberta opened it for me. She pointed to a seat for me at a table set for two. The Reverend Jameson Jones was standing over a big range.

"Hungry?" the Reverend asked.

"You bet," I said. Breakfast was my favorite meal. I tried to guess what the wonderful warm smells in the kitchen included, and gave up and concluded that they simply added up to breakfast.

"How do you like your scrapple?" asked the Reverend.

Scrapple! "Crisp on the outside, hot on the inside," I said. I hadn't had scrapple since my senior year in college. Scrapple was a Philadelphia thing. I liked it and it reminded me of college.

"Right up," said the Reverend. "Glad to meet a Pilgrim who knows his scrapple."

Sister Alberta sat on a stool in a corner, enjoying the show. "Jameson's got very specific ideas about cooking scrapple," she said. "He says women can't cook it, 'cause we keep peeking on the underside. Says we got no patience. Says it takes a man to cook scrapple."

"That's right," said the Reverend. "Admit it Sister. You can't cook scrapple. You gotta just flip it once, when it's ready. Not before. And no back and forth with it, no movin' it around either. That just tears it up."

"'Course, scrapple is one of the only things you can cook," said Sister Alberta, "though I give you some credit on your pancakes. They ain't bad either. Come to think of it – you can cook up a breakfast as good as anyone. You do make a mess, though."

"Great artists always make a mess," said the Reverend. "The Pilgrim here can help me clean up."

"It's a deal," I said, figuring that my value to this team was mostly as an audience, an audience with an appetite. They were enjoying themselves. I wondered how long they'd been doing whatever it was they did in this neighborhood, this church and this kitchen. I wondered if they were related. I wondered how old they were. I wondered how I could possibly pay them back for taking me in and feeding me.

• • •

So the Reverend Jameson Jones and Captain Ryan O'Brien, USMC, recently retired, ate breakfast together – and what a breakfast it was. Scrambled eggs, home fries, piles of thick buttered toast, pancakes with maple syrup, a pitcher of orange juice, mugs of coffee and, of course, scrapple. Sister Alberta did not really serve us so much as simply keep an eye on what we might want next and place it on the table. She cleared the table when we'd finished, placing everything in the sink except for our coffee mugs. Then she placed the coffee pot on the table next to the cream and sugar and left us alone in the room. I felt that a Reverend outranked a Captain there in that kitchen that morning.

"I can't thank you enough for what you've done for me," I said. "I owe you – big time. I don't know what might have happened last night if you hadn't taken me in. I hope it was you put those pajamas on me and not Sister Alberta."

"Yep," said the Reverend. "That was me."

"Thanks. I guess I owe you one," I said.

"You definitely do not owe me pajamas," said the Reverend. "I don't wear 'em anyway."

"More information than I need," I said.

We cleaned up the kitchen. I stuck with the sink, rinsing dishes and glasses; and the Reverend loaded the dishwasher and wiped down the table and counters. When the dishwasher was full, we soaked pots and pans in the sink and declared victory. I thought that we were reasonably competent as a team.

"Let's get you wherever it is you have to get," said the Reverend. "Sister's gone to find you something for your feet."

Sister Alberta came through the swinging door, holding a pair of sneakers out ahead of her, and said, "Here – take these things off my hands. They've been taking up space for a month now. My nephew either outgrew them by now or else they went out of style. Probably both."

They were a newish pair of Nike basketball shoes; and when I looked at them more closely, they were Air Max Soldier V's, and apparently had something or other to do with LeBron James. They were red and black, size 14. I put them on my size 12 feet without socks and declared them perfect.

"I'll bring them back," I said.

"No need," said Sister, looking sad. "My nephew doesn't need them where he is right now."

"Let's go," said the Reverend, indicating that our time in the kitchen was up, and that the subject of Sister's nephew was not a good one.

We went out the front door. Three of the choir members were on the porch, waiting for us. "Bye Pilgrim," said one. "Nice shoes," said another. The third, a boy and the oldest of the three, said nothing. My staff was leaning against the porch wall, next to the door.

"I can't take that with me where I'm going," I said, pointing to the staff. "Would you watch it for me?" I asked the tall boy. He said nothing, but smiled with his eyes, walked to the staff and placed a proprietary hand upon it. He raised it up and pointed at the porch ceiling.

"Careful where you aim that thing," I said, "you never know what it's gonna do next." Then the Reverend and I got in his car and drove away.

"Those kids can sure sing," I said. "They are really good."

"All us Black Folks can sing – dance too," said the Reverend, unsmiling and looking sidewise at me.

His comment astonished me. I took a deep breath, kept my eyes facing front and tried to interpret what he'd just said – wondering if I'd insulted him somehow, if I was about to offend him further by a foolish response, if I'd misjudged him completely, if saying nothing at all might be the best thing I could do and deciding that it was not – all the while thinking that it was not possible that the Reverend Jameson Jones had shuffled the deck, a deck that had just included lending me his pajamas, a friendly breakfast and amicable cleanup and somehow played a race card from its bottom; and knowing that whatever I said next might be important to our short relationship, and realizing that I very much cared about his opinion of me as well as that of Sister Alberta and the kids that sang in the choir; and that since I'd been trusting my instincts lately, I'd continue to do so, and so I said: "I never noticed, since I've been too busy drinking Guinness, fighting, eating boiled potatoes and having bad luck."

He looked over at me, laughed once, reached and poked me in the shoulder with his right hand and said: "maybe you'll do." He laughed again, and said: "So – you know what this means, right?"

I started to out think myself again and decided to play it safe.

"No," I said. "What on earth does it mean? That I can borrow your pajamas again if I need them? That I can stop in if ever I'm barefoot in Chester again? What exactly does it mean?"

"It means," he said, "that you might do. You said you owed us; and you asked what you could do. Maybe there is a thing or two."

While we finished up the short drive to my boat club, where I'd parked my car, the Reverend explained to me a number of things. First, I was to call him "Jameson" and he'd call me "Ryan" when it was just the two of us. When we were around the children, I'd call him "Reverend" and he'd call me "Mister O'Brien". Second, he'd be pleased to see me in church once in awhile, on Sundays – at 9:30 a.m. Third, I'd be welcome on Saturday mornings for breakfast, anytime, if I came early – 7:30 a.m. – and helped feed the children. Fourth, the eleven year-old boy I'd given the staff to for safekeeping – his name was Nashir – could barely read, and if I would read to him once in awhile, he'd be thankful. Finally, the City of Chester had just issued a citation to the Church, informing it that it was not duly licensed and inspected to serve food or provide lodging to more than three non-family members at any given time, on any given day or night – and that the permit to do so would have to be issued by way of the normal bureaucratic, time-consuming, expensive, ass-kissing process; and if I could help in that regard, he would end up in my debt. He handed me the citation and told me to read it and think about it all. His cellphone number was written on the back of the paper.

He turned in the gates to the West End Boat Club, in Essington, where my car was parked. I pointed to the five year-old Subaru Forester, with the trailer hitch on the end; and Jameson stopped next to it, shook my hand again and smiled. "Hope to hear from you Ryan," he said.

"You will Jameson," I said.

UNCLE RYAN
CHAPTER SIX

"How's your Uncle Ryan?"

It was Jack Walker, the dock master of the Club, steering the Club's monstrous forklift toward the River to pull a small powerboat. He stopped by my car and put the noisy forklift in neutral, waiting for an answer. I'd just found the small magnetic box with the spare car key, under the hitch.

"He's good," I said. "He says he misses the West End." Uncle Ryan had been a West End member for twenty years. He had been a contractor by trade and could fix almost anything. Some said he kept the Club going in the early, lean years. He'd gotten me into the boat club three years before he decided he had enough money and was tired of the cold. He had moved to Florida; and now he owned and operated a small marina on the eastern edge of the Everglades. He said he had gators for company most mornings.

"Tell him we miss him too," said Jack. Then he glanced down at my sneakers. "Nice sneaks. You look different today. Going sailing? Fishing?"

"I am different today," I said. "*Larke* is across the river, anchored. I swam the River last night."

"You swam across the River? That River there?" he said, pointing toward the Delaware.

"Long story. Today I've gotta go back to my apartment, get some stuff, wait for a high enough tide and get *Larke* back where she belongs. Anyone around to run the workboat later?"

"I'll be here," said Jack, "but I wouldn't leave your sailboat anchored out there for six more hours – especially if there's something wrong with her."

"If I had to guess, she's got a few bullet holes," I said, "but I won't really know until I take a look. What's the workboat's draft?"

"Practically nothing. Nine inches maybe," said Jack. I'd better take you now. Bullet holes? What the crap. Swam the river? Maybe I better hear the whole story. Let me park the forklift."

I opened the car and put Jameson's citation from the City of Chester on the passenger seat. Then I followed Jack out "B" Dock to the workboat. The boat had been a donation from a club member who'd gotten too old to use it. It was a seventeen foot, all-aluminum skiff with an ancient 70 horsepower Evinrude two-stroke outboard. The boat was practically bulletproof – it had already received hundreds of dings from the hard duty it'd had moving the pile driver, finger piers and floating docks. It started right up, I cast off the dock lines, and Jack steered us out of the marina and into the River.

"Where is she?" asked Jack.

"Not far," I said, pointing in the general direction of *Larke*. "Past the rock jetty. Near Chester Island."

Jack ran the workboat slow enough that we could talk; and in the ten minutes it took us to reach *Larke*, I told him what had happened the night before. Jack was an eccentric, as were lots of older boat club members – but he was a good listener. I recalled my Uncle Ryan telling me that Jack drank Jack Daniels whiskey, while another Club member named Johnny Daniels, drank Johnny Walker scotch. Uncle Ryan thought the whole thing was hilarious and that it somehow explained everything anyone ever needed to know about the West End. The night he sponsored me for membership, we'd bought a round for Jack and Johnny. Any status I'd had at the Club was just residual from Uncle Ryan's; without him, I'd just be a kid sailboater in the blue collar world of gray-haired power boaters.

• • •

Larke was listing to starboard, aground in the low tide mud. We circled her slowly in the workboat, and found a row of bullet holes stitched neatly in her port side – below the bootstripe. She'd taken on water when the tide was higher, and I wondered how much had found its way below deck and into her bilges. Jack edged the bow of the workboat close to *Larke's* stern, and I hopped aboard her. I was happy and a little surprised to see my wallet, cellphone and car keys in the small compartment in the coaming, right where I'd left them; and I put them all in my pockets and looked in the small cabin. There were about three inches of dirty water inside which meant that the bilges were full and *Larke* could have taken on enough water to sink her – but she'd been saved by the shallow water and lowering tide.

"Plug the holes, pump out the water and come back when the tide's higher," said Jack.

"Plug the holes with what?" I asked.

"Hell, duct tape might work. It's a nice straight row of holes. Wonder where they ended up. They might've done some damage inside."

I looked more carefully at the holes. They seemed to be angled downwards. That made sense, if I assumed a shooter standing in another boat, alongside *Larke*. "They all ended up somewhere in the lead keel," I said. "No real harm. Lead on lead."

Jack looked through the workboat's toolbox and found some Velcro and duct tape. "Clean around the holes, cover 'em with the sticky side of Velcro, then duct tape. That should hold long enough to get across the River to the travel lift. Pump her out a little. You get to wade in the mud."

I handed Jack my wallet, car keys and cellphone, took off my sneakers, jumped in the water and did as Jack suggested. The whole effort took about ten minutes. Then I pulled myself aboard *Larke* and left muddy footprints all over her, using the manual pump to remove most of the water from the cabin and bilges. When I'd finished I decided not to wait aboard *Larke* three or four hours until the tide was higher, but to go back to my car, drive to my apartment, get cleaned up and dressed, make some phone calls and try to figure out what to do next. As we pulled away from *Larke*, I whispered to her a promise to be back soon.

Back at the West End, I thanked Jack for his help, hopped in my car and drove to my apartment. I'd only lived there since the first of the month – ten days prior. I didn't think of it as "home" yet; and I still woke up in the mornings, alone, wondering where I was and why no one was snoring on a cot next to me – with dusty Afghan sunlight filtering through holes in my tent.

The apartment was missing the best dog in the world, and was only about half furnished, with boxes still full of inexpensive stuff from IKEA that still had to be put together. I'd been assembling one or two things a day, usually kneeling on the floor until my legs cramped and I lost my patience and began to damn the inanimate objects that came in clear plastic bags along with the confusing assembly directions written in several languages. I did have a bed, a table, a chair, a bookcase and a desk, however; and the desk was a large wooden one with room enough for several computers, a printer, two desk lamps, an in-out basket and some hanging filing bins. The desk had room to spread out papers, and was the only space I was satisfied with – it felt finished and ready for my new life.

The apartment building itself was old – a three and one-half story brick residence, on the edge of center city, close enough to work to let me walk. It was a twin, built in the 1870's and converted into four units years prior. My apartment was a walk-up – top floor. I had dormers, one each on the east and west ends of the apartment, and three along the south side. The light inside was great; and the place had nooks and crannies all over it – elegant doors, trim and moldings that had never been painted. I loved the place. Best of all, a parking place for my car came with it, only a half block away. I'd signed the lease the same day I saw the place, as soon as I'd made sure Smokey could handle the steps and after I'd seen four other apartments, all in large, modern buildings with doormen, concierges – places that, according to my real estate agent, had "lots of young people like you" in them. She'd been surprised at my selection and assumed it was a money-related decision. It wasn't.

I had about three hours to kill before I went back to the West End to get *Larke*, so I booted up the computer, stacked my mail and plugged my cellphone in to its charger. Then I went to take a shower, shave and brush my teeth. I was not hungry – I was still full from my breakfast with Jameson. The hot shower felt so good that I overdid it a little and steamed up the whole bathroom. I opened the bathroom door to let some steam out and started to blow dry the mirror so I could shave. I heard my cellphone ring; but by the time I wrapped a towel around my waist and reached the phone, it had stopped ringing. I pressed "send", the feature that told me whose call I'd missed. It had been Uncle Ryan. I called him back as soon as I'd shaved, dressed and brushed my teeth.

"Guess who I just heard from," said Uncle Ryan, after I'd called him back. No "hello, how are you, what's up", nope. Just "guess who I just heard from."

"Jack Walker," I said. Jack was tight enough with Uncle Ryan to have his number, and worried enough about me to make the call.

"What the crap, Ryan," he said, "swam the Delaware goddamn River – at night! Bullet holes in *Larke*. What's going on?"

"I can explain everything, Uncle Ryan," I said. "It was all some stupid mistake. I was in the wrong place at the wrong time. It was a one-off. It won't happen again in a million years."

"You can explain everything to me when I get there," said Uncle Ryan.

"Get here! What do you mean, 'get here'? You're in the Everglades. Living happily ever after. You and Albert the Alligator. At least that's what Mom told me when I talked to her last."

"I'm bored. I need something to do. You're it. I'm coming."

"What about your marina?" I said. "Don't you have to be there to run it?"

"It practically runs itself," he said. "Besides, Sissie can take care of things 'til I get back."

"Who's Sissie?"

"Sissie Powell. I thought I'd mentioned her."

"Nope," I said. "Maybe it's none of my business."

"I'll tell you about her when I get there. She's real interesting."

"When will you get here? Give me your flight information, so I can pick you up."

"Come on Ryan. You know better than that. I'm not flying. I'm driving. I've got Oscar with me. We already left, and we're trailering our boat. We'll call you when I get close. Oscar says hello to Smokey." He terminated the call.

• • •

I sat at my desk and thought about what I'd just heard. Uncle

Ryan. I wondered what my parents were thinking when they named me for him; and I wondered if he'd changed much. I hadn't seen him since my graduation over four years ago. He'd been my height, but forty hard pounds heavier. I remembered his hands as big and rough from his work. He'd happily taught me to fish, drove three-hundred miles each way to see my high school football games and told me he was proud of me when I'd worn my Second Lieutenant's uniform to graduation. He was usually happy, but could slide over into melancholy when he drank. He told me never to fight while drinking – that nothing good ever came of it. I never saw anyone bother him much. He never backed down from friendly arguments, and seemed to enjoy them.

"It's a god-damned debating society we've joined," he said once, when we'd been drinking at the West End's bar one Friday night and arguing with members about the need for dredging the marina, how to do it best, what it would cost and how long it might last. Uncle Ryan had been solidly in the pro-dredging camp; and I thought he'd be happy to see that the work had been done a year ago. He'd never married. Maybe "Sissie" was the one.

Oscar was his six-year old dog, a loyal ninety-pound, mixed-breed, rescued by Uncle Ryan from the very City of Chester I'd recently visited. He told me he'd been driving through town at dusk, on his way home from a hardware store that sold antique plumbing fixtures. He got a little turned around and in a very bad section of the city, when he'd passed a dog sitting under a streetlight. Something about the dog caused Uncle Ryan to drive around the block; and the dog was still there. "It was like he was waiting for me," said Uncle Ryan, when he told the story. "I stopped the truck, opened the door and he jumped right in – like it was his truck."

Uncle Ryan, Oscar, his boat and a pickup truck were headed my way. Smokey and Oscar had really liked each other. Damn but I missed my dog.

We're All Guilty of Something
Chapter Seven

I checked e-mails, decided to answer them later, ran down the three flights of stairs and the half block to the car, and headed back to the West End. On the way I tried to decide if I was happy Uncle Ryan was driving twelve hundred miles in his pickup truck, with his dog and boat, to keep me out of trouble. Once, spring of my senior year in college, he'd picked a fraternity brother and me up at a police station – after we were charged with D.U.I. City police had stopped us for driving "too cautiously" at 2 a.m. one Saturday morning. We were barely over the legal limit on the breathalyzer. Never mind that I had not been driving – the ticketing cop swore he'd seen us switch seats a few blocks back. Uncle Ryan was visibly pissed – not at me, but at the police – and he sounded off while stomping out the door of the station after the desk sergeant had said, shrugging his shoulders with casual indifference, "they're guilty, right?"

Uncle Ryan had pivoted away from the door, pointed a big finger at the sergeant and said: "you've just put points on the driver's license of a man who's about to go overseas and fight for you, jackass. We're all guilty of something!" I grabbed him and pulled him out the door before anything really stupid happened.

In other words, Uncle Ryan was someone who was capable of complicating my modest plan to grow up, live by myself in a place I'd picked out and start a career at Howell & Barrett. I knew I'd be glad to see him, as would everyone else at the West End and a few of the ladies he'd left behind; and I knew we'd have some fun together – some fishing, some beer and good conversation. But as Mom said, when I'd been admitted to Wharton, "I worry about Uncle Ryan. He's my brother, I love him, and I know how much the two of you like each other; but he can be a big distraction."

So I'd better show Uncle Ryan that I'd matured a lot, so he wouldn't spend a lot of time helping me grow up. For him not to be too much of a distraction, I needed to get *Larke* to the Club and repaired, get my inexpensive furniture assembled, my apartment organized and give at least the appearance of being ready to be a grownup. I was a grownup, I told myself. I'd been responsible, every day, for the lives of forty-two men. Wasn't that grownup?

But when I was honest with myself, I admitted that something about starting over, by myself – without the hierarchy and chain of command, without the mnemonic devices and acronyms, without all the accoutrements, history and glory that went with the Marine Corps – had me a little uneasy. I was worried. I was insecure; and I couldn't fully understand why. Oh well. Run down under the kickoff. Get up in the morning. Do my best. In other words, do those things my Pops had always told me to do whenever I'd come to him with a problem, when I'd been worrying about one thing or another. I decided to give him a call on my cell, as soon as I got to the West End.

• • •

But when I got back to the Club, everything was in the usual

Saturday afternoon state of confusion, with work parties moving finger piers and sealing portions of the "C" dock deck. Three members were tending to the scrubby native plants that we'd been forced to plant by something called the Natural Resource Damage Assessment and Restoration Program, managed by the U.S. Fish and Wildlife Service, to offset the loss of plants from the recent dredging. The effort to keep the native plants alive was part of the comprehensive permitting process that had allowed us to dredge. The habitat of the red-bellied turtle had been mentioned a few times in the narrative of the regulations club members had struggled to comprehend. I'd missed all the outrage members displayed at meetings over the issue, since all the Club had been trying to accomplish was dredging the marina back to its original state. I'd thought that if we ever encountered a red-bellied turtle, some member would be likely to shoot it; but I was proven wrong two days earlier – we'd actually seen one, basking in the sun on a half-submerged piece of driftwood; and four or five members happily watched it for hours, saluting it with an occasional beer and toasts: "looks like a good life to me, bro" and "hope you're happy pal, 'cause you cost us a lot of money."

So the Club was busy, Jack wanted to take me to *Larke* right away; and I did not phone my Pops.

"Thanks for dropping a dime on me," I said to Jack. "Uncle Ryan's already on his way. He's trailering his boat."

"What about Oscar?" asked Jack.

"Of course – he's coming too," I said.

"Good," said Jack, revving the workboat's engine and ending our conversation.

When we arrived at *Larke*, she seemed to be floating levelly and I assumed the

Velcro and duct tape repair job was working. I clambered aboard my sailboat, untilted the outboard until the propeller was underwater, choked the motor and pulled on the start cord. The motor started on the first pull; and I waved Jack away – back to the West End. Next I went forward, to pull the anchor. When I had it half way up, I heard a motor approaching. Looking up, I saw a powerboat approaching – it was white, and had a diagonal blue stripe on its side and a flashing blue light above the console. It was the New Jersey State Police. I wondered what they wanted, and if it had anything to do with the events of the evening before. I let the muddy anchor splash down into the River again and watched the boat approach. This had not been part of my plan.

The uniformed officer in the boat was alone, and a competent boat handler. She – for it turned out to be a middle-aged woman – came alongside *Larke* and handed me a line, indicating with her chin that I should tie it to a forward cleat. I did as I was told, and stood up, waiting for further instructions.

"Mind if I come aboard?" she said.

She had wiry reddish-blond hair poking out from under a cap. She could pass for Pippi Longstocking's much-older sister. I noted that she had all the usual State Police accoutrements: uniform, handcuffs, a small radio and revolver – all attached to a leather belt. She also had a billy club, two small black leather books – one in her hand and one in a back pocket. She wore black gloves, shiny steel-toed boots, a bullet-proof vest and mirrored aviator sunglasses. According to her black and white plastic nametag, she was "Bardeaux". The sum of these parts bespoke S.S. Waffenchick; and I did not expect to experience anything enjoyable in the following half hour.

"What for? My papers are up to date. The Coast Guard Auxiliary checked the boat three days ago at the West End. There's the sticker. What's this about?"

"Sir," she said, with emphasis, right hand resting on her revolver, "are you refusing me permission to come aboard?"

"No," I said, "but it's not common practice to board small sailboats with steel-toed boots. Can't I just hand you my papers?

Everything will be up to date and in order. I assume this is just some routine check. Right?"

"No," she said. "Wrong. This is not routine. In fact, it's part of a murder investigation. Now, I'm coming aboard." She reached across *Larke's* coaming, grabbed hold of the boom, near the topping lift and hauled herself aboard.

"I.D., sir."

I pulled my wallet out of my back pocket, intending to hand her my driver's license. Then I decided to show her my Marine Corps picture I.D. Maybe "Captain" O'Brien, USMC, would get better treatment, I thought. No such luck.

"Your driver's license, sir," was all she said, after she'd glanced at the card I'd handed her.

I looked in my wallet, in the slot where I kept it. No luck. I started to go through my wallet, thinking it must be there somewhere. While I was not looking, she drew her revolver, aimed it at my chest and backed away from me. Unfortunately for her – and for me too, as it turned out – her steel-toed boots slipped on the round, solar-powered, stainless steel exhaust fan I'd installed on *Larke's* small stern. She tumbled backwards overboard, her gun firing once in the air as she fell. I knew she couldn't drown in four feet of water; nevertheless, I jumped in after her, thinking that I'd done nothing, this was all a mistake; and that if I helped her surface, she'd at least stop shooting.

So we surfaced together, my hands under her arms. "God damn it," she said. "Get your hands off me! Move away from me. Put your hands in the air."

It was hard to move in four feet of muddy water on top of six inches of mud, but I managed to get myself six feet or so away from her. I faced her, raised my hands in the air and said: "now what?" I made the mistake of smiling as I said it.

"You think this is funny! You are about to be charged with a crime – and, you've just resisted arrest."

"Sorry," I said. "This is definitely not funny. I'm pretty sure I did not commit a crime. I know I'm not resisting arrest. So – now what?"

"Climb in my boat," she said. "Take these handcuffs and cuff your left hand to the console. There." She pointed with the revolver. "Now."

I moved deliberately and did exactly as she said.

"Now reach over here and pull me aboard with your right hand."

Waterlogged, and bogged down with police paraphernalia, she was heavy; but she was surprisingly strong, and with some awkward scrambling, we got her aboard.

"Sit there," she said, indicating a two-person seat in front of the console. Then she started her boat, switched on the blinking blue light and added a siren to the confusion. She headed around to the back side of Chester Island. She drove slowly, so her boat was quiet enough for her to recite my rights to me as we moved along. Then a police helicopter flew noisily into the picture and hovered over us for a minute – long enough for Bardeaux to signal to the pilot with a big, happy thumbs-up.

The helicopter moved off and settled on the Island; and we headed for the shore adjacent to it.

"What am I being arrested for?" I asked. "I don't think I'm guilty of anything. This is all a mistake."

"Trust me, It's not a mistake," said Bardeaux. "Now shut up. We're all guilty of something."

Time of Death
Chapter Eight

From my humble place in the world – handcuffed to a stainless steel post on a New Jersey State Police boat – I watched Patrolwoman Bardeaux talk to a suit who had just exited the helicopter. In the five minutes she spent discussing her intrepid capture of me – with frequent dramatic gestures in my direction – she went from wet and bedraggled, but joyous, to wet and bedraggled and very angry. She stomped one muddy foot into the Chester Island mud at the end of the conversation, threw her hands in the air, shouted something that sounded like "my collar!" and reluctantly handed something to the man she'd been talking to.

Apparently that something was a key to my handcuffs, and Detective Smyrl – "call me Smyrl," he said – efficiently unlocked my handcuffs, removed them from the post and relocked them on my wrists. He was turned out in a dark suit, a paisley tie and honest-to-God galoshes – the kind I hadn't seen since 4th grade, the ones with the metal buckles. He sported not one, but two plastic pocket protectors, one in his white shirt pocket and one in his suit coat breast pocket. Patrolwoman Bardeaux followed us as we walked away from the boat.

"You're O'Brien, right?" asked Smyrl.

"Yes."

"There's something I want you to see, O'Brien," said Smyrl.

"Are these cuffs necessary?"

"For now," said Smyrl, galoshing over the Island mud.

"She's scarier than any Taliban I met in Afghanistan," I said, referring to Bardeaux.

"She says you resisted arrest."

"She lies," I said. "It's more like I assisted arrest. She fell off my boat and I jumped in the River and helped her up."

"We'll discuss it later," said Smyrl. "The charge of resisting arrest is the least of your worries right now." He steered me along, following little red pennants, stuck in the ground, attached to wire supports.

In the small clearing, where I'd been the night before, where I'd sucker-punched Max, lost Marvin and decided to swim the River, were two people, on their knees next to a body – Marvin. He'd been shot once in the chest, and lay on his back. The medical examiners or crime scene investigators or whoever they were, were removing fluid from one of his eyes with a big hypodermic needle. My own eyes hurt to watch. Next, they rolled him on his side, slit his pants and carefully took his temperature – rectally. I noticed Smyrl, noticing me.

"Do you recognize this man, O'Brien?" asked Smyrl. "Think carefully before you answer."

"His name is Marvin," I said. "Emphasis on the *vin*. At least that's what Max called him. So did someone else, I think."

"Who's Max?" said Smyrl. "Think carefully before you answer."

"Max is someone I met last night here on Chester Island," I said. It's a long story. I'll be happy to tell it to you, but let's go sit down somewhere. Why the handcuffs? And why do you keep telling me to think carefully before I answer?"

Smyrl pulled a small plastic bag out of his suit coat jacket and held it up so I could see it. It contained my driver's license. "This was found about ten feet from Marvin," he said. "Now let's go have a nice long talk." I followed him to the helicopter.

"Have you been in one of these before?" asked Smyrl.

"Several hundred times," I said. "Ten days ago was my last – from Kandahar to Kabul."

"Buckle up," said Smyrl.

• • •

As we flew away, I looked down at where we'd been. Chester Island was spread out under us; its bland green and brown surface broken only by an angry patrolwoman, her boat, two medical examiners and Marvin. It was too noisy to talk in the 'copter, so I sat in a bucket seat, next to Smyrl, handcuffed, and tried to imagine what had happened on the Island after I'd left it last night.

After we'd landed and been escorted by a State Trooper in an unmarked gray Crown Victoria to a place identified as a New Jersey State Police Regional Headquarters, Smyrl sat me down in a small conference room, still handcuffed, and asked if I'd had my rights read to me.

"That was about the only thing Patrolwoman Bardeaux did by the book," I said.

"Do you want to hear them again? I'm taping now."

"Not necessary," I said, speaking clearly for the recorder.

"So what do you think happened on Chester Island, O'Brien? How did your driver's license get where we found it? Start at the very beginning. Leave nothing out."

I did as I was asked; and I told Smyrl everything, absolutely everything, that had happened the night before on the Island. I left nothing out, and concluded with the theory that someone named "'Bama" had taken my driver's license from *Larke* and dropped it near Marvin's body after he'd killed him.

Smyrl had not taken notes as I'd talked – he had the tape, after all – but after I'd finished, he wrote on the notepad in front of him. He seemed to be listing things as they occurred to him. Then he spoke. "So you are recently out of the Marine Corps, where you'd been stationed in Afghanistan, in an infantry company. Right?"

"Correct," I said.

"You reconnoitered Chester Island – for the fun of it – after you saw lights and heard noises. You sucker-punched someone named Max who was in a uniform and tied him up. You took his weapon, with which you were familiar. Someone else – Marvin, in fact – killed a dog you loved. You intended revenge and confronted Marvin. Marvin ran away. You untied Max and decided to swim across the Delaware River, at night. Right?"

"Yes," I said, realizing how ridiculous the whole story must sound to Smyrl.

"You realize how ridiculous this sounds to me," said Smyrl. "Nevertheless, something about this tale is so preposterous, that I'm inclined to think you couldn't be making it up – therefore it might be true. Understand: the textbook New Jersey State Police take on this is likely to be that a former Marine, recently discharged from a combat zone and suffering from PTSD, killed someone, half by accident, and then ran – I mean swam – away. Then he foolishly came back the next day – just as murderers sometimes do – to see what was happening at the scene of the crime."

"I can see why you'd think that," I said, "but I absolutely did not kill Marvin. And what was all that equipment doing on the Island? Radar – night vision goggles – boats with quiet, electric motors. Anyway, I agree to a lie detector test – a polygraph, or whatever it's called. I want one for Bardeaux, too, on the 'resisting arrest' charge."

"Never mind that. Do you have any idea approximately what time it was when you left the Island," asked Smyrl.

"Yes, I said. "The moon rose at exactly 8:21 p.m., a few minutes before Smokey was shot. After that I ran back to Max, confronted Marvin and decided to swim the River. All that happened pretty quickly. I'm sure I was off the Island by 9:30 p.m. 10:00 p.m. at the latest. Why?"

"The hypodermic needle in Marvin's eye was removing vitreous fluid, to check his potassium leak rate. It's a way to estimate time of death. Same for the thermometer. Bodies cool at a rate of 1.5 to 2 degrees per hour. Those two guys you saw are good. They'll weigh Marvin, check what he's wearing, note the environmental temperature and use everything to estimate what time he died. Your best hope is that Marvin was killed after you left the Island. And on that score – can you prove you left the Island when you say you did? Did anyone see you? Where did you spend the night? Let's take it from the time you jumped into the River."

"How long will it take to estimate the time of death?"

"They'll be pretty sure of themselves in two hours; and they'll be positive by ten o'clock tomorrow morning. Again – where did you spend the night?"

I thought it over and realized that two things had to happen for me to be released. First the time of death estimates had to indicate a death after 10 p.m., preferably even later – after midnight. Then I had to be able to provide witnesses as to my whereabouts last night. Somehow, I did not want The Church of Jesus Christ is Lord, Sister Alberta or the Reverend Jameson to be visited by police – at least not on my account, and not unless I already knew the estimated time of Marvin's death.

"I was with friends, in Chester," I said. "Who would contact them, and just how would it be done? I'd prefer you not bother them until we know when Marvin died. I'd also welcome the polygraph, anytime. How does that work?"

"We'd have one of our officers, accompanied by a Chester City police officer, visit your friends, unannounced. We'd show them your picture and ask for confirmation of your version of events. We'd ask questions in a way that would prevent them from knowing that you were using them as an alibi.

"A single-issue polygraph, properly administered, is right about ninety percent of the time; so in the case of the 'resisting arrest' issue, Patrolwoman Bardeaux's word would still matter, no matter what the test results were. Multiple-issue polygraphs are much more complicated, and I'm not inclined to fire up the bureaucracy on that yet. You're not going home tonight anyway."

"So tomorrow sometime there will be a final estimate on the time of death?" I asked.

"Yes," said Smyrl.

"What time?"

"As I said, we'll have the preliminary estimate tonight, in two hours – based on the heat loss calculations – and the final estimate, with written conclusions by 2 p.m. tomorrow.

"Am I entitled to a phone call?"

"Yes. One. Do you need privacy?"

"No. I can make it from my cellphone if you'll return it to me – on speaker mode if you want."

"Sorry. No cellphone," Smyrl said.

"I need a phone number from the speed dial," I said.

Smyrl signaled to someone on the other side of what I now realized was one-way glass; and a uniformed trooper brought my cellphone a few minutes later. Smyrl looked up Jack's number for me.

I called Jack on the landline. He answered on the third ring. He was obviously in the West End's noisy bar. "Who's this?" he said.

"It's Ryan," I said. "I have a favor to ask – before it gets dark."

"Let me take the call outside. It's noisy in here."

Back on the line in a minute, he said, "Where are you? I thought you were bringing *Larke* in earlier. What happened?"

"I had a problem," I said. "I can't get back to *Larke* now and I don't want her out another night. Can you and someone else bring her back to the Club for me? Maybe pull her and put her on her trailer? I'd owe you."

"I got lots of questions about this," said Jack, "but I'll ask them later. I'm thinking there's a woman involved with this. Right?"

I thought of Patrolwoman Bardeaux and answered yes. I knew Jack would take good care of *Larke*.

"Do you have a place for me to sleep tonight?" I asked Smyrl.

"Tell you what," said Smyrl, "I'm going to bend some rules. I'll let you stay here, in this room, until we get the preliminary T.O.D. estimates. If they're post-midnight, I'll let you stay here all night – provided you let me look into your alibi. Deal?"

I thought about a police officer visiting The Church of Jesus Christ. There was a chance that the Reverend Jameson Jones would be unresponsive to questions about me, especially if someone like Patrolwoman Bardeaux got in his face. I decided that I trusted Smyrl, though. "If you agree to be the person who visits my friends, and I spend some time with you beforehand – then I agree."

"You're not really in a position to bargain with me, O'Brien," said Smyrl. "Tell you what – I'll think about it. Get comfy."

"Where are you going?"

"I'm going to follow up on some of the information you gave me. We'll look for the weapon you say you threw in the River. We'll look at the rootstock where you say you fired it. We'll dig a bullet or two out of your sailboat. We'll compare all ballistics to the bullet in your pal Marvin."

"When will you have those results?"

"Probably not for several days," said Smyrl. "It's a weekend. The ballistics lab won't even open until Monday. In the meantime, here's a pen, some paper and my cellphone number, in case you think of anything else I should know. Use the phone only to call me – no one else. The switchboard will be monitoring the calls. Don't do anything stupid. I'm not following normal procedures with you right now."

"Thanks," I said, as he left the room.

O'BRIEN & SMYRL, LIMITED
CHAPTER NINE

So I sat, handcuffed in a small conference room, alone with one steel table – bolted to the floor, two chairs, a one-way mirror, one pad of paper, one pen and one round wall clock that said it was 5:19 p.m. I tried my best to look innocent. I felt watched; so I put what I hoped was a guilt-free look on my face. I pulled the pad of paper over in front of me, picked up the pen, and started doodling. To kill some time, I decided to make lists; and I started with a simple innocent list of Ryan to-do items. My cursive handwriting is almost illegible; and often I can't read it myself. But I think my printing is somewhat elegant – a fusion of my high school mechanical drawing class and a one-day calligraphy seminar a college girlfriend had coaxed me into taking with her.

After I quickly scribbled a list of all the easy stuff – pick up dry cleaning, return e-mails, call my Pops, get some food in for Uncle Ryan and so forth – I carefully reprinted it; and so the sheet in front of me ended up alternating an indecipherable scrawl with legible lettering. The clock now informed me it was 5:44 p.m. I'd only killed twenty-five minutes. I turned my back on the clock, vowed not to look at it for at least an hour; and I tore the first sheet of paper off the pad, and started another list – this one of everyone I should get in contact with, sooner rather than later. I took my time, and the list ended up with sixty names on it; and I decided to prioritize the names, and commit to contact at least ten people on it each day. Prioritizing the names took a long time, since I made a game out of it by adding four more to get to sixty-four and then did brackets, like the NCAA March Madness basketball playoffs. Since it was September, I headed the brackets "September Insanity". The eventual winner was no surprise – my Pops.

It was now 6:59 p.m., and I realized it had been exactly twenty-four hours since I'd glanced at my watch, on *Larke*, watching the sun set with Smokey, sipping my favorite single malt, content, and thinking about all the good things my future would likely hold. Now I was in a New Jersey State Police facility, handcuffed and alone in a small room. My dog was dead, my boat was damaged and I'd maybe been arrested for murder – and for resisting arrest. Another twenty-four hours like the last would just about put Ryan out of business.

I invested a few minutes feeling sorry for myself, and noticed that I was hungry. I tore off a sheet of paper and wrote "FOOD?" on it in big block letters and then placed it by the one-way mirror. No one seemed to be watching me, however, since it wasn't until 7:15 p.m. that a young patrolman came in and asked me if I'd like some coffee. I said yes, thanked him, voted for lots of cream and sugar and asked about food. He told me that Smyrl would be back soon, and that I should ask him about food.

The coffee was terrible – not really hot and with the powdered non-dairy creamer that did its level best not to dissolve. I drank it anyway, nursing it along until 7:39 p.m. Then I tore off the two pages of brackets and decided to draw a map of Chester Island, and mark as many events on it as I could remember. I put the deltoid shape of the Island down on paper, a north-south line, *Larke's* location, the rootstock, and headquarters. I drew a small person, with x-d out eyes to indicate Marvin's body, and a cartoon rifle to mark the approximate place where I'd dumped the M4. I added the helicopter's landing site and the approximate place Bardeaux had parked her boat. I added a small broken heart where Smokey had been shot. Then I looked at the completed map; and I was sure I'd either forgotten something, or that it was trying to tell me something important. I thought about the tides, the moon and the wind direction. I traced my approximate route off the Island, in the River. I drew in the shipping channel as I remembered it, the Commodore Barry Bridge and even the flight paths of planes in and out of Philly International. I looked at the map for a few minutes. It told me nothing.

I looked at the clock. It was 8:22 p.m. I'd been in the small room for less than three hours, and I was exhausted from trying to distract myself and to make the hands of the clock move around in a circle a little faster. I realized that I'd make a very poor inmate at whatever Supermax facility they had waiting for murderers. Good thing I was innocent. I promised myself not to murder anyone, ever.

Smyrl finally arrived at 8:41 p.m. He looked focused, as if he was solving a mind-melting Sudoku in his head. He frowned, "what's all this?" He was looking at my artwork.

I tossed the pen down. "I was trying to occupy my mind – kill a little time. "That's a map of Chester Island."

"Not a bad idea," said Smyrl. "We should probably do one of these to scale. There's a computer program that can pretty this up."

"What about the preliminary time of death estimates?" I asked. "Do you have results yet?"

"Yes, they're estimating a 2 a.m. to 4 a.m. T.O.D. for Marvin."

"So I'm off the hook?"

"If your alibi holds up, and the potassium leak-rate test

confirms," said Smyrl. "Of course, there's still the 'resisting arrest' charge to deal with."

I tipped back in my chair. "I almost forgot about that. What's next?"

"We go check out your alibi."

"Who's we?"

"We are we. You and me. O'Brien and Smyrl. The two of us in this room. Plus a driver."

"In handcuffs? I'm going to meet my friends in handcuffs?"

"For starters," said Smyrl.

• • •

And on the way to Chester, in a black and white driven by a uniformed patrolman, down the New Jersey Turnpike, off on US 322 and over the Commodore Barry Bridge, I talked to Smyrl about the Church of Jesus Christ is Lord, the Reverend Jameson Jones and Sister Alberta. I told them what their mission in Chester seemed to me to be. I told him of the kids' singing. I told him of their kindness to me when I was wet, barefoot and exhausted. I told him I did not want them disturbed or upset in any way. I told him that unless he was careful in presenting me, in handcuffs, and my need for an alibi, they might not understand what was going on. I told him of my drive with Jameson to the West End Boat Club and his request for my help with the citation from the City.

I was about to tell him about my Uncle Ryan, when he interrupted. "Where is that citation?"

"It's in my car, on the passenger seat, at the West End," I said.

Smyrl pulled out his cellphone. "Lawson – leave the sailboat alone for now and go to the – where's your car, O'Brien?"

"It's the gray Subaru Forester at the north end of the lot."

"Do you see the gray Subaru Forester at the north end of the lot?" he asked into the phone.

Smyrl waited a minute for Lawson's answer, and asked me: "is there any way into the car?"

"Yes, there's a magnetic box with a key under the trailer hitch."

"You see the car?" Smyrl said into the phone. "Good. Get the key out of the magnetic box under the trailer hitch, open the passenger side door and read me what the paper on the seat says."

Smyrl waited another minute, and said, "Good. Lawson. Stop what you're doing for now and bring it to me. Meet me directly under the Commodore Barry Bridge on PA 291. I'm in a New Jersey State Police car. We'll be parked on the south side of the street, facing east."

Next, Smyrl dialed another number, apparently the Chester City Police Department. "This is Detective Smyrl, New Jersey State Police. Can you patch me in with the officer meeting me Chester at The Church of Jesus Christ is Lord, on PA 291? You can. Great. Thanks.

"This is Detective Smyrl. I'm speaking to Officer Ortiz? The one and only Sergeant Ortiz? Listen there's a slight change of plans. Meet me under the Bridge on 291, south side. I'm in a New Jersey black and white. We'll be there in ten minutes. Thanks. You too."

Then Smyrl put his phone away pulled a key out of his pocket and unlocked my handcuffs. "Don't think we'll need these.

"We've got ten minutes and we're almost there," said Smyrl. "Officer – drive west for a few minutes. O'Brien – show me the train yard where you came ashore."

We did a U-turn when we reached the train yard, than pulled over and stopped. Smyrl rolled down his window and looked off to his right. "So you came out of those trees there?"

It was now dark out, but the yard's security lighting clearly showed trees. "Yes. And across that stony ground. I was wishing for shoes about then."

"I bet. What then?"

"I walked along the tracks until I reached Clayton Street."

"Drive slowly ahead," Smyrl told our driver.

"There's Clayton Street," I said.

"I think I've got the picture," said Smyrl. "Driver – head on down and park under the Bridge."

Shortly after we'd parked, Lawson delivered the citation, handing it to Smyrl through the car window. "Thanks," said Smyrl. "How's the ballistics going on the sailboat?"

"Fair," said Lawson. "We've got two slugs, but they're pretty beat up. We're done for the night. We'll pull more tomorrow until we get one in good condition. We can probably make do with what we'll get."

I squirmed in my seat. "What about my boat? How much damage are you doing to get the slugs?"

Lawson looked at Smyrl, then drove away. Smyrl looked at me and shrugged.

Next, Officer Ortiz arrived in a Chester City squad car. He pulled over, across the street, next to us, turned on his interior light, and rolled down his window. "Detective Smyrl?" Ortiz spoke with a lilt, turning "detective" into a four-syllable word. "De-tec-ee-teeve".

Not to be outdone, Smyrl responded in kind, "Sarg-ee-ant Or-teez."

I cringed, thinking that Smyrl had just blown our chance of local cooperation with politically incorrect and ethnically insensitive humor, when they both laughed.

"Long time, Sam," said Ortiz.

"Very long time," answered Smyrl. "Six years. You bailed on us."

"Hey de-tec-ee-teeve, my wife got a real job over here. Family first. That's what we Or-teez's always say."

Smyrl laughed. "Looks like you're making out alright, sarg-ee-ant."

And so it went. Ortiz and Sam Smyrl joked with each other, while I looked on realizing that Smyrl's first name was Sam. Sam Smyrl. Sammy Smyrl. No wonder he'd taken pity on a suspect named Ryan O'Brien. I thought his elementary school nickname just had to be "squirrel". Finally they got around to business, and Smyrl handed Ortiz the citation from the City of Chester that Jameson had asked me to look into. Ortiz said it was standard bullshit from the useless Department of Licenses and Inspections and that he could make it go away. In fact, it would be his pleasure to make it go away.

One thing, though – Ortiz had personally arrested Sister Alberta's nephew. "Pretty much for his own good," Ortiz said. "He was headed for disaster. He's in a court-adjudicated juvenile program right now – out-of-state. I heard he's doing alright there. Be out in nine months. But I'm not sure how Sister feels about me."

"Let's find out," said Smyrl, signaling to his driver to head down the street to The Church of Jesus Christ is Lord.

• • •

So we parked both cars in front of the house which was really a church or a breakfast club or a choir loft or a school or a home, or a sanctuary for pilgrims, and I watched Ortiz jog quickly up the steps and rap on the door. In the porch light, I could see my staff leaning next to the door. Sister Alberta answered Ortiz's knock, stepped outside, folded her arms and looked down at Ortiz. Ortiz waved the citation, then handed it to Sister, who read it quickly. She moved over to an old-fashioned metal glider on the porch, sat down and patted the seat next to her. Ortiz joined her. They talked for a minute; and Sister handed the paper back to Ortiz, who folded it carefully and placed it in a breast pocket.

Next, Ortiz gestured towards our car and spoke to Sister

Alberta. She squinted in the dark and peered towards us. Then she stood up and waved us out of the car, and up the steps. She had a handshake for Smyrl and a hug for me – a big strong one. "Bless you Pilgrim. I see you took care of that citation already. Less than one day. Maybe God's at work here. Let's all go inside."

Inside, Sister Alberta had us on her home turf; and she clearly outranked sergeants, detectives and pilgrims. She ordered us to the kitchen table, where I just realized I'd had my last meal – over twelve hours ago; and she made coffee for us. "The Reverend's in bed," she said, "so let's be quiet. He always goes to bed early on Saturday nights. He's preaching tomorrow. 'The Prodigal Son'. That's always a good one. We got prodigal sons all over this town. Pilgrim here's a prodigal son – right Pilgrim?"

I thought of my Pops and mumbled an aw-shucks kind of "yes", as Sister put mugs, cream and sugar on the table. When she'd finished pouring four coffees, she looked at Sam Smyrl. "So, Detective Smyrl, what was it you wanted with me?"

Smyrl looked thoughtful. Before he could answer, I said, "May I please say one thing first. I'd appreciate it. I'll be very brief."

Smyrl nodded a yes, but warned me with his eyes that what I shouldn't say was anything to give Sister Alberta a heads-up about the alibi.

I placed my left hand over Sister Alberta's right hand. "Sister, Detective Smyrl is going to ask you some questions. My name will come up in a few of them. Just answer them truthfully. And don't worry."

Sister withdrew her hand from under mine, sat up straight and looked directly at Smyrl. "Of course I'll answer truthfully. Detective Smyrl?"

Smyrl looked directly at Sister. "When was the last time you saw Ryan O'Brien?"

"When he walked out that door," she pointed out the door we'd come in, "and drove away with the Reverend Jones."

"Approximately what time was that?"

"This very morning at about – maybe 10 a.m."

"When did you first see Mister O'Brien?"

"I first saw the Pilgrim when he banged on my front door. Last night at about 11:30 p.m."

"Why do you call him the 'Pilgrim'," asked Smyrl.

"'Cause he was barefoot, shivering, and carrying a staff. That staff outside the door. He'd just swum the River. He come to The Church of Jesus Christ is Lord for a reason. Look – he's already fixed the citation this fool City gave us."

"I see," said Smyrl. "Was the Pilgrim – I mean Mister O'Brien – here from the whole time he entered last night until the time he left this morning?"

"Yes he was."

"Where did he sleep?"

Sister Alberta gestured towards the door. "Out there. On the couch. The Reverend put him in pajamas after he fell asleep."

Smyrl smiled – likely at the image of me in pajamas. "So Mister O'Brien was here from about 11:30 p.m. last night until 10 a.m. this morning?"

"Yes. That's what I said."

"Sister Alberta," said Smyrl, "I have no more questions for you now. If more come up, may I call you?"

"Certainly. Just don't call during Services."

"I won't," said Smyrl. "This is wonderful coffee. Thank you for your time. We'll leave you now. By the way – is there a way I could leave a small donation to the Church?"

Sister Alberta's face lit up, and looked at Smyrl with a smile. "You don't have to do that – but any contribution is welcome. There's a plate by the door."

We all stood to leave. "Pilgrim," said Sister, "you stayin' here again tonight?"

I looked at Smyrl, who shook his head. "No," I said. "Maybe

another time."

"Sergeant Ortiz," said Sister, "can you stay for two more minutes and talk to me about my nephew?"

SANCTUARY
CHAPTER TEN

Smyrl insisted that we drive out of our way to a hole-in-the-wall called "Walt's" for cheesesteaks. Smyrl, our patrolman driver and I sat on spinning stainless steel stools at a counter and ordered off a menu from the year 1955. I had a twenty-cent vanilla milkshake (for three dollars) and a fifty-cent large cheesesteak (for four dollars and fifty cents).

"I've been coming here about twice a year since I was a kid," said Smyrl. "Best cheesesteaks in the world. Plus I love the old menu. I'm not sure who owns the place now, but the original Walt founded the place in 1939. I assume you're in no hurry to get back to the conference room, Pilgrim."

"Is that where I'm spending the night?"

"Yep," said Smyrl. "You can have your cellphone, though."

"I'm likely to be able to go home by 10 a.m. tomorrow. Right?"

"The crime lab boys are usually on time, so I'd say yes. Plan on about ten or a little after."

I'd forgotten how good a Philly cheesesteak could be. I'd fantasized about them in Iraq and Afghanistan, but Walt's cheesesteaks were beyond even my MRE – induced visions. I remembered to do the "Philly lean" – bending forward over the plate, to avoid dripping grease and cheese. My cheesesteak had onions, hot peppers and provolone cheese; the fresh beef had been chopped to a perfect consistency; and the roll had come from a bag that said "Amoroso's". The milkshake came in an oversize stainless steel mixing cup and was so thick I needed a spoon to finish it. I believe I'd never had two meals in one day that were as good: the scrapple-filled breakfast with Jameson and a classic Philly cheesesteak dinner with Smyrl.

On the way back to Regional Police Headquarters – back over the Commodore Barry Bridge – Smyrl talked about the murder he was now investigating without a prime suspect. He covered aspects of the investigation – the likely chronology of events and where and how the case would likely be resolved. He believed as I did, that someone named 'Bama had likely shot Marvin out of some operational imperative and dropped my driver's license to point the finger at me. As far as the murderer knew, Ryan O'Brien was still the prime suspect. The case would likely be a long one, and be solved by someone coming forward with information, or with a determination as to what was actually going on that night on Chester Island, or by dumb luck. Smyrl did not believe that I was in any ongoing personal danger.

I was back in the conference room by midnight, too tired to be bored and ready for sleep. Smyrl tossed me an overcoat from lost and found in case I got chilly, showed me where the men's room was, demonstrated to me that the door was unlocked, promised to see me at about 9 a.m. and left. I decided to call Uncle Ryan.

"Hey Uncle Ryan, it's me. How goes the drive?"

"I'm your side of Richmond," he said. "Oscar says hello. See you in a few hours."

"Uh. I'm not home right now," I said. "I won't be home until about 11 a.m."

Uncle Ryan laughed. "What's her name?"

"I'll tell you all about it tomorrow. Sleep at my place. Pick up the key from my car at the West End parking lot. It's in a magnetic box below the trailer hitch. Do you have my address?"

"Yep. I pulled it off your postcard. Nighty-night."

"Night." I closed the phone and prepared to sleep.

• • •

I stretched out on my back on the floor of the conference room, spread the overcoat over me and thought about the day just past. I hadn't had so little control over my own life since the summer between my Junior and Senior years, at Quantico, where in six weeks I learned that the Marine Corps was not much like college. In fact, the Marine Corps was a perfectly unreasonable place, where random events beyond my control affected everything I did, every day. I recalled the moment I'd realized that my platoon sergeant – perhaps best qualified for the post because he loathed us – had disassembled my rifle and buried it piecemeal in a giant sand ashtray because I'd left it unguarded for thirty seconds while I followed some order or other of his. Lucky for me I had two good friends who cleaned and reassembled the rifle for me, while I was off following some other command of the sergeant's. I started to think about Michael and Walt, wondering what they were up to, thought about moving them up a bracket or two in my September Insanity list – when the day caved in on me and I fell asleep.

"What are you doing here, O'Brien?" It was Patrolwoman Bardeaux. She stood over me, still in uniform, poking my thigh with her right steel-toed boot.

Certain that this was only a dream, I rolled over, happy to be awakened from the nightmare. Then I realized that the conference room light was on. I opened my eyes again, and Bardeaux was still standing there.

"I said – what are you doing here?"

I sat up, shed the overcoat, and stood up. "This is where Detective Smyrl left me."

"In an unlocked conference room! A murder suspect! Someone who resisted arrest!"

"I'm not a suspect anymore," I said. "I've been cleared. Smyrl checked out my alibi. I'm just waiting for the potassium leak test confirmation on Marvin's time of death. The test is due back at ten – Detective Smyrl at nine."

Bardeaux slumped into a chair, and motioned me to sit. She looked bewildered, then pissed. Then she appeared to make up her mind about something. "You won't be here at nine. You're coming with me. To a real lockup. You have not been cleared of the resisting arrest charge – because I filed it. It's your word against mine."

"I'm not going anywhere with you," I said, "Detective Smyrl ordered me to stay here. If I leave, I'll probably really be guilty of something – fleeing probably."

"In fifteen minutes I'll have the paperwork I need," said Bardeaux, "and you'll be leaving – in cuffs. Just you and me. Stay right here. Wait. Give me your cellphone." She got up, showed me she was locking the door and left.

I sat there for a minute in a state of shock, wondering what I'd done to deserve the awful luck that had catapulted Bardeaux back into my life; and decided it was nothing more than the same random fate that had given me the good luck of meeting the Reverend Jameson and Detective Smyrl – and maybe none of it was luck at all but predestined events over which I had no control; but maybe I had some control (such as when I decided to trust my instincts and swim off Chester Island – a decision that had likely saved my life) – and now I needed to trust my instincts again and take action of some kind; only I could think of little to do to get myself out of the conference room, which had one locked steel door, no windows and solid walls. I raised my eyes to Heaven and noticed the dropped ceiling – two by four foot tiles.

I waited another minute, assuming that Bardeaux might be observing me through the one-way glass. I practiced my glum look. Then I threw the overcoat on the conference table, stood on it and pushed up a tile. There was a space of two feet between the tile and the old plaster ceiling. The space contained air-conditioning ducts, sprinkler pipes and electrical conduit. I didn't think the wires holding up the metal framework that housed the tiles looked strong enough to hold my weight, but the black sprinkler pipe looked like a possibility.

I chinned myself up into the ceiling, pulling the overcoat up with my feet. Next, I replaced the tile, and shinnied along the sprinkler pipe towards a partition. My eyes adjusted to the gloom; and enough light poked through various ducts and cracks in the ceiling to see a little. I worked my way past one partition and headed in the general direction of the Men's Room, dragging the overcoat along. When I passed a second solid partition, I lifted a tile and dropped the overcoat to the floor. Then I edged back to the partition and lay there listening to myself breathe. The whole effort had been no more difficult than a tricky obstacle course – and I'd always been good at them. I waited. I'd taken action. I'd trusted my instincts. I'd done what I could. I'd done my best. The rest was up to fate – fate and a nutty patrolwoman.

• • •

"O'Brien!
"O'Brien! You are in very big trouble!
"O'Brien! Where are you?"
I heard Bardeaux's footsteps coming closer – underneath me. She'd reached the overcoat. "O'Brien – you bastard! Shit!" I heard running and the slamming of a door.

I lay on my back, crossed my legs at the ankles and put my hands behind my neck. I might have smiled; and by the time I finished wondering if I'd be able to sleep, I was asleep.

I am proud of my ability to be able to fall asleep anywhere. When there's nothing to be done, no where to go and rest is needed, I can sleep – wherever I am. Sleeping between a dropped ceiling and an old plastered one, next to conduit, metal ducts and sprinkler pipe, resting on a partition in the New Jersey State Police Regional Headquarters – surely qualified as anywhere. When I woke up the first time, it was 3:37 a.m.; and a piece of hardened drywall compound was stabbing me in a kidney. I managed to break it off, shift around a little and fall back asleep. By 5:48 a.m., I had the first inkling that a trip to the men's room would be inevitable; and I listened to the quiet for a few minutes and climbed down – onto the men's room sink. I resisted the urge to write "Bardeaux sucks" on the mirror, in soap; and, instead, stretched a little and returned to my sanctuary. By 7:45 a.m., I heard voices – murmurings from another part of the building. I decided to stay put until I heard Smyrl's voice.

I drifted in and out of sleep for another hour, instantly forgetting dreams upon awakening, listening for voices and getting restless. Finally I heard Smyrl: "O'Brien. O'Brien. Pilgrim! Where are you?"

Climbing down into the men's room, I washed my face, tucked in my shirt and looked in the mirror. "I'm in here. In the men's room."

Smyrl opened the door. He was excited. "Are you alright? How did the conference room door get locked? Did you sleep alright? Come to the conference room – there's something I want to show you – something I've got to deal with." Then he turned his back and left before I could answer any of his questions or tell him about Bardeaux's visit, or where I'd spent the night. I followed him down the hall and into the room.

Smyrl's cellphone buzzed, and he answered it as if he'd been expecting a call. "The story is so inaccurate as to be basically untrue. Who gave it to you?" Smyrl smacked his palm down on the morning's edition of The Philadelphia Inquirer, open to the first page of the Local News section where he'd highlighted a story:

Murder on Chester Island
Suspect in Custody

A New Jersey State Police official confirmed that a body was found on Chester Island Saturday morning. A routine Boeing Company helicopter test overflight of the vacant Island observed the body and alerted the Marine Services Division of the New Jersey State Police.

Officers found the body of a male dressed in camouflage and shot once in the chest. While crime-scene investigators were securing the area, a suspect in a nearby boat was arrested by State Police Patrolwoman Bardeaux.

Bardeaux declined to comment on the arrest, but sources stated that Ryan O'Brien, an ex-Marine Captain, recently discharged, resisted arrest, was placed in custody and is being held overnight for questioning.

The motive for the killing or the name of the deceased is unknown, but conjecture by a knowledgeable official pointed to possible combat stress reaction (PTSD) on the part of O'Brien, who was recently in service in Afghanistan and participated in the Iraq war during an earlier deployment.

Chester Island is unpopulated, located across the Delaware River from the City of Chester and is actually part of New Jersey. Activity on the Island is normally restricted to waterfowl hunting and muskrat trapping; and what O'Brien and the deceased were doing on the island is under investigation.

I sat down and listened to Smyrl snarl at staff writer Stephan O'Leary. "I said no! O'Brien is not a suspect. He's assisting in the investigation. No. O'Brien did not resist arrest. Goddamn it – nothing that matters in your fucking scoop is true. The only stuff in the article that's true you could find on Google! The part about Chester Island being in New Jersey and waterfowl hunting and goddamn muskrats – that's true! I need to know who gave you this story. I need to know now."

Smyrl listened for a minute, then he got scary quiet and spoke in a whisper. "Listen O'Leary – you fucking cub reporter – talk to your editor. Have him call me within the next five minutes. 'Protecting your sources' my ass. Your 'sources' have lied to you and may be involved in a murder. I need to know who gave you this story, and I'm expecting an answer. Understand?"

Smyrl snapped his cellphone shut, sighed and sat down facing me. "I am truly sorry about this," he said. "This is a major fuckup. Everyone involved, including me is going to pay some kind of price for it.

"I'm not sure what we should do next. O'Leary – by the way he pronounces his first name 'Steffan' – seems clueless as to whether he should cooperate with us or stand on some fucking source-protecting principle he learned in college. I suppose we start with Bardeaux."

"Someone mention my name?" said Bardeaux as she opened the door. "May I come in? May I join the team investigating a murder?"

THE CAVALRY
CHAPTER ELEVEN

"You may," said Smyrl, "if you lose the resisting arrest charge you filed. I know you think O'Brien here grabbed you while you were in the River, but I saw the incident from the helicopter. I think he was trying to help you. I also know you had to deal with bullshit paperwork because you fired off a round by accident. Charging O'Brien here with resisting arrest is not the answer to that problem. What do you say?"

Bardeaux sat down and stared at me for a minute. "Where did you spend the night, O'Brien?"

"Right here."

"How did you sleep?"

"Like a baby. I can always sleep."

"Alright," she said, staring at me. "No resisting arrest."

I nodded. Bardeaux would get my silence in return for dropping charges. A deal. No words, no handshake, no writing – but a deal. I also sensed that someday she'd want to know how I'd vanished.

"Have you seen this?" said Smyrl, pushing the newspaper over to Bardeaux.

"No," said Bardeaux, reading the article. "It's baloney. I didn't take this reporter's call and I did not 'decline to comment' – I just didn't return his call. Now I want – no, I need – to be part of the team investigating this."

"You must have mentioned the incident to someone," said Smyrl.

"I did not. I filed only the normal log at the end of my shift and the incident report concerning the arrest. Nothing more. Nada. I swear."

I was considering how very believable Bardeaux sounded, when Smyrl's cellphone rang, and he answered. "Thanks," he said. "Anything else? Later.

"That was the Crime Scene Unit. The potassium leak test confirms. O'Brien was not on Chester Island when Marvin was shot."

While Smyrl looked a little distracted, Bardeaux shoved my cellphone across the table at me. I turned it on and saw voicemails from Uncle Ryan. I did not bother checking them, but simply called him back.

He picked up right away. "Where are you? Do you need a ride?"

"Can I be picked up now?" I whispered at Smyrl. He nodded a yes.

"That would be great Uncle Ryan," I said. "It'll take you about a half hour to get here. I'm in Jersey." I read him the address off of a business card Smyrl pushed at me. "I'll explain everything."

"I know you will," he said.

• • •

While I waited for Uncle Ryan to pick me up, Smyrl went over the entire case, covering the complete chronology of events on the

Island. He danced around the details of my alibi, simply saying it was airtight, said nothing unkind about Bardeaux's involvement and decided out loud to pay The Philadelphia Inquirer an official call later in the morning. "Seems to me that whoever called the Paper is the best lead we have. Bardeaux. Would you like to come with me? It's your name they've got in the paper somehow."

"Gladly," she said.

Next, Smyrl took out a laptop, mashed some buttons and showed us the screen. It was my map of Chester Island, all neatly drawn to scale with symbols, arrows and all the rest. He was swiveling the computer around to show it to Bardeaux and me, when the door to the conference room banged open and a big dog ran in and hopped in my lap. I laughed. "Oscar! Hey bud. How you doing?" Oscar seemed to be doing just fine.

Uncle Ryan clumped into the room and sucked up about two-thirds of its oxygen. "Ryan! What in Hell's going on here?"

Smyrl sat bolt upright in his chair, momentarily silenced by the sheer presence of the large man who'd arrived to rescue me; while Bardeaux looked like she wished she'd worn a flowery high-necked dress and was about to break into song – a slow waltz with lyrics appropriate to an Uncle Ryan on horseback, arriving with drums, a trumpet and a saber clattering at his side; while I had to keep myself from laughing or crying and somehow felt both like a little kid and a lucky young man who'd just officially and finally dodged a bullet.

"This is my Uncle Ryan," I said, "and this is Oscar. Uncle Ryan – this is Officer Bardeaux and Detective Smyrl. They've just finished drawing some conclusions about a case they're working on; and I'm free to go home with you. You might say that they are the team that has exonerated me."

"Exonerated?" said Uncle. "You mean someone thought you'd committed a crime? You? Ryan O'Brien? Captain Ryan O'Brien, USMC?"

"It was all a misunderstanding," I said.

"Can you all spend five more minutes with me?" said Uncle Ryan. "I'll listen carefully and won't interrupt."

"It'll save me hours in the long run," I said.

Smyrl looked doubtful. Bardeaux continued to look entranced, and turned the computer towards Uncle. "Most of what happened is on this screen," she said, moving over one chair and indicating that Uncle Ryan should sit between Smyrl and her.

So they spent a cozy ten minutes talking, pointing and smiling at the computer screen – almost like I wasn't there. Uncle Ryan looked up at me only once – when Smyrl told him about Smokey. Smyrl then shoved the newspaper at Uncle Ryan, who read the short article with one big finger underlining the words. He frowned at Bardeaux. "How did the paper get this story?" he asked. "How could anyone have known all this unless you told them?"

"Officer Bardeaux and I are going to the paper next, to get the answer to that very question," said Smyrl.

Uncle Ryan looked thoughtful. He looked again at the map on the computer screen. "Are the forensic guys finished with the crime scene?" he asked.

"They will be by noon today," said Smyrl.

"How many other beautiful, red-haired women are on the water for New Jersey's finest?" asked Uncle Ryan.

"None," answered Bardeaux. "Wait," she said, waiting a few seconds while her face stopped deciding to blush, "I mean that I am the only woman currently qualified to operate a boat on the Delaware River – south of Trenton – for the New Jersey State Police."

"So it would have been easy for someone watching you arrest Ryan to find out your name."

"And they already knew Ryan's name from the driver's license drop," said Smyrl. He reached into a breast pocket and handed me my license in a plastic bag. "Almost forgot."

I was feeling the need to contribute to the grownups' conversation. "How about the resisting arrest charge?"

"Probably took a contact inside – nobody important, some paperpusher or deskjockey. Let's go talk to the Inquirer," said Smyrl, nodding at Bardeaux.

"Can we get a copy of that map printed out?" Uncle Ryan asked.

"Sure," said Smyrl. "Just take a minute."

So Smyrl and Bardeaux went off to harass an Inquirer reporter named Stephan O'Leary – or his editor, or his editor's boss, or however far up the chain it took – while Oscar and I shared the passenger side of Uncle Ryan's big pickup truck – a perfectly maintained, dark blue Chevrolet 2002 Silverado, the same truck he'd had when I last saw him. "You've been a busy man," said Uncle Ryan, climbing in next to us. "In about thirty-six hours, you've done a recon job on Chester Island, got Smokey killed and *Larke* shot up, pissed off some bad guys, swam the Delaware River, spent Friday night God-Knows-Where, got arrested – for murder, convinced Smyrl of your innocence, spent Saturday night God-Knows-Where and are now off with your Uncle to fix this goddamn mess.

"Where did you spend the nights, anyway?"

I told him about Friday night's good luck with The Church of Jesus Christ is Lord, Jameson, Sister Alberta and the kids who called me Pilgrim; and then I talked about last night's sleep tucked into the dropped ceiling of the building we'd just left.

"One thing," he said. "You've picked up some serious debt – those folks at the Church for one and Smyrl for another. You owe Smyrl big time. Most cops wouldn't have gone to the trouble he did. You'd still be sitting around in some tank, waiting for something to happen. You know what?"

"What?"

"I figure I owe Smyrl too. He got my nephew out of deep-shit trouble."

"He bought me a cheesesteak too," I said.

"Where?"

"Walt's."

"That place with the 1955 menus? I've eaten there. Not for years, though. Was it as good as I remember?"

"Better," I said. "Big milkshake, too. Now I'm hungry again. How about you?"

"Let's eat somewhere, then we've got stuff to do."

• • •

So we ate lumberjack breakfasts at a diner, fueled ourselves up for whatever Uncle Ryan wanted to do next, he showed me a wallet-sized picture of Sissy Powell and told me she was one-quarter Seminole Indian and related to Osceola himself – I told him the truth, that she was beautiful – we drank four cups of coffee each, swapped catch-up stories, took some leftover waffles and a bottle of water out to Oscar and headed for the West End.

Uncle Ryan told me he'd arrived at the boat club late the night before, bought a round of drinks for the regulars – a Jack Daniels for Jack Walker – and talked a cheering crowd into helping him splash his boat in the dark. The tide had been wrong for the boat ramp, so a fleet of pickups shone their headlights on the travel lift while Uncle Ryan and Jack Walker worked the slings, the lift, the dock lines and all the rest. His boat was in my slip now, and that's where we went.

Almost everything about the boat was exactly the same as the last time I'd seen it – four years ago, one slip over, next to *Larke*. It was the same perfect 1987 Parker 21 Center Console, a gleaming white low-freeboard classic powered by a newer Yamaha fuel injected 250, and with expensive Furuno electronics. I knew the

Road King tandem axle trailer was carefully parked somewhere on the Club grounds. The only change to the boat was the word *Sissie*, in tasteful black and gold lettering, starboard side, aft. Uncle Ryan smiled at me, noticing me noticing the boat's name. I smiled back, thought of the commitment the name implied, bit my tongue and helped him lift a toolbox aboard and stow it next to two cardboard cartons he'd carried from his truck.

"Where's your fishing gear?"

"Up in *Larke*. In the parking lot," I said.

"Go get us two rods, some gear and whatever else we might need to catch a Channel Catfish or two."

'We're going fishing?" I asked, surprised.

"Sure," said Uncle Ryan, "but that's not all. Just run up and get what I said. I'll warm up *Sissie* and change the chart plotter around from my very own gator-infested swamp to the Delaware River."

I jogged up to the Club's boat storage area and pulled two spinning outfits, a bucket and my tackle backpack from *Larke's* small cabin. She looked lonely on her trailer; and her bullet wounds cried out for triage. Back on the dock, I pulled the eel trap, slithered two eels into my bucket and brought everything to *Sissie*.

It felt like old times – Uncle Ryan and me going fishing in his boat, on the River, with Oscar up on the bow – nose in the wind and smiling. Missing from the picture was Smokey; and I thought I'd some dues to pay somewhere to someone for her death. The guy who'd shot her, Marvin, was dead, but whoever set up the whole deal was really responsible. Someone named 'Bama needed to hear from me eventually. I almost didn't mind that he'd set me up for a murder, but he'd gotten Smokey shot and given me a hole in my heart.

"Where's your head?" asked Uncle Ryan.

"What do you mean?"

"What are you thinking about?"

"Smokey," I said.

"Remember the time she tried to retrieve the catfish you threw back? She was over the side and in the water before we could stop her. She dove for that cat – fucking dove. I never saw anything like it. Can you imagine the story that fish got to tell its grandchildren! Ha!"

Then Uncle Ryan assumed the basso voice of grandfather catfish talking to his grandchildren: ". . . and there I was, captured by the deadliest fishing team to ever ply the muddy waters of this great River – Ryan O'Brien and his famous Uncle Ryan – I managed to escape by luck and daring and just as I thought I was safe, a monster, a black thrashing monster had me in his jaws and was taking me back to Catfish Hell. I don't really know how I escaped – pure luck and the grace of the whiskered one herself."

I laughed, remembering the incident. It was from a Club Catfish Tournament my senior year in college. We'd been culling fish as we caught them, keeping only the three largest for the weigh-in. Grandpa hadn't made the cut. Uncle Ryan had won the tournament twice, but never with me aboard. We'd always weighed in three nice fish, but finished shy of in-the-money. That particular Catfish Tournament had cost me a girlfriend, who couldn't understand why I wanted to spend the day fishing with Uncle Ryan, and carousing with a bunch of blue-collar drunks afterward – instead of going to some fancy event her sorority had concocted. My excuse – "I'll always want to fish with my Uncle" just made things worse.

"Where can we pick up a quick fish or two?" asked Uncle Ryan.

"Jetty end, channel side, downriver," I said. This was fisherman's shorthand for let's fish the deep end of the five-hundred yard long rock jetty, Jersey side, anchor downriver and let the incoming tide take our bait close to the jetty structure.

"Aye Mate," said Uncle Ryan, getting *Sissie* up on plane, while I watched for the occasional floating log West Enders called "gators" that could tear the bottom out of a boat. We were anchored and fishing with chunks of eel for bait in ten minutes and had three decent sized catfish in the live well in another ten.

AUNT DEB'S DITCH
CHAPTER TWELVE

"Now What?" I asked.

"Anchor aweigh," said Uncle Ryan. "Stuff to do."

"What's in the boxes?" I asked, after I'd pulled *Sissie's* anchor and we were underway.

"That's the 'stuff' we're going to use to figure out what's going on. Trust me."

We circled the jetty, heading first upriver to avoid the shallows around the rocks; then we looped towards the Jersey side and the other end of the jetty. At this point we could observe the south side of Chester Island. The forensic guys were still on the Island; and a boat identical to the one Bardeaux had used to arrest me was pulled up to the usual spot.

"Good," said Uncle Ryan. "We're not too late."

"Too late for what?" I asked.

"I figure someone saw Bardeaux arrest you yesterday. I figure they called the Inquirer after they got her name from someone. They already had your name from your driver's license. I figure that as long as forensics is here, whoever it was is still watching. I figure we'll see if we can find them, maybe we can solve this thing for your pal Smyrl. Remember, we owe him."

We eased *Sissie* around a point of marshy land. It was to our left, as Chester Island was on our right.

"Anywhere from here on, someone could have seen you get arrested, while they watched the Island," said Uncle Ryan. "Let's anchor and look like we're fishing."

"Let's actually fish," I said, "though this isn't really much of a place to catch anything."

"That's why we've already caught a couple," said Uncle Ryan. "Think of them as props."

So we anchored two-hundred yards from the Jersey side of the River in six feet of water, four-hundred yards from Chester Island. I rigged up the chunked eels, got the rigs into the water and the rods in rod holders. It made no sense to hold a rod when catfishing. They hooked themselves if you just left them alone; but if you did the tuna-jerk, they got away every time. The large circle hooks prevented the fish from swallowing them, and a hands-off approach to the rods was best.

"Don't – as in DO NOT – look up right now," said Uncle Ryan. "Keep watching the rod tips. But there's a truck parked up on Floodgate Road." Floodgate road was a gravel road that ran along the bank of the River. It was eight feet above water level; and I'd never been on it, and I'd never seen anyone else there either. The whole area wasn't much more than swamp, some flood control dikes, trees and bushes.

I followed his command and kept facing *Sissie's* stern and the rod tips. One rig was attracting attention from something too small to be caught; but eels are so tough that nothing without real teeth could take them off a hook. I left it alone. "What do you want to do?"

"I want to keep on pretending we're fishing. I want to maneuver *Sissie* to where we can get a picture of the license plate. I want to run up the bank and confront whoever's up there, beat a confession out of him, turn him over to Smyrl and go have a few beers. I want to win the lottery, too."

"That all sounds good to me," I said. "Especially the 'beating' a confession out of him. Can I help with that? For Smokey?"

"No. I was just kidding about that part. The license number to Smyrl should be good enough. Maybe the guy's a birdwatcher. You've been arrested enough for the week."

So we moved *Sissie* again, this time east towards a small creek with the mysterious name of "Aunt Deb's Ditch". I'd always wondered if whoever named the muddy tidal creek intended to honor Aunt Deb or insult her. We anchored again, this time on the license plate side of the truck.

"OK," said Uncle Ryan, "I'll hold up a fish. You take a picture. Make sure you get the license plate."

He took a catfish out of the live well and held it up. As I got ready to take the picture with my smartphone, the man with the truck walked around to its rear and stood in front of the license plate. "What the crap," I said, "he's blocking the picture."

"Don't look at him," said Uncle Ryan. "Where does that road go? Can he get out either way?"

"I don't know. Check your chart plotter."

"Nah," said Uncle Ryan, "we've got to try something else. Pull the anchor. Don't look at him."

We move back around to the other side of the small point of land – behind a stand of trees and out of sight of the truck. "You wanted recon, right?" asked Uncle Ryan.

"That was Friday night," I said. "I'd been drinking single malt. Now I'm sober. A lot has happened since that version of Ryan O'Brien went recon. I'm different now."

"I wasn't really asking," said Uncle Ryan. "You – Captain O'Brien – are the only logical candidate for this assignment."

"Let me guess," I said, looking at the satellite view on the chart plotter. "Through two or three hundred yards of that tick-infested swamp there, swim fifty yards of Aunt Deb's Ditch, take a couple of pictures, send them to Smyrl, come back, don't be observed."

"I doubt there are ticks there," Uncle Ryan said, smiling and giving me a gentle fist bump, "the snakes probably ate them all." Then he trimmed the outboard motor up and carefully ran *Sissie* aground, bow-first, on the muddy shore; and after I placed my smartphone in a plastic zip-loc, I stepped out into the muck.

There was no point in trying to keep dry or out of the mud, since I knew Aunt Deb's Ditch was out there waiting. I kept to the trees and made good time. I did not need to crawl or camouflage myself with mud. By the time I reached the Ditch, I was sweating. Smokey would have enjoyed every minute of it.

• • •

I looked across the water and saw a gravel road up on a bank. It was either Floodgate road or one that connected to it. The truck was parked out of sight to my right; and the only way I could get close enough to take a picture was to swim the Ditch, climb the bank, and move west along the road. I waded into Aunt Deb's Ditch. It was waist-deep, the bottom was muddy and I shuffled along, holding my smartphone over my head. Toward the middle, it was neck deep, but then it got gradually shallower. I stopped at the foot of the bank and listened. It was quiet.

I scrabbled up the bank, using small bushes and trees for handholds. I slipped a few times, but made it to the gravel road and turned right. I was about four-hundred yards from the truck. Every minute or so I stopped to listen, since I felt exposed on the road; and I figured I'd duck into the trees if I needed to hide. On my third stop, I heard a motor, getting louder. The truck was headed my way.

This changed things. Maybe it made things easier, I thought.

Maybe this was one of those lucky tactical opportunities I'd read about but never experienced in Afghanistan. I'd hide behind a tree, let the truck pass, lean out, take a quick picture and be done with the exercise. I readied the smartphone by removing it from its zip-loc and making sure it was turned on. I noticed that there was no cell signal. No matter. What mattered was that I was about to get a picture of the license of the truck belonging to the man that was responsible for Smokey's murder.

Noise from the truck was getting slowly louder. It sounded as if it was grinding along on the rutted gravel road in low gear. I got another grand idea. Recognizing that this idea came from the same brain that chucked a piece of driftwood out into the River and got Smokey shot, I gave the thought another two seconds of deliberation. I still liked the idea; and I'll defend it to anyone – it was decisive, improvisational, bold – and, best of all, I was trusting my instincts. I thought to take two pictures: one of the driver, then one of the license plate.

Cover was limited on the driver's side of Floodgate Road, but I figured that the driver of the truck would be paying too much attention to the road to notice me; and I planned to hold very, very still while I took the pictures. I crouched behind a man-sized evergreen bush. As the truck approached, I raised the smartphone up to about driver face-level, and waited. As the truck rattled by, I took the first picture; and as soon as it was past me, I leaned out and took a shot of the rear of the truck. Then I held very still and waited for the truck to drive away.

Big problem. After it'd move about fifty yards down the road, the truck stopped. Then the reverse lights came on and it began to back up. I knew that whoever was driving the truck might be armed and that I could not swim Aunt Deb's Ditch fast enough to keep from getting shot, so I crossed the road – in full view of the driver – and headed off into the swampy thicket on the other side of the road. After scrambling into the bush about thirty yards – to where I could just make out the road and the truck – I heard a truck door slam, then a pissed-off voice.

"Hey you! You in the bushes! Come out of there!"

Now I knew exactly what I had to do; and it was not whatever the guy with the truck told me to do. It had happened to me before, only a few times. In confusing or uncertain circumstances, I'd somehow known exactly what to do; and this was one of those times. I called back, "Who are you? What do you want?" Then I moved further west, paralleling the road and I called out again: "I'm only coming out if you tell me who you are." I wanted to give him the impression that I was moving away from him.

"Never mind who I am," he said. "Who are you? What are you doing here?"

I'd moved another dozen yards or so west. "Alright! I'll come out. Give me a minute. I'm tangled up in these briars." I moved a little more and shook a small tree. "I'm coming!" Then I reversed course and headed back towards the truck. I'm pretty good in the woods – not crazy good, like Geronimo, or live off the land for two years good, like Jim Bridger – but as the Walter Brennan character in some old western or other said: "no brag – just fact", I'm much better than most; and I knew I could reach the truck before Mister Pissed Off.

I got to the truck. No one in sight. No keys. I hadn't expected to be that lucky. I reached in, put the clutch in neutral, popped the emergency brake and started pushing the truck. As soon as it was rolling, I turned the steering wheel, aimed the truck left and watched as it rolled down the bank and into Aunt Deb's Ditch. I noted that it had Alabama plates. Watching the truck settle into four feet of muddy water was the most satisfying thing I'd seen for years.

I was tempted to hide in the bushes to see 'Bama's reaction – now I was sure it was him; but I decided instead to get back to Uncle Ryan and *Sissie*. I jogged east around a bend in the road, waded the Ditch again and got myself back to the big River – several hundred yards from *Sissie*. I called to Uncle Ryan. Oscar saw me first and barked. I waved when Uncle Ryan finally saw me and jumped aboard *Sissie's* bow when he reached me.

"You look pretty pleased with yourself," said Uncle Ryan.

"I am. Get me to cell service, somewhere out there." I waved towards the Pennsylvania side of the River. I looked at my smartphone pictures and realized that I'd missed the shot of the truck's driver, and had only a blurred image of the side of the truck.

Sissie showed her stuff and it was too noisy to talk until we'd reached the shipping channel, mid-River, where cell service looked to be reliable.

I dialed Smyrl's number – it rang to voicemail. "Damn." I texted him:

CALL ASAP – EMERGENCY

Smyrl called me right back. "This better be good," he said, "Bardeaux and I've worked our way up to a very senior editor here at the Inquirer."

"It's better than good." I said. "I've got pictures of 'Bama's truck – Alabama plates – and better yet, I can tell you where he is right now. Do you have access to the map we drew?"

"It's on my laptop. Just a sec." A minute later, he said, "Okay. Got it."

"Find Aunt Deb's Ditch. East-south-east of the Island. The truck is in four feet of water, in the Ditch, and not going anywhere. 'Bama is probably armed, definitely pissed off and trying to figure out what to do. He's likely somewhere along that gravel road – 'Floodgate Road'."

"Okay," said Smyrl. "I got all that. I've got lots of questions for you. Stay put, wherever you are and let me get back to you as soon as I've made a few calls."

"We're to 'stay put'," I said to Uncle Ryan.

We edged out of the channel, back toward Jersey. Uncle Ryan switched the chart plotter to fish-finder mode and was watching it. "Fish marking," he said. "All men are equal before fish," I said, quoting Herbert Hoover.

Sissie says "give a man a fish and he has food for a day; teach him how to fish and you can get rid of him for the whole weekend."

"Good things come to those who bait," I said. We fished.

CATFISH GOT WHISKERS
CHAPTER THIRTEEN

"Usual deal?" I asked.

"Of Course," said Uncle Ryan. "A point each for first fish, last fish, biggest fish, smallest fish, most fish. One point for anything not a catfish. Ten points for a striper. A hundred points for a sturgeon. Minus one point for an eel. Minus two points for losing your bait. Minus ten points for a snag and rig loss. The usual awards, given contemporaneously with each fish."

"Deal."

Normally, we'd each fish two rods, change rigs and bait often, keep score out loud, and drink beer. Since we'd started out on a serious mission, one that was still double top-secret-crypto to me, we had no beer. But fishing without beer is better than beer without fishing.

"Fish on!" said Uncle Ryan. "I call two pound Channel Cat. One point – first fish."

Oscar barked enthusiastically.

"Okay," I said, "It's the Most Illustrious Order of Saint Patrick for you – Sir Ryan."

"Hey, fish on!" I said. "I call three pound Channel Cat."

"Alright!" said Uncle Ryan, "It's The Most Ancient and Most Noble Order of the Thistle, for you – Sir Ryan."

Just then my phone rang. It was Smyrl. "Where are you?" he said.

"Out here. In the River. Fishing. Where are you? Any luck with 'Bama?"

"Not 'Bama," said Smyrl. "Max – the guy you sucker-punched. At least I guess that's who it is. It's probably 'Bama's car, though."

"What do you want Uncle Ryan and me to do?"

"Nothing for now," said Smyrl. "See if you can stay out of trouble for a few hours. Max says he was birdwatching and his car accidentally rolled into the Ditch while he wasn't looking. He thinks he left the emergency brake off. He's got binoculars and a bird book for cover."

"What happens next?"

"We work the car – its plate, fingerprints. We work Max back in your favorite conference room. We don't mention you by name. We'll see where it goes. Probably take us three or four hours. You're free to keep fishing or whatever it is the two of you want to do. We may call you later to corroborate Max's version of Friday night. Later."

"He hung up," I said to Uncle Ryan. "We're free to go about our business. What are in those boxes anyway?"

"Stuff we need to set up. You win – so far. Two to one. You got the biggest fish and last fish, I got the first fish. Reel in." He turned off the fish-finder and returned to chart plotter mode. He aimed *Sissie* at Chester Island. When we reached the Island, he nudged the bow of the boat onto muddy ground, I jumped off with the anchor and stuck its flukes into the mud.

"You bring that box," said Uncle Ryan, "I'll bring a few tools and this box. Show me where the body was."

We walked across the damp, grassy Island, to the spot where

Marvin had been shot and my driver's license dropped. There were lots of footprints, and the place was muddy. Oscar sniffed the air and barked twice. It seemed years ago to me that I'd been here last, not two days. "This is it," I said.

Uncle Ryan selected a relatively dry place and put down the box he'd been carrying. "Over here Ryan." He opened his cardboard carton with a utility knife, then my box. They contained electronics.

"What we've got here is high-quality, solar-powered, wireless, day/night security cameras. When we're finished, images will be transmitted to a receiver, forwarded to a router that will send them to a computer – your computer. We've got six of them to plant today. The hardest thing we'll have to do is to hide the solar panels but still have them get enough sun to keep on working. We can do it."

"How much did all this stuff cost?"

"It's probably worth about nine-thousand dollars, retail, but it didn't really cost me anything. I got it from a rich guy I took fishing a month ago – he makes this stuff. I won it from him on a bet. He bet me I couldn't put him on a bonefish over nine pounds. We got three over ten. He was happy to lose the bet. I was going to use this stuff on my marina, but never got around to installing it. I don't think I really need it anyway. It was already in the truck when I left to come see you.

"We'll pick three locations, put two cameras at each location and call it a day. This is a logical first location. If someone finds one camera, the second one might still show us something."

• • •

So we placed cameras in a tree and in a thicket, aimed at the site where I'd punched Max and Marvin's body had been found. As usual, I was amazed at Uncle Ryan's ability to do stuff with his hands, without seeming to think about it. He looked at a diagram of the setup – camera, solar battery, connectors – once and threw it away. When he was satisfied, the three of us returned to the boat and he turned on the chart plotter. "Now we've got to find the place where the bad guys launch their boat. Where do you think we should look first?"

"Well," I said, looking at the chart plotter, "they need a place with road access and no steep bank. That leaves out most of everything I see here. The bank down Floodgate Road is too steep. We could look up the Old Canal there." I pointed downriver a half mile or so; and I switched the chart plotter to satellite mode with labels. "There's a gravel road up here – 'Stump Road' – that might get close to the canal."

"What's the water like up there?" asked Uncle Ryan.

"Shallow. But navigable. I've fished up there a few times. It's a great place to go if it's too windy to fish on the River."

So we ran *Sissie* down the Jersey side of Chester Island, past two old wooden wrecks that showed at low tide; and we turned left into the Canal. Another half mile straight south on the canal and we came to a bend, and in a quarter of a mile we came to a fork. Stump Road would be off to the right, through trees and bushes.

"Recon time again," said Uncle Ryan. He nosed *Sissie* into the bank; and I jumped off. "Twenty minutes, tops," he said.

"Right," I answered, looking at my watch.

I snooped around in the woods, and found a network of ATV trails. They were likely made by kids, but they could also provide a way to get a boat to the Canal. I walked along one of the trails in what I thought was the direction of Stump Road, but ended up on a power line. Where the power line crossed the Canal there were tire tracks and footprints, and no steep bank. I was sure this was where someone could have launched a boat. I called Uncle Ryan on his cell and asked him to move *Sissie* a little further along the canal, and soon I was waving to him to come take a look.

"This is perfect," said Uncle Ryan. "We'll hang cameras on the power line towers and no one will think twice about them. They'll think they belong to South Jersey Energy."

"How do we get them up on the towers?" I asked.

"You're kidding, right?" said Uncle Ryan.

"Oh." I looked up at the nearest tower. It looked unclimbable.

"You're not going up very far," said Uncle Ryan. "Just up to that first cross-beam. Let me get all the stuff you'll need."

"It'd be a shame to survive Iraq and Afghanistan and die falling off that tower."

"Do you want me to do it?" asked Uncle Ryan.

"Absolutely not," I said. "If you fell off the tower, Mom would kill me and then we'd both be dead. I'm going."

With everything I'd need in a plastic five-gallon bucket and with one end of a rope tied to its handle and the other end to my belt, I muscled my way up the first ten feet of the tower. After that there were steel rungs and the going was easy.

At about thirty-five feet, Uncle Ryan signaled that I was high enough. "Do you know what to do? Were you paying attention?"

"Yep," I said. "I do. I was." And I proceeded to haul up the bucket and start to rig things up just like I'd been shown.

Uncle Ryan walked back to the boat and was messing around with something, when I saw some movement out of the corner of my eye. It was a truck, moving slowly down the power line, toward *Sissie*. The truck was two small hills and one left-hand turn away from being in sight of Uncle Ryan; and I called him on my cell.

"Uncle Ryan. There's a pickup truck headed your way. Suggest you move away – back around the bend."

"What about you, partner?"

"I'll hold very still. No one ever looks up."

I watched Uncle Ryan back *Sissie* away from the landing, spin her round and move back down the Canal. From my vantage point up the tower I could see where he stopped, cut the motor and began to drift. I could see him start to fish, casting a small lure back and forth across the Canal, from bank to bank. When in doubt, fish.

As the truck approached the small landing, it stopped and turned around. The truck had a boat trailer attached, and the driver maneuvered the back wheels of the trailer up to the water's edge, then into the water until the canal water covered the keel rollers. Then he got out of the truck and fiddled with the cable that would connect to a boat and allow it to be pulled onto the trailer. Then he driver stood there, lit a cigarette, looked around and made a cellphone call.

I could see the small boat heading up the Canal before Uncle Ryan, but I couldn't hear it. Electric motor. I called Uncle Ryan and told him about the approaching boat. "Pretend to be fishing."

"Pretend? Fish on!" I could see his rod bending and a small splashing at *Sissie's* stern. Oscar was barking. "This puts me ahead!"

The trailer blocked the truck's license plate, but I took pictures with my smartphone anyway, since the security camera wasn't set up yet. The driver of the boat slowed down as it approached *Sissie*, demonstrating courtesy towards a fisherman playing a fish. He and Uncle Ryan waved at each other, and then the skipper of the small boat drove it right onto the trailer. The truck driver passed the winch line to the skipper, who reached over the boat's bow and hooked it onto a D-ring. The truck driver cranked the hand crank until the boat was settled on the trailer, and then pulled boat and skipper out of the Canal. Once the boat was away from the water, both men fiddled with tie-downs, straps and the plug at the boat's stern. They were competent and had done the drill before. I took pictures.

After the truck, trailer, boat and men were out of sight, I finished up with the security cameras and climbed down from the tower. Uncle Ryan maneuvered *Sissie's* bow into the bank and I hopped aboard. "Last fish – one point. Fish not a catfish – another point. Score now three to two – Uncle Ryan." He showed me a nine-inch yellow perch. "I should get an extra point for catching this on a lure." He nodded towards a small crankbait.

"That's my rod," I said. "That's a violation and disqualification."

• • •

We headed back out the canal and talked about what we'd just seen. We had no real pictures, no license plate. The small boat's registration number had been on the side away from Uncle Ryan. He said he'd recognize the boat's skipper if he ever saw him again. We agreed that we had nothing worth reporting to Smyrl. We had two more security cameras to set up. It was late afternoon.

We decided to set the remaining cameras up on access points to Floodgate Road; and we took turns climbing the steep bank and rigging up the gear. Uncle Ryan was twice as fast as I was setting things up. When we were finished, we headed back to the West End. The tide was high enough to use the Club's boat ramp, and Uncle Ryan decided to pull *Sissie*. So on a Sunday afternoon, late, with Club members comfortably tired from a day of boating or from working around the marina, and likely a little less than sober, Uncle Ryan demonstrated his boat handling and trailer maneuvering skills. In about five minutes, he had *Sissie* up the ramp, on the trailer, tied down, and hosed down.

Both Jack Walker and Johnny Daniels were on the wooden walkway, watching. They were drinking something hard and glittery in plastic cups. They didn't say anything to us, but they looked at each other and smiled when Uncle Ryan was satisfied with his boat, truck and trailer. Johnny pointed a finger at me and gave me a thumb's up – saying, in so many words: "now that's how you pull a boat."

After Uncle Ryan parked his truck, boat and trailer, we headed into the clubhouse. A major rebuilding of the Club six or seven years before had left the West End with a large rectangular bar, usually full of happy members by Sunday afternoon. We secured a corner spot at the bar, ordered draft beer and looked at a menu. Johnny, Jack and the other regulars came in and sat around us. Uncle Ryan had kept his membership in the Club, even after he'd moved to Florida; and his book of script, worth fifty-dollars in drinks, was unused. So he laid it on the table and signaled Dee, the barmaid, to use it up on everyone there. She took paper ketchup holders and placed them upside-down next to patrons; and folks at the bar raised a glass to my Uncle.

The Club's kitchen was usually under new management. Chefs would come into the Club, look around at the attractive waterfront setting, and believe that they could make money selling fancy lunches and dinners to the Club members. By the time they realized that the Club was private and that only members and guests of members could be served liquor, and that Club members would not support fancy food – the hours of the kitchen were scaled back and the food evolved into bar food. We ordered two pepper and egg sandwiches each, cheese fries and another beer.

We listened to the talk around the bar, argued about who'd won our fishing contest, ate our dinners of bar food, enjoyed each other's company, and did not become involved in discussing the West End's latest controversy: whether or not the dredger we'd hired had actually fulfilled his contract by dredging the entire nineteen thousand cubic yards of muck out of the marina, or whether he'd shorted us by thousands of cubic yards. Consensus at the West End always ran to conspiracy; and most folks believed that there were many reasons we'd been cheated – including the number of barges that had left with the dredging spoils and their rated capacity, the soundings performed by Club members immediately after the dredging was competed and undredged areas visible at blowout low tides. Whether the Club owed the dredger money or vice versa was another issue hotly debated.

"Don't you miss all this?" I asked Uncle Ryan.

"A little," said Uncle Ryan. "I do miss the monthly meetings. They should be filmed. Reality TV. 'As the Club Turns' or 'All My Club Members'." Just then his cellphone rang, and after looking at the caller ID, he hopped off the bar stool and went into the pool room to take the call.

He came back in a minute, looking worried. "Gittum up, Scout," he said to me, indicating with a nod of his head that it was time to go. He left his script on the bar, told Dee to use it up on his friends, said goodbye to the assembled crew and herded me outside to my car. Oscar jumped into the back seat, Uncle Ryan into the passenger side, front. "Home James."

VERILY
CHAPTER FOURTEEN

I drove while Uncle Ryan sat in the Subaru's passenger seat, fiddling with his cellphone. He was texting; and his big hands were made for plumbing, or stone masonry, or wrangling cattle, or fishing for king crabs, or lumberjacking. "Damn. I hate these tiny keys. I screw up half the time. It takes me five minutes to say 'hello'."

"Why not just call her?"

"How do you know it's a her?"

"It's gotta be Sissie," I said. Who else could it be?"

"Yeah smartass, that's right. It's Sissie. And I can't call her right now. She doesn't want her brother Mikey to know she's talking to me."

"Mikey?"

"Yeah. Her kid brother. He's back. He's a pain in the ass. He's the one thing Sissie and I don't agree on. She'll want to give him a job – another job, we don't need help, he'll screw up six ways from Sunday, I'll lose my patience with him, Sissie will lose hers with me, we'll argue, Mikey will disappear for a few days, Sissie will blame me, I'll blame Mikey, Mikey will come back – probably high, Sissie will want to give him another chance, I'll mope around about it and give in, Sissie will hug me and thank me and then the whole damn sequence will happen again. Come on down to my marina for Groundhog Day. Watch the show. What the crap. I'm probably going to head home tomorrow after rush hour."

"Sounds grim."

"Yeah. Good word. 'Grim'. Glad you went to Penn so you could describe my life with the perfect word."

"Sorry Uncle Ryan, I don't have any experience with that kind of thing. I just don't know anything about it. How old is Mikey?"

"He's exactly your age. Twenty-seven."

"College?"

"Nope. Did graduate from high school, though."

"Jobs? Skills?"

"He's a motorhead. He can fix cars, boats – pretty much anything made of metal that has moving parts. But he never sticks to a job. He gets bored. He's never had the same job for more than six months."

"Sounds like lots of twenty-seven-year-olds," I said. "Maybe he'll grow up."

"Yeah, but he's nothing like I was; and that's the problem. I don't understand him. Sissie says I don't relate to him – whatever that means. She says that it's my fault. She never tells him he doesn't relate to me.

"Sorry to hear there's trouble in Paradise. If I can help somehow, let me know."

Uncle Ryan looked over at me. "Thanks. I think I'll pass on having Ryan O'Brien fix this one for me."

"Hey Uncle Ryan – excellent sarcasm. I didn't even know you did sarcasm."

"Pay attention to the road. By the way our goal tonight is simple – to assemble the rest of your furniture, set up the computer links to the cameras, go out and have a few drinks and get a good night's sleep. I figure this will be your first night in your own bed in awhile."

"Verily," I said, pulling into my parking spot.

"Listen to him, Oscar. Verily. See what an Ivy League education will do to you. Verily."

• • •

In a hectic two hours, we dedicated one of my three computers to the security cameras, tested the setup by watching absolutely nothing at all happen on Chester Island, assembled the rest of my furniture, walked and fed Oscar, showered and were headed out the door. Uncle Ryan seemed relaxed from the structured routine and I looked forward to a quiet night, some decent food and conversation with one of my favorite people on the planet.

"Where would you like to eat?" I asked.

"Let's see. Not far away – a short walk. Drinking – yes. Driving – no. No reservations. No loud music. Decent food. No need to go somewhere else after we eat. Beautiful women – your age, of course."

"Interesting criterion," I said. As soon as I said 'criterion', I knew I was in for a ribbing.

"What the crap, Ryan. Did you use words like 'criterion' and 'verily' in Afghanistan? Seriously? What would you have told your platoon about my requirements for dinner?"

"I'd tell them there might be beautiful women their age. They wouldn't care about the rest of it."

"How would they behave when they got there?'

"That's a really great question. I'd say it was insightful, but you'd give me crap about that. First they'd be very shy. When all you do is swear at each other 24/7, and often think about getting killed, you worry about being able to speak to women at all. You become concerned that you've might have forgotten how. After the men – kids, really, most of them – had a few drinks, they'd loosen up. Pretty soon they'd be the life of the party. First they'd want to sing. Then they'd want to dance. Finally they'd likely want to fight – at least a few of them. Cooler heads would prevail. We'd be shown the door; and only if the owner was very tactful, would we go peacefully. We'd all go back to our tents and fall asleep – remembering little the next day. The troops would recall only that I took them somewhere cool, that they had a great time, that they were immortal, that they were Marines and that they'd follow Lieutenant O'Brien anywhere."

"Okay," said Uncle Ryan. "I'll follow you anywhere too, Lieutenant."

We ducked into a place called the Pub & Kitchen. A small sign on the door said "No Reservations."

"Check!" said Uncle Ryan. "One criterion. Three, actually: short walk, no driving and no reservations."

We went inside. "Check!" said Uncle Ryan. "No loud music. And check again – beautiful women everywhere – your age. Let's eat here."

We settled into a table for four in a corner where we could both have our backs against a wall, and where we could talk. We ordered drinks from a pretty waitress, and then debated whether my Founder's Porter was darker and therefore more manly than his Yards Love Stout. We briefly considered drinking one each of every draft beer, ale, stout, lager and porter at the bar; but we decided we did not want – absolutely did not want – any of the pale ales, winter solstices or something described as raison d'être. So we traded, and from our waitress – who I now felt was really good-looking – I ordered the Love Stout and Uncle Ryan ordered a Founder's Porter.

"I think I liked the stout better," said Uncle Ryan. "I liked the malty, cocoa flavor. Sweet. And – I swear – I think I tasted oysters in there."

"And I think I liked the porter better. I'm pretty sure I tasted caramel."

So we switched glasses back, looked at a menu and ordered. Now our waitress – the same young woman – was lovely. Then we talked. Man talk. Porter and stout talk. Favorite uncle and blessed nephew talk. We recalled fine times, touched many bases and ate good food. We ordered another round of porter and stout from the same knockout waitress; and we ate dessert she recommended. We managed to politely turn down her suggestion on after-dinner drinks and had yet another round of porter and stout. We became full. We became maudlin – although I did not say that word out loud. We tipped our gorgeous waitress generously; and we reluctantly, but courteously – as officers and gentlemen should – retired to the bar to free up the table. After we were reseated, our waitress came up behind Uncle Ryan, tapped him on his shoulder and lit up our corner of the world with a megawatt smile. Then she handed him a Grant – a fifty dollar bill.

"I'm not sure if I just passed a test or am just plain stupid," she said. "Did you realize this was a fifty? I'd rather have you guys come back next Sunday – than accidentally leave me this, realize it later and then never see you again."

Uncle Ryan swiveled on his bar stool, faced her and smiled. "It wasn't a test. I meant to leave a double-sawbuck. If it had been a test, though, you surely would've passed it." He traded presidents, and pocketed the Grant and handed her a Jackson. "Why Sunday?"

"I only work here Sundays," she said.

"Well I'm going to be in Florida next Sunday, but Ryan O'Brien lives here. No reason he can't be here. What do you do the rest of the week when you're not working here and passing tests?"

The waitress glanced at me briefly, then turned her full attention back to Uncle Ryan. "I go to school. I have homework. I work part-time. I work out. I walk my dog. I do my laundry. The usual."

"Ryan here's just out of the Marine Corps. Just moved back to town," said Uncle Ryan.

I excused myself then to go the men's room, since I wasn't about to listen to Uncle Ryan brag about me; and I certainly did not want to demonstrate to him that I was just as shy as the men in my platoon, and that I'd lost most of my confidence regarding women, for the same simple reasons my men had – I'd been too busy staying alive and been too exhausted to think about them much; but our waitress was very pretty, and although I tried to remember exactly what she looked like, I realized that I was left with few specifics – only a vague impression of a slim figure, an unaffected cheerfulness and a certain grace; and I decided not to mention 'unaffected' or 'grace' to Uncle Ryan, but might recall for him, later, that she worked out and that she had a dog; and glancing in the mirror and I saw a familiar crew cut and solemn blue eyes; and then I watched someone I recognized as Ryan O'Brien square his shoulders and march out to the bar.

Our waitress was off serving someone else with the same cheer and grace she'd shown us. I felt betrayed. Uncle Ryan tried to cheer me up. "She seemed interested in you," he said. "Wouldn't give me a phone number, though. Said it was against her personal policy. Smart girl."

"I suppose. Does she have a name?"

"I didn't get a name. I did give her your name and phone number, though; and I told her where you lived. Was that alright, Lieutenant?"

"I suppose. After all, we're practically engaged. She's had my name and phone number forced on her by my Uncle Ryan while I was in the men's room pissing."

"I predict you'll hear from her."

"She has a dog," I said. "And she works out."

Uncle Ryan clinked his glass of stout to my glass of porter. He laughed. I wasn't sure whether he was laughing with me or at me, but he did have a great laugh and so I laughed back – with him, at me.

As we walked back to my apartment, my cellphone vibrated. It was Smyrl, working very late. "I just sent you an e-mail. Read it and see what you think."

"Let me get back to my place. I'll barely be able to read this screen. It's dark and I'm borderline drunk. Gimme fifteen minutes."

Uncle Ryan and I read Smyrl's e-mail on the large screen of one of my computers.

O'Brien:

Here's everything I know – that I am allowed to tell you. You were right. Max is an idiot. He believes he is working for a contractor who is in turn working for Homeland Security. He's always been paid in cash by someone he knows only as 'Bama.

He knows nothing about a murder, and he does not know your name. He remembers you decking him; and thinks he owes you one – if he ever sees you. He knows that Marvin went missing and that 'Bama went back to the Island to find him.

He was told by 'Bama to watch the Island from Floodgate Road and report to him by cellphone. 'Bama has not answered his cellphone today. Max does know that someone saw him on Floodgate, but he does not connect that to his truck going into the Ditch. I think he really believes he left the emergency brake off.

He says that the last time he saw 'Bama, early today, he and the operator of their boat were headed somewhere together, with the boat and trailer hitched to 'Bama's truck. Since you and your Uncle Ryan were out and about in his boat – did you see anything worth reporting?

If so, send me an e-mail. If not, call me tomorrow at 10AM.

Max is spending the night in a real lockup, while we verify some of his creds.

Smyrl

Oscar whined once. Uncle Ryan decided to take a short walk. I dialed Smyrl.

"Smyrl," I said, "I might have something of interest. But to get it to you, I'm going to have to use this phone to send you a few pictures."

"Pictures of what?"

"Pictures of two guys retrieving a boat, taken up the Old Canal this afternoon. Maybe 'Bama's one of the guys. Let me send them to you. Call me back after you've got them."

I fiddled with the smartphone and forwarded the pictures I'd taken from the power line tower. Smyrl called me two minutes later.

"What the crap is this, Ryan? Were you flying over the Canal? Tell me exactly where these were taken from, the direction you were facing and how far away from the subjects you were. I can't make out features or license plates or anything, but maybe our guys here can enhance them tomorrow morning."

So I told him where we'd been, although I didn't mention the surveillance cameras. Somehow I felt Smyrl would be displeased with me over our freelance project; and I also felt that somehow I'd be disloyal to Uncle Ryan if I told Smyrl what we'd been up to. Smyrl reminded me to call him the next morning at 10 a.m.

I ran down the stairs to find Uncle Ryan and Oscar, but they were right on my front steps doing nothing.

"Nice night," said Uncle Ryan.

"Very," I said.

"You mean verily, don't you?"

"Verily."

TERMINATED
CHAPTER FIFTEEN

The last dream I had in the morning, the one that got me up for good: snippets of recent happenings, combining people and events that would never mix in real life – a milkshake from Walt's, slurped while resting in Jameson's pajamas between ceilings at the New Jersey State Police Regional Headquarters, with Bardeaux shooting random holes in that ceiling, because she heard the alarm go off on Johnson's Suunto 10X Wrist-top Computer watch, while Smokey barked at her – and I somehow did not worry, because I sensed it might be a dream. Even so, I was relieved when I awakened and knew, absolutely knew for certain, I'd been dreaming.

I shuffled to my bathroom and rid myself of the last of the Founder's Porter. It was pre-dawn, but edging towards daylight outside; and Uncle Ryan and Oscar were sound asleep on my couch. I decided to monitor the security cameras, to make sure I knew how they worked. I selected the split screen option that showed views from all six cameras at once. They all seemed to be working, but nothing was happening at any of the sites. I selected the playback option and set the time for the previous midnight, then fast-forwarded through the morning hours. At the fastest speed setting, I could view one hour of camera time per minute, but the speed was too fast for me to really comprehend what I was seeing. I slowed the speed and found myself comfortable at three minutes per hour. I slowed to actual time when I saw five deer approach the water at the power line. When they looked in the direction of the camera, their eyes lit up, ghostlike. At any rate, the cameras worked; and I could monitor them at my convenience and report anything unusual to Smyrl.

Uncle Ryan leaned over my shoulder and looked at the screen. "Pretty good, huh?"

"Works like a charm, Uncle Ryan. I can't believe you knew how to set this up."

"Uncle Ryan – spymaster. I should be on the road by ten, ten-thirty. What should we do in the meantime?"

"I owe myself a workout – a run and some stuff at my health club would be perfect. Then breakfast."

"I'm not running with you," said Uncle Ryan. "Oscar and I will walk, maybe a slow jog. After that, though, I'll pump some iron with you – see how weak I'm getting in my old age."

"Let's do some of this before rush hour. What day is it anyway?"

"It's Monday."

So the three of us walked west to the Schuylkill River trails, where we turned right, upriver, and headed for the Art Museum and Boathouse Row. "I'll run now, and meet you two about here in forty-five minutes or so," I said.

"Bye bye," said Uncle Ryan, as I jogged off.

I felt sluggish at first, the by-product of late nights, too much porter and the weird events that had happened since the moment I'd made the foolish decision to reconnoiter Chester Island, in the dark, on Friday night. That night seemed like half a lifetime ago, not less than three days. With the exception of the killing of Smokey, all the rest of it would be little more than interesting – a story to tell my grandchildren. The death of the best dog I'll ever own – and be owned by – was something I still needed to deal with; and Marvin, Smokey's shooter was dead, so there was no revenge to be had there; but 'Bama, and whoever else was responsible for that mess still needed to hear from me.

After a half mile or so, my body became attuned to running, and I stopped thinking about plans, events, people, problems and all the rest of what our relentless intellects force us to consider; and I simply ran; and when I run I think about running, and nothing else, although I might consider running related things – my heart rate, my pace, how far I've gone, whether my left calf is hurting for a reason that matters, whether I can catch the guy fifty yards ahead of me, what my time is, here, at the two-mile mark – but I am unable to think of much else; and the people who say they drift off into some altered state while running, where mysteries of the universe are revealed, where quantum mechanics becomes clear or where the final last, perfect words of their novel – "On the bank in the thickening dusk, in the will o' the wisp dusk, abandoned but vigilant, a motor-cycle" – spring unbidden into their minds, I find not believable.

I turned around after twenty-five minutes, at the three and a half mile mark, and picked up the pace a little. I found Uncle Ryan and Oscar talking to a woman jogger; and I stopped to listen.

"He crapped in that ground cover, way over there by the River," said Uncle Ryan. "What's the problem?"

"Well the problem is, for one – he's supposed to be on a leash, and for two – you're supposed to pick up his excrement," said the woman. I noted that she had on lime green spandex tights, an unzipped light-weight runner's jacket lined with Gore-Tex and partially covering a heart rate monitor, ECCO BIOMS running shoes, Wick-A-Way socks, a black plastic runners' wristwatch and a billed cap that said "P.D.R.".

"Pick up his excrement! His excrement! You're kidding. You mean his crap? Why would I want to do that? His crap is over there in the ivy, fertilizing it. What's the harm?"

"Nonetheless," said the woman, "we have rules for a reason. If everyone let their dog run loose like you do, people like me couldn't run here; and if no one picked up their dog's poop – well, then where would we be."

"Well I, for one would be right here, minding my own business," said Uncle Ryan. "Oscar and I would be harming no one and trying hard not to interact with people like you."

The woman turned to me, hoping I'd be a voice of reason. "Can you explain to this man here what I'm trying to get across? Maybe he'll listen to you."

I tried a diversion. "Do the letters on that cap stand for the Philadelphia Distance Run?" I said. "Was that this year's? I missed it. It's my favorite race."

She bit. "No. It's and old hat. Now it's called the Philadelphia Rock 'n' Roll Half-Marathon. I did better than I expected this year. The weather was perfect."

I looked her up and down, and estimated she was in her late forties or early fifties. "I guess it's hard to finish anywhere the money in your age category. What with all the other thirty-somethings."

She couldn't help herself, and laughed. "I wish," she said, "although I haven't missed a race since I was in my thirties."

I feigned disbelief and commented on her shoes, while Uncle Ryan and Oscar edged away. "Are those as amazing as they say? Aren't they considered the very most expensive running shoe?"

"I'm just trying them out," she said. "I've only had them a day or so, so it's too soon to tell. They are very light."

I excused myself. "Well, I've gotta go. I'll go see if I can talk some sense into him. See you another day. I'll expect a full report on those shoes." Then I caught up with Uncle Ryan and Oscar, who had edged away at the start of my diversion and were now fifty yards away and walking quickly.

"I am so very fucking glad I live in the Everglades," said Uncle Ryan.

"I hear you," I said. "I may have to visit – often."

"Would that call for a 'verily'?"

"Verily," I said.

• • •

Uncle Ryan fed Oscar and let him up on my couch; and then we headed for my gym. Actually it was not really a gym – it was something called a Fitness-Plex – a place of mirrors, hot tubs, steam rooms, rows of machines, television monitors and padded rooms where very fit people conduct classes in yoga, Pilates, and numerous celebrity specials. There were two rooms for Spinning, the indoor cycling craze where Spandexed people enter a darkened room, listen to loud music and exhaust themselves collaboratively on stationary bicycles, as well as squash and racquetball courts and two swimming pools.

Membership was a perk granted me by virtue of my employer, Howell & Barrett; and although I was a little embarrassed about the sheer yuppiness of the place, a place where very few members of the 2nd Platoon, "L" Company, Third Battalion, Sixth Marines would feel welcome – let alone be able to afford – there was one modest corner of the establishment given over to free weights; and that's where Uncle Ryan and I were going. We contemplated bench press contests, factoring in complex body weight adjustment algorithms and a generally enjoyable nephew/uncle time – results to be reported posthaste to my Pops. But it was not to be.

According to his name tag, the middle-aged clerk behind the Ushaped counter was "Stan". Stan frowned. "I'm sorry sir, your membership has been rescinded."

"Rescinded? What does that mean?"

"It means you had a membership here, and now you do not."

"As of when? I was just here last Thursday."

"Let's see. As of this morning – about an hour ago. Your ex-employer's Human Resources Department called to say you'd resigned your position."

"I certainly did not resign my position," I said. "There must be some mistake." Stan looked down at my card, the one with a black X on it. "I am sorry Mister O'Brien. There's really nothing I can do."

"Do you have a name for someone in Howell & Barrett's Human Resources Department?"

"I do. A Ms. Tarry-Brigham-Smith is who you'll need to call."

"Can she tell you over the phone to rescind the rescinding of my membership?"

"I suppose that might be possible. She rescinded your membership by phone."

"Would you give me her direct number, please?"

"I'm afraid that would not be possible."

Uncle Ryan had gone from an interested non-participant, to someone itching to get in a word or two. He leaned on the counter. "Of course it would be impossible for you to write the number down. But it would be very possible to just turn the book so Ryan here can see the number. That way you're off the hook. Do it right now."

"May I borrow your phone?" I asked.

"Certainly," said Uncle Ryan, reaching across the counter and handing me the phone.

I did not wait for comments from Stan. "How do I get an outside line?"

"Dial nine first," said Stan, surrendering to the inevitability of the Ryans, who were taking up most of the available oxygen.

A female voice answered my phone call. "Ms. Tarry-Brigham-Smith."

"Hi," I said, "this is Ryan O'Brien – a recent hire by Howell & Barrett. I'm at the Fitness-Plex and there seems to be a bit of a problem. I was hoping you could help."

"Oh yes," said Ms. Tarry-Brigham-Smith, cheerfully. "I phoned the Fitness-Plex this morning – concerning your employment here."

"Did you intend to tell them I'd resigned my position? Because I did no such thing."

"Oh. Of course. Yes. It's simply our policy to use the word resigned when dealing with a third party in such matters. It's much kinder and gentler than terminated. Don't you agree?"

"Are you informing me I've been terminated? I don't even start work until a week from today. Informing me I've been fired through Stan here at the gym doesn't seem very professional on your part."

"I attempted to call you on the phone number you've listed on your application for employment – I have it right here – and the phone was answered by some young man that answered 'Phi Kappa Sigma'. I believe he must have been joking. He said he'd heard of you, but was quite sure you no longer resided at that number; and he had no other number for you – in fact, he thought you were in Afghanistan of all places. I've sent you an e-mail confirming your termination. Hopefully that notification went to a valid address."

"I can't believe this," I said. "Why did this happen?"

"You were arrested." said Ms. Tarry-Brigham-Smith. "You were arrested, charged with a felony and, you resisted that arrest. I read the Inquirer article myself and brought the matter to the attention of our Managing Partner, who personally made the decision – a decision that was clearly correct. The terms of your employment contract – which you signed – with Howell & Barrett outline your personal responsibilities regarding legal matters. I'm sure you know that Howell & Barrett maintains an impeccable reputation – a reputation that is vital to its success. Charges of resisting arrest and murder are obviously something we can have nothing to do with – hence your justified termination."

I could feel the start of tunnel vision – that focused vision that gradually excludes almost everything but whatever it is that I am looking at directly. This is a precursor to something I'll admit is most properly termed: rage. Rage happens to me very infrequently, but when it does I do not know what I am doing – or saying.

Uncle Ryan grabbed the phone from me, raised his voice half an octave, and spoke into it clearly: "Thank you for your time. I'll go read my e-mail and get back to you." Then he carefully placed the phone back in its cradle, thanked Stan, turned me around and frog-marched me out of the Fitness-Plex. He'd have won the bench press contest hands down.

"I could tell you were going to lose it," he said, after we had walked a half block. "That won't help. It wasn't Stan's fault. It's all fixable."

"I'm not sure I want to fix it," I said.

"What does that mean?"

"Exactly that. I – am – not – sure – I want – to – fix – it."

Uncle Ryan mimicked me, something he knew I hated. "I understand the words, but I – am – not – sure – I – know – what – they – mean."

"Please let go of my elbow," I said. "Let me walk with you for a block or so; and I'll try to explain." He did, we did, and I did.

"I'm just trying this on myself," I said, "and I haven't thought it through; but I very much wonder if I am cut out for a desk job at Howell & Barrett – working with folks like Tarry-Brigham-Smith, where I'll probably rotated first into their back office, data-checking, number crunching, hedging bets and spending lots of time staring at computer screens and meeting with people who have absolutely zero idea of what I've been up to for the last four years while they devised complex algorithms and became masters of the universe and high-fived each other with the creation or marketing of each new derivative or hedge fund; and I even wonder if they really have even the slightest need for someone like me who has been away from all of this for so long it's probably all changed into something not recognizable; and maybe the real reason they terminated me is that they simply don't need me anymore, especially now that the economy is in the tank . . . ."

"Stop it! Enough!" Uncle Ryan grabbed my elbow again. "Who hired you?"

"You mean his name?"

"Yes. Of course. His name."

"Sam Barrett. He hired me four years ago."

"What did he say to you when he hired you?'

"He said I'd be worth more to him in four years, that the time would go by faster than either of us could believe. Then he shook my hand and said 'you're hired'. He also said 'Semper Fi'. He's a former Marine himself."

"So he was enthusiastic about your working for him?"

"Seemed like it," I said.

"And his position at the firm is what, exactly? Is it his name at Howell & Barrett, or his father's grandfather's?"

"Bud Howell and he founded the firm. In 1976, I think. I'm not sure what his exact title is now. He's in his mid-sixties and probably functions as a Board Chairman – handles a few important relationships, worries about the big picture, stuff like that."

"Did you like him when he hired you?"

"Very much. He seemed like a straight shooter. What wasn't to like? He liked me back; and he hired me."

"Don't you think you owe this man – a man who hired you – who you like – who might actually know what you've been doing for the last four years and maybe from personal experience – the number one or number two guy at the firm – don't you think you owe this man at least a talk before you toss your dream job in the shitter?"

"I think I might like to simply work for you at your marina."

"Who said I was hiring? And who said working at my Marina would be something you could call 'simply'? Anyway, I've already got Mikey as my designated fuck-up relative."

"Sorry about the 'simply'. I meant you don't have a Human Resources Department. And you know I wouldn't be a fuck-up."

"Tell you what, Ryan O'Brien. If you give the job at Howell & Barrett everything you've got for one year – a complete year – and you still want to come wrestle gators with me, it's a deal. You'll be worth more to me in a year anyway. The year will go by faster than you can believe. Semper Fi."

Uncle Ryan laughed and shook my hand and we walked back to my apartment. I had a lot to think about.

CLEMMIE
CHAPTER SIXTEEN

The ride to the West End was a quiet one. Uncle Ryan was worrying about Sissie and her kid brother Mikey and thinking about the long drive on I-95 back to his marina in Florida. I was considering all the things I needed to do; and I was sorting through them and sequencing them. Oscar had his nose out the crack in the back seat window, experiencing the smells of West Philadelphia, the Schuylkill River, highways, an oil refinery, a four-story high pile of rusting junked cars, the George C. Platt Bridge, Philadelphia International Airport, the river town of Essington and, finally, the West End Boat Club.

After Uncle Ryan had readied *Sissie* for trailering, we gave each other manly, back-slapping hugs. We did not discuss my career at his marina.

"Be well," said Uncle Ryan.

"You too. Don't let Mikey ruin Paradise for you."

Uncle Ryan opened the door of his truck, and Oscar hopped in. "I expect updates on your life. Monitor the cameras. I'm back in a flash if anything really exciting happens. Don't get arrested.

Don't get shot. Call your Pops."

"I hear you," I said, watching my uncle get in his truck and wheel the trailer out the gates of the Club. I would miss him greatly; and in a strange way I was happy to see him go. It was time for me to grow up, figure out what I wanted to do and make it happen – all by myself. I was still a little too worked up from my conversation with the woman with the hyphenated name from Howell & Barrett's Human Resources Department. I was somehow happy I'd forgotten her name, as it diminished her importance. I turned to *Larke*, and prepared to inspect and fix whatever damage had been done to her.

I had a car full of what I might need for repairs: rubber gloves, epoxy resin, de-waxing solvent, a disc sander, sandpaper, a catalyst, bottom paint, boot stripe primer and finish coat, paint brushes, foam rollers, a jack, a three-foot piece of two-by-four, cleaning liquid, a bucket, boat wax, towels, and a tool box full of tools. All of the bullet holes in *Larke* were below the waterline, but Lawson had had to jigger fiberglass in the boot stripe to remove two of the bullets. I wondered why I could remember his name, and not the head of Human Resources at Howell & Barrett. It was very telling, a shrink would probably say – that I remembered the name of a guy who dug bullets out of my sailboat but couldn't recall the name of a woman in authority who had terminated me.

Screw that. No complicated thinking for me for the two hours it would take to get started on gussying up the prettiest little sailboat on the River. So I placed the two-by-four under *Larke's* keel, jacked her up enough that I could get at the bullet holes in her hull, mixed epoxy and let it start to thicken while I prepared the damage by some sanding and de-waxing. I gobbed the epoxy into the bullet holes, filling them to overflowing. Next I dragged a hose over from the water source and washed the dried mud off *Larke's* deck. I noticed boot heel marks where Bardeaux had fallen off the stern; and I scoured them off with a scrubbie. Bye-bye Bardeaux. I towel-dried the deck and applied marine polish – first to the deck and then to the hull. Two hours. Except for the hardening epoxy, *Larke* was beautiful. I sat down on the tongue of her trailer, in the shade, to think.

I began by attempting to be honest with myself. I recognized that I had been a spectacular failure the previous three days; and that I needed to be somehow different. I was without real supervision or guidance for the first time in my life; and I was failing Grown-Up 101. I needed to become an adult. I needed to be responsible for myself; and I needed to accomplish this by myself. Nothing bad that had happened to me in the last few days had happened without my involvement. But for Ryan O'Brien, and his actions, none of it would have happened. It hadn't happened to me; I'd been responsible for lots of it.

I decided that I needed to work to undo as much of what had happened as I could: get my job back – I could always quit it if I wished someday; repair *Larke*; help Smyrl find 'Bama; get Johnson's Suunto back or buy him another; pay back a little of the debt owed Smyrl, Uncle Ryan and the good folks at The Church of Jesus Christ is Lord. There was nothing I could do about Smokey except remember her.

Next I hauled an electric cord over from the power source and used my disc sander to sand the lumps of epoxy down to just above the surface of the hull. Then I sanded by hand, using finer sandpaper. When I was finished, I had a row of pink bullet holes that would need priming, a day of drying time, a finish coat, another day of drying time and finally some polish. The portions of the holes below the water line would just need bottom paint. I purposely did not think about my failures while I sanded and primed; but when I was finished, I somehow had a plan. I dialed Smyrl.

• • •

"You've reached Detective Smyrl. Please leave a message after the beep."

Crap. "Detective Smyrl . . . this is Ryan O'Brien . . . I'd like to talk to you about two things: one – your progress on the murder; and two – getting a statement from you about my innocence. I've been terminated at my dream job because of the Inquirer's article. Thanks. Hope to talk to you soon."

I hung up and spent a few minutes mixing the primer and preparing to paint over the epoxy. Just as I was at a critical stage – rubber gloves on, paint in tray, foam roller wet, reaching towards hull – when the phone in my pocket started up with "Semper Fidelis". It was the Sousa marching song, not the Marines' Hymn; and I'd selected it after I'd been unable to obtain the piccolo solo from "The Stars and Stripes Forever". By the time I'd placed the paint tray and roller down and taken off the gloves, the phone stopped with all the inspiration. I did not recognize the phone number; and so I waited for the voicemail, and played it back after my phone indicated it was finished.

"Hi. This is Clemmie. Hopefully you are really Ryan O'Brien and that was really your uncle who gave me this number, and this is really your apartment I'm outside with my dog. I'm the waitress you met last night at the Pub and Kitchen. In case you're interested in a dog walk, I'll wait here for five minutes."

What the crap! Uncle Ryan had worked his charm. He'd been right. She did call. Her name was Clemmie! I started to punch the return call button, when Sousa started up again. It was Smyrl. Damn. I took the call.

"Hey."

"It's Smyrl – I'm getting back to you."

"How are things going? With the case."

"We've got lots of possibilities. We're following up a bunch of very minor leads we got from your pal Max. We've enhanced the photos you sent us of the boat retrieval guys. We've dusted the truck for prints. All that stuff. You should come in sometime later today to talk again. To go over the time line again – and the map. How soon can you get here?"

"I can be there in an hour, but I'll be dressed in my boat painting clothes. Is that alright?"

"I've never seen you dressed up," said Smyrl. "I probably wouldn't recognize you in a suit. Come over however you're dressed."

"See you in an hour."

• • •

I wondered about the name Clemmie, wondered if it was short for Clementine – as in "Oh My Darling". I hit "redial".

Her voicemail:"This is Clemmie. Is this Clemmie? Please leave a message. Leave a please message."

Hmm. Either a sense of humor or crazy. I'll play along, I thought. "Is this Ryan? Missed I your sorry call? Me please you back call." I put the rubber gloves back on, rolled the primer carefully over each of the epoxied bullet holes, cleaned up, removed the gloves and hoped Clemmie would call me back.

As I hopped in the car and began the drive to the Magic Kingdom of Smyrl's little conference room, I wondered if I'd just made a very big mistake in my phone message to Clemmie. Maybe she was dyslexic, or was learning disabled in some way – had some problem processing words – or English was not her native language. Maybe I'd just insulted her. Maybe I'd just failed some test, caught in a trap set in her voicemail. Crap.

Sousa rang when I was just leaving the Club; and I pulled over onto the grassy shoulder of the road to answer the call. "You passed the test, Ryan," said Clemmie.

"That's because I didn't know it was a test," I said.

"Well, it was; and you passed."

"Where are you?"

"I'm walking my dog. I gave up on you."

"I'm not home right now. I was working on my sailboat."

"Your Uncle didn't tell me you had a sailboat."

"That's because he's a powerboater. Sailboats don't count to powerboaters. They call us 'blowboaters' and other derogatory names. Then when gas and diesel prices hit the roof, and powerboaters can't afford to use their boats, we sailors rub it in."

"He told me lots of other stuff about you."

"I bet. Don't believe any of it."

"It was all good – some of it too good to be true. I need to meet you someday – just to see how much of it's fiction. He layered it on pretty thick."

"That's my Uncle Ryan. He can sling it."

"He didn't tell me his name was Ryan too. Are you named for him?"

"Yep. He's my Mother's favorite brother. In fact, he's everyone's favorite everything. He's probably your favorite customer. Right?"

"Ha. Maybe. We'll see how accurate his propaganda was. Anyway – I'm sorry I missed you today. It's a good dog walking day."

"Rain check please I may have?" I said.

Clemmie laughed. "May you. Two days. Your front steps – Wednesday seven a.m.?"

"Deal."

"Roger. Over and out." Clemmie terminated the call.

Holy shit; I'd just talked to a beautiful woman with a sense of humor who walked her dog and used words like "roger" and "over and out" and didn't sound silly doing it; a cheerful beauty who for some reason wanted to meet me – a man-child fuckup who'd crashed and burned much of his life in just three short days. I knew

I'd better get very busy fixing that life; and realized that I had Clemmie's name and phone number as good-luck charms. So I smiled and punched up a favorite CD – a mix made for the car; and since I was confused about a lot of things, I opted for a most confusing song; and sang along with the lyrics that never failed to further confuse:"Ain't it just like the night to play tricks – when you're tryin' to be so quiet? We sit here stranded . . . ." And although I can't sing worth a lick, I sounded better than the weird genius who wrote the song, so I sang louder and drowned him right on out of my happy car – that smelled of epoxy, paint, sweat and boat. And dog. I could still smell dog.

•••

Smyrl was succinct. Bardeaux was quiet. I was attentive. The case was summarized. The computer chart was updated. The pictures I'd taken of 'Bama and his boat skipper had been enhanced and enlarged. The skipper had been identified. A warrant was out for him – for questioning. 'Bama was still a mystery. His truck had yielded no prints except Max's. Bardeaux excused herself to make phone calls – her departure seemed planned.

"Anything else to tell me, Ryan?" asked Smyrl.

"Yes. I don't trust Bardeaux. And Uncle Ryan and I set up six cameras: two on Chester Island, two on Floodgate Road and two more near the boat landing where I took those pictures."

"Cameras?"

"High-quality, solar-powered, wireless, day/night security cameras. They feed to a computer at my place. I'll monitor them."

"Can we monitor them too?"

"Yes. I can give you passwords into the website. Monitoring them is tedious. Maybe you can help me. A division of labor or something. Please don't let Bardeaux be one of the monitors."

"Is there something you want to tell me specifically about Bardeaux?"

"No. I just don't trust her completely."

"Because she arrested you?"

"Partly that. Mostly because she was so damn happy to be arresting me. And I never resisted arrest. She made that up; and she was sticking to the charge until you told her you'd seen the incident. Do you trust Bardeaux?"

"I've no reason not to."

"Where do things stand with the Inquirer and a correction or retraction? What was the reporter's name?"

"Stephan O'Leary. Remember – it's pronounced 'Steffan'."

I wrote the name down. "Did he reveal his source?"

"Not yet. He doesn't want to. A committee of journalists at the Inky are meeting later today on the matter. They call it an 'issue of journalistic integrity' and take the whole thing very seriously. We can probably subpoena the name or names, but don't want to do that unless we have to."

"I need a written correction from them – published," I said.

"You said in your voicemail that you lost your job over the article."

"Yes. A statement from you would be helpful too. In fact it wouldn't just be helpful – it would be essential. Can you do that for me? Today?"

"You write it, we'll print it here and I'll sign it. How's that?"

"I was hoping you'd say that. I took the liberty of sending myself an e-mail with a draft attachment. May I use that computer to access it?"

"You took me for granted," said Smyrl.

I laughed. "Highest form of flattery. You can take me for granted, too. Seriously – I owe you; and I know it. Without you, I'd either be in jail or out on bail talking to a lawyer. I mean it – I owe you."

He pushed the laptop over to me. "It's already on line."

I accessed my e-mail, pulled up the statement and let Smyrl read it. "Seems reasonable," said Smyrl. "Send it to me, I'll forward it to an office here, someone will download it and print it on letterhead. I'll sign it. Five minutes. He excused himself to make phone calls; and his departure seemed planned – for Bardeaux came in and sat down across from me.

"O'Brien," she said, "do you want to tell me where you were Saturday night?"

"I was right here with you," I said.

"You disappeared." She leaned across the table and said, slowly: "you fucking vanished. How did you do that? Where did you go?"

I thought about telling her the truth and decided instead to not lie. "I was here. I was using a theory learned in the Marine Corps. That's why you couldn't see me."

"Bullshit, O'Brien," she snapped. "What's the name of this theory?"

"A lot of it is classified," I said. "But I suppose if I can't trust you – well who can I trust? I used third-tier absentials to disappear."

"What a crock," said Bardeaux. "I'm gonna look it up."

"You won't find much. Most of it is military and classified. And it doesn't work for me all the time. I'm not completely proficient in its use."

Bardeaux sat back in her chair. Smyrl arrived with the letter I'd requested. We promised to keep in touch – once a day. By e-mail. Phone if necessary. In person if essential. I left.

DARKER THAN AMBER
CHAPTER SEVENTEEN

It was a little after three o'clock – too late to drive home, get cleaned up, dressed and go off to tilt at the windmill named the Inquirer. Plenty of time to begin paying other dues, though. I punched in Jameson's number.

"Jameson. This is Ryan O'Brien."

"Pilgrim. How's it going? Sister Alberta told me about your Saturday night visit. Police still involved in your life?"

"I'm in the clear – thanks to the good Sister. Other parts of my life could be better."

"How so?"

"Maybe we'll talk when I see you. That's why I'm calling. I've got a few hours. I could read to that boy. What's his name – Nashir?"

"That'd be good. He's come played with your staff everyday since you left it. He's here now. Come on over."

"I'm dressed in painting clothes. Is that alright?"

"Got shoes on?"

"Yep. A shirt, too."

"Look forward to seeing you."

"Twenty minutes."

• • •

Nashir smiled his shy smile at me and silently handed me my staff when I climbed the steps to the porch of The Church of Jesus Christ is Lord. I handed it back. "Hold this for me for a few minutes, Nashir. I need to talk to the Reverend. Be right out." Nashir looked skeptical, like he'd been disappointed before – like I'd disappear for another three days.

We were standing in the Church foyer. "Am I teaching him to read, Jameson? Or am I just reading to him?"

"I'm hoping you're doing both," said Jameson. "First you're reading to him. If he gets interested, maybe we'll figure out what to do next. We've got him in the Chester Community Charter School. They've tried Phonics, Look and Say, some experiential approach and a Context Support Method. None of them have really worked. He's polite, listens, seems to have a good attention span and is not a disciplinary problem. But he doesn't seem to really get it. Maybe he's just not interested. He doesn't ask for the book. He's passive."

"Any advice for me?"

"You might as well read him something you like. I think all the little kids' stuff they've tried has no interest for him. We think he's twelve or thirteen, but because of language difficulties, he's been placed in the fourth grade. I think he's smart."

"Language difficulties?"

"He's from Juba, in South Sudan. Been here two years. God knows what he's seen in his short life. Maybe stuff like you saw in Afghanistan or Iraq."

"Alright," I said. "I owe Sister and you big time for last Friday night. I'll do my best. I've got a favorite old paperback in my car. I was reading it for about the fourth time. I'll go get it. We'll read on the porch."

Nashir looked forlorn as I ran down the steps to my car; and then his face lit up when I ran back up the steps holding a book. We sat in Sister Alberta's glider, Nashir held the staff, while I held the book – *Darker Than Amber* written by John D. MacDonald in 1966. I loved all the Travis McGee books by MacDonald. This was one. My Pops told me once I was another Travis McGee wannabe – and then said that that wasn't so bad. "Go for it," he'd said, laughing.

I decided to start with the teaser on the back of the dog-eared paperback:

> *McGee was moored beneath the bridge and having a lot of luck with a Wounded Spook and some hungry fish. Suddenly there was a screech of brakes overhead. The girl came down, feet first, skirt fluttering, through the orange glow of the bridge lights. She chunked into the water off the bow of the skiff, taking the plug and McGee's line straight to the bottom. A motor roared. The car rocketed off.*

Jeezus. MacDonald could flat-out write! I couldn't wait to read more, even though I already knew Travis would rescue Jane Doe, or Vangie, or Miss Western or whoever she was – only to lose her again to a murderer; and that McGee would bloodily avenge that death and go back to musing about the meaning of everything, drinking a little too much gin and considering the state of the world from his houseboat-cum-barge-cum-trawler, *The Busted Flush*.

About then, I realized that a kid from South Sudan might not know what MacDonald was talking about – might not have a frame of reference for much of what I'd just read. I looked at Nashir. He smiled at me; but it was not a smile of comprehension.

"So – the name of the guy in the book is 'McGee'." I pointed to Nashir and said "Nashir." I pointed to me and said "Pilgrim." I pointed to the book and said "McGee." Nashir nodded and smiled.

"So," I said, "McGee was in a boat – a boat. The boat was moored – anchored – under a bridge." I pointed to the Commodore Barry Bridge and said: "bridge."

Nashir nodded and smiled.

"So, McGee is fishing." I pantomimed fishing with a rod and reel. "He's using a lure – bait – called a 'Wounded Spook' and he's catching fish. Lots of fish." I signaled ten fish with my fingers.

Nashir stood up and thumped the staff twice on the porch, laughed and sat down – all ears, it seemed. Maybe he'd fished once.

The whole Ryan – Nashir waltz went on for thirty minutes or so, and I thought that it was possible – not likely, but possible – that he understood at least some of the seventy words or so that comprised half of the teaser on the back cover. At this rate, it would take about two years for me to read the whole book to Nashir. Maybe we needed to try some other book – an age appropriate book, or a reading-level appropriate book, something by Doctor Seuss. I felt discouraged.

Nashir tapped on the book, smiled and nodded. "Please more," he said.

Please more! The first thing Nashir had said to me. Although he apparently sang in the choir, it was the first thing I'd ever heard him say to anyone. Please more!

• • •

And so I read, re-read, explained and mimed the rest of the

short back cover teaser, insisting that Nashir respond by talking, smiling and giving me a thumbs-up when he thought he understood; and together we learned that McGee dove in the water, bloodied his own hands tearing off the wire binding cement to her feet, brought the woman up, dried her off, noticed she was beautiful and would likely ensnare him in something deadly – and we had especial difficulty with metaphors, similes and MacDonald specialties – phrases such as ". . . heart like an ancient gutter . . . ." and "Eurasian beauty with the look of angels . . . ." – and we went over and over again the troubling English language use of words that have multiple meanings, such as the naming of a fishing lure a "Wounded Spook" (of particular interest to Nashir); and when we were finished we'd spent two hours reading one-hundred and fifty-six words and, goddamn it, Nashir got it! He understood. I thought that just maybe this whole extravagant undertaking was possible.

I handed Nashir the book and left him sitting in the glider with it; and I went inside to report to Jameson.

"Well," said Jameson, "I looked out the window a couple of times. Something sure was going on out there. Looked like some kind of magic in the air."

"He's pretty smart," I said. "At least I think so. He comprehends stuff if I repeat myself enough and we go over everything six ways from Sunday. I'm not sure we're really reading though – it might be more like charades. He's able to think in the abstract. I'll leave the book with him. I think he'd like that."

"He can't take it home," said Jameson.

"Why not?"

"It'll never get back here. He's living in a foster home with a bunch of kids. Some of them are older than he is – it's complicated. Trust me on this one. The book stays here. Just like the staff. Nashir already knows this anyway."

"Whatever you say."

"When can you come back?"

"Maybe tomorrow afternoon," I said. "I've got stuff to do in the morning. I'm not sure how long it will take. I might get very busy next week if I can manage to get my job back."

"What about your job?"

"It's a long story. Maybe there'll be a happy ending I can tell you about tomorrow or Wednesday."

"I hear you. Just don't promise Nashir anything and then not come through."

"Can I say I'll try to come tomorrow afternoon?"

"If you spend enough time on the idea that you'll do your best and that you'll definitely be back by Wednesday after school. Can you do that?"

"Yep. I can. Should I give him a ride home?"

"Absolutely not. You'll just confuse the neighbors. Terrible idea."

So I went back outside, and spent fifteen minutes giving Nashir the book and explaining that the Reverend Jones would keep the book for him and that I'd be back – probably tomorrow, but the next day for sure. He understood. We shook hands on it. He thumped the staff on the porch three times. When I left Nashir was swinging on the glider, turning pages of the book.

• • •

Driving home, north on I-95, I got stuck in traffic. I noticed that my gas gauge signaled low and the tiny dashboard gas pump icon was blinking. I needed to take a piss. I wasn't much of a Travis McGee. He never got stuck in traffic, ran out of gas or needed to urinate. I exited the Interstate, onto PA 420, headed south three blocks to a gas station. There I pumped my own gas, moved the car away from the pumps and borrowed a restroom key from a glass-enclosed attendant. The key was attached to a nine-inch length of broom handle, the restroom was reasonably clean and some of the graffiti was interesting – some merely crude. I laughed at the classic: "Back in five minutes – Godot!" that was printed carefully on the metal panel that screened the urinal from the toilet. I thought about trying to explain that to Nashir.

I pulled out my own pen and wrote, in small, tasteful block letters: "I was here – an artifact . . . a tall, pale-eyed, sandy-haired, shambling, gangling, knuckly man . . . on my way to *The Busted Flush* at Slip F-18 at Bahia Mar Marina in Fort Lauderdale" and signed it simply "Travis" – doing my part for the immortality of good old McGee; and walking back to my car, I considered just how old he would be now, in the year of our Lord 2015; and while driving, I did some elementary math and since Travis seemed to me to be in his late thirties or early forties in the 1960's – that meant that about fifty years ago he was about forty – making him ninety now; and I bet he was still a handful, especially with the ladies at the Sunset Assisted Living Facility.

I decided to drive into the City a back way – through the inner suburbs, then through West Philadelphia. I did this because traffic on I-95 was unbearable, and because I wanted to take my time, to think about everything I needed to do; and for fun I decided to consider matters in terms of "what would Travis do".

I found U.S. Route 13, called Chester Pike, and turned right – East – towards the big City. On autopilot, my eyes took in aging suburbs – mostly older homes interspersed with two story commercial properties – stores on the first floor, apartments above. The road had almost everything America had to offer: elementary schools, churches, hospitals and every kind of small business. One or two upscale areas offered boutique clothing, gift and jewelry stores while other stretches of the road featured nail salons, tattoo parlors, small used car lots, abandoned gas stations and "We Buy Gold" signs. The road was a SEPTA bus route, and people of all sizes, shapes and colors waited on corners for the next bus. Chester Pike connected six or seven small boroughs, and led eventually to Baltimore Pike and the City of Philadelphia. The atmosphere along Baltimore Pike ranged from litter-strewn, every-other-house-abandoned, lock-your-car-door ghetto to the slowly-getting-gentrified area around the University of Pennsylvania. In other words, I saw everyday America – warts and all – something I'd missed terribly for the ten months I'd spent in Afghanistan. I imagined that Nashir's South Sudan looked nothing much like this either; and I had no inclination to find out by visiting.

• • •

During the drive I considered Travis's list: Smokey, Johnson's Suunto 10X, my job at Howell & Barrett, a murder and the police. Travis would likely deal with each of these in his inimitable and direct manner. He'd find out who was responsible for Smokey's death and kick his ass – probably 'Bama's. Then he'd rip the Suunto off someone's wrist – again probably 'Bama's. He'd likely turn over a desk or two at the Inquirer and get the retraction, charge into Howell & Barrett's Human Resources Department and end up sleeping with Ms. Hyphenated name. The police would be skeptical of Travis's involvement at first, but appreciate him when he solved the murder. With the substantial money he stole from whatever organization 'Bama was fronting for, Travis would set up a trust fund for Nashir's education and donate lots of money to The Church of Jesus Christ is Lord. Then he'd retire to *The Busted Flush* and drink Boodles Gin, watch the sun go down and wait for another adventure.

When I got home, I parked my car and ran up the steps to my apartment. I knew I couldn't be Travis McGee. I hoped that I could figure out how to be Ryan O'Brien.

WHAT WOULD TOWNES SAY
CHAPTER EIGHTEEN

I showered, pulled on comfortable old sweatpants and sweatshirt and looked around my apartment. I liked what I saw. It was the first time I'd ever lived alone; and privacy and the ability to simply do whatever I wanted, without considering the needs of sweaty Marines, noisy fraternity brothers or younger siblings was a welcome novelty. I made myself something to eat – canned soup, two peanut butter and jelly sandwiches and a beer – subsistence that was smack dab in the wheelhouse of my culinary competency. I'd thought about peanut butter and jelly sandwiches – constructed my own way – the whole time I'd been in Afghanistan.

The food in-country had been three kinds. MREs – Meal, Ready-to-Eat – were packets of food prepared in the U.S. and freeze-dried; and troops complained about them constantly, calling them "Meals Rejected by Ethiopians", "Meals Rejected by Everyone", "Meals, Rarely Edible", "Morale Reducing Elements" and so forth. I thought the complaining was pretty good-natured and healthy; and some of it was very clever – the frankfurters in one package were called the "Four Fingers of Death". Since most of the meals were low in dietary fiber, they sometimes caused constipation and were called "Meals Requiring Enemas", "Meals Refusing to Exit", and "Meals Refusing to Excrete". My favorite was "Three Lies for the Price of One: It's Not a Meal, It's Not Ready, and You Can't Eat It". Damn – I missed the clever, complaining genius of some of the troops; and I hoped that equivalent investment banking humor existed and that Howell & Barrett had at least a little of it.

The second kind of food was hot chow prepared by cooks in mess areas and occasionally in the field – if an operation was large enough to warrant it. This was my least favorite food, since it was often a mystery, usually out of a giant, simmering pot, and casually plopped out into your waiting mess kit by a sweaty Marine who was pissed that he'd drawn that duty. Since Marine Officers always ate last, after the troops, the pickings were sometimes slim on the safe stuff: bread, apples and oranges and anything that came wrapped.

The third kind of food was local stuff, bought by troops from vendors when the circumstances seemed safe enough. A lot of the food had strange – to us – names: qorma (an onion-based stew, usually including lamb and lots of spices); paloa (rice-based, with meat – usually lamb – and stock added, including fried raisins, slivered carrots and nuts); and khameerbob, which is a pasta in the shape of a dumpling, filled with whatever is available, again often lamb. Some Marines really got into the local food, and became very knowledgeable about it. I never fully trusted it, and wasn't that big on lamb; so I limited myself to eating local only on occasions that called for some show of appreciation or unity or acceptance of local customs. I did like the bread, though, especially naan, and I bought it when I could.

So I made my peanut butter and jelly sandwiches the way I always did: wheat bread, butter on the jelly side slice, then jelly, and then peanut butter – lots of it – on the other slice. Sometimes I warmed the bread in a toaster. One of the best things about my meal was the clean up – pretty much zip. Into the recycling bin with the soup can and beer bottle, into the sink with the soup bowl, spoon and pot.

I wandered over to the computer that was monitoring Chester Island and environs, and played with buttons for awhile, fast-scanning through ten hours of nighttime viewing in about a half an hour. Absolutely nothing had happened in view of any of the cameras; and the monitoring was mindless, allowing my neurons to wander where they would. They concluded that being a civilian was really different than being in the Corps – and not just because of peanut butter and jelly sandwiches. In the course of one day – not yet over – I'd gone for a run, been terminated from my job, said goodbye to Uncle Ryan, made a start on repairing *Larke*, made a date to run or dog walk with a pretty girl named Clemmie, and read, pantomimed and charaded a favorite book to a kid from South Sudan named Nashir. In Afghanistan, I would likely have done one thing, it would likely have been something dangerous, have taken all day, probably been exhausting, resulted in me becoming filthy dirty, and would certainly not have involved women.

Checking my e-mail on a different computer, I had messages from friends and family. None of them were urgent. I didn't want to talk to Pops until I'd at least resolved my job situation. There was an e-mail from Smyrl mentioning the monitoring he was starting on the cameras and setting up an interactive log so I could share the task with two of his administrative people; and I opened the log, used the PIN Smyrl provided and logged in the ten hours of viewing I'd just completed.

I killed the time before bed by watching a little television, roaming the internet, reading, and laying out my good clothes for tomorrow's tasks. Then I hit the sack. I thought about how I was going to handle tomorrow – first the Inquirer, then Howell & Barrett. My last thought before I dozed off, was that tomorrow I would become someone who did stuff, not someone who stuff got done to – I would be the actor, not the actee. I slept well.

• • •

Walking up Broad Street to the Inquirer Building – the distinctive bone white Beaux Arts almost-skyscraper with a clock tower – I felt as if I belonged in the City. I was pretty sure that my suit, tie and shoes were adequately stylish. My briefcase was of Italian leather, a graduation gift from my grandmother, elegant and, except for my car, likely the most valuable thing I owned. I needed to let my hair grow out a little, from the buzz cut to something more businesslike, something that said "I go with the briefcase", not "I'm a former killer".

As I approached the Inquirer, I noticed a steady stream of cars pulling into an adjacent parking garage; and the foot traffic down the sidewalk alternated with the drivers in an impatient but reasonably polite dance – "you go – my turn – alright, now your turn" – that was somehow nice – civilized. When it was my turn to cross the entrance to the parking garage, a new Saab convertible pulled up, bumper-to-bumper with the car ahead of it – blocking the sidewalk.

I smiled, certain that the driver of the car would back up as soon as he saw what he'd done; and I gestured to him by holding my arms apart and then thumbing a suggested direction, backwards, for him to move. In absolutely no way was I threatening, rude, or disrespectful to the young white male who looked directly at me and flipped me the bird. The pretty young woman in his car sniggered; and he laughed along with her at the five or six peons on either side of his car, unable to walk to work.

I put my briefcase between my feet and turned up the palms of my hands, as if to say: "what the fuck?" He cocked a finger at me, meaning me and not all the other folks there; and he pulled the hammer of his thumb back and pulled the trigger – making his gun hand jump three times. Three shots. Then he repeated the one-finger salute. I considered options.

Travis McGee would do something violent and extremely cool at this point – perhaps smash the driver's side window, grab the car keys, fling them down a sewer, and invite the passenger in the car to lunch (she'd accept, of course); but it was unlikely that the creep driving the Saab would have flipped Travis the bird, since Travis's demeanor was almost always threatening enough to cause the more likely scenario of a window roll-down and a "sorry sir"; and my Uncle Ryan would have smiled at the asshole, reached up and somehow undone the hood of the Saab and ripped out the carburetor, closed the hood, stomped on the carburetor and disappeared; and my Pops would have embarrassed the young couple with that look he had – the one that said "I'm so disappointed in you" – that the passenger would have gotten out of the car and never spoken to the driver again, even though the Saab would quickly reverse to let pedestrians pass.

None of these options would work for Ryan O'Brien, however. I was obviously not frightening enough to act like Travis, knowledgeable enough to disable the car like Uncle Ryan or mature enough to act like my Pops. So I did the first thing that came into my mind – I hopped up on the hood of the car and lightly danced across it – thinking "East Side, West Side, All Around the Town" to myself – dropped to the sidewalk on the other side and walked away. Perhaps what I'd done was the right thing, since I heard applause, laughter and cheering from the rest of the pedestrians. I quickly forgot about the incident, as I entered the Inquirer building and tried to find the right floor – the one for "Local News", the floor that might house Stephan (pronounced "Steffan") O'Leary.

• • •

The security guard behind a marble counter appeared to be my best bet for finding O'Leary, since his name was not on the large directory next to the elevators. Most of the names I recognized there were sports writers, one or two editors and the political cartoonist. It seemed I'd have to call Stephan from the lobby and have him grant me access. I was about to ask the guard for assistance, when I heard a commotion behind me.

An angry, loud, male voice said: "Goddamn it to fucking hell. How could I know the guy was a nut case? It's not my fault."

"The hood of my car is scratched," said a woman. "You were driving. It is your fault."

"The guy didn't look like a whack job. How could I know he was crazy? The scratches will compound out."

"Oh, like you know how to compound out scratches – 'Steffan'." She drew out Stephan's name, making it into two syllables.

I moved around to the side of the counter and looked away, using my foot to slide my briefcase along the floor, out of sight. "Bing." Saved by an opening elevator door, taking the loud and angry debating team up, up and away.

"So how can I help you?" said the security guard. "Are you here to see someone?"

"Well, yes," I stammered, "that was Stephan O'Leary, right?"

"Are you here to see him? Why didn't you just say hello?"

"No, I just thought I recognized him. He seemed to be in a very bad mood."

"He's never in a good mood," said the guard. "Who are you here to see?"

I uttered the only name I could come up with – that of my favorite sportswriter. "Phil Sheridan."

"Your name?"

"Ryan O'Brien."

The guard smiled and punched a four-digit number. "Someone to see you Mister Sheridan. A Ryan O'Brien." He seemed surprised at Sheridan's response. "Okay Mister O'Brien – go on up. Fourth floor."

"Thank you. By the way, which floor is Stephan O'Leary on?"

"That'd be the fourth floor as well."

I got on the elevator, randomly punching buttons for three floors – two, five and six. I'd get off on one of them, kill a little time and leave. No sense getting into it with O'Leary. Maybe the written letter from Smyrl would be enough to get me my job back.

At the second floor stop, a mail boy got on, pushing a cart full of letters. He punched the button for the fourth floor. When we stopped there, Phil Sheridan was waiting for me. "You must be Ryan O'Brien," he said, extending his hand and yanking me out of the elevator.

"Mister Sheridan," I said.

"Call me Phil." He looked me up and down. "What can I do for you?"

"Probably nothing," I said. "I really came here to see Stephan O'Leary, but now I'm doing everything I can to avoid him. Your name was the only one I could think of. I'm sorry."

"Well, I suppose it's flattering that you came up with my name under pressure. It's also interesting that you're avoiding 'Steffan'. Why not come to my humble cubical and tell me about it." He turned and walked away, expecting me to follow him. I did.

I sat in the one extra chair, Phil sat at his desk and we talked. I told him I'd been arrested, cleared – fully exonerated – and that I was trying to get the Inquirer to correct the article in its Local News section, written by O'Leary – an article that had gotten me fired before I even began work. I told him I planned to take a notice of pending correction to my employer, along with Smyrl's letter, and try to undo the firing.

"Where will you be – hopefully – working?"

"At Howell & Barrett."

"I'm surprised they're hiring," he said.

"They offered me a job four years ago, when the economy was booming. The job was to start after my time in the military."

"I should've guessed from your haircut. Where'd you serve?"

"In the Marine Corps – last in Afghanistan. Before that in Iraq. At Camp Lejeune when not overseas."

"What rank were you?"

"I was a First Lieutenant. I made Captain on the day I got out."

"Thank you for your service. That's what we civilians are supposed to say. Right?"

"I suppose so. You're welcome. Thanks for your columns. You made me smile a few times in Afghanistan, when I could get a two-week old Inquirer. All I ever read was the Sports Section."

"Well then you're welcome, too. Why are you avoiding O'Leary?"

"I walked across the hood of the car he was driving. He was blocking the sidewalk, he wouldn't move and he flipped me the bird. I couldn't think of anything really appropriate to do – so I walked across the hood of his car. Of course I didn't know it was him."

Phil laughed, a nice manly guffaw. "Was it a little Saab convertible?"

"Yes."

"Was there a female passenger in the car? Pretty blond."

"Yes. She seemed as big a nitwit as O'Leary."

"Well," said Phil, "I can see why you need to avoid the guy. Maybe we can do an end run. You said you had a letter from the Detective involved?"

"Yes. It's right here." I handed Phil Smyrl's letter.

He read it quickly. "Seems good. I've got an idea, but let's make a couple of extra copies." He came back from the nearby copier, handed me the original and one copy. Let me see what I can do with Stephan – with this."

Phil came back in about five minutes, laughing. "You should hear his version of things. According to him, you jumped on his hood before he turned onto the sidewalk, then you gave him the finger and ran away when he got out of his car. You were 'deranged' and likely homeless. He didn't mention your briefcase."

"What bullshit. Did he read Smyrl's letter? Is he willing to corroborate it?"

"He said he'd look at it later, when he calmed down, that he was still too upset to think about much else than the 'incident' he'd experienced. Get this – he asked me if I knew anything about compounding scratches out of cars."

"So – should I wait around?"

"Only long enough for me to write you something. Hell, I'll use Inquirer Sports letterhead. I'm already done with my real job here for the day. Sit there. Gimme a minute or two."

"Can you get in trouble for this?"

"Who knows? We're laying off another forty employees next week. We're moving from this building to another 'iconic' old building – the old, empty Strawbridge's Building in a few months, the Deputy Managing Editor I report to handles not only Sports, but Business and the Sunday Edition as well. In other words, I'm not even sure who it would be that I'd get in trouble with – and, anyway, I feel like doing this. So don't interrupt me for the next six minutes. Okay?"

"Okay." I watched as Phil fiddled with his computer, laid the original letter from Smyrl out next to it and began to type. He paused every so often and laughed. When he was done, he hit "print" and a nearby printer spit out a one page letter. "What do you think?" he asked, handing me the letter. It read:

To Whom It May Concern – at Howell & Barrett:

The article that appeared in this past Sunday's Edition of The Philadelphia Inquirer, regarding a murder on Chester Island and the apprehension of a suspect, contains numerous errors of fact. Our bad. We are in the process of correcting said article. Specifically, Ryan O'Brien is not only not a suspect, he is actively assisting the New Jersey State Police in their investigation of the crime. His assistance in the ongoing investigation has been termed "invaluable", as O'Brien brings significant field experience from recent deployments to Afghanistan and Iraq as an officer in the United States Marine Corps as well as particular familiarity with Chester Island and the waters and lands surrounding it.

As Townes Van Zandt opined: ". . . snow don't fall on summer's time; wind don't blow below the sea . . . ." and only in a fictional dystopian world would someone of O'Brien's character and integrity, someone who risked his life repeatedly for America, be somehow punished for his innocent involvement in tangential aspects of this matter. Because it is possible that the Inquirer's reporting of this crime has caused the temporary termination of O'Brien from Howell & Barrett, as well as possible mental anguish, the Inquirer has offered him legal consul, gratis, and guaranteed him subsequent honest and timely reporting of both the investigation itself and any impact on his employment the matter may have had. It is our collective opinion here at the Inquirer, that although the article in question was clearly: our bad; termination of O'Brien's employment without due process was: your bad.

Sincerely,
Phil Sheridan
Senior General Topic Columnist – Sports

"Well, what do you think?"

"I think you, Sir, are an underpaid, under-appreciated genius; I think I'll frame this; I think it would have given me a laugh even in Afghanistan; I think it's perfect. Lord knows what anyone at Howell & Barrett might think – but you know what?"

"What?"

"If this doesn't do the trick, I don't want to work for them anyway. Thank you so very much. I owe you."

"Nope," said Phil, "now we're even."

We shook hands. We laughed. We promised to keep in touch. We laughed again. I left.

ARROGANT DITZ
CHAPTER NINETEEN

Well now that was interesting, I thought, as I walked the nine city blocks between the Inquirer Building and Howell & Barrett's offices. I'd managed to – sort of – accomplish my mission of getting something on Inquirer letterhead that might help undo my job termination. Phil Sheridan's willingness to pen something original, funny and on topic was pure luck; but, as they say – better lucky than good. I thought about the incident with Stephan O'Leary, his girlfriend's car and me; and a little too much of me was pleased with the brilliant whim, the spur-of-the-moment idea of dancing across the car's hood, and too little of me realized that I'd been an immature dope acting on impulse.

Howell & Barrett occupied the top four floors of a boxy, functional, no-frills fifteen-story building on Market Street – the same space where I'd been promised a job by Sam Barrett four years ago. According to the directory next to the elevator, Human Resources was on the 12th floor; and when I exited the elevator, I was met with a tasteful waiting area, windows overlooking Market Street, glass security doors and a receptionist.

She was attractive, in her late-forties, I guessed, efficient, and in full command of her reception area – the tiny piece of the universe in which I found myself. "Good morning, Sir. May I help you?"

"Yes. Thanks. I'm here to meet with someone in Human Resources. I don't remember her name, but I spoke to her yesterday by phone."

"Do you have an appointment?"

"No, but I'm sure she'll see me. She said she'd been trying to contact me."

"But you don't remember her name?"

"It was three names, a 'Ms' with a hyphenated last name. Something, something Smith."

"Ms. Tarry-Brigham-Smith."

"Yes. That's her. Thanks for your help."

She smiled. "Since you don't have an appointment, and you did not remember her name – can you at least tell me what you wish to see her about?"

I couldn't think of any concise way to say that I'd been terminated at the instigation of Ms. Tarry-Brigham-Smith for something I hadn't done, something that involved a murder, the shooting of my dog, the nighttime swimming of the Delaware River, my discovery of The Church of Jesus Christ is Lord, the New Jersey State Police and the Philadelphia Inquirer, and that I carried with me written proof that the termination had been a mistake – so instead, I didn't lie.

"Certainly. It concerns employment. I'm due to start work next Monday; and there's been some confusion that I need to clear up with her."

"I'll call her. Your name, Sir?"

"Ryan O'Brien."

"Nice. I like that. It rhymes."

"Parents. What can you do with them," I said.

"Hey. I'm one myself."

"One what?"

"A parent – of course." She punched in a number. "Janice? This is Sue – in reception. I have Ryan O'Brien to see you."

Sue looked over at me. "Yes," she said into the phone. "Certainly. I'll ask him.

"Mister O'Brien, Ms. Tarry-Brigham-Smith asks if you can make an appointment to see her – perhaps come back sometime as early as this afternoon, after lunch. She's in a meeting right now."

"Tell her I just want to hand her two documents, and that this will take about ten seconds. I'd like to give them to her myself. They have an important bearing on my employment. Important to me, anyway. If I may, I'll wait here."

Sue said: "Janice – he wishes to wait here and hand you some written material. No – I already suggested he come back this afternoon."

I decided to try to get Sue out of the middle. "May I speak with Ms. Tarry-Brigham-Smith myself – it might be easier?"

Sue did not ask "Janice" for instructions, but transferred the call to the phone on the small coffee table in front of me. It rang once, and I picked it up. "Hello, Ms. Tarry-Brigham-Smith?"

"O'Brien?"

"Yes."

"I don't have time to see you right now. I'm in the middle of an interview."

"No problem. I simply wish to hand you two letters – one from the New Jersey State Police and one from The Philadelphia Inquirer. They exonerate me. You can 'un-terminate' me."

"Can't you give them to Sue?"

"How much longer will your interview take," I asked. "Maybe I can wait."

"Another half hour – then there are the tests to administer. I won't be completely finished until after lunch – as I said earlier."

"How about I wait here a half hour, hand you the letters and you can read them while you're administering the tests?"

"I suppose so. I'll be out in a half hour."

• • •

We hung up. Sue looked over at me. I looked at her. She smiled. I smiled back. She got busy. I had a half hour to kill. I sorted through magazines and selected one about golf – a game I did not play. I looked at the feature article explaining how to add fifty yards off the tee by utilizing the B.L.I.S.T.E.R. acronym – which stood for: balance, leverage, incline, strength, tangent, equilibrium and radial. Each of the seven steps was accompanied by complex drawings showing vectors, trajectories, algorithms, and something called Monge's Theorem of Three Circles and Common Tangents. The implication was that if you had an advanced degree from M.I.T., you could become one helluva golfer. I sighed and put the magazine down.

Sue was temporarily not busy. "Not a golfer?"

"Nope," I said. "You?"

"Ha. Nope backatcha. I'm a divorced golf widow. I hate the game. It ruined my marriage."

Sue seemed to be laughing – at herself, her ex-husband, at golf. "A Million Stories in the Naked City," I said in my best baritone, "and this has been one of them."

"You're not old enough to remember that movie," said Sue.

"Neither are you."

"Too bad all the cute non-golfers are too young for me," said Sue. "Don't take up the 'activity'. Note I don't call it a 'sport'."

"I promise," I said. "I don't even own clubs. I admit to fishing, though. Are there fishing widows?"

Sue laughed out loud. It was a good laugh. It was hearty. "My mother was a fishing widow while we kids were little. Then she gave up raising us and joined him. She kicked his ass fishing – out-fished him all the time."

"Sounds like my kind of woman," I said.

"Know what? My dad didn't care. He loved it. He bragged about her to his buddies."

"Happily ever after?"

"Absolutely," said Sue. "Happily-ever-goddamnit-after."

Just then we noticed a short, curly-haired woman holding open the glass security door and listening. "Am I interrupting something here?"

"Nope," said Sue. "Just talking fishing, golf and the meaning of life. Time flies sometimes. Janice – this is Ryan O'Brien. Mister O'Brien – this is Janice Tarry-Brigham-Smith."

Janice fluttered her right hand at me through the door, indicating that I should hand her something. She did not enter the reception area, did not shake my hand and did not look me in the eye. "Alright," she said, "let me have the documents."

I unflapped the briefcase. I found a copy of Smyrl's letter. I found Sheridan's missive. I took three steps towards Janice Tarry-Brigham-Smith. I handed the letters to her. She took them. She said nothing. She turned away. She walked away.

"Well," said Sue, "that went well."

"Somehow I don't think I'll be working here," I said.

Sue pointed at the chair I'd been sitting in. "Sit for a minute."

I sat.

While watching me, Sue took two calls and directed them elsewhere. "This is not my real job," she said. "I'm covering for someone who's out sick."

"I'm surprised they can spare you from wherever it is you do work."

"They can't, but my boss is out for two weeks, recuperating; and I can do his mail, answer his calls and keep him up to date from here."

"Who's your boss?"

"Sam Barrett. That's why Janice didn't want to talk to you – in front of me. She's not usually quite so rude."

"Sam Barrett! He's who hired me – four years ago. He seemed like a great guy. In fact, regardless of what happens here with the firm, I owe him the courtesy of checking in. I just finished four years in the Marine Corps; and he told me he wanted to hear about it when I got out. He said we could trade war stories."

"Well, Semper Fi to you, Ryan. That'd probably be very good for him right about now," said Sue. "He's at the Hospital of the University of Pennsylvania. He had his prostate removed yesterday. He's already called twice today. He's bored. And by the way, he is a great guy."

"I'd very much like to talk to him. I'm afraid I've got some explaining to do about some things that have happened. Actually, I'd like his advice. When would be a good time to see him?"

Before Sue could answer, Tarry-Brigham-Smith rapped on the glass security doors and gestured to me to follow her.

Sue buzzed me in and said, "Good luck."

· · ·

I sat in one of the two "guest" chairs in what I suppose was Howell & Barrett's Human Resources Department Office. T-B-S threw my letters on her desk. "Back in a jiff," she said.

I looked around the office and realized that although the modest furnishings – the desk, chairs, file cabinets, computer monitors – were familiar; the purpose of the office, as displayed by the two walls of books, loose leaf notebooks, brochures, pamphlets and posters was as foreign to me as was the babble I'd overheard in a dusty wool-merchant's tent in Kandahar my first week in Afghanistan. Massive leather-bound volumes of something called

The Age Discrimination Act of 1975 was next to equally compendious volumes of *Americans With Disabilities Act of 1990*, which was adjacent to a worn spiral-bound publication titled "Supporting and Building the Desired Organizational Culture", which was displayed beside a stack of pamphlets that had "Sexism in the Context of the Patriachal Corporation". A poster on one wall said "The Boss is Not Your Enemy – Neither is SHE Your Friend", and on the other wall were certificates signifying that Ms. Janice Tarry-Brigham-Smith was qualified to deal with "Race/Color Discrimination & Employment Policies/Practices", discuss "Race, Gender and Age Stereotypes" and to foster "Creative Destruction in the Workplace". There was no mention anywhere of investment banking, stocks, bonds, derivatives or clients.

T-B-S returned to her office and sat facing me. She seemed more relaxed in her own digs, where I suppose I was somehow less threatening. She read the letter from Smyrl. "Hmm," she said, "almost seems like you wrote this one yourself. I had no idea you were assisting Detective Smyrl. I assume he'll take a confirming call from me?"

"Of course," I said. "That's why he gave you his e-mail address as well as his cellphone in the letter." I did not say: you fucking arrogant ditz.

She turned to the letter from Phil Sheridan. She seemed to read it at least twice, then looked up at me and said: "what on earth does 'snow don't fall on summer time; wind don't blow below the sea' have to do with anything?"

"It's a metaphor," I said. "He's taking the time to be eloquent and saying that in a just and fair world, those things that never happen – wind blowing below the sea and snow falling in summer – would happen before I'd lose my job over something that I'd clearly not done."

"Oh. Who is this Townes Van Zandt?"

"He's legendary. He's a philosopher/writer who lyrically expressed with power and vigor ideas that connect the mystical to the mundane, the spiritual to the commercial. I'm surprised you haven't heard of him."

"Is he living?"

"No one except Professor Van Zandt can answer that," I said. "Like many geniuses, he was or is reclusive. No one's seen him in years. There have been undocumented sightings."

"I see. I wonder how I've not heard of him."

"What was your major in college?"

T-B-S became positively chatty, enthusiastic to be discussing her qualifications to give me a hard time about my job. "I majored in Human Services and minored in Communication. But I have a broad understanding of all of the Social Sciences and I took courses in Public Administration, Political Science, Industrial Psychology, Sociology, Collective Bargaining and Labor Law, Gender Studies, African American Studies and Latino Studies."

"Well, maybe that explains it," I said. "He's really a philosopher. You do seem extremely well-rounded and qualified to be a rock star in the Human Resources world." Since I wanted to get the conversation back to my job, I again did not say: you fucking arrogant ditz. "Will those letters suffice?"

T-B-S thought a minute, and pulled a loose-leaf notebook off a shelf. It was titled *Howell & Barrett Human Resource Polices*. "This is still a work in progress," she said, "but I think the answers can be found here somewhere." She paged back and forth. I watched.

"Here we go," she said. "Good news. It says: A previously 'terminated' employee may apply for a position at Howell & Barrett. Howell & Barrett will not consider the cause of the termination in evaluating the applicant for rehire, but consider the applicant's qualifications as if he or she had not experienced termination."

I tried unsuccessfully to get my head around what that sentence meant to me. I couldn't. "In other words, if I was fired for actually murdering someone, Howell & Barrett couldn't consider that fact when I applied for a new job?"

"Well, yes. But that's not the point. From a practical point of view, a murderer would be in prison and therefore unable to apply for a job. Maybe a better example would be someone fired for substance abuse, on the job, – and considered for rehire at a later date."

"Well, I was not really 'terminated', was I? Don't the two letters cause a rescinding of the termination? After all, the reason you caused me to be terminated turned out to be untrue."

She thought a minute and came to a conclusion. "You were terminated. All the paperwork was completed and you are not now an employee of Howell & Barrett. There is no such thing in here about a 'rescinding' of a termination. Therefore to work here you must be rehired by us."

"Okay. Here I am. Rehire me. We know there's a position open – mine."

"The hiring process takes approximately two weeks now. There is an application for you to complete, interviews you must have, tests to administer to you, references for you to obtain, and psychological evaluations to be completed. Only then can a decision be made about a hiring."

I made a conscious decision to not stand up and turn over T-B-S's desk and pull all the bullshit books off her shelves. I opted for calm, but I was faking it. "But the only reason I now need all this stuff is because you – Ms. Janice Tarry-Brigham-Smith terminated me unfairly."

"There was absolutely nothing unfair about your termination. Policy is in place about unfavorable publicity, and being mentioned in the only real newspaper in town as a murder suspect who resisted arrest is about as unfavorable as you can get."

"Howell & Barrett were not even mentioned in that incredibly inaccurate article. How was there unfavorable publicity?"

"I can think of five or six reasons how your arrest could ultimately bring unfavorable publicity to the Firm. But – listen closely – I do not have time to debate this with you. Whatever the 'fairness' – you were terminated. The only way for you to work here is for you to go through the very same employment process as everyone else. Any other process would be unfair to other applicants."

I could think of nothing helpful to say, or do. I sat there, dumbfounded, staring at T-B-S.

She opened a desk drawer, pulled out a glossy binder and extended it towards me. "Here is an application for employment. Do you want it?"

I did not say any of the clever, obscene things the angry angel perched on my right shoulder was suggesting. I established a personal best – a trifecta of not saying, for the third time: you fucking arrogant ditz. Instead, I stood, reached for the binder, pasted an insincere smile on my puss and managed to say: "Why certainly. I appreciate your professionalism – it's positively chimerical, our discussions have been fulsome, and you are as indocible a person as I've ever met. Thank you for your time. I'll get back to you soon."

I was too upset to even be friendly with Sue, when she asked how it went. "Catch-22," I said, punching the elevator button. "Franz Kafka wrote the script in there," I said, looking now at Sue. "She's an arrogant ditz," I said, as the elevator binged.

"That good, huh? Don't surrender yet Ryan O'Brien – here," she said, extending a slip of paper in my direction.

I managed a wan smile, pocketed the slip of paper and rode the elevator down to the ground floor.

I'M AN OKAY MAN
CHAPTER TWENTY

By the time I reached the Market Street Bridge over the Schuylkill River, I'd worked through the denial stage of whatever it was that had just happened. I conceded that I was still someone who still got stuff got done to him; and I felt about the same as I did when I'd been a rookie Second Lieutenant – chewed out by a Captain for having a tarnished brass belt buckle five minutes after I'd returned from a three day field exercise. I'd survived that, and all of the other indignities, disrespectings and nonsense that went with being part of a giant testosterone-laden bureaucracy – and I'd survived. I would survive this.

I surrendered to a lavish anger that marched me north along the Schuylkill's east bank, past the Art Museum to the elegant old structures overlooking the Fairmount Dam, where seeing patient fishermen fish for carp and catfish did not calm me; and so I walked on, thinking about how I'd been wronged – assigning blame, cursing my luck, considering methods of vengeance, and recollecting the physical revenge in Poe's *The Cask of Amontillado* and imagining T-B-S crying out "for the love of God O'Brien" as I mortared her into my basement wall; and recalling the psychological retribution of Heathcliff, relentlessly destroying Hindley and becoming his erstwhile master; or remembering a most satisfying revenge – the complex, long-term, remorseless vengeance of Dantes, who after his fourteen years imprisonment in the Chateau d'If, and disguised as the Count of Monte Cristo, gradually induces the abject ruination of the three men responsible for his unjust imprisonment – until I found myself at a bridge, a non-allegorical bridge, which I crossed on Girard Avenue, and which aimed me directly at the Philadelphia Zoo;where I decided to stare in a wolf's yellow eyes and borrow inklings of savagery, and let an elephant remind me how to never forget.

• • •

Except that the Zoo had no wolves – they'd been gone for years, shipped to a wolf conservation center in upstate New York. Elephants? Nope. Released to an elephant sanctuary in Western Pennsylvania where they wandered a seven-hundred acre conservation center with elephants from other zoos and circuses. Good for them. I was reduced to trying to find some other animals for inspiration, but with little success. The Zoo had many animals that I would not otherwise experience, some of them endangered – but they were inauthentic somehow, or at least not as real as the imagined wolves and elephants.

The animals that seemed not unhappy to be in the zoo were either reptiles – for whom happiness was an improbable concept anyway – or small and unusual mammals. Short-eared elephant shrews and Eurasian harvest mice wandered safely and content within the habitats of several species of lemurs. Birds – Mandarin and Mallard ducks, geese, peacocks and chickens – were noisy and hyperactive; although a solitary Bald eagle glared at me fiercely for seconds from a caged perch. All the hoofed animals seemed hungry and oblivious. The larger primates – the Western lowland gorillas and the Sumatran orangutan – appeared dignified but glum. Bears were busy sleeping. Most of the large cats – the African lions, the Amur tiger and several species of leopards – were somnolent, displaying a disinterested lethargy when I attempted to get their attention.

Only the cheetahs displayed attentiveness, and were therefore somehow less-attenuated versions of wild animals. There was a smaller degree of difference between the cheetahs at the Zoo and cheetahs on the Serengeti, than there seemed to be between other animals and their real habitats. There were three cheetahs – at least that I could see – and they had a fairly large habitat. It seemed to me that they could escape if they thought about it and were clever. The cheetahs implied savagery was of an immediate – see it, chase it, kill it, eat it – variety, however, and although I found them thought-provoking, it was inapplicable to my employment situation.

I sat in front of the cheetahs for awhile, watching them watch me; and then I called Jameson.

"O'Brien," he said.

"Jameson," I said.

"You're not coming today, I suppose."

"Correct. Please explain this to Nashir for me."

"Will you be here tomorrow?"

"I promise."

"Alright. Here's a head's up. Nashir is spending a lot of time with *Darker Than Amber*. And he's not just looking at the cover."

"That's good. Right?"

"I guess so," said Jameson. "How's the job situation?"

"Not good. I don't think I have one; and all I seem to be able to do is walk around and be pissed off about it."

"Where are you now?"

"I'm on my way to the hospital to see someone, but as we

speak, I'm at the Philadelphia Zoo, sitting in front of the cheetahs. They're staring me down."

"Say hello to them for me," said Jameson. "Good luck with the rest of your day."

"Thanks."

I opened my briefcase, removed the employment application and looked at it. It was comprehensive. It was twenty-two pages in length. I folded the application lengthwise and tried to push it into a nearby trash receptacle, but the receptacle was full, and the fucking thing wouldn't fit. I considered throwing the application into the cheetah habitat. Let them deal with it. Instead, I sighed and put it back in my briefcase. I watched the cheetahs again for a few minutes, and then decided to leave the zoo; and since I'd told Jameson I was going to the hospital, I headed off to the hospital.

• • •

A feature on my smartphone provided a map of the neighborhood I was walking through. It was named "Mantua"; and it was an interesting place – a place that looked capable of distracting me from my angry self-absorption. So I turned off 34th Street and headed west on Wallace Street, into the neighborhood's broken heart. Wherever blighted city areas in Philadelphia are heading, Mantua looked like it was trying to get there first. There were many hundreds of vacant lots – apparently the result of tearing down houses that had once been there, for many of the houses left standing had the outlines of zigzag stairs and ruler-straight floors and partitions etched on their windowless side walls. Houses left standing alone had the look of sentinels, watching over vacant lots, clusters of row homes and new low-rise public housing.

The few people I encountered in Mantua seemed to have little to do. They sat on porches or stood on street corners. A few waited at bus stops. One young man walked towards me and I noticed his pant leg rode up displaying an ankle holster atop Nike Air Jordan retro sneakers. He wore baggy jeans and a raggety blue hoodie; and he stared down at the sidewalk as we passed. I almost told him that his holster was showing; and then I thought that that was a really dumb idea and that he probably wore it that way on purpose.

Turning left and heading south on 37th Street took me across Spring Garden Street, out of Mantua and into Powelton Village, which appeared to be a place of Victorian houses, community gardens, trees and people with places to go. Compared to Mantua, it bustled, and I wondered about the circumstances that gave the two communities such different trajectories. At least I wasn't thinking about my job.

I walked through Drexel's Campus, across the traffic of Market, Chestnut and Walnut Streets and found myself entering Penn's Campus. I realized I'd had nothing to eat since breakfast and was starving, and I ate from John's Lunch Cart – a scrapple and egg hoagie – while seated on a stone bench across Spruce Street from the Hospital, listening to the screech of ambulances and the thwop-thwop of helicopters.

I reached in my pocket and pulled out the slip of paper Sue had handed me on the way out of Howell & Barrett – before the long walk, the missing wolves and elephants, the cheetahs, Mantua, the ankle holster and lunch. It read: "Sam Barrett – Room 679, Founders Pavilion, H.U.P.". The Hospital of the University of Pennsylvania was confusing – floors didn't seem to line up, elevators were slow and full, and I got contradictory directions to Sam's room. Eventually I found him; but first I heard him.

• • •

"I can't lie down anymore," said the loud voice that turned out to be Sam Barrett, successfully annoying his nurse. "If I don't stand up and walk around I'll go nuts. Who cares about my prostate if I'm insane? I'm gonna push this I.V. around the halls. Do I have any boundaries?"

"You can go anywhere on this floor," answered the nurse. "Don't go in any patient rooms. Don't go on elevators. Try not to bother staff."

"Thanks." Sam wheeled his I.V. out the door, almost running me down. "Who the hell are you?"

I looked him up and down. He was still short, nearly bald and trim. His color was a little off – a hospital grey. I managed not to laugh at the I.V., the tied-in-the-back hospital gown, the high black orthopedic socks and the booties. I did smile, though. "Nice booties."

"Do I know you?" Sam said.

"I met you once, four years ago. I'm Ryan O'Brien."

Sam stuck out his hand, his left one, since his right was shepherding the I.V. unit over a threshold. "Where've you been? Sue called me three hours ago."

"I walked here."

"Jeezus. That's about fifteen blocks. That's five blocks an hour. The pet turtle I had as a kid could get here faster than that."

"Sue didn't tell me you were expecting me. I guess I took a detour."

"Let's get away from my room," Sam said. "I feel like I'm at my own funeral in there. It's full of flowers. Only thing missing is a coffin."

"I did not bring you flowers."

Sam and his booties and I.V. shuffled and clattered down the hall to a small visiting area. "Thanks for that." He indicated that I should sit and that he would continue being vertical. I sat.

"I'm bored out of my skull," he said. "Talk to me about the outside world. What have you been up to?"

"How long have you been in here?"

"Since yesterday at 5 a.m. Surgery, recovery – groggy in my room – flowers – visitors – crappy night's sleep with hospital beepings, buzzings and nurses constantly checking on me – lousy food – no cable television – a noisy, crazy patient across the hall – wife crying at my bedside for no reason – surgeon visit this morning to tell me how gifted he is and how lucky I am to have selected him. In other words, I've been here for years. Now you go. What have you been up to today? Whatever it is, it must be better than what I've done. Talk."

I talked. I told him of my trip to the Inquirer, walking on the hood of the car of the man I'd wanted a favor from and how Phil Sheridan bailed me out.

Sam interrupted. "I like Sheridan. He writes great stuff. Let me see the letter."

I unflapped my briefcase, pulled out the letter and handed it to Sam.

Sam stopped his hospital pacing, the shuffle-clank of the booties and I.V. He read. He laughed. He sat down. "This is really good. I need a copy of this. This is hilarious." He laughed some more. "Of course I didn't know any of this stuff about a murder and your arrest. I've got lots of questions about that – but I'll ask them later. What did you do next?"

"I went to your firm to give Phil's and Smyrl's letters to your Human Resources Department."

"Wait. Who's Smyrl?"

I handed him Smyrl's letter. "Jeezus O'Brien – you sure keep busy. But let me get back to that. What then?"

"Then I failed to impress your Ms. Tarry-Brigham-Smith, she told me I'd been terminated and told me to reapply for my job if I wished. She implied that I would not be successful. I don't know if I impressed Sue, your secretary, but at least she was civil – in fact, she was competent and funny. I liked her and I think she did not dislike me. She gave me your room number."

"Then what?"

"I walked around. I went to the zoo, looking for elephants and wolves."

"What for?"

"I wanted their help in deciding what to do about my job. I know that sounds silly – unprofessional – but I thought somehow they could help."

"Did they help?"

"No. There are no wolves or elephants at the Philadelphia Zoo right now. The cheetahs were thought-provoking, though."

"What thoughts did they provoke?"

"For one, they convinced me to throw away my job application. I tried to stuff it in the trash, but it wouldn't fit."

"Do you have it with you?"

"Yes. It's in here." I handed him the application.

"It's got mustard on it," Sam said.

"I told you I tried to fit it in the trash can."

"Do you want to work for me?"

"I want to work for you, but I'm not sure I want to work for Howell & Barrett. Maybe that doesn't make any sense to you, but it does to me."

"Look," said Sam. "I sort of do know what you mean. The whole Human Resources thing would piss me off too. I'm not at all sure I could get a job at Howell & Barrett now. Do me a favor."

"Okay."

"I like that. You didn't ask 'what' – you said 'okay'."

"I've decided to trust you on this one. What've I got to lose."

"Alright," said Sam. "Here's the deal. I'm giving you an employment test – right now. It will take less than five minutes. If you pass, we'll do an end run around Human Resources."

"Okay."

"Here's the test. It's verbal. You don't need a pen or paper or a calculator or a laptop or internet access. Accept the premise of this test."

"Okay."

"Ha. I still like that. You'll never be a 'yes' man, but you might be an 'okay' man. Here's the test. Listen."

I listened.

• • •

"You are working at Howell & Barrett, and decide to come in early – at 7 a.m. to catch up on stuff. You need a pot of coffee and know how to make it – it will take exactly five minutes to brew and you drink it black. You need to take a one-minute piss. The men's room is on the way to your office, one-minute from the kitchen and one minute more to your office. You need to access your computer in order to work on a project; and your computer will take two minutes to boot up and run through the security protocols and be ready for you to use.

"Got that?"

"Yes," I said, suspecting some trick.

Sam read my mind. "No tricks. Here's the question. Here's the whole test. What is the shortest period of time that you can be at your desk, with coffee, working?"

I looked for complicated answers and couldn't think of any; and so I said: "assuming no running – seven minutes. A little faster if I run."

"How do you figure?"

"I start the coffee, while it's brewing, I hit the men's room, take a leak, walk to my office and turn on the computer, walk back to the kitchen, pour the coffee and walk back to my office. Faster if I ran."

"Forget the running – especially with the hot cup of coffee. Congratulations. You're hired."

"I don't get it."

"You sequenced your work. You realized there was a proper sequence to minimize the time required. You accepted my premise. You did the simple math. You did not overthink things. Again – you are hired."

"You mean there are people who've applied for jobs at Howell & Barrett who couldn't answer that question?"

"Ryan – there are people working at Howell & Barrett who couldn't answer that question. In fact, none of the employees who made it over all the hurdles your pal Tarry-Brigham-Smith constructed – even with sublime grade-point averages, impeccable referrals and perfect board scores they could not answer that question correctly. Some of them simply added up the total minutes. As I recall, they all said twelve minutes, although one said ten. One woman told me she didn't drink coffee and wouldn't make it for anyone else. One young man told me he drank tea and wanted to know how long it would take to brew some. Two others decided the whole question was somehow inappropriate and that they'd properly deduced that the best answer was to refuse to answer it. One guy guessed four minutes and wanted to debate me on how he could pour the coffee before it was completely finished perking. A woman told me she'd have purchased her coffee at Starbucks, to save time – but then she couldn't do the addition and came up with ten minutes. She said she needed more time in the ladies' room. All of them were pissed off at me and the test. So, again – congratulations. You answered the question and you don't seem pissed off. Can you start work tomorrow?"

"I am not at all pissed off," I said, "but I can't start work tomorrow." I was thinking about my morning meeting with Clemmie and my afternoon reading with Nashir.

"I thought you were an 'okay' man."

I laughed and explained why I couldn't – or rather wouldn't – start work tomorrow. I'd made two promises and had to keep them.

Sam laughed back at me and said he understood. "But I wonder if you could pick me up at get me out of here late tomorrow morning. I want to talk to you some more about what's been going on with you. I have some ideas, but they need to percolate more. I just need a ride home. An hour and a half round trip – plus a half hour to get me out of here."

"Okay," I said.

"'Okay'. I love it. Thanks. I'll call you when I'm ready. Leave me those letters and the application for employment. I'm going to see if I can get a job at my own firm."

REUNION
CHAPTER TWENTY-ONE

It was Wednesday, 6:45 a.m. I was outside. I was sitting on my steps. I was waiting for Clemmie. I wondered if she'd bring her dog. I hoped it would be a large quiet dog, not a little yappy one. I hoped Clemmie would like me. I hoped that I wouldn't disappoint her somehow. I did not wonder if I'd like her. I did not wonder if my porter-influenced recollection of her was flawed. I was wearing running shorts and shoes, a tan USMC cap and an old blue hoodie. I'd take off the hoodie if she came for a run, without a dog.

I felt something in my pocket, and pulled out a solitary Good & Plenty, a pink one – not pink, really, but that unique Good & Plenty color that was part dark pink, bright salmon and fuchsia. I knew it was four years old and would be very stale, a narrow cylinder of sweet black licorice leftover from pre-Marine Corps days – the last time I'd worn the hoodie. It reminded me of Smokey, since when I'd walked her, I had dog treats in my right hand pocket for her and Good & Plentys in my left hand pocket for me. I wondered if Clemmie would be on time; and I imagined that she was responsible and likely to be punctual. I looked at my watch. 6:57 a.m.

I was looking towards my right, since I thought Clemmie would arrive from that direction – north and west was the general direction of Penn and Drexel – and she'd told Uncle Ryan that she went to school. I wanted to see her before she saw me.

WHAM! I was hit from my left and knocked off the steps and onto the sidewalk. I went fetal for a second, thinking I was being mugged. Then I heard whining and felt something licking the back of my neck. It was a dog. It was a black dog. It was a Labrador retriever. It was SMOKEY! It was Smokey, whining, licking my face, shaking all over; and it was Clemmie, running up grabbing for the leash.

"Omigod!" she said. "I'm so sorry Ryan. I've never seen Smokey like this. She got away from me the second she saw you."

I lay on my back, hugging Smokey, while she tried to become part of me. "Give us a minute. This is my dog. I thought she was dead."

"Your dog?"

"Long story," I said. "I'll explain everything in a minute." Clemmie took a seat, and watched the Smokey and Ryan show. Smokey whined. I got something in both eyes and had to wipe them on the sleeves of my hoodie. We calmed down and I took a seat next to Clemmie, with Smokey half on my lap. There was a small shaved spot on her left flank, and a bandage.

"You talk," I said to Clemmie. "I'm still a little worked up. I hope I'm not flunking this test."

"You're still passing tests, O'Brien," she said. "Anyone who can cry over a dog is okay with me."

As soon as I was able hold onto a coherent thought, I realized that it was likely to have been Clemmie behind the rootstock on Friday night – fooling with guns and ammo and hanging out with Max, Bama, and the murdered Marvin. In a second or two, she'd realize that it had been me on the other side of the rootstock, and that my actions had caused the fuckup of 'Bama's mission and Marvin's death – unless she'd already realized that and was acting, in which case Clemmie and Ryan were not destined to become a thing. In that case, Clemmie needed to talk to Smyrl.

"How'd you end up with my dog? And how did you know her name was Smokey?"

"My sister brought her to my apartment Saturday morning. She told me her name was Smokey; and she asked me if I'd watch her for a few days. She said Smokey had been in the Delaware River, retrieving a stick; and that someone had shot her. She also said that Smokey had retrieved the stick even though she'd been bleeding badly. Emily left Smokey and the stick at my apartment."

"Your sister's name is Emily?"

"Yes."

"If everything you've told me is true, Emily might be in serious trouble – and in danger."

"Of course it's true. What kind of danger?"

"What's Emily like?"

"Emily's always in some kind of trouble. She likes life on the edge. We're twins – not identical – and she's the adventurous one. I'm the boring, responsible one."

"There's a whole lot I need to tell you about the night Smokey got shot. Someone was murdered the same night. Are you willing to talk to the police? They'll need to know Emily's name."

"I don't want to get her in any more trouble."

I might be a sucker, I thought. At least I might be as far as Clemmie was concerned. But I decided to tell her what had happened Friday night. "How much time do you have?"

"I've a class at 9:30 a.m. I should study for a half hour. My place is twenty minutes from here. I'll need ten minutes to shower and dress. It's a fifteen minute walk to class. It's 7:15 a.m. now. I can eat something in five minutes. So I need to be at my place at about 8:30 a.m."

She sounded like Sam Barrett giving me his employment test. "Let's walk Smokey to your place, then we'll do laps around the block until you have to go."

"What about Smokey?"

"What about her?"

"I've been taking good care of her."

"I can see that. I thank you for it, but she's my dog."

Clemmie sighed. "I suppose you're right. I didn't have a dog for lots of reasons; and mostly because I don't really have time for one. But in the four days I've known her, I've come to love her."

"Well keep right on loving her. See her as much as you want. In fact, when – well, if – I'm at work, you could walk her sometimes. I'll get you a key to my place." As soon as I said this I realized that if Clemmie was lying about her sister I shouldn't be giving out keys to my place – especially with one of my computers streaming video of Chester Island.

We stood up to walk, and I realized I hadn't really looked at Clemmie closely. I guessed her height at five-eight or so, hair – dirty blond, at least wavy, maybe curly, of indeterminate length because it was casually bunched on top of her head, eyes – blue, figure – trim, condition – fit, makeup – none; and she still had that casual grace that I'd remembered from the Pub & Kitchen. She was beautiful, but either didn't know it or didn't care.

She noticed me noticing her. "Am I passing a test, Ryan?"

"Perfect boards," I said. "Merit Scholarship."

"Now please tell me about what happened Friday night. Tell me everything. And start at the beginning."

"I was anchored off Chester Island, in the Delaware River last Friday night. Smokey was with me; and I saw lights moving around on the Island." That was how I began, and Clemmie did not interrupt me until I got to the Smokey-gets-shot part of the story.

"What, exactly did the voice behind the rootstock say?"

"I don't remember exactly, but it might have been a woman and she was pissed that Marvin – the guy who ended up dead – shot Smokey. Then she was even more pissed off when Marvin left her there alone."

"Did she say anything else?"

"I don't think so. I left then, trying to find Marvin myself."

"Then what?"

I told her about untying Max, of Marvin's escape, of my swimming the River and of people on the Island looking for me – first on foot and then by boat.

"You swam across the Delaware River – at night?"

"It wasn't as hard as it looks. I went very slowly. I came ashore in Chester."

"You might be crazy."

"I am almost certain that I'd be as dead as Marvin if I had stayed on the Island."

"So Emily was on Chester Island, at night, with a bunch of people with guns, one of whom was killed; and no one knows what really happened. And I don't know where my sister is now." Clemmie dabbed at her eyes with her sweatshirt sleeves. "I'm not going to class. Let's go talk to the police."

I told her about Smyrl and how competent he seemed and asked if I could call him and mention Emily. "Of course," said Clemmie.

I dialed Smryl – voicemail. "Smyrl. This is O'Brien. My dog is alive. She was rescued by someone who was on the Island last Friday night. That person is now missing. Her name is Emily . . . ." Uh oh. I didn't know Clemmie's last name. I looked over at her with a raised eyebrow.

"Her name is Emily Putnam," she said.

"Emily Putnam," I said to Smyrl's voicemail. "Call me when you can." I terminated the call and put the phone back in my pocket. It was 8:30 a.m.

• • •

Sousa's "Semper Fidelis" blared from my pocket. "Smyrl!" I said into the phone.

"No," said Sam Barrett. "Not Smyrl. Sam Barrett. I'll be out early – in a half hour. Pick me up out front at 9 a.m." He hung up.

I told Clemmie I'd promised to pick Sam Barrett up and take him home; and that I should keep my promise. I asked her if she'd watch Smokey for a few hours.

"Nope," she said. "We're coming with you. I've got a million questions. You're not getting out of my sight until you answer them."

So we jogged as much as Smokey would allow, and got to my car in fifteen minutes. The back of the car was filled with tools, paint, solvents, a bucket, towels and all the other stuff I was using to repair *Larke*, so we put Smokey in the back seat, and Clemmie took the passenger seat, front. I drove west on Market Street, south on 34th Street, and into the pickup lanes, behind taxis, buses and cars. By the time we edged to the pickup area, it was 9:05 a.m.; and Sam Barrett was sitting outside a large revolving door in a wheelchair, tended by an aide.

"Go get him, Clemmie – please. He's probably annoyed with me for being five minutes late. I'll get Smokey into the back somehow."

Clemmie hopped out of the car and headed for Sam. I opened my car's hatch and began to consolidate my gear, to accommodate Smokey. I'd just cleared a space when Sam threw his small suitcase into it and shut the hatch. "Jeezus, O'Brien. You're late. Your car is full of crap. You brought a dog. At least your girlfriend is beautiful. I'm in the back with the dog. Let's go."

Clemmie told Sam she was not my girlfriend and offered to sit in the back; but Sam had already bonded with Smokey and he was firmly settled into the back. I said the only thing I could think of: "where to?" Then my phone rang; and I answered it quickly, before Sam could criticize the music.

"Smyrl?"

"Nope. This is your Uncle Ryan. What's up?"

"You made it home okay."

"Yep."

"How's paradise?"

"Good. They missed me. I should go away more often. What's with you? Did you talk to Sam Barrett? Do you have a job?"

"I can't really talk now, Uncle Ryan. But real quick: Smokey's okay, Sam Barrett is in the back seat of my car with her right now, and Clemmie – the beautiful Pub & Kitchen waitress – is in my passenger seat. We're driving Sam home from the hospital. And so far this has been a very special day." I glanced over at Clemmie.

"Whoa. Call me when you can."

"Roger that." I terminated the call and began threading my way around the busy streets, heading for the Schuylkill Expressway to take Sam home. Smyrl called. I answered.

Smyrl asked me about Smokey and about Emily. Then: "where is Emily? I should talk to her."

"I don't know where Emily is."

"Then how do you know about her; and who brought your dog back?"

I glanced over at Clemmie. "Emily's sister."

"Then I should talk to her."

"Well, I'm not sure that's possible," I said.

Clemmie snapped her fingers, asking for the phone. I handed it to her.

"Hi. This is Emily's sister. I'm Clemmie. How can I help? Uh huh. Saturday morning. No. I haven't heard from her. I'm worried. Yes. I'll ask Ryan.

"Ryan – Detective Smyrl would like us to come talk to him as soon as possible. He thinks Emily is in danger."

Sam weighed in: "Ryan. Jeezus. Let's all go talk to the detective. I've been thinking about all this all night. Go. I can go home and be bored recuperating anytime. This is interesting. Go."

"Tell him we'll be there in an hour," I said. She did.

• • •

So when we got to the Schuylkill Expressway, we went east instead of west, over the Walt Whitman Bridge and onto the Atlantic City Expressway. Clemmie kept my phone, since the State of New Jersey was anal about cellphones and driving. Clemmie and Sam told me to talk, begin at the very beginning and tell them everything. I surrendered and started talking.

So that is how Sam Barrett (wealthy co-founder of Howell & Barrett and City of Philadelphia mover and shaker, recently minus a prostate), Clemmie (beautiful student, twin, dog-lover, recently minus a sister), Ryan O'Brien (bewildered ex-Marine, recently minus a job) and Smokey (best dog ever, no longer minus an owner and now resting her head on Sam's lap) drove to the Regional New Jersey State Police HQ, in a six-year old Subaru Forester, with a hitch, crammed full of repair-my-sailboat stuff and Sam's luggage – while I yammered on, uninterrupted, reciting the litany of events that had happened to me in the last five days. Clemmie turned around and looked at Sam when I said "swam the river", again when I admitted to "sleeping in the ceiling", once more when I told them I'd "pushed a truck into the River", yet again when I told them I selected *Darker Than Amber* to read to Nashir and, finally, once more, when I divulged my walking on a car hood in Center City; and every time Clemmie looked at Sam, he laughed.

Five minutes out from Smyrl, I ran out of things to confess and fell silent. Clemmie placed her hand on my left shoulder and kneaded it. I couldn't tell if she did this in sympathy, wanted to mold me into someone different, wanted to exorcise my bad-luck demon or wanted to touch the magic-me – someone who had turned not-boring. "What do you think, Sam?" she said.

Sam pondered. Then: "I feel the most like a gypsy grandfather I've ever felt in my life. I'm in a car with two interesting young people, a wonderful dog – who is now snoring on my lap – and enough gear in the back to start a boatyard; and we're headed off to talk to a detective with the name of – Sam Smyrl. I need to see how all this plays out."

"That's how you feel, Sam. I asked what do you think?"

"I think that Smyrl, O'Brien, Clemmie, Sam and Smokey need to figure out the reason why people were on Chester Island, armed to the teeth, and that will lead to a murderer and your sister. I also think that we'll need to do this very quickly – for your sister's sake, and because the longer this is unsolved, the harder it will be to figure it all out. That's what I think. What do you think, Clemmie?"

"I don't care about Chester Island and whatever happened there. I just want to find my sister. How about you, Ryan?"

"I want to solve the murder, find your sister, enjoy my dog, spend lots of time with you and get my job back at Howell & Barrett. I want a time machine to go back to Friday night and do it all differently – except that then I wouldn't have met you. Look. Here we are."

Let's Not Forget About Emily
Chapter Twenty-Two

Sam and Clemmie went inside, looking for Smyrl, while Smokey and I headed for shady ground cover to give Smokey the chance to take a leak and sniff around a little – she obliged. We started back to the car when my cellphone binged – indicating an e-mail message had been received. I'd blocked most e-mail from finding its way to my phone; and I saw this one was from Lance Corporal Simmons – a Fire Team Leader in my platoon. I still thought of it as my platoon.

The message was awful. A day that so far been full of remarkably good occurrences – Smokey's resurrection, Clemmie, Sam's help – had just turned dreary, blighted by the news that Platoon Sergeant Johnson had been wounded in Afghanistan – Saturday morning. There were no details, other than that he was in Landstuhl Regional Medical Center in Germany and would be flown to Dover Air Force Base when his condition permitted. I felt like I'd been punched in the stomach; and I went to hands on knees – the vomit position – just in case.

Fuck. Sergeant Johnson. Wounded. At Landstuhl – the place

where serious wounded were sent. My fault. I'd left the platoon, left Afghanistan and left Sergeant Johnson. Then I'd lost his Suunto. My fault. Sergeant Johnson. Wounded. Wounded about the same time I'd lost his Suunto. Fuck. I had to find that wrist watch. I promised myself I would.

Smokey whined, and I went down on my knees to give her a hug – really to let her give me some comfort. I pulled the solitary pink Good & Plenty out of my pocket and bit it in two – half for me, half for Smokey. It was a vow, a communion, a promise, to give the Suunto – the very one with the "J" scratched on the back – to Johnson. I decided not to be separated from Smokey; so the two of us followed the other half of our team into the building.

• • •

Inside the conference room, the Sams were already seated next to each other, talking – apparently about me. Clemmie was listening.

"Here he is now," said Smyrl.

"He's brought his dog," said Barrett. "You can never tell what he's going to do next."

Clemmie said nothing, but looked at the ceiling over the conference table, and smiled, as if to say I know where you slept last Saturday night. Then she looked more closely at me, and she frowned.

I sat down next to Clemmie, across the table from the men. "Smokey's part of this too. She was on the Island last Friday with me; and if she could talk, we'd solve this whole mess right now. We need to figure this out – I need to figure this all out soon."

"Why 'soon', Ryan," asked Smyrl.

"I'll explain later – but this all needs to be over with soon. Sam Barrett already told us that the longer this is goes on, the harder it's going to be to solve. I agree. We need to solve it – soon."

Smyrl looked puzzled, but decided not to question me further. He had been recapping what he knew. Sam Barrett and Clemmie were listening. I tuned out, since I'd heard it all before. I focused on my personal need to be at Dover Air Force Base when Johnson arrived there – with his Suunto. Smokey lay on the floor at my feet, quickly realizing that no food, balls, squirrels, or sticks were imminent and that attending to the yammering of humans was the usual waste of time – so she sighed and tuned out with me – and that's where we both were until the door banged open and Bardeaux walked in.

"Mind if I join you?" she said.

Smokey got to her feet and began to growl. I felt the hairs on the back of her neck bristle. She continued growling at Bardeaux.

Bardeaux's right hand moved to her holstered gun. "What's that dog doing in here?"

"My dog," I said. "Smokey! Sit! Good girl. Now lie down and be quiet."

"She must smell my cat," said Bardeaux.

I exchanged glances with Smyrl, then Barrett. "That must be it," I said, as Bardeaux took a seat at the end of the table, as far away from Smokey as she could get.

Smyrl finished summarizing, and then questioned Clemmie about her sister. He was good at his job; and by the time he'd finished, we all knew a great deal about Emily Putnam. Emily had not returned Clemmie's phone calls, the automatic message stating that the phone's in-box was full. Smyrl spent extra time on the exact model of Emily's phone; since he believed that the phone had a GPS feature that might be useful if the phone was turned on. He thanked us for coming in, seemed truly pleased to have Clemmie and Sam Barrett involved, and said he needed technical help to set up monitoring of Emily's phone. The most important thing I learned was that Clemmie's name was not Putnam – Emily had been married once, for two months – but kept her ex-husband's name. Clemmie's last name was Olsen.

We left Smyrl and Bardeaux in the conference room. Smokey growled at Bardeaux on our way out; and I noticed Bardeaux's hand involuntarily reach for her holster. "No need for the gun," I said, "I've got her."

Bardeaux stared at Smokey, then me. It was not a friendly stare.

• • •

"That was interesting," said Sam Barrett as we loaded into my car. "Smyrl seems to be very competent. Do you have his phone number and e-mail address, Ryan? I'd like to stay in touch with him."

"I do."

"Are you willing to tell us what's bothering you?" said Sam. "Something's on your mind. What happened after we left you outside with Smokey?"

"I don't think you'd understand."

"Try me."

"Okay. My platoon sergeant was wounded Saturday morning in Afghanistan. I spent at least part of every day with him for the last nine months; and he's a friend, a great guy and superb Marine. He's at Landstuhl. He'll be flown to Dover when he's stabilized. I don't know anything more about his condition; but I need to be there when he arrives, and I need to have something he gave me – a Suunto wrist computer/watch – and it's probably with 'Bama, wherever Clemmie's sister is now. Does that make sense?"

Sam was quiet for a minute, then he spoke softly. "Perfect sense, Ryan. I don't talk about this to anyone, not even my wife, but I want to tell you why I think I can honestly claim to understand how you feel.

"I was in Company H, 2 – 5, at Hue City in February 1968. I was a twenty-three year old platoon commander. The North

Vietnamese had lied about a truce – the 'Tet Truce' and took the City. We were part of the operation to retake Hue. We crossed the Phu Cam Canal at An Cuu Bridge. We'd already had casualties from three days of fighting; and we took more from sniper fire, booby traps and counter-attacks from spider-holes – usually at night. I had four men killed and seven wounded. The last death was a Navy Corpsman attached to us. The North Vietnamese booby trapped a dead body – one of ours – and he was killed checking it out. My Company Commander was wounded later. He got a Navy Cross and a Purple Heart; and he deserved them. Of all the movies made about Vietnam, I hated FULL METAL JACKET the most. Maybe it was a good movie – I don't really know – but most of the action was supposedly set in and around Hue, and all I could think of was that Corpsman, crawling out to get blown up by a dead body.

"But seven months after Hue, as soon as I got Stateside, I found that Navy Corpsman's family – wife and two young kids – and went to talk to them. They were in a second floor apartment in Norfolk, still trying to wade through the alphabet soup of government programs devised to help with the death – Tricare, Housing, D.G.P., D.I.C. and all the rest of it. I stayed around for a week, yelling at Navy bureaucrats and helping the family get organized. My Company Commander stayed in the Corps. He made Lieutenant General. I got out and co-founded Howell & Barrett.

"I'm not saying I know how you feel. No one knows that but you. But if I can help somehow, I'd like to."

"We studied the Tet Offensive and the Battle of Hue in Basic School," I said. "I don't think anyone will be studying what we've been doing in Afghanistan years from now. Have you kept any connections with the Corps?"

"Yes."

"Could you find out about Sergeant Johnson's condition?"

"Yes."

"Would you?"

"Yes."

"Thanks for being a 'yes man' for a few minutes. Would you start finding out now?"

"Yes," said Sam, carefully retrieving his cellphone from his pocket under Smokey. "Ron," he said into the phone. "I've got a favor to ask." He proceeded to ask Ron to look into Sergeant Albert N. Johnson Jr.'s condition, at Landstuhl, and determine when he might be headed to Dover. Sam exchanged pleasantries with Ron. They seemed like they were friends.

"Who's Ron?" I asked.

"Lieutenant General Christmas," Sam said. "He was my C.O. at Hue. He's retired, but still very much connected."

"Wow," was all I could think to say.

• • •

Sam changed the subject. "Do you think Smokey was trying to tell us something about Bardeaux?"

"She sure didn't seem to like her," said Clemmie.

"She's never been bothered by cats. She ignores them." I said.

"So what could her growling mean?" said Sam.

"I think you already have an opinion," Clemmie said, "and I'd like to hear it."

"Me too," I said.

"Okay," said Sam. "It seems to me that this sweet dog here – a dog whose head is back on my lap, by the way – wouldn't growl at a human being unless she'd met her before. I think the meeting must have been unpleasant. I think it's possible that Smokey and Bardeaux met last Friday night."

"I've never trusted Bardeaux," I said.

"Run over the sequence where she arrested you again, Ryan,"

said Sam.

"As soon as I couldn't find my driver's license, she pulled her weapon."

"Did she know your driver's license was left on the Island?" asked Clemmie.

"I don't see how," said Sam. "Smyrl had the driver's license, not Bardeaux."

"I'm probably lucky she didn't shoot me," I said, "and the 'resisting arrest' charge was completely bogus. She was pissed when Smyrl took over, and really pissed when Smyrl released me. There is one thing I never told Smyrl – that I slept in the ceiling to get away from Bardeaux."

"Why didn't you tell him?" asked Sam.

"At the time I thought Bardeaux was just upset that she'd lost an arrest – one that would look good on her record. She agreed to drop the resisting arrest charge and so I said nothing."

"I'm going to text Smyrl. I'll tell him to give me a call when Bardeaux is not around." He began to fiddle with his phone, a little frustrated with his generation's glacial texting speed. When he finished, he asked me when I could take him to Chester Island.

I told him that *Larke* wasn't in the water and that she was undergoing bullet-hole repairs and was at least a day away from being ready to be dunked – and that was if I did some work today.

"Well then, let's go watch you fix bullet-holes."

"Fine by me. How about you Clemmie?"

"I'd like to see *Larke* anyway, I've already missed all my classes for the day. So yes – especially if we can get something to eat at your boat club."

• • •

An hour later, we were parked beside *Larke*, hatch of my car up, I was stirring paint; and Clemmie and Sam had admired my boat, traced the row of bullet holes with their fingers, and were following Smokey to the boat ramp, where the tide was high enough to throw a stick or two for her. I used masking tape and a small foam roller to apply the cream paint to the bootstripe that ran parallel to the waterline on *Larke's* black hull. When I was satisfied, I cleaned up and went to look for the rest of the team. They were not at the ramp, but a furry-wet black dog was lying under the awning, on the deck, just outside the back door to the West End's bar – facing the River. Smokey was ignoring a half-feral black cat that had adopted the Club. Sam and Clemmie had entered the bar in search of food.

I found them at a corner of the bar, drinking draft beer and sharing a mound of cheese fries. Pals. Sam was lacing his half of the fries with Old Bay Seasoning. Clemmie was relying on lots of salt. I was a little jealous and felt left out, and at the same time was somehow happy that they liked each other. In a sense they were enjoying each other because of me. The usual crowd was not there; it was a quiet Wednesday afternoon and on the late side for lunch.

"Mmm," said Clemmie, eating a fry. "These are good. Have one, Ryan."

"She's right," said Sam. "Best food since my surgery. That's not saying much, though. Have a beer. Let's decide what to do next. I take it we can't go to Chester Island today."

"Paint has to dry, and we need a high tide to use the boat ramp anyway. Soonest we could launch would be tomorrow at noon. Don't you need to be back in the real world by then? Both of you?"

"I'm not due back at work for a week and a half. Sue is at least as competent as I am," said Sam. "So I'm in. I need to see where all this happened. I might bring some stuff."

"Clemmie?" I said.

"It's back to class for me," she said. "One day of hooky is enough. I've got the rest of today, though. What's on the agenda for the rest of the afternoon?"

"At 3 p.m. I need to be in Chester, at The Church of Jesus Christ is Lord, teaching Nashir to read. I promised him; and I already let him down yesterday."

"Sounds good to me," said Sam. "Count me in. I'd like to meet Jameson."

"I'd like to hear the kids sing," said Clemmie.

I started whistling me and my shadow and they laughed. "I'd love the company" is all I could think of to say.

Walking to the car, Sam's cellphone rang. I noticed that it was the default, phone-company ring. There was nothing fancy about Sam. It was Smyrl calling him back; and I could hear only Sam's half of the conversation, but he was doing most of the talking.

Sam told Smyrl of our concerns about Bardeaux, mentioning Smokey's reaction to her and of my sleeping in the ceiling to avoid her. Then he said: "On those video cameras – the ones on Chester Island – can you display them differently? You can. Good. Split the shot of the murder site off from the camera watching that camera. That way if anyone fools with the main camera, we'll get a shot of them. Then tell Bardeaux about the first camera, but don't tell her about the second one. Okay? You will? Good. Thanks."

He handed his phone to me. "He wants to talk to you, Ryan."

"Smyrl."

"O'Brien. You slept in the ceiling? This ceiling here? Saturday night?"

"I did."

"To avoid Bardeaux?"

"Right."

"Why didn't you tell me?"

"I thought it didn't matter. She was dropping the resisting arrest charge. We all got sidetracked by the Inquirer article."

"Anything else you haven't told me?"

"I don't think so."

"Stay in touch." Smyrl hung up, and I gave Sam his phone back. It rang again almost immediately.

Once again, Clemmie and I were treated to Sam's half of a brief conversation. "Ron. Okay. Sunday the 30th? Right? Okay. I owe you – 'Captain'."

"You called him 'Captain'," I said.

"And he calls me 'Lieutenant'. That way, I'm always twenty-three and he's always twenty-eight. When you get to be our age, you'll understand."

"I think I already understand. What did he say about Sergeant Johnson?"

"He'll be flown to Dover on Sunday the 30th. Ten days from now."

"How is he? What are his injuries?"

"The General didn't know. Or wouldn't say. He said he'd try to find out more."

I knew what I'd be like for the next ten days; and it didn't look good for Clemmie and Ryan. I knew I'd get a little weird, be distracted and sometimes unavailable. I'd made a promise to myself about the Suunto. I was going to get it back before Sergeant Johnson landed at Dover.

Maybe Clemmie read my mind; and after a few minutes of silence, and about the time we were crossing the Commodore Barry Bridge, she said, "Let's not forget about Emily."

"It's a Deal," She Said
Chapter Twenty-Three

Twenty minutes later we were parked, in Chester, on West 2nd Street – A.K.A. PA291 and Rosa Parks Highway, almost under the Commodore Barry Bridge – in front of the Church of Jesus Christ is Lord.

"This doesn't look much like the Bryn Mawr Presbyterian Church," said Sam.

"It is modest," I said.

"Unassuming," said Clemmie.

"Unpretentious," said Sam.

"Cut it out," I said. "It sounds like you're at a wine-tasting. Wait 'til you hear the kids sing. And wait 'til you experience Reverend Jameson Jones."

"We're just kidding," said Sam. "We'll be good. We won't embarrass you."

And they did not. Clemmie spent the next hour sitting in the room that served as a chapel, listening to the kids sing. They were working on a version of Beulah Land, and they sang for Clemmie, happy to have her full attention, as she sat in a folding chair in front of them, radiant, grinning, tapping her feet. She did not try to sing. Sam spent the hour in the kitchen with Jameson; and they came out at the end of my session with Nashir in good spirits – two men from extraordinarily different places in the world, who had spent the hour examining their similarities, not their differences.

Nashir insisted on holding *Darker Than Amber* – a paperback that looked even more ragged than when I'd given it to him; and he quickly read the teaser on the back aloud to me. He knew that the Wounded Spook was a fishing lure; and he acted out some of the action – the casting of a lure, a car rocketing off, McGee diving into the water. My concentration was not perfect – I kept thinking about Sergeant Johnson – but it did not matter. Nashir had obviously been studying the book – probably to the exclusion of other homework – and he was obviously learning to read. He turned to the First Chapter.

WE WERE ABOUT to give up and call it a night
when somebody dropped the girl off the bridge.

Wow! Nashir read that first sentence, the grabber that MacDonald often used to cause fans in 1966 to march to the bookstore counter with their dollar-fifty. Then Nashir stood up and read the next five pages to me, acting out the part of Travis McGee. That's right, an eleven year-old kid from South Sudan imagining himself diving into midnight waters under a bridge in Florida and tearing the pads of his thumb and fingers unwinding the wire that tied cement blocks to the ankles of a beautiful woman. Reading. Nashir did a great job on everything relating to plot, a mediocre job on backstory and a terrible job pronouncing lots of words. But he was reading. Jameson gave me a thumbs-up from the doorway.

"I don't know exactly when I can come back," I said to

Jameson. "I've got something to settle first. Anyway, Nashir's doing great. I don't need to be here every day."

"But you will be back, right?"

"I'll come when I can. I promise." The second one I'd made today.

• • •

We were back in my car, threading our way through the tired City of Chester and looking for access to The Blue Route, also known as I-476, and sometimes called the Mid-County Expressway. We'd head north and drop Sam off at his house in Bryn Mawr. His wife had already called him and informed him he was overdue.

"Well, this has been a fun day," said Sam.

"No it hasn't," I said. "It's been a shitty day."

"Sorry, Ryan, you're right. I was too busy thinking about a murder on Chester Island, appreciating Smyrl, enjoying cheese-fries with Clemmie, and being entertained by Jameson. I forgot about Sergeant Johnson. It won't happen again. Let's do what Clemmie suggested and not forget about Emily. In fact, let's talk about her for awhile. Tell us about her, Clemmie. Tell us things you didn't tell to Smyrl. What's she look like?"

Clemmie half turned towards the back seat, so Sam could hear her better. "I told you we were twins – fraternal twins – but we look nothing alike. Emily's petite, she's got straight black hair, a heart-shaped face and delicate features. Her eyes are a very pale blue. Perfect teeth, of course. She's a knockout. All of my boyfriends end up with a crush on her."

"Not me," I thought. "Never." Then I considered the "all my boyfriends" and wondered if I'd make the list. Shit. There was a list.

"Okay," said Sam. "We know what she looks like. What's she

like?"

"She's very bright – close to perfect board scores. She was a gymnast when she was little. She's an exhibitionist. She needs excitement. Sometimes I can't believe we're related. She's very unconcerned about money – she's extravagant and reckless with it. Generous too, I suppose. Here's one quick story that might explain her. She got two-hundred thousand dollars in a settlement from her ex-husband – poor, love-struck Timmy Putnam – and she gave fifty of it to Gram and Gramps – paid off their mortgage – twenty-thousand to me to pay off student loans, and then tried to spend the rest on a motorcycle."

"A hundred and thirty-thousand on a motorcycle?" asked Sam. "Jeezus."

"She wanted a 1952 Vincent Black Lightning. She first heard of one in a song by Richard Thompson, and was obsessed with the idea; but she couldn't find one at that price. So she settled for a rebuilt World War II Royal Enfield. I admit it is very cool – it's olive green and has metal courier boxes mounted over the back wheel. She only paid seventy-thousand for that, so she paid my rent and her rent a year in advance, gave a big party and banked what little was left.

Just then we looked down on the Blue Route, from an elevated spot near the I-95 junction and access. Traffic was crawling. "Take PA320 North," said Sam. I did.

"What else?" asked Sam.

"Isn't that enough?" I thought. "What a flake."

"Well, she's named for Emily Bronte and Emily Dickinson. I'd say she's absolutely nothing like either of them – an introverted poet and a sickly novelist who died when she was thirty."

I couldn't help myself. "Are you named for anyone?"

Clemmie laughed. "Yes I am – and my name really is Clemmie. It's not short for Clementine. And I am nothing at all like the only Clemmie I've found in literature. My grandfather named both of us – me after a book he liked a lot. Actually, Emily's more like the 'Clemmie' character. I hated the book and didn't finish it."

"Why did your grandfather get to name you?" asked Sam. "I never got a vote with my grandchildren."

We were now crawling along through Swarthmore, a pretty, green college town. I stopped to let an older man pull out of his driveway; and he honked thanks and reached out of his window and gave me a thumbs-up. I noticed a small USMC sticker on his bumper. "I probably know him," said Sam. Then he said: "turn right here. This is enough of this traffic. Let's go on Baltimore Pike for awhile. We'll be heading in the opposite direction of traffic. Back to your grandfather, Clemmie."

"My grandfather and grandmother raised us. I don't know my dad, my mother died when Emily and I were three. When we were born, my mom was already living with Gramps and Gram. She let Gramps name us."

"Are your grandparents living?" I asked.

"Yep. Going strong. Eighty-four and eighty-two. I get myself home at least once a month. They live upstate – a four hour drive."

"What do you drive?" I asked. "What kind of car?"

"No car, Ryan. I take a bus. Two buses, actually. I transfer in Allentown."

Clemmie talked more about her life until I realized that we were almost to "Walt's"; and I suggested that we stop and pick up cheesesteaks for the road. I thought Sam would enjoy the menu from the 50's. As I turned into the small parking lot next to the shop, my phone started blaring and I answered it.

"This is Uncle Ryan – again," he said. "Can you talk for five minutes?"

"Sure – just a minute."

I whispered: "Clemmie – please get me a large cheesesteak – raw onions, provolone cheese and hot peppers. And a vanilla milkshake. Get yourself whatever you want. Sam – you'll love this place. It's even older than you are."

Sam removed Smokey's head from his lap and climbed out of the back, while Clemmie accepted the twenty-dollar bill I handed her. They went into "Walt's".

"I'm back Uncle Ryan. What's up?"

"Well, I want to know what's going on with you. Smyrl, Bardeaux, the murder, Smokey, Clemmie, Sam Barrett – the whole deal."

"Sure. But this should probably wait 'til tonight. I've got Sam, Clemmie and Smokey in the car. We're stopped outside of "Walt's" and they're inside getting cheesesteaks for the road."

"Okay. Tonight for sure. I need a full report. A half-hour type of report. And I might put you on the speaker. I've got someone who wants to listen to you."

"Sissie?"

"No – a guy. And older guy who's had a lot of background in stuff like you're experiencing. He's interested. He might have some ideas."

"Whatever you say. How about eight o'clock?"

"Sounds good."

"Later."

"Verily."

• • •

Alone for the first time that day, I reached into the back seat, patted Smokey and thought about Johnson. I felt myself slipping into a gloomy obsessive state that would require me to do something physical, soon, and to stop thinking about doing something. Once when I was in high school, my Pops told me I was certainly no Lord Byron and that I likely suffered from the opposite of Weltschmerz; and that instead of recognizing that physical reality would never satisfy the demands of the mind, my mind never bothered concerning itself with the pure joy of physical action. I still don't know what he meant, but understood that if I couldn't meet Johnson's flight – with his Suunto in hand I'd not forgive myself. It was also likely that I'd screw up any chance of a relationship with Clemmie, cause Sam to reconsider efforts to employ me, and encourage myself to do something violent. With these thoughts in mind, I decided to fake it for the next hour, to be cheerful, and to drop Sam and then Clemmie off as soon as possible. Then I'd go look at videos of Chester Island, mope, talk to Uncle Ryan and try to get some sleep.

The ride to Sam's should have been at least pleasant, but I failed at Cheery – 101 and even a "Walt's" milkshake annoyed me somehow, as I was unable to get at the ice cream at the bottom of the container and drive at the same time. I refrained from swearing out loud.

"Want me to drive for awhile?" said Clemmie.

"Please," I said. I pulled over into a K-Mart parking lot. We did a rotation: Clemmie drove, Sam moved to the passenger seat to navigate and I moved in next to Smokey in the back seat, where I managed the last of my milkshake and started on my cheesesteak. Clemmie adjusted the rear view mirror and started to drive. She seemed competent. Sam seemed tired. I fed bits of my cheesesteak to Smokey.

At Sam's house in Bryn Mawr – let me be honest, it was an estate, replete with beautiful grounds, six or seven chimneys and a circular drive – his lovely wife, Ellie, met our car, helped Sam out and offered us a pro-forma invitation to come in. Clemmie answered for both of us, thanking Ellie for the invitation, but saying she had to get some studying done and needed to leave. I managed to thank Sam for his help. Sam reminded me of our noon trip to Chester Island next day, while Ellie frowned at him as if to say: we'll see about that.

"Are you going to move to the front seat," said Clemmie, "or am I your chauffeur?"

"Sorry," I said, disengaging myself from Smokey. "Need directions?"

"Nope." Clemmie drove right down Lancaster Pike – Route 30 – towards the City. "Talk to me. Tell me stuff. What's going on in there?" She tapped my head with a finger.

• • •

Uh oh. Trouble ahead. My head was, of course, full of random thoughts that, set free, would likely flutter into the air and then, like carpenter bees on steroids, drill holes in the barnacled, oaken hull of the Good Ship Ryan O'Brien, at least in any clear-eyed assessment by the beautiful, wise and manifestly sane Clemmie. I could admit that it was very likely that I would fall in love with her, and soon, and that I was truly different than most guys I knew in that regard – most guys needing apparently to be loved first; or I could go on about Sam giving me hope regarding my job, and that he offered me new thoughts about getting older that were good ones, and that I'd be required to spend significant time, energy and effort being worthy of his friendship – if friendship could possibly go with work (and I thought maybe in this case it could); or I could mention Nashir's channeling Travis McGee, and explaining just why I found that to be wonderful – requiring a monologue that would, in itself, use up the rest of the trip to Clemmie's apartment; or I could tell her a story or two, or three about Smokey, stories that would provide her with insight into just how important the wondrous creature napping in the back seat was to me and how we owned each other; or I could avoid answering by asking Clemmie questions about her courses, her major, her hopes and dreams – but that would be somehow cunning, and inappropriate given that I was projecting love in the near future; or I could attempt to explain, at length, the relationship guys –

Marines, for sure – have with other guys when they've been at war together and seeing each other scared witless but not showing it – but that would be beyond my limited verbal skills and take weeks anyway, and lead to a possible weepy-eyed discussion of Sergeant Johnson, and the significance of his giving me his Suunto 10X Wrist Top Computer and how urgent it was for me to have it with me when I met his flight at Dover on the 30th – and how I'd likely be distracted and bad company until I did; and by the time I'd run through and rejected each and every one of these terrible ideas, my mind became a just-erased blackboard, and so I opened my mouth and wrote this on it:

"The next time you visit your grandparents, I'd like to drive you."

Clemmie looked over at me. "I wasn't expecting that."

"Well, I'm full of surprises."

"It's a deal," she said.

Devlin Meyer – Salvage Consultant
Chapter Twenty-Four

Dropping Clemmie off at her apartment could have included an awkward dance – a two-step involving a provisional "do you want to come in" from Clemmie, hinting at some indefinite period of probationary behavior ahead for me; thus requiring a response from me that was sure to be deficient – "sure, I'd like to, but I really have stuff I need to do, so I'll take a rain check". But Clemmie preempted all that by hopping out of the car and telling me to stay double-parked for a minute – that she had something she wanted to get from her apartment for Smokey. So I stayed put while she ran inside and came out with a stick – a well-chewed piece of driftwood.

"This is the stick Smokey retrieved, even after she'd been shot. She should have it."

I did the only thing I could think of: I got out of the car, accepted the stick and hugged Clemmie. I hoped a heartfelt hug would serve better than a bunch of imperfect words.

After Clemmie disentangled herself from my embrace, we agreed to talk later that night. We also agreed that any news about Emily would be shared immediately. Just before I pulled away, she reached in the car window and knocked lightly on the top of my head.

"Be careful," she said, "I'm counting on that ride to go see my grandparents."

"Me too."

Smokey got busy with her stick.

• • •

By the time I'd parked the car, walked and fed Smokey, checked e-mails, showered and changed clothes, eaten something, and trashed junk mail, it was nearly time for me to call Uncle Ryan. I sat down and pulled up the videos of Chester Island, Floodgate Road and the power line; and I noted that, as usual, nothing at all was happening. It seemed to me that nowhere on Earth was so much nothing occurring as at the remote boondocks New Jersey riverfront locations where we'd expended thought and energy placing expensive, high-tech cameras. I did notice that Smyrl had changed the view of the two Chester Island cameras; and I assumed he'd also informed Bardeaux as Sam had requested. I supposed that Sam had some clever idea about Bardeaux, the cameras and proving something that was too nuanced for Ryan-man-of-action to comprehend.

I made notes in preparation for talking to Uncle Ryan, to be able to give him a quick summary, a chronology, of events. I wondered who the older guy was that he wanted to sit in on my debriefing. Uncle Ryan usually made up his own mind about things without a lot of outside input. My Pops said that seemed to be true of pretty much everyone he knew named Ryan.

At exactly 8 p.m., I called Uncle Ryan. He answered

immediately. "I'm putting you on the speaker, Ryan. I have someone here who has a lifetime of experience in just the sort of confusion you're involved in. He's a mostly-retired salvage consultant. His name is Devlin Meyer."

"Hello Devlin," I said.

"Hello Ryan," croaked the broken voice of an old man. "Please speak clearly, I'm hard of hearing. I hope I can help."

"Thanks," I said; and I proceeded to give my best twenty minute summary of everything that had happened. Uncle Ryan deferred to Devlin, who asked a few good questions.

"I don't know if this will be helpful," Devlin said, "but here's what I'm thinking. One – there was nothing involving terrorists or terrorism as we think of it happening on Chester Island that night – otherwise you'd be dead. Two – it's about money, since it's always about money. Three – the girl, Emily, is the likely key to this; find her, find 'Bama, solve mystery. Four – I gather you have a personal interest in this that you have not told me about. Am I correct?"

"I didn't tell you about a computer wristwatch that I lost on the Island, and the man who gave it to me, Sergeant Johnson." I explained he'd been wounded and that in just under ten days he'd be flown to Dover and that I needed to have the wristwatch with me then.

"So that's your personal interest in this, right?" said Devlin.

"That and the fact that I will be falling in love with Emily's sister sometime soon."

Devlin and Uncle Ryan laughed at that. "Okay," said Devlin, "five – you're on the clock with respect to the watch. That's going to make everything harder. Do you have your boat in the water? Can you get to the Island in a hurry if you need to?"

"*Larke* will be in the water at high tide tomorrow – around noon. She doesn't get anywhere fast, though. She's a sailboat. Plus, the other side knows she's mine, and would recognize her."

"You need a runabout, something like my little *Munequita*."

"Or better yet, something like my *Sissie*," said Uncle Ryan.

"One more observation," said Devlin. "You're itching, just itching to do something – anything. You're thinking that anything's better than sitting around worrying. You need some physical action. Right?"

"Very much right," I said. "How do you know that?"

"You remind me of myself, before I got to old to do much of anything. That's what I'd want to do – something action-action. Tell you what Ryan – let your Uncle Ryan and me talk about this for a day or so, while you don't do anything too stupid. Let us know if anyone hears from Emily, if the security cameras pick up anything interesting, or if Detective Smyrl has any ideas. Okay?"

"Okay," I said. "Thanks for your time. I hope to hear from you soon."

We terminated the call, and I lay down on the couch to think about things. Devlin was a "semi-retired" salvage consultant, too old to do physical salvage work – whatever that was – but still able to think clearly about my predicament. Uncle Ryan seemed to respect his opinion; and he'd certainly been a fast study. I hoped to meet him someday. In the meantime, there wasn't much for me to do except scroll through the security cameras' logs, get a good night's sleep and get *Larke* into the water in the morning. I sat at the computer that was dedicated to the cameras and began to fiddle. I suppose I was willing something to happen in front of one of them – and sure enough – shazam! It did.

The cameras on the Island were staring at the usual grass and trees, and the Floodgate Road cameras showed nothing but empty dirt and gravel road and a glimpse of a rising tide. But the camera that I'd wired to the power line tower showed a truck, trailer and small boat backing towards the Old Canal. The driver was alone, and stopped short of the muddy embankment. I knew he'd have to wait for a higher tide to launch the boat; and I figured that would be about 11 p.m. I also realized that he'd have to be back to the launch site by about 1 a.m. in order to retrieve the boat – before a lowering tide made it impossible. I decided to pay him a visit.

"You're sitting this one out," I said to Smokey as I threw together a small backpack full of stuff that might be useful. I did not include my only pistol – a Sig Sauer .40. I did not have a carry permit for it, and didn't think I'd need it anyway. I wasn't exactly sure what I was going to do, but believed that I'd figure it out during the drive to the site. At least I'd be doing something.

• • •

Forty-five minutes later, after driving a little too fast south on I-95, over the Commodore Barry Bridge, and east on US 322, I followed the GPS app on my phone east on NJ 44 and, finally, left on Stump Road. My car wouldn't permit me to turn off its headlights in the dark, so I backed it into a canopy of trees about four-hundred yards from the launch site, and decided to walk carefully to the Canal. After putting on a dark jacket, I headed in that direction.

The boat had been launched, and the truck and trailer left near the water, ready to retrieve the boat. I considered disabling the truck – a slashed tire or two or a battery cable disconnect were within my skill set – but I wasn't at all sure that the boater was not an innocent fisherman, crabber or trapper. I did pull off a wire to the trailer's right rear light – under the assumption that it might make it easier for me to follow. I wrote down the truck's license plate and the trailer's registration number. Realizing that what I was doing was being captured by the camera I'd wired to the nearby power line tower, I waved in that direction and pantomimed my next action: to follow the truck and trailer. I doubted that anyone would be watching the cameras – live – but hoped to at least see myself on screen later. If something happened to me, maybe Smyrl would have a useful clue about it.

I returned to the edge of the tree line, where I could see the launch site and still get to my car in time to follow the truck. I doused myself with insect repellent against the mosquitoes and prepared to wait quietly. Just then my cellphone blared out its urgent Sousa ring.

"Ryan," said Clemmie, "I thought you were going to call me."

"Sorry," I said, "I got involved with something on the security cameras and forgot. What's up? Have you heard from Emily?"

"Why are you whispering?"

"Was I whispering?"

"Yes."

"How's this?" I talked a little louder.

"Ryan. Where are you right now?"

"What do you mean?"

"I mean – where are you?"

"I'm in New Jersey, in the boondocks. I'm going to follow a truck that might have something to do with Emily."

"Are you alone?'

"Of course. And I shouldn't be talking on the phone. I'm going to turn off the ring for now. I'll call you later, as soon as I can. Okay?"

"Okay. Later."

I disabled Semper Fidelis and sat on a tree stump. I vowed never, ever to be anything less than honest with Clemmie. She'd picked up on my whispering and realized that I wasn't at home. Her powers of observation and deduction were obviously greater than my powers of dissembling. I texted a message: "In case I am delayed – could you walk Smokey early a.m.?"

She answered almost immediately. Apparently being three years younger than I made her three times as fast texting: "Yes. Key?"

"On lintel over door."

"What's a 'lintel'?"

"The door frame – top."

"Why not say 'door frame'?"

"Two words – 'lintel' one."

"Oh. Goodnight, Ryan."

"Goodnight, Clemmie."

"Goodnight John Boy."

"Ha. Goodnight Mary Ellen."

• • •

I sat there in the damp New Jersey boondocks night, waving off the few mosquitoes that were hungry enough to ignore my repellent and thought good thoughts about Clemmie. I hoped she was thinking good things about me. I wished Uncle Ryan was with me. For one thing, he'd know how to disable my car's headlights, so I could follow the truck more closely.

I waited. It was a wait much like those I'd experienced in Afghanistan. The biggest difference was that in Afghanistan, we'd watched and waited through the nights, usually hoping that nothing eventful happened; and there were lots of us – sneezing, coughing, farting and whispering through endless nights, all of us happy to see another dusty, red sunrise. I didn't miss anything about Afghanistan or Iraq. I did not want to go back to either hellhole. I did not want to be a platoon commander again. I did not want to wear a uniform again. But I did want to hand Sergeant Johnson his Suunto; and I wanted it badly enough to risk a few things to do it.

My thoughts wandered around, waiting for the boat to return to the truck and trailer; and I considered Devlin Meyer. Something about him seemed familiar, but I couldn't come up with what it was that was tickling my memory. I shelved all random thoughts when I heard the hum of an electric boat motor. I stood and watched the operator of the boat gently guide the boat onto the trailer, reach over the bow and hook the trailer winch cable to the D-ring, step onto the trailer tongue and crank the winch handle. After he'd secured the boat, he hopped in the truck and drove it twenty feet or so, moving the trailer and boat up out of the water. Then he retrieved something from the boat and put it in the back of his truck, checked his trailer tie-downs, started up the truck and headed in my direction.

I moved through the trees to my car, waited until the truck was a hundred yards past me, jumped in the car, and quickly shut the door to dim the dome light. Ryan-the-dopey-technophobe could have disabled that by simply throwing a switch on the light, but hadn't. The headlamps were another matter; and I knew that as soon as I hit the ignition some magic photoelectric sensor, probably embedded in the instrument panel, would activate them automatically.

The next time Uncle Ryan was in the vicinity of my car, I'd have him show me how to disable the lights – but of course I'd probably never need to know how to accomplish that once I began my distinguished career as a highly-paid investment banker at Howell & Barrett, and was husband of Clemmie and father of two or three perfect children (one of them named Ryan – after Uncle Ryan, of course): and living in a quiet, safe community in the suburbs, coaching Little League baseball (and/or softball), mentoring children from the Church of Jesus Christ is Lord, staying in touch with Nashir in his dorm at Harvard (shit no – make that Penn – there was no sense in ruining the lad), working out and staying healthy and in good shape, vacationing once a year at Uncle Ryan's (who was happily married to Sissie by then), and staying in touch with Sergeant Johnson (who had had a full recovery). Shit. Stop it Ryan. Focus. You just imagined your obituary.

I waited until the truck and its taillights disappeared over a small rise on Stump Road, then hit the ignition and began to follow. My GPS told me there was nowhere for the truck to go until after it had gone under highway US 130 and reached Main Street in the small river town of Bridgeport. As long as I was close enough to see which way the truck turned on Main Street, I'd be good. West. In keeping with both my own personal Manifest Destiny, and Horace Greeley's suggestion, I also turned west.

VROOOM – WAAANNNGGG – GONE
Chapter Twenty-Five

There were undoubtedly protocols for following another car – or in this case: car, trailer and boat. In fact, there were probably whole chapters in the alphabet soup of agencies' – F.B.I., D.E.A., C.I.A., D.H.S., and N.S.A. – regulations that would have been useful to have read, committed to memory and used. But since I knew nothing about tailing, I used what common sense I could muster and followed the one-eyed trailer – not too closely, not too far. I assumed that Travis McGee had done this hundreds of times in his career, and would have acted as my consultant, were there money in it for him: "Back off a little, Ryan. That's it. Now pass him – tail from in front for awhile. Okay, now pull in to that gas station and let him pass you again. That's it."

I wondered what there would be in this for a salvage consultant such as Travis. I was only looking for a wrist computer and Clemmie's crazy sister, Emily. And to be honest, I didn't really care about Emily, but Clemmie did; and I wanted to make her happy with me. In other words, I was acting selfishly – as some philosophers believed all humans do at all times. I didn't see how there was money involved in anything that had happened to me since Friday night. But Devlin had said ". . . it's always about money." Maybe I was missing something.

The one-red-eyed trailer was an easy tail. The driver was choosing back roads and heading mostly west and south. South Jersey topography is flat, so I could see the taillight from a quarter of a mile away; and I decided to maintain that distance. I realized that I'd promised to call Uncle Ryan and Devlin if the security cameras showed anything interesting, or if I decided to do anything "too stupid." But New Jersey is adamant about not using cellphones while driving; and although there were no cops in sight – in fact there was nobody at all in sight – I decided to save the call until I stopped. I didn't think I was doing anything stupid anyway; and if I decided to call anyone, I should probably call Smyrl first. I was in New Jersey.

After twenty minutes, the truck pulled into a small gas station, at a crossroads in a little town called Woodstown. I drove on past, pulled over a half mile down the road into the driveway of a closed-up farmers' market, doused the lights, waited a minute and dialed up Smyrl. He didn't pick up, and I left a voicemail asking him to call me, and giving him the truck and trailer license numbers. Then I tried Uncle Ryan and left him a similar voicemail when he didn't pick up either. I sat there in the dark, considering if I was a tailor or a tailee, and hoping the truck, boat and trailer would soon zip past me.

Then: VROOOM – WAAANNNGGG – GONE, a motorcycle passed me, headed back in the direction I'd come; and then BRAAAAAP – BRAAAAAP, it downshifted. I sat, dumfounded, rejecting every adjective for speed I could think of as inadequate: like a bat out of hell, like blue blazes and like greased lightning – none of them made the cut. And the thunderous noise of whatever one-eyed monster I'd thought I'd seen was earsplitting. For a moment, I thought I'd imagined the cycle. Half out of curiosity and half out of disbelief, I decided to follow it, at least back as far as the gas station.

When I got back to the station, I pulled next to the gas pump farthest from the truck, boat and trailer. The motorcycle was at the gas pump next to the truck; and the motorcycle operator was off the bike, talking to the station attendant. She – that's right, the crazy, pedal-to-the-metal motorcyclist was a woman – removed her helmet, shook out short, dark hair and was forcefully telling the attendant not to fill her tank. The State of New Jersey insists on pumping your gas for you – an anachronism legislated under the theory of maintaining working class jobs; and as the attendant headed my way, I saw the motorcyclist and truck driver exchange fist bumps. Then she opened up one of the two courier boxes mounted over the motorcycle's back wheel; and he handed her something from the truck bed.

"Quite a bike," I said to the gas station attendant.

"Yeah. She didn't want any gas, though."

"Well, I don't need much either. Top me off with premium."

"Right."

I watched the truck, boat and trailer pull out of the station, headed back the way we'd come; and I watched the motorcycle mama put on her helmet and BRAAAAAP – BRAAAAAP, VROOOM – WAAANNNGGG – GONE, back into the New Jersey night the way she'd come. I'd never catch her.

"She's something," I said. "Know her?"

"Never seen her before."

"How about the cycle? Seen one of them before?"

"Nope. You didn't need much gas. Six bucks."

I paid the attendant in cash, got in my car and headed off after the motorcycle.

• • •

I figured that there was no need to drive over the 50MPH speed limit. The motorcycle was miles away by now; and I'd only manage to find it by luck. But the County Road I was on was taking me through farm country, mostly empty. I thought that might help. My phone serenaded me with Semper Fidelis.

"Ryan!"

"Uncle Ryan."

"What's up?"

"I was tailing someone, but I lost them – at least for now."

"How about some background."

I told Uncle Ryan what I'd been doing and why. I asked him for his thoughts. I told him to ask Devlin to give his opinion.

"So right now you're driving down country roads in South Jersey, looking for a motorcycle?"

"Technically, yes."

"You mean verily?"

"I suppose. Verily."

"My first thought is that you should get in touch with Smyrl. That's also my second thought and my third thought."

"I have a call in to him. He hasn't returned it yet. Meantime, I need to be doing something; and it seems to me that this might be a long shot – but it's better than doing nothing."

"Okay. I understand. Then here's my last thought: look for the motorcycle in an organized way. Don't just guess where it went, but follow some orderly process of elimination. I'll talk to Devlin."

"Thanks Uncle Ryan. I'll call you if anything happens."

"Call me before midnight, even if nothing happens."

"Okay."

• • •

By the time we'd finished talking, I found myself in a small town named Alloway. I drove around the streets of the small town, looking for a parked motorcycle. No luck. I consulted the map app in my phone; and given the direction we'd come from, it seemed to me there were only two logical roads that the motorcycle could have taken. I took the right hand option, Quinton-Alloway Road, which led to the even smaller town of Quinton and two more possible routes for the motorcycle. The right hand option was County Highway 650, a.k.a. Quinton-Hancocks Bridge Road, which led me to another two-road option. Options seemed to be multiplying much too fast for me to deal with in one night. I pulled over to the shoulder of the road, played with the map app – scrolling around – and I pondered.

Assuming that the motorcyclist was taking a direct route eliminated lots of options that would have taken me north – likewise east. All the south and west options led eventually to water, either the Delaware River, the Cohansey River or any number of small creeks. There were six possible terminations; and I decided to abandon the every-option plan and simply drive to each terminus in a north-south order. Just then Smyrl called; and I filled him in on what I'd been doing.

"What are you going to do if you are lucky enough to find the motorcycle?"

"That depends."

"On what?"

"On whether the motorcyclist is by herself or with someone."

"Herself?"

"Yes. Herself."

Smyrl informed me that he was in Trenton, at a mandatory powwow involving the latest political reorganization of the New Jersey State Police command structure, requiring general ass-kissing, random begging for more resources and useless chatting up of superiors. He explained that he was terrible at this part of his job and could not wait – absolutely could not wait – to get back in the field where he belonged, which would be in two days. In the meantime, I was to try hard to not do anything "too stupid."

"Everyone seems to be giving me the exact same advice."

"Well, you're the one who slept in the conference room ceiling. Anyway, it's good general advice. Tell you what – I'll try to follow the very same advice here in Trenton. I'll try hard not to do or say anything too stupid either. Okay?"

"Okay." We did not talk about the security cameras, Bardeaux, Chester Island, or Clemmie's sister; and I headed off down a country road for the first of six possible places that might unveil a souped-up, olive-green World War II Royal Enfield motorcycle and Emily Putnam.

The roads I drove were empty; and I wondered – did people live in this place? The very dark enabled a sky festooned with brilliance, and not of the razor sliver of a moon, but with that of stars wheeling slowly. I turned off the radio and opened the car's moonroof; and promised myself, again, to learn the names of at least a few constellations, to teach to children someday. As I drove, west, then south, then west again, I felt that the earth was not round, but flat only, enabling all roads, creeks and streams to writhe about in mortal fear of Death at the hands of the immense, tidal, muddy Delaware River – a River that became a Bay and then an Ocean. The reluctant Cohansey hid in its own serpentine coils before surrendering eventually to an estuary, and a Cove so named.

Between me and the Delaware, there were trees like white cedar and stunted pin oaks, and then endless meadows of grass: smooth cordgrass, soft rush, water willow, cattails and the sedges – all grass that billowed in a wind, looking like a flooded prairie, but home not to buffalo and antelope, but muskrats, otters, mink and beaver. An infinite number of insects lived out there too: mosquitoes, ticks, chiggers and the greenhead fly. Uncle Ryan called the greenhead the Jersey State Bird. And Emily was out there somewhere, conspicuous in her noise and speed, on a mechanical horse fabricated for war over seventy years ago.

• • •

I drove every likely road between Alloway Creek on the north and the Cohansey River on the south; traveling on roads named Frog Ocean, Hells-Neck, Jerico, Gum Tree, Back-Neck, Bacon's-Neck and Telegraph; to towns called Stow Creek, Shiloh, Peck's Corner and Greenwich. Greenwich was the last town I planned to visit before I gave up my needle-in-a-haystack operation. I drove slowly down Greenwich's Ye Greate Street; and thought I'd like to come back sometime, in daylight, maybe with Clemmie, and take a careful look at the colonial homes and churches there. After Ye Greate Street dead-ended into a farm overlooking the Cohansey River, I decided to take a look at the docks and marinas, a half-mile west on Market Lane. There was a nice boat ramp there, boat slips for about fifty boats, a travel lift and parking for seventy or eighty additional boats. The operation looked to me to be thriving; but since it was nearly midnight, everything was closed. I parked and walked out on one of the docks; and from its end, off to my right and down the Cohansey, I could see the lights of another marina. I looked at my map app and saw that it was Hancock Harbor and that it was about a half mile away as the crow flies, it was three miles away as Ryan drives. I decided to make it my last stop – then I'd call Uncle Ryan, drive home and go to bed.

Standing on that dock, looking west, I saw a blue, brazen lightning flash far out over the Delaware – as if from some demon realm. I counted quickly, waiting to hear the thunder, but never did. Instead, a wet wind forced me back into my car; and I closed the moonroof and drove off, car rocking from that wind, now a dervish. Next came rain – pitter-patter at first, then huge drops pelting the car and far outranking my windshield wipers. I felt like a blind Argonaut, feeling the tiller of my steering wheel rather than seeing the road. At a walking pace, something loomed. It was a long-abandoned gas station with one slant-roof bay standing; and as the plague of nickel-sized hail struck, I took shelter there. I locked my doors against the night.

Soon the hail covered the ground, undersized lucent eggs, spawned in Heaven. The slant-metal roof of the garage beat a rat-a-tat. I knew that such a storm couldn't last, since the Earth wouldn't long abide such a pummeling from whatever directed the assault. I thought then of the war I'd left and then of War itself and how unceremonic it had become – no bright banners or warriors dancing, but only an impersonal letting of blood by mostly invisible hands. In two brief days in Basic School, we'd been introduced to the concepts of Absolute War, the Just War Theory, Deterrence Theory and been introduced to Peace and Conflict Studies by a guest lecturer – an Episcopal priest. Of course there was no time for such considerations in any of the endless days we'd spent in Iraq or Afghanistan; and I doubted that any Legionnaire crossing any Rubicon ever wondered much about such matters, as he would have been too busy thinking about blisters on his feet. Something in me, however, objected to the drones we were utilizing so effectively – an objection based upon nothing, I supposed, other than the sheer impersonality of the technology; with Sergeant Johnson taking the pro-drone position ("whatever it takes") and Lieutenant O'Brien the anti-drone stance ("Jeezus – Johnson – that UAV is being controlled by a geek in Arizona!").

Damn. I'd done it again. I'd thought of Sergeant Johnson; and as if the thought itself conjured up the apparition, a face appeared at my passenger-side window and with the slap of a hand on the pane, a woman said: "Hey! Open up. Let me in!"

YIN-YANG
CHAPTER TWENTY-SIX

She tried to open the door while I tried to unlock it; and we stymied each other two or three times before she got the door open. I looked for straight black hair – check; a heart-shaped face – check; and pale blue eyes – too dark to tell. She leaned in, looked at me – wet – looked at the clutter in the back of the car and in an unexpected, deep, slow voice, said, "unusual weather we're havin' – ain't it." Then I got it: she was imitating, perfectly, the Cowardly Lion in the poppy field in the Wizard of Oz, when it was snowing.

"Toto, I've got a feeling we're not in Kansas anymore," I said.

"Here's looking at you, kid." Humphrey Bogart. She got in the car. "You don't look like a mass murderer."

"Neither do you."

"Got any towels back there?" she said, flicking on the dome light and glancing my way. Pale blue eyes – check.

"Sure," I said. "Here." I handed her a clean boat towel.

She took the towel and dried her hair, then ran her fingers through it. Then she reached her right hand to me – to shake. "Emily," she said.

"Ryan," I said, smiling at the calloused, firm handshake. "What've you been doing – lumberjacking?"

"Nope. What are you doing here, Ryan?"

"Waiting out the blow. You?"

"Same deal. But what's got you here at this godforsaken spot anyway?"

"I've got a small sailboat. I'm looking for places to trailer her."

"Her?"

"Of course. How'd you get here?"

"Motorcycle."

"Where is it?"

"Over there," she said, pointing ahead and off to the right.

The hail had stopped its awful pinging off the metal roof. The rain was steady, and the lightning had passed over us and was now lighting up the sky far to our east. I flicked on the headlights, started the car and edged it around until the high beams lit up the motorcycle.

"Nice bike."

"He's more than that."

"He?"

"Sure. He."

The way she spoke to me – as if I new nothing of motorcycles – made me respond: "it's a Royal Enfield – a World War II model. Right?"

"Right. Not many sailboaters would know that," she said. "I figure they're just about as opposite as can be – sailboats and motorcycles. Your boat's all quiet and slow. My bike's all noise and speed."

I thought to get clever, flirty, all double entendre and ask her if she only liked fast and noisy – but I thought of Clemmie and didn't. "Yep. They'd be an odd couple for sure. Are you going to get back up on that bike after it stops raining, or can I drive you somewhere?"

"I hate to leave the bike here, but I need to get going. Maybe I'll take you up on that ride. Let's push the bike behind the station."

She got out of the car; and I did the same. We walked towards the cycle together. She slipped and fell to one knee; and she grabbed my arm, up high around a bicep and pulled herself up, leaning against me. "I'm beat," she said. "Push the bike over there for me." She pointed. "I'll wait in the car."

By the time I'd reached the Enfield, Emily'd started my car, locked the doors and was driving away. She beeped twice – quiet little honks. Like she wasn't stealing my car – the car with my wallet and cellphone in it.

I stood there and watched the tail lights disappear down the road. Fuck. Fuck. Fucked. It was two and a half miles arrow straight to the Cohansey River. I turned to the motorcycle – the useless Royal Enfield; and I decided to hide it. I wheeled it into bushes on the far side of the road and tipped it over – a $70,000 sacrilege lying in the mud. Then I started running.

• • •

I was lucky, blessed that the Cohansey River was over two miles away, for the rage that aimed me at Emily for the first mile – a dark red, tunnel-vision inducing miasma – would have ended in disorganized violence. In the recent words of both Smyrl and Uncle Ryan, I would have managed something "too stupid" to undo. What I needed was organized violence.

The very rhythm of the running, in a drizzle that was in the process of becoming a mist, induced a capitulation of that fury: to anger, then a useful resentment that permitted thinking in addition to acting. So I ran and I indulged in big-picture, irrelevant thoughts. I wondered if everything I had done, was doing and would do was somehow preordained – not in a religious sense, since the vagaries of Shia and Sunni Islam had blown the cover off religion for me, first in Iraq, then in Afghanistan; as Muslims murdered each other over who was the rightful successor to the Prophet over a millennium ago – but in some non-random, knowable thermodynamic process, starting with a great big bang, including the formation of the Earth, the comings and goings of Ice Ages, comets, continents and humans.

What nonsense! Of course there was nothing predetermined about anything I ever did, was doing or would do. Free will forever! I just wished the rain would stop. Then I wondered who would stop it – as in the perfect lyrics by John Fogarty about shelter from the storm, towers growing and five-year plans and new deals being wrapped in golden chains. And now I was a half mile out from wherever I was going and minutes from whatever I was going to do; and all I knew for sure was that I hoped it could be something not just violent, but useful as well. I was tired of the Smyrl-O'Brien-Barrett versus Emily-'Bama-Bardeaux chess match.

Just outside Hancock Harbor Marina, I stopped running, moved off the road and walked towards the water. There had obviously been a storm-caused power outage, since everything was dark except a few battery-powered boat lights. The marina included boats-in-the-water, boats on trailers in a parking lot, parked cars and, on the north end of things, a restaurant called Bait Box. I decided to find my car, then find Emily, and maybe find 'Bama. I worked the marina from south to north and found my car, parked between two boats on trailers. It was unlocked; and I opened the door. The keys were on the driver's seat and my wallet was still in the driver's side pouch on the door. My cellphone was missing. I removed my wallet, locked the car doors and hid the keys on top of the rear left tire. Find car – check. Now for Emily.

Some perfect combination of atmospheric conditions placed a thick fog over the River, but not over land. The marina sheds, the restaurant, cars and trailer boats were all visible, but the docks and piers that jutted out onto the River were shrouded. Emily was not visible on land, and so I began searching for her on piers and docks that reached into the River.

"I'm over here, Ryan. You're pretty fast. I thought you liked it slow. I left your wallet and car keys in the car."

She was on the next finger pier to my left. "All I want from you is my cellphone," I said. "If you give it to me I'll tell you where I hid your motorcycle."

"I have the phone. But stay where you are or I'll throw it in the river."

"I don't trust you."

"Well, I don't trust you."

"Jeezus, Emily. I was helping you with your motorcycle – in the middle of nowhere; and you stole my fucking car. Why should I trust you?"

"You didn't tell me you knew my sister. You probably knew who I was all along. Right?"

I eased into the River, and stood in waist-deep water. "How do you even know I know Clemmie?"

"She called you on this very phone. She wanted to know if she should walk Smokey in the morning. I figure that means you're the guy that shot Marvin. So you lied to Clemmie, you've been lying to me. You're a liar. Plus a murderer."

"What did you tell Clemmie?"

"I told her you were great in bed, that we were busy fucking our brains out and that she should forget about you, and that I wasn't giving you up until I was finished with you. She asked to speak to you. I told her you were out buying more condoms."

I took two steps along the pier. The water was armpit-deep. "Why would you do that to your sister?"

"To keep her away from jerk-offs like you. You're a murderer."

"Listen Emily. I did not shoot Marvin. I was not on the Island when he was shot. That was me behind the rootstock, when

Marvin shot Smokey and left you stranded. But I did not shoot Marvin!"

"I don't believe you."

I decided to take another approach. "Thank you for saving Smokey, anyway. That was the only sane thing you've done since that night."

"She's a great dog. She's too good for you. You should give her to Clemmie."

"Well, if I don't survive the night – make sure Clemmie gets her. Now let me think a minute. Okay?" I went quiet and edged along the pier to where I could see Emily's legs – just her legs. The rest of her was standing up in the fog.

"Ryan," she said. "Say something."

I figured it was now or never, and I exploded out of the River, grabbing for Emily's nearest leg. I used it to pull myself up onto the pier and I tackled her while she flailed away at me. She did not scream. She said nothing – she just went berserk. She was a major handful, but she was a petite handful and I outweighed her two to one; and I had her straddled, arms pinned in less than a minute.

"Now what?" she said.

"Now you listen for a minute. You give me my cellphone. I leave. You go do whatever crazy thing you want to do next. But I'd be happy to never lay eyes on you again. And if you have a shred of decency you tell Clemmie the truth."

"Your phone is in my left pocket."

"Don't move. Don't talk. Don't fight me while I get it."

She held still while I maneuvered the phone out of her pocket. It was mine. "I'm getting off you now. Then I'm going to tell you a few things. Then I'm leaving. You can stay here or come with me – your call."

I got off her as I'd promised. Emily sat up, cross-legged. I hunkered down and said, "How much do you want to hear?"

"I've got about five minutes. Make it quick."

I did. I told her what had happened on Chester Island the night she'd been playing soldier there. How I'd swum the River before Marvin was shot; and how that had been proved. I told her she should come in, talk to Smyrl. Then I asked her what she'd been doing there.

"Not your concern," she said. "We were doing something pretty terrific in the big-picture scheme of things. Until you came along and screwed everything up."

"Think about this Emily. I did not shoot Marvin – someone else did. Someone else murdered Marvin. If it wasn't you, you're involved with a murderer. You should come with me. I'm leaving now."

"I can't leave."

"Okay. Here's one more thing you should know. I want to forget all about everything that happened on the Island that night. I truly do. I want to get on with my life. But I can't. I lost a wrist computer that night. It's not mine. It belongs to someone I care about. It matters to me. I want it back. I'll get it back." I stood up. "Coming? Staying?"

"If I get that stupid big wristwatch back for you will you just go away?"

"If you tell Clemmie the truth and get me the Suunto, I'll stop thinking about this. I'll go away."

"Okay. The wristwatch will be arriving in about ten minutes. I'll call Clemmie now. Let me have the phone."

I handed her my phone, hoping she was telling the truth for a change. Apparently she was. "Clemmie. This is Emily again. I'm calling to tell you I made all that up about Ryan and me." Pause. "No, I had a reason for it, but that probably doesn't make sense anymore." Pause. "He'll explain when he sees you." Pause. "Yes – here he is." She handed me the phone.

"Ryan."

"Clemmie."

"What are you doing?"

"It's a long story. You didn't believe the stuff Emily said about me. Did you?"

"I never know what to believe from Emily; and I don't know you well enough yet."

I held on to the yet. "I'll explain everything as soon as I see you. I'm almost done here. Can you tell Emily to come with me? I'll bring her to your place."

"Let me talk to her."

Emily refused to take the phone. "I'm not going with you. She'll understand someday."

"She won't talk to you. And I've gotta go for now. I'll call later." I terminated the call. "How can the two of you be so god-damn different?"

"I'm the evil twin," said Emily. "Clemmie's the good twin. It's always been that way. It's the way it is. Black-white. Good-bad. Yin-Yang."

"What bullshit."

"It's not bullshit, Ryan. Clemmie's incapable of doing anything other than what she should do. She's responsible. She was the easy child. I'm pretty much the opposite."

"You seem fond of each other. She says mostly good things about you. You obviously care about her."

"That's all true. But it doesn't change much about how different we are. By the way – where'd you put my cycle?"

"It's in the bushes – across the road from the station. You'll find it. It will be muddy."

"Okay. Here's the deal. My boyfriend will be here in a few minutes. By boat. He's wearing the watch. You go back to the parking lot, wait there, I'll get the watch and bring it to you. Then you'll drive away and stop thinking about all this. Okay?"

"Is your boyfriend nicknamed 'Bama?"

"Yes he is. But that's no concern of yours."

"He is probably the one who shot Marvin. He tried to frame me for the murder. He's a bad man. You should get away from him."

"You're wrong. He's a very good man, doing something wonderful and necessary. I'm helping him. I love him."

"Someone who knows about this kind of thing says it's all about the money."

"He's full of shit. There is nothing about money in any of this."

"I'll forget the Suunto for now if you'll come with me."

"Fuck you Ryan. Listen. I get the watch. I walk off the pier. I hand it to you. You go. We're done. Okay? Now get off the pier."

I walked backwards off the pier, watching Emily fade into the fog.

MORTON'S FORK
CHAPTER TWENTY-SEVEN

The storm blew itself out over the Atlantic, leaving a sky full of stars; and in the bifurcated worlds of river fog and clear skies, I sat on the tongue of a boat trailer and listened and thought; and I listened because there was nothing to see, but perhaps something to hear; and I thought because there is no way for bipedal, big-headed, tool-using, world-eating omnivores not to think; and I considered Emily and how she'd lied to her own sister about me – a hurtful scatological lie – and likely lied to me as well; especially the part about her involvement in something very good, something she said she believed was big picture good (whatever that meant) – either an intended falsehood or an innocent untruth based on belief in something she'd been told by 'Bama; and so maybe she'd lied to me about retrieving the Suunto, and she intended only to leave, by boat, in the fog; and so I sat and thought and listened; and I heard the hum of a small outboard motor off to my right – downriver; and then I heard quiet; and then I heard fog-muffled voices.

I heard Emily say: "It's about time. What took you so long?"

I heard a man's voice: "I got here in seventeen minutes. What more do you want."

"Let me see your watch." As if this was part of a dispute about time.

"Get in the boat."

"No. Let me see your watch."

"I don't have time for this. Get in the fucking boat. Now."

"Not until I see your watch. The big one."

"If I have to get out of the boat to put you in it, I'll be pissed and you'll be sorry."

"I'd already be in the boat, if you'd let me see your watch the first time I asked. Now – let me see your watch."

"Fuck it. Go crazy some other time. I'm putting you in the boat."

A very small part of me felt sorry for 'Bama, trying to deal with Emily. After all, I'd had no luck at it. But the rest of me, a very big and angry part of me, wanted Johnson's Suunto; and I placed my cellphone on the tongue of the trailer and moved quickly out onto the fog-shrouded pier.

He saw me – my feet and legs anyway – before I saw him; and when I got close enough to see what was going on, he was reaching for something in the bottom of the inflatable dinghy he'd edged alongside the pier. It turned out to be an M4 carbine, the same weapon I'd last seen on Chester Island. Lucky for me it had a noise suppressor, because the suppressor caught on the dinghy's passenger seat. There is no way to outrun a bullet, but I got lucky and did the blind, violent barbarian thing and launched myself at 'Bama – left foot squarely stomping on the rifle, right fist aiming at his jaw. But he ducked, and my knuckles only grazed his forehead. My knee hit him in the chest; and just before the two of us splashed into the muddy Cohansey River, I sucked in a lungful of air.

We came up in waist-deep water, splashing and throwing

ineffective haymakers at each other. He was a little bigger than I was, but I'd surprised him; and I stood with my back to the dinghy, to keep him away from the rifle. We paused a minute, eying each other. He threw a big roundhouse right hand at me; and I ducked it and grabbed at his wrist – but it was wet and slippery and he pulled away. I felt the Suunto on his wrist – Johnson's Suunto. My Suunto.

We stood and looked at each other, breathing hard. "I want that watch," I said. "It's mine."

"Fuck you. It's mine. I've had it for years."

"You're full of shit. They're new. They haven't existed for years. It's mine. I want it back."

'Bama looked up, over my shoulder. "Emily! Get in the dinghy. Pick up the rifle and shoot this idiot. Do it now."

I had my back against the dinghy and I was close to the rifle. But I knew that the minute I turned around to reach for it, 'Bama would be all over me. "Don't do it Emily. I can prove it's my watch."

"Do it Emily. Do it or its all over," said 'Bama.

I felt the dinghy rock against my back. I supposed it was Emily getting into the dinghy and picking up the rifle. "What's all over?" I said. "I just want the watch back."

"Everything we've been working for will be over," said 'Bama. "Emily. Shoot the bastard."

It's a very bad feeling to have the sense that someone's about to shoot you in the back with a high-powered rifle – and to know that there's nothing you can do about it. But Emily didn't shoot. And she still didn't shoot. "I think Emily's sitting this one out, 'Bama. Let's get to it."

He looked disappointed for all of about one second, then he waded towards me and started punching – not a thoughtful jab, jab left, right cross or anything planned, but a hell-bent, get-it-over quick pounding – the kind bigger guys think will work with people smaller than they are. I covered up pretty well, arms to the sides of my head, like Uncle Ryan showed me when I was just a kid; but still some of his punches were landing – and they hurt like hell, especially two right hand shots to the same spot in my ribs. Then I took a turn hammering him. I'd fought bigger guys two or three times; and sometimes they got discouraged when the fight looked like it wasn't going to be over quick. And Emily still didn't shoot.

I jabbed twice with my left, feinted with my right and nailed him good with a left hook to his right ear. He blinked, shook his head and decided he might like to wrestle instead of fistfight. He came at me, arms reaching for my waist and I tried to knee him under the chin, but the River got in the way. He stomped on my right foot. I tried to kick him in the balls, but the underwater kick was slow-motion and ineffectual. He had one hand in my belt; and I pried it off by bending back his thumb until it was just shy of the breaking point. He stepped back, and we looked at each other again.

"Next comes biting, strangling, tearing off ears and eye-gouging," I said, smiling – trying to look like I couldn't wait. "Maybe even one of us will die tonight. Is that wrist watch really worth it? It really is all I want from you."

Emily spoke: "You said you could prove it's yours. How can you do that?"

"Take it off, 'Bama. Give it to Emily. There's something scratched on the underside and I can tell her what it is." I did my best to look rested, ready for the next round, but I didn't feel that way. 'Bama could definitely use his size to eventually win a fight with me; he'd wear me down, especially in the water where my quickness was limited; and all I could do about it was to make him pay more than he was willing for the win. "Go on. Give it to Emily. Let her see what we're fighting about."

"Sure," he said. "But that doesn't mean we're finished." He

removed the Suunto and tossed it over my head into the dinghy, where Emily picked it up.

"Okay, Ryan – how do you know it's yours?"

"There's a 'J' scratched underneath. It stands for Johnson, as in Sergeant Johnson – Platoon Sergeant of the Second Platoon, 'L' Company, Third Battalion, Sixth Marines. The platoon's still in Afghanistan. Sergeant Johnson's in a hospital in Germany. He's wounded. I need to give it back to him."

"That's so very sweet," said 'Bama. "Is he your gay lover?"

I laughed. "If you were fighting him, you'd already be dead – asshole."

"There's a 'J' on the back, 'Bama. Like he said."

"Well then fuck it. Give him the watch and let's be off."

I reached a hand up over my right shoulder and felt Emily place the Suunto in my palm. "Thanks. And thanks for not shooting me too."

"I'm still considering it," said Emily.

Still facing 'Bama, I talked to Emily. "No you're not. Clemmie says you're very smart; and if that's true, what you're thinking about is whether or not you should give the rifle to your boyfriend. You know he'll shoot me with it; and you're wondering if he'd shoot you too."

"Don't listen to him Emily," said 'Bama. "I'd never hurt you, and you know it. Throw me the rifle."

"Don't do it Emily. You'll have my dead body to get rid of. And you'll have to explain it to Clemmie, too."

"Shut up – both of you. Beat each other to death if you want – but shut up while I think for a minute."

'Bama and I stared at each other. Emily was silent. Then the dinghy moved a little. It felt like Emily was getting out of it. I figured she was headed for my car, and I said: "The keys are not in the car, Emily. I hid them."

Phut, phut, phut went the rifle, making deadly little splashes in the water next to me. "I told you to shut up," said Emily. "Next person to talk gets shot."

I felt the dinghy move a little more. Emily was paddling it out into the River. "Ryan – hold on to the bow. 'Bama – catch the stern. Neither of you talk." She paddled a little more, then was content to let the fog-shrouded River's outgoing tide take us toward the Delaware River. We were about four miles as the crow flies from Cohansey Cove and the Delaware, but the River snaked around so much that the total distance was probably closer to ten miles. I didn't remember anything about the Cohansey tides, and how fast they moved; and the fog prevented me from seeing the shore.

So the three of us floated, silent and fog-bound down an empty river, two of us holding on to either end of an inflatable dinghy and one person in the boat – the crazy Goddess with life-or-death-on-a-whim power over two healthy men – with the rifle.

• • •

I listened to Emily talk to herself. At first the muttering was incomprehensible, too quiet to be understood. Then it began to make sense to me – not sense in the sense that it was rational, but sense in that it included a recognizable and sequential thought process. She was trying to decide what to do; and it seemed she'd deduced that she had four options: 1 – shoot me; 2 – shoot 'Bama; 3 – shoot both of us; or 4 – shoot neither of us. She was trying to use rational thought to deduce which irrational action to take; and she was using words she'd learned somewhere – words like hard determinism and paradox and self-contradiction and cognitive distortion. She mentioned Spinoza and Hobson and someone I'd not heard of named Buridan, and said something about his ass.

Eventually, after twenty minutes or so, she muttered: "So what I've got here is a Morton's Fork here, except that instead of two equally unpleasant alternatives, I've got four. Four tines on my Morton's Fork. What to do?

"What to do? If I kill Ryan, Clemmie might never speak to me again. If I kill 'Bama, the project is kaput – and I lose another boyfriend. If I kill them both that will cause both bad outcomes. If I kill neither of them, Ryan will probably shut the project down; and 'Bama will likely kill me. What to do?"

Of all things, she decided to ask us what to do. 'Bama and Ryan, who'd just tried to kill each other and given the chance would try it again were asked to provide input, limited input, into the dilemma. "'Bama," she said, "You have five minutes to convince me what to do. Ryan. You're next."

'Bama might have been an eloquent person, capable of a convincing dissertation, of charming and winning the heart and mind of a lady; but he'd been half-drowned, beaten about the head, had his thumb nearly broken, was hanging on to the stern of an inflatable dinghy in the fog and headed for the giant Delaware River; and he had been dealing with Emily for days – enough to make most any man gibber like an idiot.

He used his five minutes to beg, cry, promise and finally whine about the importance of 'the project' – a project that had been in the works for "over two years" and which couldn't be allowed to crash. He begged Emily to shoot me, let him in the boat. He would forgive everything.

"Time's up, 'Bama," said Emily. "Okay Ryan. Go."

I was not going to beg a crazy woman to not shoot me. I figured I'd just as likely say the wrong thing anyway, so I just talked, and I told her what I'd been doing and that I didn't think I was finished with life just yet. "I've been in Iraq and Afghanistan, where people were trying to kill me, and somehow they didn't. I met Clemmie when she returned Smokey to me – a dog you saved from bleeding to death – a dog that loves me and has waited for me for four years. I'm teaching a kid from Africa to read – he lives in Chester in a group home and seems to need me. I have a good job lined up. The only reason I'm even here is to return this Suunto, this wristwatch, to Sergeant Johnson when his plane arrives in Dover, Delaware. I'm likely going to be another of a long line of men who fall in love with your sister. I don't think you should shoot either of us. Throw the rifle in the River and either come with me or go with 'Bama."

I didn't tell her that if she did shoot me, Smyrl, my Uncle Ryan and Sam Barrett would most definitely figure out who did it; and that Uncle Ryan would not be expecting the New Jersey State Criminal System to take care of matters – he'd handle it himself.

"Thank you. Now both of you be quiet," she said.

We drifted downriver for another twenty minutes. I figured I was at least two miles from my cellphone, my car, my wallet. I admit that I was afraid – not physically afraid to die, but afraid that I'd die without adding up to anything, that I'd die and there'd be nothing left of Ryan O'Brien, that only family and a few friends would mark my passing. It would be a particularly foolish way I'd died.

Finally, Emily spoke. "I've made a decision. 'Bama – lean over here, I want to tell you something."

'Bama moved a little, rocking the dinghy, and Emily whispered something to him. I figured I was in big trouble; and I considered submerging and making a break for it. Then 'Bama said, "No Emily. Please. Please." Then: phut, phut, phut. And silence.

"Do you figure you can get yourself back to your car, Ryan?" said Emily.

SINE MORIBUS VANAE
CHAPTER TWENTY-EIGHT

"Yes," I said, pushing off from the dinghy before Emily could change her mind. I swam against the tide for a minute, getting out of her sight as fast as possible – then turned left and swam for shore. Shore was all mud, small creeks, cattails, cord grass and sedge. The going was slow; but at least I was alive and I wasn't barefoot. I knew there was likely a direct route back to my car, but I was afraid to leave the River; and so I followed the course of the serpentine Cohansey, wading through creeks, sucking my feet up from black mud and forcing my way through tall grass. I was thankful the sun wasn't up, to bring the greenhead flies; and I was even more thankful I was still alive, knowing it had been a near thing.

After an hour and a half, I reached the marina; and I sat on a floating dock and splashed mud off my feet and legs. Then I held on to the dock and dunked myself in the River, shook myself and retrieved my cellphone. The car, keys, and wallet were all where I'd left them; and I drove away, home, trying to put thoughts of Emily out of my mind. I drove slowly while texting Clemmie that she did not need to walk Smokey in the morning; and I told her I'd call her later in the day to tell her everything.

"Emily is alive," I also texted. "Alive but crazy," a thought I kept to myself, "and a murderer." Then I went right to Uncle Ryan's voicemail and told him I was okay and would call him at 10 a.m. I said I had lots to tell him and to have Devlin Meyer around if he was available. I drove home, gave Smokey a short walk, showered and passed out in my own bed – my blessed very own bed.

• • •

I woke up, believing myself to be rested, knowing I was in a good mood; and I decided to attempt to have an absolutely average and dull day. It was what we'd always wanted in Afghanistan and never managed to get: a day of unexceptional happenings, a day of simple garden variety routine. Another Platoon Commander in "L" Company got up each morning stepped outside his tent and said: "Bring on the quotidian!" Almost no one knew what he was talking about; but I did. "Bring on the quotidian!" I said to Smokey; and the two of us decided to start the day with a nice long walk – a walk that might include a scrapple and egg hoagie from John's Lunch Cart with all the overworked, underpaid interns and residents outside the hospital on Spruce Street.

So Smokey and I ambled, generally west to the Penn Campus, past Franklin Field. Along the way, I watched other people working on their own quotidian days. None of them seemed to be likely to have been almost murdered – and twice in less than a week. I'm certain that none of them had been forced to swim across the Delaware River, at night or listen to a crazy woman decide not to kill them in a foggy Cohansey – just the night before. But I stopped that line of thought, realizing that it was exactly what I'd decided not to do. So Smokey and I ordered, paid, waited in a short line and were handed breakfast. We ate it in front of College Hall, watching the statue of Ben Franklin watch us.

The bench I was on and Smokey was under should not have been comfortable enough for me to fall asleep – Smokey could fall asleep anywhere. But just when I was thinking that Ben's quiet gaze made me a little nervous, I believe I did fall asleep; and I imagined his look in my direction was accusatory. He seemed to be asking me how on Earth I could be trying so hard to have a boring day when he was stuck up on a statue with so many interesting ideas still percolating in his polymath mind. "Why by the time I was your age," he'd say – if he could talk – "I'd already started up Poor Richard's Almanac, fathered a son, started the first library in America and thought up a half-a-dozen inventions. I started this very University when I was not much older than you are now. And there you sit, hoping to be bored, wishing that nothing of interest will happen. You should be ashamed."

"But Ben – may I call you Ben?" I dreamed.

"Everyone does – Ryan," he said.

"But Ben – things are very different now. Everything's very complicated. I've been in the Marine Corps – off in Afghanistan and Iraq fighting for most of the last four years."

"I've heard of Afghanistan. Where's Iraq?"

"I think you knew it as 'Persia'."

"Why were you fighting there?"

"I don't really know."

"You were in Persia and Afghanistan, fighting – for four years – and you don't know why?"

"Like I said – everything is complicated now. There were lots of reasons we were there. I think some of them were good ones and maybe some of them were not so good. Anyway – a lot has happened to me in the last few days; and I just wanted a break from it all – even if it was just for one day."

"I'd give anything to be alive again," said Ben. "I love

complicated. I wish a lot would happen to me for a few days. Do me a favor, Ryan. When you wake up, shoo the pigeons away for me."

"Sure Ben."

"Thanks Ryan. Another thing you should know. The real motto of this University is, as I intended it: Sine Moribus Vanae. I knew that it could be interpreted as 'loose women without morals' – but the operative words are 'could be'. It could also be interpreted in other ways. I intended ambiguity. The prudes who changed the motto to Leges Sine Moribus Vanae were wrong to do so. You would likely call them 'assholes'."

"I didn't know that," I said.

"One more thing," he said. "I dislike the pacifist 'Quaker' as the mascot of this University. I believe that it is very likely that it was Quakers who changed the motto. At least you had none of them in Afghanistan. Right?"

"Right," I said. "Is there anything you are particularly happy about now?"

"Many things. For just one example, I am pleased that my likeness is on your one-hundred dollar bill, and that they are called 'Benjamins'. It is enjoyable for me to consider the many interesting transactions involving them – and, circumlocutorily, me."

"Oh," I said as I woke up. I looked at my watch, shooed the pigeons from the statue of Benjamin Franklin – statesman, politician, scientist, inventor, diplomat, and capable nag.

• • •

By the time we'd wandered back to our apartment, it was almost time for my call to Uncle Ryan. I wondered if Devlin Meyer would still be interested in my doings. A part of me hoped that he was.

"Hi Uncle Ryan."

"Hey Ryan. Devlin's here too. What's up?"

I told them what had happened last night, as sequentially and impartially as I could. I offered the conclusion that Emily was both crazy and a murderer. When I'd finished, there was silence, then Uncle Ryan spoke: "What do you think, Devlin?"

"There's a lot of food for thought there," Devlin croaked in his ancient voice. "Let me ask a couple of questions. Okay?"

"Sure," I said. "Fire away."

"How smart is Emily?"

"Very. Clemmie says she's a weird genius. I.Q. off the charts."

"How honest is Emily?'

"She's extremely dishonest. She seems like someone who'd rather tell a lie than the truth."

"Did you see – personally see – 'Bama get shot?"

"No. It was too foggy. Also – I was at the other end of the dinghy and getting ready to make a break for it."

"Did you hear anything – any talking – after the shots?"

"No. But I was too busy swimming away, in case Emily changed her mind about shooting me."

"Let me think for five minutes," said Devlin.

So for the next five minutes, Uncle Ryan and I talked about what we'd done that day, what our plans for the rest of the day were and generally chit-chatted away the five minutes Devlin needed to consider matters. Uncle Ryan agreed that Benjamin Franklin was a cool dude; and that if he were living, I should sponsor him for membership in the West End Boat Club.

"Here's what I think," said Devlin. "It is very possible – even likely – that Emily is neither crazy nor a murderer, and that she did not shoot 'Bama. It was an act – a set-up – for your benefit. It was the perfect way for you to stop thinking about 'Bama as anyone of interest in whatever's going on. It was the perfect way for 'Bama to stop thinking about being pissed at Emily and maybe even killing her, because he'd be thrilled with how clever she'd been. All that nonsense about Morton's Fork or whatever, was just a con job – a very good one.

"'Bama's still alive. There's still something going on and it's still all about the money. The good thing is that 'Bama and Emily – and Officer Bardeaux, if she's involved – don't know that you know what's really happened. They think that you think 'Bama's dead and Emily murdered him. You have an advantage. Understand?"

"Maybe. But I don't want anything more to do with all this. I've got Johnson's Suunto back, Smokey's alive, I might get my job back and I've met Clemmie. I just want to live a normal life – a boring, humdrum life. I'll tell Smyrl what happened and let him worry about it. It's not my concern. Is it?"

Devlin was silent for a moment; and then he seemed to be on the verge of getting pissed at me. He coughed twice and croaked his answer. "Damn it Ryan, I'd give anything to be young enough to be involved in whatever the hell it is you don't want any part of. I'd love to be able to work my way through all the stuff you think is confusing. Wait 'til you're ninety and need a fucking cane to get around. You should be ashamed. And one more thing – just because you don't want anything more to do with this doesn't mean that whatever this is won't want more to do with you."

I realized that Devlin was using very different words to tell me almost the same thing Benjamin Franklin said to me earlier. I felt a little defensive. "Well, I am going out to Chester Island in a couple of hours – with Sam Barrett. I suppose I haven't really stopped being involved in this yet." I was? Was I really going out to the Island where it'd all started? Did I want to? No. Was I going? Yes. I'd just said so.

"What are you doing out there?" asked Devlin.

"Sam wanted to see it. I'm doing whatever he wants. He says he might bring something with him. I think it's fifty-fifty that his wife won't let him go."

"Will you take Smokey?"

"Should I?"

"Take Smokey. Listen to Sam. Report anything to Smyrl. Tell your Uncle Ryan too."

"What about you Devlin?"

"I'm going away. I've got something to do in *Munequita*. It'll take me a couple of days."

"You didn't tell me about that," said Uncle Ryan. "Is that a good idea?"

"Your Uncle thinks I might not be up to driving my little runabout. Yes Uncle Ryan, it is a very good, very important and long overdue idea." Then I heard a door shut.

"I don't know what that was all about," said Uncle Ryan. "I'd better go see."

"Right. Bye."

"Later."

• • •

It is one of Life's great pleasures to have practiced something that matters to you often enough to be able to do it without thinking – no checklists, reminders or manuals required; and so at 11:30 a.m., Smokey and I launched *Larke* at the West End's boat ramp – we managed to hitch the trailer to the car, back the car down the ramp, unlatch the winch cable, tie a line to *Larke's* starboard-forward cleat, tie the other end of that line to a cleat on the dock, dump the boat off the ramp, park the car, use the line to turn *Larke* around facing the river, untie the line, jump down the five or six feet from the dock to *Larke's* deck, start the motor (second pull) and head for the boat slip.

I enjoy getting *Larke* into the water, unaided. Folks with boats understand what I mean when I say that having "help" when docking or launching often only makes things more complicated –

better to just do it yourself. When someone volunteers assistance, I usually decline, telling them that I need the practice. Sometimes I ask them to watch and give me a grade; and although the kibitzers at the Club always give me a passing grade – I never get the A+ I deserve; and this is because of the inherent power-boater bias against sailboats. I tell them I only used two gallons of gas getting *Larke* about a hundred miles downriver and up the Inland Waterway to Avalon, New Jersey; and they ask me how long it took and laugh when I admit it was three days. They tell me they can do the trip in five hours; and I ask them how much gas they'd use, and they admit to some unaffordable number. And so we live in congenial co-existence – the sailors who can get anywhere for free and jury-rig failings of stays, shrouds, halyards, sheets and lines and the power-boaters who can overhaul engines, re-jigger outdrives, and re-wire electrical systems.

As I was unhitching the empty trailer from my car, I saw Sam Barrett drive into the Club; and I waved him over. He'd brought some stuff in an older model, black Chevrolet Silverado. Except for the color and the fact that it was spotless, it was Uncle Ryan's truck. He showed me the gear he'd brought with him for the sail to Chester Island; and he told me how he thought we should use it. I brought him up to date on everything that had happened the night before, and told him of Devlin's opinion about it all.

We lugged his gear down to *Larke*, loaded it, helped Smokey aboard, and cast off.

"Sail or motor?" I said.

"Sail," said Sam.

Sam turned out to be a good sailing partner. He knew enough about sailing to know that he didn't know everything, that every sailboat is different and that he was not the skipper; and he was content to let me handle everything except the jib sheets. And so the three of us – four if you count *Larke* – worked our way towards Chester Island – mostly running with the wind over our starboard beam, but against the last of the incoming tide. It's funny, but the very quiet of sailing often makes the people aboard quiet too; and we were mostly silent as we edged up to the Island where so much stuff had happened the Friday past.

CHESTER ISLAND TANGO
CHAPTER TWENTY-NINE

We lowered and secured sails, anchored, and carried Sam's gear ashore, wading in three foot-deep water; and when everything was stacked neatly on the muddy shore, I motored *Larke* into deeper water, in advance of the outgoing tide. By the time I waded back to Sam, he'd assembled a high-tech, lightweight metal detector and was testing it by zapping it over some coins he'd thrown in the grass.

"We're good to go," said Sam. "You carry the shovel; Smokey can sniff around at whatever."

Sam looked like a giant insect, sweeping his appended proboscis back and forth across the grass, listening to whatever it was he heard in the wireless headphones. He was enjoying himself. This was a vacation for him. I trailed along behind, unable to talk to Sam because of his headphones. I was alone with my thoughts; Smokey wandered, never out of sight. "It's working," said Sam. "Dig here."

I unearthed an old beer can just under the surface – a Miller High Life – probably left by a goose hunter a decade before. I wondered if this was the kind of artifact we were destined to find. We worked our way counter-clockwise around the Island, working from the shoreline to about thirty yards inland. Sam stopped and removed his headphones once and said: "I'm going to ignore the first ten feet of shoreline – it's too full of trash."

As he started to put the headphones back on, I asked him how long he was allowed to do this. "Eleanor asked me to be home by 4 p.m.," he said, "so I figure 5 p.m. is my outer limit – after that I'd pay too high a price. But if we find something – all bets are off." He grinned like a big kid.

Sam went back to work. The task seemed to me to be futile, since at the rate we were going, the Island was too big for Sam to cover in less than three weeks. But he seemed to have some system in mind; and as we completed the section of Island facing the Delaware, he doubled back the way we'd come, moving inland. I put my mind in neutral. Chester Island was an empty, benign place in daylight, unlike the frightful place it had been in the dark last Friday night. I wondered why no one had ever thought to develop it. Surely it had some use – smack dab in the middle of millions of people. Smokey disappeared into some dead-looking bushes; and when I followed her in, she was snuffing around, interested. I called her. Usually obedient, she ignored me, and Sam noticed. He came in waved his magic detector in the general direction of Smokey.

"There's something in there," he said. He ran the detector back and forth. "It's pretty big. Dig here."

I dug where Sam pointed and quickly hit something that felt like wood. I cleared dirt off two identical boxes – about five feet long and a foot wide. Sam brushed the dirt off one of them and we saw "Anza Mk-I" stenciled there in black letters. Below that were symbols that looked to me like Arabic. The boxes were secured with three metal bands and rows of galvanized nails.

"Jeezus, Sam. Is this what I think it is?"

"The mother lode," said Sam.

"We'll never get them open without tools."

"Use your magic phone, take pictures and e-mail them to Smyrl, to me and to yourself. Tell Smyrl where we found them. Then let's cover them back up, mark the spot with something and get out of here. This calls for a libation."

I spread my T-shirt on the ground and pinned it there with four small sticks, right over top of the spot, and we left, doing the complicated tango we'd used to get onto the Island, only in reverse: Ryan to *Larke*, up anchor, *Larke* to the shallows, gear-dog-Sam-Ryan aboard and outa there. We did not sail against the tide, but motored back to *Larke's* slip, docked and headed for the Club. Sam was very pleased with himself.

• • •

We sat, Sam and I, on the grand patio, under the large maroon canvas awning at the West End Boat Club, sipping light beer mixed with crushed ice; and we gazed out over the River, towards Chester Island and waited for something to happen. Smokey stretched out on the grassy bank in front of us, content.

"I wonder what Smyrl will do with this," said Sam.

"Maybe it will get him out of Trenton a day early."

My phone did its thing, causing Sam to smile. It was Smyrl. He asked me where I was, who I was with; and then he commanded us to stay put.

"Don't go anywhere, Ryan. That goes for Sam as well. Homeland Security – the real DHS this time – and the FBI are now involved, and they want to interview you."

"What about you?" I asked.

"I'm still handling the murder. That's all I'm doing. You did manage to get me out of Trenton, though. Thanks. Bye." He terminated the call.

I told Sam that we weren't going anywhere for awhile, and why. He seemed to be delighted. "I hope it's the FBI," he said. "I've got a lot of confidence in them. DHS – not so much."

"What's wrong with DHS?"

"Maybe nothing. Maybe I'm just an old fart that doesn't like change – but DHS has become too big, too fast. They've now got responsibility for Immigration Services, for U. S. Customs and the Border Patrol, for TSA – the folks that abuse you at airports, for the Secret Service, for FEMA and for the United States Coast Guard. The Coast Guard! I bet I know how the Coast Guard feels about being part of DHS. On the other hand, the FBI has been around for a hundred years, has a budget of about one-tenth that of DHS and is full of competent people – many of them former Marines. I suppose I think of the FBI as the Marine Corps and DHS as just a new, big-government, money-sucking, disorganized, amorphous blob."

We'd carried the binoculars up from *Larke*, and were taking turns with them. Other Club members became interested, and pretty soon we had a small crowd of the usual suspects, drinks in hand, offering thoughts, opinions and witticisms. In a few minutes, we saw a black helicopter circle and land – it had a gold band and logo on it; and two minutes later we saw a second black helicopter arrive – with "FBI" in large white letters. We couldn't see what they were doing.

"Before we get all busy with whatever happens next," said Sam, "I wanted to get you to sign your new employment application. I filled it out for you." He reached into the briefcase he'd retrieved from his car and pulled out my application. It still had mustard stains on it from the Philadelphia Zoo.

"How did you know enough about me to fill out the application?"

"I used my own personal data – other than date-of-birth, physical description and so forth. I told you before: I want to see if

I could get a job at Howell & Barrett."

"Sam – you are Barrett. Of course you can get a job with yourself."

"That's not what I meant, and you know it. Just go along with me on this."

"Okay." I signed the application and gave it back to him.

"That's my man. Okay."

"One condition, though," I said. "Can you pull some strings and get me back into the gym? I'll be able to wait for an eventual job if I can work out. If I can't you'll be hiring some fat, soft slob who doesn't deserve the job."

"Okay."

"So you're an 'okay' man too. Thanks."

· · ·

"While we're waiting for whatever happens next, what is it you'd like to do at Howell and Barrett?" asked Sam.

"I'm not sure I know what you mean," I said. "I figured there would be some training program, some step-by-step sequence, an incremental chance to get ahead over time. I thought you would be telling me what you wanted me to do and I'd just say 'okay' and go ahead and do it."

"Of course it will work that way. But before you start work and get all tar-babied up with the typical way we do things, I'd like to hear if you have any ideas of your own. Okay?"

"Okay. But let me be honest – I didn't think about this much in Afghanistan. I was busy keeping a platoon of Marines alive. But since then, I've thought of three things – stock market related things – that I'd be interested in."

"Give them to me in order of complexity."

"Okay. Here's number one. From what I can tell, there are such a proliferation of Exchange Traded Funds that there are nearly unlimited ways to invest in almost anything. Let's take an easy example: gold. There are ETF's for actual gold, for gold mining companies, for gold in various geographic regions, double and even triple impact ETF's, long and short alternatives and so forth. Even though all of these are driven off the same thing – price of gold – they have different performance metrics."

"True. How does that make anyone money?"

"I'm not sure. But I wonder if most of these come back – or nearly so – to the identical price-of-gold historic trend lines. Over time, of course. And I wonder if when there are deviations – intraday or whatever – there are buying and selling opportunities in anticipation of the return to 'normal'."

"Is that something you could research yourself?"

"Yes. I don't think that would be too hard. Backtesting should be easy. I'm pretty sure I could do the work myself."

"What's your second idea?"

"Let's call this one 'disaster investing'."

"Not sure I like the name – but go ahead."

"Okay. Every time there's a disaster of some kind – be it man-made or a natural disaster – stocks are affected. The wrecking of a cruise ship sinks the stock of the cruise line, a hurricane like Katrina ruins the insurance companies that insure property, and the crash of a plane impacts the airline stock."

"Unless we're shooting down airplanes ourselves and shorting the stock, I don't see how there's money to be made there. The disasters are not predictable."

"No. You're right. But that there will be disasters is a given. They happen every year. So to be prepared with information and prepared to act – long or short – after the disaster is what I had in mind. I think there might be observable reactions in the market to the disasters – and money to be made there."

"Interesting. Is that one you could handle yourself?"

"I think I could do the set-up work – the parameters, the

criteria – and I'd need help with some of the grunt work."

"What's your third idea?"

"This one's pretty far out. I definitely could not handle it myself. In fact, Howell & Barrett might need more computer capacity. This one we'll call 'absential investing'; and it would be based on a consideration – not of the things we can observe about a stock or an industry – but about the things we cannot observe."

"You may be losing me. I can get the theory, but can't see a way to do it. Got an example?"

"Only a Marine Corps one – not an investing one." I told Sam about Major Davis and night navigation, and first and second-tier absentials; and I wondered aloud if we ended up knowing a lot about stock market actions that investors did not take, whether by deduction we'd know something valuable about what actions they would take – and I thought that that would be valuable somehow.

"Hmm," said Sam. "Let me think about that one."

• • •

We sat back and watched Chester Island through binoculars – comfortable with each other. I wondered if the ease I was experiencing with Sam would vanish as soon as I started work. Before that happened, I decided to ask him some other big-picture, Ryan-O'Brien, meaning-of-life questions. I knew I'd value his thoughts if I could get them.

"Let me ask you this Sam. If you were me would you declare victory and quit winners on this whole Chester Island thing? Or would you stay involved somehow?"

"What do you mean?"

"I guess I mean that one hand, I've got Smokey back, I've got Johnson's Suunto back, I probably have a job and I've got a girl I like. Oh, and I've got a responsibility for Nashir and some debt with Smyrl and Jameson and you."

"There's no debt owed me," said Sam. "I'm having a blast."

"Okay. What I mean is – is the Chester Island Tango over? Should I get on with life? Accept the quotidian?"

"That's a question we need to hand off to someone smarter than I am – Socrates maybe."

"He's dead. And the only quote of his I can remember is: 'the unexamined life is not worth living'."

"He didn't much like working for pay, either – although I don't remember the exact quote," said Sam.

"I guess what I'm asking the older, smarter man sitting here next to me sipping beer is simple: what would you do if you were me?"

"That's such a complicated question. I usually refuse to answer it; but it's been a great day – one for the books. Here's a thought: the only things I regret in life are the things I didn't do. I'm too old to do lots of those things now. I'd give a lot to have the energy and stamina I had when I was twenty-seven."

"So you're saying I've got the rest of my life to get old; and then the rest of eternity to be dead. I should get off my ass and stay involved with this, at least until it's wrapped up."

"I guess I'm saying you've got to figure it out yourself. I don't know what I'd do if I were you. 'Old' is the operative word for me right now. I'm only three days past surgery and I'm tired. I'm ready for a nap."

"You're telling me pretty much the same thing as two other people. One of them was a statue of Benjamin Franklin who told me he was bored standing there with nothing to do but be annoyed by pigeons. Smokey and I fell asleep in front of the statue – the one in front of College Hall at Penn. I suppose it was just a dream."

"Who was the other guy?"

He's a ninety-year old man living alone on a boat the Everglades. He said he'd give anything to have a go at whatever it is this is all about. One more thing he said: 'it's all about the money'. I can't figure that one out."

"Did he say anything else?"

"Yes. He said that this thing might not be finished with me, even if I wasn't finished with it. Then he got annoyed and left."

"Maybe he was right," said Sam. "Look." A helicopter was headed our way. It had "FBI" on the side in white letters. It circled the Club and landed in the gravel area the West End used to store boats in the winter.

Except for Indians
Chapter Thirty

FBI agents rounded the corner of the West End, and mounted the steps to the patio. There were two of them. One, a woman, a forty-something, wore boots, black cargo pants and a black jacket and ball cap that both read "FBI" in white block letters. The other, a man, a thirty-something, was dressed in the stereotypical dark suit with a white, starched shirt and a red and blue striped necktie.

"Anyone here named Ryan O'Brien?" asked the female agent. I raised my hand, like a third-grader – not quite sure I wanted to be called on.

"How about Sam Barrett?" asked the suit.

Sam raised his hand. "Over here," he said.

The agents paced over to us, we stood, and the woman said, "I'm Special Agent Ayers, this is Special Agent Rizzo. We need to talk. Where can we get some privacy?" She nodded at the West Enders standing there, drinks in hand, looking interested.

Jack Walker herded the group to the other end of the patio, where they could still watch, but couldn't hear. Someone wondered if Agent Ayers was a "G-Woman". Ayers and Rizzo turned two beige plastic patio chairs to face Sam and me.

Agent Ayers spoke. "Normally, we'd spend a few minutes getting you comfortable with us – you know, building a rapport, asking you neutral questions about your hobbies, the weather and so forth. Unfortunately, we don't have time for that. We need to be very direct. We need to ask you questions; and you need to give us truthful, succinct answers. This is possibly a matter of national security. Okay?"

"Okay," Sam and I said in unison.

"Which of you knows the most about this mess?"

Sam looked at me, and I volunteered: "I do. I've been involved with this one way or another since last Friday night. Sam just since yesterday."

"Okay. We are going to follow one standard protocol, or we'll get our asses handed to us on the inevitable review. We need to interview you separately. Rizzo – you take Mister Barrett over there; and I'll talk to Mister O'Brien here." Sam and Rizzo moved about twenty feet away, arranged two chairs and began to talk.

• • •

Agent Ayers produced a small recording device, poked a button and said: "Mister O'Brien – tell me as quickly as you can, what's happened. You mentioned last Friday night. Let's start there."

I'd had some Marine Corps training in interrogation techniques, but never had to use them. I recalled that there were behavioral signs of a truthful person, so I sat upright, looked Ayers directly in the eyes and tried to appear relaxed. I told her what had happened last Friday night and since. She interrupted only occasionally, with a pertinent question or two.

I'd told the story so many times, to Jameson Jones, to Detective Smyrl, to Uncle Ryan, to Clemmie and to Sam, that I didn't have to think much about it. I felt like my Pops telling us bedtime stories that all began with "Once upon a time, not so long ago, and not so far away," and ending with ". . . but that's a story for another night at another time." He always put his kids into the stories, mentioned us as part of an adventure about once a minute; and we loved it. Agent Ayers didn't love it, but she seemed to be listening very carefully to the narrative; and she looked out at the River when I mentioned swimming it, smiled when I told about pushing the truck into the water and frowned when I mentioned sleeping in a ceiling to avoid a police officer. The whole recitation took about twenty-five minutes.

Then she did the classic interrogation thing, and asked me: "So what, Mister O'Brien, do you think this is all about? Guess for me."

"I don't know, but I guess 'Bama was part of something last Friday night that I interrupted. I think the others involved were clueless about what they were really doing – except maybe for Emily. On one hand I don't think they were terrorists as we think of them, or I'd be dead; on the other hand, I assume there were hand-held surface-to-air missiles buried on the Island; and I can't think of any reason anyone would want them other than terrorism – "

Agent Ayers interrupted. "The boxes were empty. Full of dirt."

I thought about that. "Then they're somewhere else, maybe on a boat – maybe on the boat that Emily and 'Bama were on, the one the dinghy was from, the one on the Cohansey River somewhere in the fog."

I finished talking, and when Ayers ran out of questions, she looked over at Agent Rizzo and Sam, and signaled for him to come over. "Go sit with Mister Barrett a minute please, Mister O'Brien." I did as she asked, and she and Rizzo talked quietly for a few minutes.

She waved us over. "Here's what we're going to do. Mister Barrett, you're free to go, we've got your cell number and address.

Please take our calls if we call you."

"Certainly," said Sam.

She turned to me. "If you wish, we would be willing and even grateful for you to stay more involved with this – for the next few hours, at least. Can you show us exactly where you last saw the woman you called Emily and the man you called 'Bama?"

"Sure. There's a chart hanging on the wall in the bar. I can show you there. Or I can show you on my phone, or on Agent Rizzo's laptop."

"Not what I had in mind. Will you show me – physically – from the air, where you last saw them?"

I thought of the unanimous advice I'd had in the last day; and it was an easy call. As a proxy for Benjamin Franklin, Devlin Meyer and Sam Barrett – and for my eventual too-old-to-do-much self, I said simply: "Yes."

As we got up to go, Sam remembered Smokey, volunteered to take her to his house, and I agreed. I visited the Men's Room, accompanied by Rizzo. I wondered if he wasn't letting me out of his sight. Ayers was on her cellphone, reporting in to someone, I supposed, and letting them know where we were going next.

Sam and Smokey left in Sam's pickup truck. Rizzo carried two aluminum cases of computer gear into the West End's pool room and set up a small command center there. The room was not in use at the moment; and boat club members agreed to stay out of Rizzo's hair while he did whatever FBI Agents did, when they looked serious, competent and intimidating.

Agent Ayers and I headed for the helicopter, which was already rotating its blades in a slow-motion thwop-thwop, as the pilot waited for us to board. When we were seated, Ayers handed me a headset, adjusted one on her own head and signaled for me to do the same. "These are so we can talk. Been in helicopters before?"

"Yup. Never one as flimsy as this. The ones I've been in are armored and carry twenty troops and all their gear."

"Military?"

"Yes. Afghanistan. And Iraq."

Ayers seemed disinterested in anything other than the task at hand, which seemed to be for me to navigate us to where I'd last seen Emily and 'Bama. "Will you be airsick?"

"No." Helicopters were insect-like. This fragile machine was a mosquito. The armored monsters used in war were hornets or flying beetles. "Can you talk to the pilot?"

"We both can. Tell him where to take us."

"The easiest way to find the Cohansey River from here would be to simply follow the Delaware and check off landmarks. So turn right and head for the Commodore Barry Bridge."

"Aye," said the pilot.

"Call off the landmarks for me," said Ayers. "I'm not from here."

"Where are you from?"

"Doesn't matter. No chit-chat. Where are we?"

"That's Raccoon Creek. The next creek will be Oldmans Creek." What was a six hour sail for *Larke* and me was a five-minute trip by helicopter. "Then comes the Delaware Memorial Bridge. Follow the bend of the River – left."

I called out landmarks I'd seen before from the River – the Salem River, Alloway Creek, and the Salem Nuclear Plant. Everything looked different from the air. The shoreline formed a distinct face – a profile, west-facing, with the promontory of the reactor site looking both man-made and like a chin. The profile was every bit as distinguished as that of Roosevelt on the dime.

"Could that be a target?" I asked, pointing to the two reactor towers.

"Not likely," said Ayers. "The missiles we're looking for probably wouldn't do the job on those. Besides, there's a coast guard boat stationed in the River, off the plant."

"I remember them. They made me go around them once, on

the Delaware side of the River. They told me it was for my own safety. They said there were young, itchy trigger-fingered National Guard troops with rifles and live ammo stationed there. There's Stow Creek – and there's the Cohansey River."

At Ayer's command, the pilot hovered over the River's mouth – a small delta of islands and a cove, at a place where the Delaware River had widened to five miles across; and then he aimed the helicopter upstream – carefully following each bend.

Under us was all slow-moving, muddy water and marsh grass; and it had the feel of something primal, not merely ancient like the dusty cities of Iraq, home to abundant, squabbling humans for millennia, but prehistoric and almost undisturbed by man – except for Indians, abiding once in isolated and tranquil camps where they summered, fished for six-hundred pound sturgeon, coated themselves with mud to keep off the flies and wove unique, conical headgear from the sedges; and where they blithely and without remorse killed and enslaved those of other encampments, separated from themselves by a muddy mile or two and only a forgotten generation or three and looking exactly alike except for the tell-tale hats, constructed differently – the land below thus in relative witness to only unrecorded and small-scale misdemeanors compared to the noteworthy, historic carnages of the Fertile Crescent I'd overflown eighteen months before, each and every slaughter in the eventual process of being catechized and avenged – if not today, perhaps tomorrow or the next day. Away from the River and north were farms.

"Show me where you were last night."

I talked to the pilot: "turn left, slow down, follow the River. There's the marina. I was parked there." I pointed to the parking lot. "We were downriver when Emily decided not to shoot me. Probably two miles." We circled the area twice.

"Where can we put down?" asked Ayers. "I want to think a bit and make some calls."

"The parking lot's full, but there's a field west of the marina. Whatever they grew there's been harvested."

"Put her down in the field, Matt," said Ayers to the pilot. "Then shut everything down. I can't hear myself think."

•••

So Matt the Pilot put her down, shut her down and then did pilot things with switches, toggles, controls and instruments. Ayers took off her headset, pulled out an old-fashioned clipboard and ballpoint pen, and began writing. "I'm a throwback," she said, holding up the pen. Then she focused on some numbers she was summing.

"How can I help?"

"You can't. In fact, I'm considering possible confirmation bias in the theory you've offered when I asked you 'what you thought this was all about'."

"What does that mean?"

"Once folks settle on a theory, they tend to self-confirm that theory by observing subsequent events within its framework. The FBI is big on worrying about self-confirmed bias. Someone's named it 'confirmation bias'; and the seminar I attended used climate science as a big-picture example of it in action. You know – we're having a hot summer, so it must be Global Warming. At any rate, I need time to think about alternative theories about what might be happening; and I need to make recommendations as to a course of action by the Bureau that covers all hypotheses. This clipboard and this pen help me think – they're like Sherlock Holmses's violin."

"Didn't he use opium too?"

"I don't know. I think he had a cocaine addiction. I don't. He was fictional. I'm not. I'll be at least thirty minutes. To Matt the Pilot she said: "Go have a walk around." To me she said: "you too

Watson."

I dropped out of the helicopter, feeling naked without helmet, pack, body armor and a squad of armed young men following. Matt was already touching various parts of his machine with care – an opened tool case was on the ground. I knew that there would be no voluntary conversation with him while he attended to the machine he probably loved, dreamed about and had secretly named. I thought of a similar machine, likely lying on its side in the mud and grass and I decided to visit it. "Matt," I said, "tell Agent Ayers that I'll be back in twenty minutes." I took off jogging, headed for Emily's abandoned motorcycle.

• • •

Two ten minute miles, a check on the cycle, maybe move it somewhere and a jog back – that was my thinking as I moved along at a relaxed pace, with none of the rage that had propelled me in the opposite direction just the night before. The leisurely jog permitted thinking, so I thought, asking myself questions: what about self-confirmed bias, was I subject to that, was I missing something important, had I told Agent Ayers about Devlin Meyer's belief about money being involved – I hadn't, had I? Soon I was back at the crossroads, the abandoned gas station and the place where I'd left Emily's motorcycle.

It was still there, glaring up at me from the weeds, muddy and annoyed at the abuse it had suffered at my hands. Like a seventy year-old monarch, standing in a chill morning watching the broken wheel of a carriage being fixed by a backwoods blacksmith, the cycle implied that it had better things to do than to lay in the mud waiting for Emily. I agreed with it; and I lifted it up and wheeled it out to the gravel shoulder of the road. In spite of the mud, in the light of day and vertical, on its kickstand, the Royal Enfield was a noble beast, a World War II olive green and clearly a he, as Emily had insisted. The panniers over the back wheel seemed to be unlocked; and so I looked inside.

The right side pannier held one of Uncle Ryan's security cameras – the left a solitary key. The key fit in the ignition. I straddled the cycle. I turned the key. Considering a mere overnight in a muddy New Jersey field a trifle compared to the cold rain of the four battles of Monte Casino, the engine overhaul prior to Anzio, and the new brakes installed for use in the alps, the engine coughed just once and started. I kicked up the stand and motored carefully towards Ayers, Matt the Pilot and the helicopter.

AN BRISTE LASADH
CHAPTER THIRTY-ONE

I rode the motorcycle and thought: so this is what a motorcycle is all about. I loved the experience. It was nothing like driving a car. Car-driving is passive and safe. The driver of a car is a look-out-the-window spectator on autopilot. Riding the Royal Enfield required all my attention and felt very unsafe. It connected me not only to the road and surrounding fields, but to the air, the sky, the sun, the weather – it was noisy, fast sailing – on land.

We went fast. I wished I knew the cycle's name. I was certain Emily had given it a good one. I told myself that the faster I went, the less likely I'd be to fall over; and I was certain there was some formula – probably involving baffling terms such as speed, acceleration, force, torque, mass and so forth that would support my opinion. So we went even faster, and we found ourselves aimed just to the right of the helicopter at a very noisy sixty-five miles per hour.

Out of my left eye, I saw Matt the Pilot stand and watch us; and when I'd slowed, turned around and headed back the way we'd come, there was Agent Ayers watching too. I imagined that fun time for Ryan was over, and I eased the cycle over the field to our audience and shut it down.

"Smyrl told me you were capable of the unexpected," said Ayers.

"It's beautiful," said Matt the Pilot. "I think it's a World War II Enfield. I mean a 'Royal Enfield'. 350cc. Durable. British-made."

I parked the cycle, lowered the kickstand and stood away from it. It was still muddy, of course, but seemed noble and glorious anyway. "It's Emily's," I said to Ayers.

"The Emily?"

"Yes. She paid seventy-thousand dollars for it. I suppose it's a classic."

"Who told you that?"

"Her sister. Clemmie. I mentioned her at the West End – in your interview."

"You didn't mention the motorcycle."

"Didn't I? If you say so. Is it important?"

"Probably not. But it makes me wonder if there's anything that is important you forgot to mention."

"Like my own small version of confirmation bias?"

"Right. Whether you know it or not, you've had a theory or theories about this in your head since last Friday night. It – or they – are not all true."

"Maybe."

"Well, for one, for four days you thought your dog was dead – she wasn't. Every thought you had for those four days involving your dog was wrong. Right?"

"Smokey. Her name is Smokey. I suppose you're right."

"I am right."

I was not in the Marine Corps anymore; and some Company Commander couldn't make my life miserable over a tarnished belt buckle, and a sergeant couldn't disassemble my rifle and plant it in a giant sand-filled ash tray. I was a fucking civilian who volunteered to help the FBI sort this out. "Okay. You are right. You couldn't be righter. You are the most right person I know. Okay?"

Matt the Pilot excused himself and walked around his 'copter, needing to be away from whatever came next.

• • •

Agent Ayers glared at me. I supposed she was giving me the traditional ten count before she unloaded. If she was still channeling Sherlock Holmes, it would be understated but hurtful and patronizing – something along the lines of: "Elementary, Watson. You know my methods – it is a capital mistake to theorize before you have all the evidence – it biases the judgment. When you have eliminated the impossible, whatever remains, however improbable, must be the truth. Of course the motorcycle ('motorbike' in Holmsian) plays a role in transpiring events. In fact, I am quite certain that the stolen matched black pearls are located in the false bottom of the starboard pannier."

But Ayers surprised me. She let me off the hook. "Is there anything else you've forgotten to mention?"

I sighed. "Not that I can think of right now. Unless what someone else thinks is important actually matters."

"What do you mean?"

"An old guy, name of Devlin Meyer, lives on a boat in my Uncle Ryan's marina – he's got an opinion."

"And that opinion is?"

"That whatever is going on is all about money."

"I can't see how messing about on Chester Island, at night, burying empty missile boxes, or even using ground-to-air missiles makes anyone money."

"I can't either. I'm pretty sure I have not used that opinion in any of my very own confirmation biases."

"Who is this Devlin Meyer?"

"I don't know. He's very old – maybe ninety. He lives on a boat. He is a retired 'salvage consultant' – whatever that is."

"Sounds like a crank."

"Maybe. But Uncle Ryan is a very good judge of people, and he respects Devlin. Devlin is the one who told me it was unlikely that Emily shot 'Bama. Before he said that, I was sure that she had. He also said that there was an advantage to me somehow, since Emily didn't know that I knew – whatever it is I know."

"Interesting thinking for a ninety year-old. I suppose a follow-up is in order, but not now. The idea that it's all about money is definitely outside all the various hypotheses I've considered; and I've got to act on what I know. I've already got alternate theories about 'Bama being either alive or being dead."

"I don't suppose you can tell me what you intend to do."

"Right. I can't."

"I don't want to know anyway. I want to take Emily's motorcycle to her sister and let the professionals handle everything else." I saluted, and got a quick grin from Ayers.

Matt the Pilot had returned from his bunker on the other side of his big machine. "You can't ride the motorcycle in New Jersey without a helmet."

"Are you sure?" I said. "I see folks without helmets on motorcycles all the time."

"That's in Pennsylvania. New Jersey enforces helmet laws."

"Any suggestions? I don't think I should leave it here."

"We could take it with us," said Matt. He was enthusiastic about this idea. "We could rig something. We could carry it on the starboard side, just over the landing skid. The two of you would have to sit on the port side, though."

"How long would it take to rig?" asked Ayers.

"No more than ten minutes. Where are we going next?"

"Back to the West End. Alright – stopwatch on. Go to it."

I was beginning to like Matt. He was a member of that brotherhood of left-brained men who could fix things without reading the manual – and, in fact sometimes couldn't read the manual – and who took metal shop and wood shop in high school and stuck with it, and filled their parents' coffee tables with ball-peen hammered copper and brass ashtrays and who still had the bookshelves they used to hold the books that only their wives read. These were the same men who became astronauts, engineers and pilots if they were lucky and good and hard-working enough, and who became carpenters, plumbers and roofers if their luck, skill and work ethic was average, and who – if their luck was bad enough – used their mesothelioma settlement check for a one-time trip to Atlantic City with their former wife and their monthly disability checks for beer and cigarettes.

Ayers and I wheeled the Enfield over to the helicopter and lifted the cycle up long enough for Matt to secure it to the copter's starboard side with nylon straps.

Ayers glanced at her watch. "Six minutes. Let's go."

So we flew back to the West End, the helicopter an osprey, the Enfield a fish; and when we landed, we had the usual small crowd watching. As soon as the blades stopped thwop-thwopping, the onlookers crowded around while we detached the motorcycle from the helicopter. Ayers headed for the clubhouse, Rizzo and FBI duties.

"You go first," I said to Matt. "You deserve it."

His face lit up. "Okay." He could have been the Gary Cooper – Will Kane character in High Noon saying: I've got to, that's the whole thing; and he hopped on the Enfield, fired it up and rode it to the entrance to the Club. He waited until he turned the corner, out of sight, before he hit the gas and we heard the cycle's VROOOM – WAAANNNGGG aimed east, up Essington's Second Street. On the return trip, to everyone's delight and applause, he downshifted – BRAAAAAP – BRAAAAAP – inside the Club grounds and ground to a gravel-crunching stop five feet from the crowd.

"You're up," he said.

I couldn't say no in front of Club members who still regarded me as a sort of junior member, almost a kid, a sailboater who'd been allowed to join and get a decent boat slip because of his Uncle Ryan. Besides, three of the Club members watching – Paul, Tommy and Richie – rode motorcycles, and turning down a chance to ride the Enfield in front of them would have been cause for a lifetime of ribbing. The trio considered themselves bikers, which over time I'd come to realize did not mean getting tattooed, cooking up crystal meth, or biking out to Sturgis to drink and fight; but meant debating the relative merits of different models of Harleys, riding to the Eastern Shore for crabs and beer twice each summer, and polishing their cycles on Sunday mornings in their own special place in the West End parking lot. So I repeated Matt's short trip on the cycle, and managed some of the same noise and speed; and I believe my status at the Club rose – at least a little.

• • •

Agent Ayers called to me to join her inside, Matt got out his toolbox and began servicing his helicopter; and Paul, Tommy and Richie decided to clean up the Royal Enfield. When I entered the pool room – command center, I saw that Rizzo's efforts were all high-tech – streaming live video, multiple spreadsheets and related charts and graphs, databases up, file-sharing and messaging ongoing; while Ayers was sitting there thinking, relying on her ballpoint pen and clipboard.

"There doesn't seem to be a real person named Devlin Meyer," she said to me as I sat down in a corner booth. "Do you know how to spell his name?"

"No. I could ask Uncle Ryan."

"That's okay. If you talk to him anyway, ask him. Otherwise forget it."

"What can I do now to help?"

"Probably nothing. Give me about twenty minutes to think and work with Rizzo here, then we'll talk."

The two of them began talking in FBI jargon. It was close to a foreign language, full of acronyms and initials – SAC, ASAC, Brick Agent, flash bangs, GOV, high speed/low drag. I tuned out and decided to look at my phone to see if I'd had calls or texts while we were helicoptering around. There were three text messages from Clemmie. Each said "call me." I did, and she picked up on the second ring.

"Ryan."

"Clemmie."

"Where are you?"

"At the West End."

"You're at your boat club!"

"Yes, but . . . ."

She was pissed. "Ryan O'Brien – you bastard! You're fishing or sailing or drinking while I'm sitting here worrying about my sister. I skipped two classes today! You text me 'Emily is alive' – that's all you tell me – and you promise to call. You don't. You are failing this test. No – I take it back. You flunked. What about Emily?"

"But Clemmie, I couldn't call." At this point, Agent Ayers came over and signaled for me to end the call. She did this by covering my phone with one hand, a finger across her neck with the other and mouthing "now" with her mouth.

I ended the call. "That's going to cost me a girlfriend," I said. "She's worried sick about her sister."

"We'll go talk to her. She isn't supposed to know the FBI is looking for Emily, in case Emily calls her."

"Who will interview her? When will that be?"

"It might as well be me, and it might as well be now, and you might as well drive me. There's no GOV here, you know where we're going. But we need to surprise her."

"Great. I just hung up on her, now I'm bringing the FBI to surprise her. She doesn't deserve this. She's a great person. A terrific person who used to think I was okay too."

"Let's go."

We went.

• • •

During the half hour ride in my car to Clemmie's apartment, Ayers doodled on her clipboard, made three jargon-filled calls on her phone and then turned to me. "Call your Uncle Ryan now. Ask him about Devlin Meyer."

I handed her my phone and told her to speed dial my uncle. She did, and handed the phone back to me. "Don't mention the FBI."

"Uncle Ryan."

"Ryan. You're overdue. What's up?"

"I've only got a minute and I'm in my car. Let me put you on the speaker and put my phone down. I'll tell you all about it later. I've got a question for you. How do you spell Devlin Meyer's name?"

"It's just like it sounds. On our log-in sheet it's: 'D-E-V-L-I-N M-E-Y-E-R'. Why? Does it matter?"

"Someone working on the case is interested and wants to know."

"The murder case?"

"Well, yes."

"Is it Smyrl? Let me talk to him."

"No, it's not Smyrl. You can't talk to them right now. Later maybe."

"Well," said Uncle Ryan, "if I were to be talking to someone I trusted, and if I thought it was important, well then I'd tell them that Devlin Meyer is not his real name."

"What's his real name?"

"I don't know. Before he left on his mysterious boat ride, in his little runabout, he admitted that he'd combined his mother's maiden name with that of a friend. He said he just wanted me to know. 'In case,' he said. Then he took off."

"Well okay. When he gets back, ask him. I don't think it's super important, but someone's just touching every base. I think they wonder what Devlin means by 'it's all about the money'."

"Fine, but I'm not sure he'll be back. He's ninety years old, he's out in a skiff and we're got line squalls headed our way. Plus, I made him take Oscar with him when he left the dock yesterday, and Oscar turned up here this morning with a note in a plastic baggie tied to his collar. In it Devlin said not to look for him – no matter what. In other words, I don't really know who he is, why he's here or if I'll ever see him again."

"But he's left his big boat there, right?"

"Yes, and he's got Mikey living in it. The two of them hit it off. Mikey's never worked so hard around here; and Sissie says we owe it to Devlin."

Ayers whispered to me to ask the next two questions. "What's his big boat like?"

"It's a glorified half houseboat, half trawler. It's old, wooden and has a lounge, a big galley and a master stateroom with a king-sized bed. Oh. And you can see where it's had its original name removed."

"What's its new name?"

"*An Briste Lasadh.*" He spelled it for us, and Ayers wrote the name on her clipboard.

"Do you know if that's a foreign language?" I asked.

"No idea," said Uncle Ryan. "I do know this. Devlin is a great guy. A man's man. I think he was taking someone's ashes to scatter. He had a wooden box – an urn maybe. Listen – I've got to go. I'm in the middle of something and, like I said, there's a line squall coming. Call me tonight if you can."

"Thanks Uncle Ryan."

Ayers looked at me and shrugged. "He knew there was someone listening, didn't he?"

"You can't fool Uncle Ryan. You'd like him – 'though he's more of a Sam Spade or a Travis McGee than a Sherlock Holmes. And I know exactly where he was – he was out in his boat, *Sissie*, looking for Devlin. Here's Clemmie's. Now to find a parking spot. There aren't many around here in the student ghetto."

"Don't worry about it. Double park. Display this." She took a small sign from her clipboard that read: "FBI OPERATION". It listed a phone number to call. I put it on the dashboard; and sat in the car as Ayers commanded, while she climbed the stairs to Clemmie's apartment.

ICE CREAM FOR BREAKFAST
CHAPTER THIRTY-TWO

It had been a full day. I was tired. I'd fought a man who'd had
killing me in mind. I'd had a crazy woman sit behind me in an
inflatable dinghy with an M4 carbine, and consider whether or not
to shoot me. I'd had a sail in *Larke* with Sam, an FBI interview,
helicopter flights, and motorcycle rides – all on not much to eat
and a few beers to drink; and as I began to wait, a petty god – a
minor contributor, once, to the violent narrative of a dead religion
– sensed that I was susceptible and caused me to sleep and worry,
hoping I would be entertaining enough to captivate other jaded
deities invited over to watch, with Jell-O shooters of ambrosia and
mead chasers and a manna-wing eating contest – thereby
attempting an incremental social climb of one small step on the
timeless staircase that begins in a dusty basement of hell where no
one lives and nothing ever happens and ends, before eternity is
finished, in one of the busy and appealing heavens. So bidden, I
obliged, sleeping and worrying – backwards and first anxious over
the whereabouts of a ninety year-old man I'd never met who was
out in a line squall somewhere between the south coast of Florida

and the Keys in a little boat he'd called a runabout and named *Munequita*, toting a friend's ashes in a wooden urn and unconcerned about his own life. So why should I worry?

Next came Uncle Ryan, who was out in the same line squall amidst crackling thunderbolts, abrupt winds, sudden eight-foot waves and dime-sized hail – out with Oscar in *Sissie*, with the human Sissie worried sick; but already so competent as to have run his boat hard aground on the lee side of one of the countless small and empty islands and hurried his anchor fifty yards into grass and mud and huddled under his oilskin poncho with Oscar, telling the dog not to worry, and that after all, he, Oscar, had survived much worse when he was a puppy, alone on the mean streets of the slow-motion disaster of a city named Chester. Oscar was not, of course, worried about himself anyway, but concerned only for Uncle Ryan – the perfect person he'd managed to find, own and keep; and his occasional whine was only to tell Uncle Ryan not to worry. And so, worrying about each other, neither of them required my concern.

I skipped worrying about Agents Ayers and Rizzo and Matt the Pilot, since they were FBI, competent, armed and trained, so no one needed to worry for them – although worrying about them seemed a little appropriate, especially if one was a criminal or could in any way be mistaken for one. But there in my own, unstolen car, with a valid driver's license in my wallet and no unpaid parking tickets residing in a City of Philadelphia computer, I was not a criminal – and could not possibly mistaken for one, except for someone named Bardeaux, who likely didn't really mistake me for a criminal, but was possibly one herself and therefore not worthy of my worry either.

Worrying about Sam Barrett was an option – after all, he was sixty-seven years old and had just undergone surgery for prostate cancer. But he had a wife, Eleanor, to worry about him; and I suspected that she knew best how to worry about Sam from years of love and practice and would do a much better job of it than I ever could. Besides that, he not only had a job, but owned the company – or half owned it – where I hoped to work someday; and anyway, if he knew I was worried about him it would piss him off no end.

I thought of Emily and 'Bama as one combined potential worry; and quickly realized that even though Emily was Clemmie's twin sister, I should be worried about them, but not for them. He was a murderer; she was crazy. They were the ones carrying around Pakistani ground-to-air missiles for some project that had been in the works for "two years". Besides, 'Bama had tried to kill me and Emily had stolen my car and, much worse, lied to Clemmie about me. She'd told Clemmie I was out looking for more condoms – surely a hateful, hurtful lie – unless she'd been lying to me about saying those words to Clemmie. They were stricken from my worry-list.

Concerned that I was not cooperating with the planned viewing of Human Worry, and potentially diminishing his social status, the god, who introduced himself as "Narvi", sent me thoughts of Sister Alberta (she with the incarcerated nephew with the size 14 sneakers), of Jameson Jones (Reverend with complete responsibility for a small and likely penniless church as well as the proper preparation of the legendarily hard-to-cook, patience-requiring foodstuff called scrapple), of Nashir (an orphan, from one place, country and continent nearly bereft of hope to another such place where a fictional character named Travis McGee was throwing him a slender lifeline); calculating that even Ryan O'Brien, an oblivious not-to-worry type (and why should I be, given survival of recent events as well as far-away places named Iraq and Afghanistan) would crank up his latent worry skills for his impatient audience. Surely these were folks worth worrying about. Then – BAM! BAM again – on the windshield.

It was Agent Ayers. "Rise and shine, Watson."

I did, stumbling out of my place of incipient worry.

"I see that you can sleep anywhere."

"Pretty much."

"Good for you. Your turn with Clemmie."

"She'll talk to me?"

"She was pissed. But I did my part for true love – something I know nothing about, by the way."

"Don't you need my car?"

"A GOV is minutes away. Adios. I'll be in touch. Thanks for the help." She reached out her right hand and gave mine a brief, firm shake. She turned me around and gave a little push up the walk to Clemmie's apartment.

. . .

The eventful day, a lack of sleep and little food had me feeling far below par. I suppose I looked less than my best as well, something Clemmie confirmed when she opened the door to her apartment.

"Ryan. You look terrible."

"I feel worse."

"Come in. I just spent an hour with Agent Ayers. She's a trip."

I made a tentative entrance, and stood just inside her door. "She's very competent."

"Come all the way in here. Ayers has me even more worried about Emily than I already was."

"Why's that?"

"Sit down." She pointed to an old sofa. "I'm not supposed to talk about it."

I sat. Clemmie stood. "Not even to me?"

"That's what she said. She might have even said especially to you."

"I thought you were pissed at me. Are you?"

"Not anymore. Ayers told me what you'd been doing today – at least some of it."

"Well you should be."

"Should be what?"

"Pissed."

"If that's what you want."

"It's not what I want. It's probably what I deserve."

"Okay. How's this?" Clemmie pasted an angry look on her face, pointed a finger at me and let me have it. "Ryan O'Brien, you bastard! Why didn't you call me this morning? You knew I'd be worried sick about Emily. If this is the best you can do – well, it's not good enough. All those nice things your Uncle Ryan said about you are bullshit! You flunked this test! What have you got to say for yourself?"

"Wow!" I said. "I'd do a lot to stay off your blacklist."

"It's not a blacklist, Ryan – whatever that is. It is my own very personal shit list – a list that is a very bad place to be. You've worked very hard to get on it; and you'll have to work harder to get off it." Then she smiled, took her finger out of my face and said: "how was that?"

"Frightening," I said. "Terrifying. Worse than anything I experienced in Iraq or Afghanistan. May I attempt an apology?"

"Sure. Give it a shot. Good luck. You'll need it. It better be good."

"Okay. Here goes. I, Ryan O'Brien offer you, Clemmie Olsen, a sincere apology for not calling you this morning. I should have called you as soon as I got up. I realize that you must have been worried about Emily. I've got some lame excuses for my behavior, but none of them are valid. I am sorry. I'm not sorry because you're angry with me and I don't want you to be – I'm sorry because I made you worry enough to miss classes. Again – I'm sorry. I hope very much that we can get over this."

"Okay. I hear you. That sounded sincere."

"Good – because it was."

"Was what?"

"Sincere."

"Right. Now I have a question for you."

"Shoot."

"Do you want to stop this dance we're doing right now, or do you want me to keep playing the music."

"Music?"

"You know: you apologize, I sort of accept the apology, you feel guilty, I'm a little distant, you get worried and buy me something – flowers, probably, I enhance my control over our relationship a little, you take me out to dinner someplace too expensive and dressy – someplace neither of us really wants to go, and the whole thing goes on for three or four days until we kiss and make up."

"That sounds terrible – except for the kiss part. I guess I want to know how you really feel about this; but maybe I should go first."

"Okay. You go first."

"Alright. Here goes. Sometimes you find out – at least I find out – how I really feel about something or someone when I find myself telling someone else how I feel. It's like the decision was made in my own mind, kept secret from me until I told someone else. Know what I mean?"

"No, but I might if you ever cut to the chase."

"Clemmie. I've recently told three or four people that you are someone 'I'm going to fall in love with'. I am headed in that direction."

"That's sweet, Ryan. I like you too. My turn."

"Okay."

"I was more worried about you than I was about Emily. I figured you were out late fooling around with something that almost got you killed once, got you arrested once and that whatever you were doing might be the end of you. And that would be the end of us. And I didn't want that to happen. And I feel weird about this, since we've only known each other for a day and a half."

"It's been a busy day and a half, though."

"True. But I'm not finished."

"Okay."

"All that stuff I said about apologies, making up, flowers, guilt – all that. I don't like any of it. It all seems phony to me. I don't want any of it."

"Not even the kiss?"

"Stop about the kiss. Here." She kissed me. It was not a this-is-the-start-of-something-big kiss, but neither was it a hi-nice-to-see-you kiss. It was something in between – kind of an I-have-some-promising-affection-for-you kiss.

"Thanks," I said.

"You're welcome," she said. "And let's hold off on the "L" word for now."

"Well, I haven't really used it. I only told other people that I was maybe going to fall in love with you. I didn't tell you, yet, that I had fallen in love with you."

"Okay. I hope you have fallen in like with me, though; because I like you right back. And now that that's all sorted out, I think you need some food."

"Sounds great. What've you got?"

"Not much. Macaroni and Cheese, hot dogs, ramen noodles – the usual impoverished college student stuff."

"It all sounds great. How about two or three microwaved hot dogs, mac and cheese and the ramen noodles for desert?"

"Fine. Sit there," she said, indicating a stool next to a Formica kitchen counter. "I've already eaten. I'll make this for you, then I've got to duck out to get notes from someone from today's classes. Let's forget the ramen; and I'll bring back ice cream for desert."

"I'll buy."

"You sure will."

Clemmie heated up a pot of macaroni and cheese, handed me a napkin, a knife and a fork, and nuked the hot dogs after slicing them a few times. "Mustard?"

"Please."

"To drink?"

"Options?"

"Tap water. Orange juice, an old can of beer or an old ginger ale."

"Water."

"Excellent choice." She ran the faucet for a few seconds, filled a large glass and put it on the counter.

Then she wrapped the hot dogs in slices of bread and stuck toothpicks in them to keep the wrapped and put them on a plate; then she emptied the macaroni and cheese into a bowl and put everything in front of me.

Then Clemmie headed for her door. "Back soon. Twenty minutes."

• • •

I don't know if Clemmie returned in twenty minutes or not, because in fifteen minutes I'd eaten, washed my dish, knife, fork and glass, placed them in the dry rack and fallen asleep on her couch – shoes beside me on the floor.

When I woke up at 2:30 a.m., the lights were out and Clemmie was in her bedroom with the door almost closed. I fought the need to use the bathroom for a few minutes, then gave up and got up. The bathroom could only be accessed through Clemmie's bedroom. I put on one dim fluorescent kitchen counter light, and shuffled over to the bedroom door, opened it enough to enter, and felt my way along the wall to the bathroom. The bathroom had no windows, and was pitch black, so I shut the door and turned on the light. I was as careful and quiet as possible. When I was finished, I replaced the toilet seat in the down position, turned out the light, opened the door and started back along the wall out of the bedroom. I was certain that I'd not awakened Clemmie.

"Ryan. Is that you?"

"Yes. I'm sorry I woke you up."

"I was half awake anyway."

"Thanks for letting me sleep on your couch."

"Come here."

I sat on the edge of her bed.

"You can sleep here if you want."

It was a double bed, there was room for me.

"Are you sure this is a good idea?"

"Well, I'm awake now anyway, you're up and awake. Better we be awake here together than awake in separate rooms. So yes, I think it's a good idea."

I lay down beside her. Clemmie threw a cover over me. We stared at the ceiling together, both lost for words. After five minutes of silence, we let our hearts take over, and we were very wide awake for the next two hours, with no talking, just touching and loving – with tenderness and awareness of need. I don't pretend to know precisely what happened that night to the two of us; but I am dead certain that we were not engaging in a simple pleasant social favor. Clemmie was a woman of pride and emotional complexity; and I hoped I would have the years I would need to understand her; and I hoped she would always find me worthy of the act of love. When we exhausted our physical selves and felt that sleep was a distinct possibility, Clemmie wedged herself into my side and mumbled: "I love us. Ice cream for breakfast."

Bring On the Quotidian
Chapter Thirty-Three

I did not wake up when Clemmie got up. She showered, dressed, ate and left me a message that said she'd gone to classes and wouldn't be back until mid-afternoon. When I finally rolled out of bed, I found my car keys on top of a note that said she'd moved the car to a legal parking spot around the corner; and next to the note there was a perfect tiny map with an "X" on it to indicate the car's location. I ate the other half of the gallon of ice cream for breakfast, as an acknowledgement that I'd heard Clemmie's whispered words correctly last night – especially the "I love us". I left her a note that was as borderline banal as the two she'd left me, telling her that I would call her after her classes, that I wouldn't forget this time, and that I wanted more ice cream for breakfast soon.

And so late that Friday morning I began what stretched into three days of normal life, a life without fights, guns, arrests, ground-to-air missiles, helicopters, motorcycles or much in the way of excitement of any kind. It was as if a genie popped out of the bottle and granted me my wish when I'd said "bring on the quotidian." And because I acknowledged to myself that I'd fallen, hard, for Clemmie, the quotidian was just fine; and for the first time in my life, I felt no risk, no vulnerability in my commitment to a woman.

I must have looked or acted differently somehow, because when I drove to Sam Barrett's to pick up Smokey, his wife Eleanor asked me right away about Clemmie, "that nice young woman you were with the other day." She laughed at me when I pretended to be puzzled. I was grateful that Sam preempted further discussion by asking me what else had happened after he'd gone home and I'd gotten on a helicopter.

He was disappointed when I told him the missile crates were filled with dirt. He'd hoped his metal detector had ended a terrorist plot. "I'd like to see the motorcycle," he said. "It must be something special for $70,000."

"I'm keeping it at the West End. Next time we're there, you can ride it."

"I'd like you to come to work on Monday."

"Great. Do I have a job then?"

"It's almost official. I've given your application to Ms. Tarry-Brigham-Smith, using my grades, references, board scores and so forth. After I've been rejected for a job in my own company, I'll talk to Bud Howell about it. Hell, he couldn't get a job at Howell & Barrett either. In the meantime, you'll work on a contract basis, on one of the ideas you had – the only one with potential."

"Which one?"

"The disaster investing idea. The other two were rejected by the committee that considers new ideas. No one really understood the absentials theory. It was considered quirky and interesting, but potentially requiring half of the computer resources in North America. They gave me credit for creativity, though. They figured I'd come up with it in the hospital, while drugged."

"You came up with it?"

"I wanted the committee to really think about it. I knew they'd give something they thought came from me serious consideration. Don't worry. You'll get credit – or blame – eventually."

"How about the other idea?"

"Someone did backtesting, using a commodity. They used the price of gold, the value of a large gold mining company and two related E.T.F.'s. They found all kinds of correlations and investment buying possibilities when, intraday, the company's stock traded down relative to the commodity and the E.T.F.'s. Opposite opportunities existed on the short side. But they believe that any significant buying or short-selling of the stock would affect the outcome. In other words, the theory makes sense, but you probably can't use it to make money. The experiment itself upsets the results – something like the observer effect in quantum mechanics. I didn't know that, of course, but one of the geniuses who couldn't pass my coffee-making employment test did. Maybe a small daytrader could use the approach. More importantly – I've made sure your Fitness-Plex membership is active."

· · ·

When I left Sam's, I called Uncle Ryan, to make sure he'd made it through the line squall okay. He picked up on the first ring, told me he and Oscar had had an adventure, were both fine, that Devlin was still missing and that the Coast Guard presumed he was dead. Michael was living in *An Briste Lasadh* and was working hard enough around the marina to lose his nickname, Mikey – a suggestion that had been Devlin's. I hinted a little about Clemmie and he observed that he was at least partially responsible for that connection. I told him of my adventures with the FBI, and we both felt deprived of Devlin's advice in the matter. We both remembered Devlin's repeated suggestion that it 'was all about the money', although neither of us could figure how that could be. We promised to keep in touch; he wished me luck in my job. I terminated the call, smiling.

It was apparently my lucky cellphone day, and I got Smyrl to answer his own phone. Although he was officially still the detective investigating Marvin's murder, he was unofficially off the case while the FBI did their thing. Besides, he said, he'd been assigned the murders of two tourists in Atlantic City – brutal, extravagantly publicized knife killings in a casino parking lot; and his superiors had him going 24/7 on that crime. When I observed that an awful lot had happened since Marvin's killing last Saturday morning – early – he literally did not know what I was talking about; and I realized that the world he lived in was pretty much always like that. There was nothing quotidian about Smyrl's working life. I told him I'd stay in touch and to keep his galoshes buckled, and he laughed and told me to please stay out of New Jersey for awhile. Just before he hung up, he remembered that the Inquirer had agreed to issue a correction concerning their article naming me a suspect in Marvin's death.

Feeling lucky, I called the Reverend Jameson Jones and hit the trifecta of three cellphone hits in a row.

"Pilgrim."

"Reverend."

"When will we see you next?"

"I'm thinking of tomorrow morning. How's the scrapple supply?"

"Always good. Breakfast for the children, eat, clean up some reading with Nashir. Right?"

"What time?"

"Best be here at seven-thirty, seven-forty five. Bring your girlfriend."

"Clemmie?"

"Well you better not have some other girlfriend this fast."

"Who said she was my girlfriend?"

"Sister Alberta. She's not usually wrong about such matters. Is she?"

"Well, I wish she'd have told me. Saved me some worry. See you tomorrow. I'll ask Clemmie."

• • •

Then I went home to my apartment and enjoyed an afternoon of glorious routine: dog-walking, e-mail answering and laundry-gathering. At the nearby Laundromat, I washed all my clothes and sheets together, on hot; and then dried everything together in one of the giant driers. I found the dry-cycle particularly relaxing. There was nothing I was supposed to be doing, other than sitting right there on that bench outside of that Laundromat, in the sunshine on that beautiful day, waiting for those clothes to dry. For the first time in days, I felt that whatever god had been moving me around on his or her colossal chessboard, requiring blind, immediate obedience, had taken a break from the game; and I would have been content to sit there with Smokey underfoot until the fine copper light of late afternoon fizzed to dark.

The ding-buzz of the drier announced the completion of my laundry; and I folded it, stacked it in a plastic tub and carried it home on top my head, left arm balancing it, right hand holding Smokey's unnecessary leash. Happiness is as contagious as misery, and people I passed on the two blocks of sidewalk to my apartment smiled back at me. Perhaps I grinned at them first. Perhaps the whole Ryan-Smokey-laundry show was amusing. I didn't know or care. I was happy enough for the whole City of Philadelphia; and I was glad that it showed.

I put clean sheets on the bed in the hope that there would be ice cream for breakfast at my apartment soon. I neatened the apartment. I did some food shopping. I reviewed the remaining Chester Island security camera and the four others Uncle Ryan and

I had planted. There was nothing of real interest on any of them, except my own pleasure in recognizing the same six deer within view of the camera on the power line tower every morning at dawn, coming to drink from the weedy bank of the Old Canal and invariably raising their heads, stretching their necks and gazing directly at the camera, set thirty-five feet over their heads and thirty yards away – their eyes ghostlike and knowing. I printed out a frame to show Clemmie, to ask her what she thought about the deer; since I wanted to know what she thought about everything.

When I called Clemmie that afternoon, I found out that she thought she should be responsible and study that night, to make up for slacking off over worries about Emily. But she agreed to be with me Saturday and Sunday – at least up until she had to work Sunday afternoon. She told me to pick something to do one day and she'd pick something to do the other day. I picked Saturday – morning at the Church of Jesus Christ is Lord, and the rest of the day to be determined; and Clemmie told me she'd think about what we'd do on Sunday.

• • •

By seven-thirty Saturday morning, Clemmie, Smokey and I were in Chester, and in the kitchen of the house-that-doubled-as-a-church. Clemmie was setting the table for the kids that would start arriving at eight, Smokey was under the table enjoying the breakfast smells, Jameson and I were slicing scrapple and beating up dozens of eggs. Sister Alberta looked in a few times, nodding in approval; and told us to use our last names in front of the kids.

So the kids waited on the porch and we called them in to feed them four at a time, ten minutes per sitting. Nashir ate in the last sitting, and seemed even quieter than usual. Miss Olsen made toast and poured orange juice, Mister O'Brien got the hang of scrapple-frying and stuck with that, while the Reverend Jones dealt with scrambled eggs. By nine o'clock, the children were finished eating and Sister Alberta was leading them through some of the same hymns I'd heard before. We chefs, waiters, dishwashers, friends and lovers ate breakfast while listening through an open door.

I joined Nashir on the porch at ten o'clock; and we sat down to continue reading *Darker Than Amber*. Nashir handed me the battered paperback, frowned, and turned to the middle of the book.

"I don't understand this – these pages," he said.

I looked at the book and scanned the four or five pages that were giving Nashir difficulty. It was a section of the book where Travis McGee asked questions of a black maid who turned out to be an undercover regional director of CORE, a University of Michigan graduate who was helpful in McGee's investigation of the murder that fueled much of the book's plot. But Nashir understood all of that – what he couldn't comprehend was some of Travis's musing about black-white relationships. Nashir read these words to me, daring me to explain them:

> . . . *about the demanding of racial equality for those with whom, except for the Struggle, they would not willingly associate. They say Now, knowing that only fifteen percent of Negro America is responsible enough to handle the realities of Now, and that, in the hard core South, perhaps seventy percent of the whites are willing to accept the obligations of Now.*

I took the book in hand and turned to the copyright page and pointed to the "1966". "That was then. This is now," I said, hoping that would be sufficient to get us back to the simpler visual story of murders and a taut-stretched plot boiling over with action and complex characters. No such luck.

"But what does that mean" asked Nashir, "the fifteen percent, the Now, the seventy percent?"

"The book was written forty-seven years ago," I said. "It's all different now."

Nashir banged the butt of the staff on the ground in frustration. I thought about John D. MacDonald, who'd frequently aimed his millions of words at Florida's environmental problems – brought about by the influx of people; and he'd nailed the State's languid sleaze and breath-taking beauty. But he'd rarely forced Travis McGee to ponder cultural and political issues, since he'd made him too busy with the exigencies of plot: murder, violence, robbery, money, needy women and fighting the good fight for unlikely causes. I doubted that MacDonald himself could explain to Nashir what it was he was trying to have McGee say to himself about race relations in 1966, one year after the Watts race riots, the year the Black Panthers formed, one year before Thurgood Marshall was appointed to the Supreme Court, two years before the assassination of Martin Luther King, before affirmative action, before the War on Poverty, before crack cocaine, before rap music and before an African-American President of the United States. So I punted.

"I don't really know what it means," I said. "These words were written twenty years before I was born. I think we should read this book for the story it tells us, for the adventure and excitement in it. We should enjoy the book. And by the way, Nashir, if you can read this book, you can read most any book."

Nashir looked skeptical, so I passed the buck. "Maybe the Reverend Jones can talk to you about this. He's older than I am, and guess what, Nashir – he's black and I'm not. I'm white. I'm mostly Irish. We've got our own issues. We're still arguing about a battle that happened in 1690. What do you say we get back to the story?"

We did; and Travis took the information he'd been given by

Noreen Walker – that was her name – and disguised himself as a rich drunk, an act that would begin the unraveling of the head-scratcher that had been Vangie's murder – Vangie being the "Amber", as in Darker Than. When Clemmie and I drove away, I felt only a little guilty about the conversation Jameson was going to have someday with Nashir.

• • •

The rest of the day – my choices – were spent on or near *Larke*: sailing until the wind died, fishing until the tide reversed from outgoing to incoming and the catfish went elsewhere, walking barefoot between the tide-lines along the driftwood-strewn shore of Little Tinicum Island, throwing sticks for Smokey to retrieve, sitting at the West End's bar, where upside-down paper cups signifying that Club members had bought us drinks multiplied to just shy of my ability to drive us to my apartment, where we surprised my clean sheets with passion and where Clemmie told me what she wanted to do Sunday.

ONE BIRD, ONE STONE
CHAPTER THIRTY-FOUR

Sunday morning Clemmie kicked me out of my own bed – the one with the rumpled sheets – much earlier than I'd planned. "What is it you guys say? Rise and shine – 'another day in which to excel'."

"How do you know about that?" I asked, as I headed for the shower.

"My high school boy friend went to the Naval Academy. He said it to me in a few of the extremely rare letters he bothered to write to me his Plebe year. He seemed quite taken with the motto. I found it very annoying. I told him to excel with someone else."

I found myself halfway to the bathroom, naked, and turned around to face Clemmie. "Well, they are crazy busy that first year," I said. "What happened to him? Does he have a name?" I felt I'd struck a mid-point between defending him and the jealousy I surprised myself by feeling. I knew jealousy was inappropriate. I, Ryan O'Brien, was the man in Clemmie's life now, not some high school ex-boyfriend. Right? Besides some writer who's name I couldn't remember, in a book I'd loved but also couldn't remember said "jealously is a disease, love is a healthy condition."

"You need a cold shower," she said, nodding her head and looking at my crotch. "It's impolite to point."

"Aye, aye."

Clemmie told me what to bring for the day's excursion. It consisted of old trail running shoes, some nylon long pants, T-shirts, a USMC ball cap and some junk to eat. We stopped at her place and she ran in and came out with a pre-packed gym bag. We ate sugary donuts and drank coffee while she drove my car. I was ordered to study some colored maps of a place called French Creek State Park. The maps were orienteering maps, five-color, in a 1:10,000 scale and very detailed. They had courses on them from previous events that Clemmie had attended.

After I'd spent fifteen minutes or so looking at the maps, Clemmie told me about orienteering: how to read the map, how to hold the map while walking, how to use a compass, what e-punching was and a few technical aspects of the sport. She called the event we were going to a "meet" and said that since it was a nice day, there would probably be about two-hundred folks of all ages competing – on different courses, depending on their age, sex and experience.

"You should probably do a Yellow Course," Clemmie said. "It's a notch up from the easiest and is mostly on trails."

"How long will it be?"

"Maybe three kilometers."

"That's only two miles. I'll finish that in, like fifteen minutes."

"No you won't. The distances are as the crow flies – you'll have to run further than that."

"How much farther."

"Maybe as far in miles as it says in kilometers. Three miles."

"So I'll be twenty minutes or so. I think I should do a longer course. What will you be doing?"

"I was going to do a Green Course. It's probably about five

kilometers; and I should be able to do it in seventy or seventy-five minutes. That's if I don't make any big mistakes."

"That's fifteen minutes per kilometer. That's twenty or twenty-five minutes per mile. You can walk that fast. Aren't you going to run at all?"

"Listen Ryan, you don't know enough about this to have an opinion. Wait 'til you've done this at least once before you start telling me how fast either of us should be. Okay?"

I should have said simply yes and let it go, but testosterone made an unfortunate appearance and caused me to say: "Maybe I should run a Green Course too. I've done lots of map and compass exercises without a problem. I think I might even be able to beat you."

"That's ridiculous, you'll be lucky to finish. But okay. Lets each run a Brown Course. That's the shortest advanced level course."

"How long will it be?"

"Probably about four kilometers."

"That's too short. I think we should do a Green Course."

Clemmie was clearly annoyed with me. "Nope. Brown it is. I have to get to work this afternoon. And let's make it interesting. How 'bout a bet. Put your money where your big Marine Corps mouth is. Okay?"

"How much?"

"I don't have any money, so it will have to be something else. How 'bout if you lose you have to clean my apartment – to my satisfaction. If you win, I clean your place. Deal?"

"Deal."

• • •

We arrived at the Park and followed orange and white signs to the meet site, where there were colorful banners saying Delaware Valley Orienteering Association, DVOA and registration. We registered. I rented a compass and an e-punch – the little gizmo that would record my splits on the course. Clemmie suggested that I get some instruction, but I turned her down, believing that I already knew how a compass worked, I could read a map and I was in excellent physical condition. At the start, I watched Clemmie run off, out of sight, on a trail heading northeast. She wore a light blue and red nylon outfit that she called simply her "fast" clothes. I noticed that her shoelaces had been double-knotted and taped to her trail runners, that she'd affixed a clue sheet to her wrist, that her compass was unlike mine and that she spent very little time deciding which way to run. The person managing the start told me I could start five minutes after Clemmie. I did.

I ran off in the same direction as Clemmie, and stopped to read my map at a trail junction. The clue for the first control was a triangle within a circle; and the legend on the map informed me that that represented a "charcoal platform". I had no idea what that was, and I decided to take a careful compass bearing and simply look for the orange and white control. I soon found one, but it turned out to be the wrong one – one on the north side of a large boulder. However, it was one of my controls – my next to last one, in fact; and so I took a bearing from it and ran off in the direction of the control I was looking for – the charcoal platform. And I found it – in the middle of a pleasant, room-sized level area full of ferns and dark earth. It would have been a fine campsite.

I ran off again, heading in the general direction of the second control, the clue for which was two black triangles and some other, adjacent, lines with a dot in the middle and some numbers in decimals. There was no help from the map legend, so I ran around in what I hoped was the general vicinity of the control until I found it – between two large boulders. I looked at my watch, which had a stopwatch feature, and saw that I'd been about twenty-six minutes getting to the first two controls. There were twelve controls in total, and I calculated that I'd be well over two hours at the rate I was going. So I went faster. And therefore went slower.

By the time I completed the course – and I did manage to finish – in two hours and thirty-five minutes, I accomplished a number of things: I fell twice, hard, in rocky ground and tore my pants and bloodied my right thigh; I managed to read my compass backwards, thus taking a bearing 180 degrees from my intended route and ending up, puzzled and gazing at a lake named, appropriately, "Hopewell"; I ran into some awful plant that stuck thousands of tiny, brown deltoid-shaped pods all over my left side; I read the contour lines backwards, or upside down twice, and mistaken small, shallow valleys – later understood to be "reentrants" – for spurs; I was gashed from briars in both of my forearms and bled onto my map; I slipped on a moss-covered log and snagged the back of my T-shirt, causing it to rip and flap for the rest of the run; I lost my hat somewhere, after wasting time replacing it on my head numerous times; I ran through a swamp of Skunk Cabbage and Jack-in-the-Pulpits and mucked my shoes and pants up to my knees; I splashed across a stream that was designated "uncrossable" to wash off the mud; I passed the same elderly man four times – he was always walking and was waiting for me at the finish; I ran completely off the map at one point, and was redirected back onto the map by a family of hikers that included a girl of six or seven who whispered to her father, "he's bleeding"; I almost gave up once, but didn't, since I didn't really know where I was anyway and was unsure about how to find the parking area; I thought about Clemmie off and on, and wondered if she'd finished, how it wouldn't be too bad to have to clean her apartment once and thought that she'd likely make fun of me and that I deserved it; and I decided that it would be somehow inappropriate to sprint from the last control to the finish, even though it was only a visible fifty meters or so, down a trail.

Clemmie was waiting for me at the finish, and she had her

goddamn magic, picture-taking cellphone out recording, for posterity, my first attempt at orienteering.

She was laughing. "Hey Marine. You finished!"

"I'm not sure how I feel about the photo op."

"I wish I had a before shot. You look like you just won a war all by yourself. I guess there's not much need to ask how it went out there."

"Maybe later."

"If it is any consolation, I didn't expect you to finish. I shouldn't have let you go out on an advanced course your first time."

"I insisted."

"You did. Let's go to download and turn in your e-punch and compass. Think you'll want to do this again?"

"Maybe in a few months, after I've healed."

At download, a slip of paper with my splits was spit out of a small printer. Clemmie grabbed at it and laughed. "You were forty-three minutes on the fifth control. It was a three-hundred meter control. That's what – about two hours per kilometer. Three hours per mile – not three miles per hour – three hours per mile. Let's see, that's like walking the length of a football field in fifteen minutes. You could crawl that fast."

"That's the leg where I ran off the map; and you're going to keep this up, right? You're going to rub it in for the rest of the day."

"Nope. I'm done. I did enjoy that, though."

"Hey. I deserve it."

"I meant what I said earlier. I'm surprised you finished. You probably beat a few people, too."

We turned to the results printout, stapled to a nearby post. My time hadn't been included yet, but it was apparent that I'd beaten one person's time, and that two people had not finished the course and that another had mispunched. Twenty-seven people had beaten me, including Clemmie. She'd finished a respectable seventh in 59:05. In other words, she'd finished in less than half my time.

"Who's the person who won – this 'Sandy' somebody? She did it in 44:08. She must be fast."

"That would be me," said the dark-haired woman sitting at the computer, trying not to laugh at me. "I ran early and am taking a turn at the e-punch. I had a decent run today."

"What's with your knee?" She had a heavy brace on it.

"No cartilage left. I mostly walk. I heard what Clemmie said to you; and she's right. If you finished an advanced course your first time out, you have nothing to be ashamed of. Plus you look like you gave it your best effort. We hope you'll try it again soon."

"Maybe I'll try a little instruction before I go out next time."

"There are plenty of folks who would be happy to help. No charge."

We said our goodbyes. Clemmie thanked Sandy, and Ed, the course setter and Mary, the meet director. Mary handed me my hat. Someone had found it in the woods.

I put my arm over Clemmie's shoulder on the way to the car. "I've got a lot to be humble about," I said. "Feel like driving?"

"Thanks for doing this with me," she said. "There's something about this sport I really like; but I know it isn't for everyone."

"I'm too tired to think right now. You drive, I'll nap."

I was asleep before we'd left the State Park, and didn't wake up until we were parked in front of Clemmie's place.

"Wait here," Clemmie said. "I'll be out in ten minutes and you can drive me to work. Okay?"

I got out of my car, stretched and waited. Miracle of miracles, Clemmie was out in ten minutes, dressed for work. We drove to the Pub & Kitchen, I let her out and promised to meet her after work. We kissed. She left. I drove to my apartment.

After giving Smokey a short walk, I showered, snacked,

watched the news on television, checked e-mails, and scanned a few hours of the Chester Island security camera. I looked at my orienteering map and considered just how incompetent I'd been in the woods. I killed seven hours doing nothing much; and decided to walk Smokey to the Pub & Kitchen to pick up Clemmie – two birds, one stone. She was due to be finished work at midnight.

• • •

As Smokey and I walked the darkened streets of Center City, past a trash-strewn alley, I felt a chill wind on the back of my neck, a bad juju; as if the Ryan piece – clearly a one-move-at-a-time-pawn – had been moved one diagonal square by the hand of the same drunken God on the same damn colossal chessboard, the Deity that required blind and immediate obedience from me.

"Not this time," I swore to myself, as I started to run towards the restaurant. Smokey ran with me; and she growled as we entered the Pub & Kitchen. The last few customers were leaving, cleanup beginning, and I was told that Clemmie had left an hour ago.

"I think she left with her boyfriend," volunteered the bartender, stacking glasses.

"I'm her boyfriend," I said. "What do you remember about him?"

"Not much. I was busy. You shouldn't have that dog in here."

"Listen fuckhead," I said, reaching over the bar and grabbing the bartender's apron, neck-high, "something's wrong. Tell me exactly what you remember. Do it now. I'll leave as soon as you've finished."

Another waitress saw what was going on, and soon there was a manager, two waitresses, a chef, two customers and a janitor watching me. I was sure that by then someone had called 911; and I let the bartender go, backed up and made a short, loud speech: "I have reason to believe that something's happened to Clemmie. You all know Clemmie, right? I need to know if any of you remember anything at all about who Clemmie left with."

"What's your name," asked one of the waitresses.

"Ryan."

"She talked about you tonight. She said you were going to pick her up. I got the impression that the two of you are in love."

"We are. Who remembers what? I'm not kidding. Something's up. Something bad. Think! Clemmie. Who remembers anything about when she left."

"I do," said the bartender. "A guy came in and talked to her, and she left with him right away. Didn't finish up her tables or anything. We covered for her. There was another guy outside. The three of them walked that way – south."

"Thanks," I said. "Sorry for the commotion. Here's my cell number. Please call it if you see or hear from Clemmie."

Smokey and I left the restaurant, walking fast, then jogging, heading south, away from my apartment, away from Clemmie's apartment and into the Philadelphia night.

BRING HIM
CHAPTER THIRTY-FIVE

Smokey and I jogged around the corner, away from police responding to any 911 call from the Pub & Kitchen. I didn't want to waste time explaining to a cop how I thought my girlfriend – of three days – had been abducted, when by all reasonable thinking all she did was leave work early with another guy. I'd never be able to explain events of the last week to him – or her, if God forbid a Bardeaux doppelganger knocked on the front door of the House of Ryan. In either case, I could hear the first question: "So you assaulted the bartender back there because your girlfriend stood you up?" Then there would be a big discussion about what constituted assault, the need to go back to the restaurant and hope the bartender was over me grabbing him and calling him "fuckface" – the cop either bored and wanting to be out fighting crime or happy to charge me with something to get inside the station house where there was hot coffee.

So we sat on a worn set of white marble steps – steps that had likely seen a hundred and fifty years of feet heading into and out of the row house – and I ignored the insistent nudge of cascading thoughts demanding action; and I took a few deep breaths and patted Smokey.

"What should we do, girl? What do you say?"

She whined a little, frustrated, I suppose at being unable to tell me what was obvious – that there was not much I could do that required running, fighting or combat of any kind, no matter how much I'd been programmed by the Marine Corps to do something requiring immediate physical exertion. Besides, she'd observe, if she could, that if my belief in a cosmic chessboard and a besotted deity about to sacrifice the Ryan Piece was in any way rational, better to sit, think, and let her catch her breath.

So I considered what I'd most like to do – phone Clemmie and talk to her; and because it was expected that I would do exactly that, I decided to text her instead. It was a careful text:

> Clemie – Sorry I missed you. I overslept. Hope you got
> home OK. Tuckered from orienteering. First day of work
> tomorrow. Call you after. Love, Rian

Clemmie would know I wouldn't let her down and that I knew something was up. Besides, I intentionally misspelled our names. Clever Ryan – and Smokey. Clever Clemmie, too; as she responded with:

> Rian – no problem. Bartender drove me home. Good luck at
> work tomorrow. Love, Clemie

So, three things: my name, bartender's involvement and her name, all bogus; and all pointing to something really wrong. I patted Smokey's head and we thought some more. It seemed to us that somehow, this had something to do with Emily. The rest of Clemmie's life was so routine, so ordinary – school, study, work, boyfriend – the only abnormal, bizarre factor in her life was:

Emily. I texted again, more cleverness:

> Clemie: I'm not sure, but when I was walking Smokey
> tonight, I think maybe I saw Emily. Is that possible? Rian

The answer came back almost immediately, beginning these exchanges:

> Where?

> Here, in the City.

> Where?

> Exactly where?

> Yes. Exactly.

> I think she went into a house over on Spruce Street.

> Which one?

> I don't remember the address. Is it important?

> Yes. Favor to ask. Please get it for me.

> Okay. Will take me thirty minutes or so. Okay?

> Okay. Thanks.

Oh my. Now there was food for thought. Someone was looking for Emily. I wondered why anyone would actually want Emily around – she was an unpredictable nutcase. She was a human tornado, screwing up whatever she touched; and I'd hoped that my last sight of her – the crazy Goddess in a fog-shrouded dinghy holding life or death in the form of an M4 carbine in her hands – had been my last; and then it came to me: Clemmie was a hostage! Give us Emily and we'll give you Clemmie! Emily had likely abandoned the two-year "project" 'Bama had mentioned while he begged for his life at the stern of his own dinghy, floating down the Cohansey River, me holding on to the bow. She should have shot him that night, instead of just pretending to kill him. 'Bama had Clemmie. 'Bama wanted Emily.

Twenty-nine minutes left until I was required to text a fictional address to 'Bama, the equivalent of mashing a button that would spark the pushing and pulling on other capricious buttons, levers, flywheels, cogs, pinions, sprockets – actions and reactions within one of those fickle equations involving multiple human beings and limitless possible indiscriminate consequences; and one of the developments might be, could be, the death of one Clemmie Olsen. Fuck. I needed to be either Travis McGee or Sherlock Holmes – or both. Travis would give a convenient address to 'Bama, wait in the shadows until two thugs arrived to retrieve Emily, then knock one of them out and beat the crap out of the other until he confessed to Clemmie's whereabouts. Then Travis would get himself to Clemmie, fast, and attempt a rescue. That would be most personally rewarding for many reasons, but the main thing wrong with this scenario was that Travis's lady loves often died – died utterly revenged by Travis – but died nonetheless. Scratch Travis.

I was no Sherlock Holmes. But I knew one – a distaff Sherlock; and so I called Special Agent Ayers at 1:15 a.m., with twenty-eight minutes left until I needed to make a fateful call.

"This better be good, Ryan," Agent Ayers said after one ring.

"Sorry to wake you up," I said. "I need Sherlock."

"I'm at work. I'm busy. Lots happening. Be quick."

"Okay. Clemmie's been abducted – likely by 'Bama. I think Emily's flown the coop and he wants her back. I owe him a text message in twenty-seven minutes telling him where I last saw Emily. I haven't really seen Emily. He thinks that I think I'm texting Clemmie."

In the ensuing five seconds, I suppose she ran through all the possibilities, all the iterations of what I'd said. She considered my likely confirmation biases, considered and eliminated the impossible and was looking squarely at whatever remained. "Where are you?" she demanded.

"I'm sitting on steps of a small row house near the corner of 20th and Rodman – east side of the intersection."

"Don't do anything. Stay right there. Again – Ryan – do not do anything until I get there. Hear me?"

"Yes. I hear you."

· · ·

In ten minutes, two robust, unmarked black SUV's rounded the corner and idled. From the rear window of the lead vehicle, Agent Ayers waved me over. "Get in." Then, "I see you have a dog."

Ayers slid over and Smokey and I got into the back seat. Smokey barked twice and climbed over Ayers to lick, wag tail at and otherwise be excited to see the other passenger. That other passenger was Emily. Emily and Ayers. Ayers and Emily. I was Watson. The rest of the world was Sherlock Holmes crying elementary! – or Stephen Hawking edging up to the mind of God – or Immanuel Kant thinking in terms of space, time and causality. I guess I was dumbfounded – and looked it.

"I saw the light, Ryan," said Emily. "I figured it out – at least part of it."

"She's been on our side since noon of what is now yesterday,

Ryan," said Ayers.

"Noon! Why not warn Clemmie? That's ten hours before 'Bama abducted her."

"Well it would have been much earlier if some screwball hadn't stolen my motorcycle – Ryan. I had to hitchhike. Where is it anyway?"

"It's at my boat club, detailed and under a tarp. Answer my question. Why not warn Clemmie?"

"I wanted to keep her out of this. I thought 'Bama would look for me; and I bought some time by leaving him a note, saying my grandfather was sick and I needed to see him. I guess he checked up on that somehow. And by the way Ryan, I was never going to shoot you that night on the Cohansey. Crazy was just an act."

"I don't think it was all an act," I said. "You have at least a few screws loose. Otherwise you wouldn't have been involved with 'Bama's project anyway."

Emily started to answer, but was interrupted by Ayers. "We don't have time to go over all this now. Ryan's got to text 'Bama with an address."

"I already texted that I thought it was a house on Spruce Street," I said.

"We've got nothing on Spruce," said Ayers. "We've got a house on Delancey. Can you sell that?"

"Probably. That's only two blocks south of Spruce. Right?"

"Right. And you've got six minutes before you're due. Let's get in position." Ayers then gave the driver an address and made a phone call. I could only hear part of her side of the conversation; but I gathered she'd talked someone out of their Delancey Street digs for a few hours, and that she planned to set a trap there.

While we drove to the Delancey Street address, Ayers made several other phone calls. I noted that she was calm and assertive on the phone. When we got to the address, I saw that it was a small condo. Ayers got out of the car and knocked on the door. A young man and woman with a small dog opened the door, each with a briefcase and a gym bag. Ayers shook their hands and pointed to the second SUV; and the couple walked quickly to the car and got in. I learned later that they were Assistant Prosecutors for the City, happy to help the FBI – and very pleased to be staying at the Four Seasons for the rest of the night at FBI expense. Two agents then got out of the car, jogged to the steps of the condo, conferred with Ayers and went inside.

Things were happening fast, and I was reminded of a small unit assault, run by a competent squad leader – each of three coordinated fireteams moving quickly, covering each other and maneuvering towards an objective. Half the fun watching was knowing that the enemy was watching too, and that they were getting nervous, realizing that they were about to lose the hill, the ravine, the house or whatever it is they were defending. Calm, competent and inevitable – same as Ayers.

By the time Emily and I were inside the condo, and it was my turn to do something that mattered, I understood the basic plan. I would text 'Bama the address, people would come for Emily, they would be captured, they would be interrogated, they would talk, Ayers would know where 'Bama was and arrange for his capture as well as the retrieval of the two Pakistani missiles.

"Okay Ryan, you're up. Text exactly as I dictate, please. No surprises."

"Okay," I said.

Clemie: I'm at the house now. The address is 1725-1/2 Delancey Street. Rian

R.U. sure? I thought it was Spruce Street.

I thought it was Spruce, but it's this house. It has a little parking spot next to it. I'm sure.

Okay. Thanks. Go home. Get some sleep. Call me after
work. Love, Clemie

Okay. Goodnight. Love, Rian

"Good work Ryan. You actually followed orders. Now you're
over there in that chair. Do nothing. Got it? Nothing."

"Got it." I moved to the chair and waited. We all waited.
Fifteen minutes passed. Ayers talked quietly into her phone a few
times. Emily sat, hushed for a change.

"The same car has passed here, twice, slowly," said Ayers.
"Good. Show time."

I heard a car door close outside the house and the doorbell
rang.

"You're up, Emily," said Ayers.

I give Emily credit. She walked quickly to the door and opened
it a crack. "Can I help you?" she said.

I heard a muffled response from whoever had rung the bell,
and Emily opened the door a little wider – and a man stepped into
the house. It was one man, and in the twenty seconds it took for
two agents to have him lying on the floor on his stomach,
disarmed and handcuffed, two FBI SUV's had boxed in the car
and had the driver on the sidewalk, likewise disarmed and
handcuffed.

"I hope you're really FBI," said the guy on the floor, talking
over his shoulder.

"We are," said Ayers, flashing a badge. "Why do you care?"

"Because you won't accidentally shoot me out of
incompetence," said the guy. "And you'll likely let me go as soon
as we get everything straightened out." He rolled over and looked
up at Ayers. "I'm a retired cop, name of Mike Hurt, a licensed P.I.
I've got a carry permit; and I was simply going to tell Emily here –

if this is Emily – that her sister is sick and needs her. We – my partner Frankie is licensed too – were supposed to volunteer to drive her."

"Drive her where, Hurt?"

"I don't know yet. I'm supposed to confirm that this is Emily, ask her to talk to my client, maybe come see her sister, and then get directions. Looks like we've landed in something above our pay grade. What's up? Can we help?"

"Maybe," said Ayers. "Check his I.D. If it checks out, get someone to vouch for him, then take the cuffs off then give him back his piece. Bring his partner in – same deal. Let me think."

"We owe my client a call pretty soon," said Hurt.

"How was that supposed to work? Where were you going to take Emily?"

"I'm to take her picture with this phone, send it to my client and ask Emily to talk to him. I don't know yet where we are supposed to go. I thought he'd work that out with Emily."

"What's your cellphone number?"

I gave her the ten digits.

"Get Rizzo to monitor that number," said Ayers to the Agent talking on his cell. "GPS whoever he talks to."

"He's too smart for that," said Emily. "He won't talk long enough for you to track him – unless maybe I can really piss him off. When you're ready, take my picture, call him up and let me see what I can do."

"This might actually work," I said. "Emily pisses me off every time I talk to her."

"Quiet O'Brien," said Ayers. "Okay, Hurt. We're ready. Take Emily's picture and send it to your client. Text him: 'she agrees'."

So Mike Hurt, retired cop, licensed P.I. took Emily's picture, texted carefully and sent it to Clemmie's kidnapper. Then we waited for a callback.

"Put it on the speaker," said Ayers when the phone jingled.

"Let me talk to Emily," said the voice. "Be quick."

Emily took Hurt's phone, cleared her throat, and said: "'Bama. You asshole. What have you done? I was coming back tomorrow morning anyway. I just went to collect my motorcycle. If you hurt Clemmie, I'll fuckin' kill you."

"Shut up, Emily, and listen. Go with the good detective – right now. Bring no one else, talk to no one else. Get in the car and head west to the Expressway, then east to I-95."

Ayers made a circular motion with her hand, as in "keep him talking."

"Can't I come in daylight?" asked Emily. "I don't trust you."

"That's it Emily. Hanging up now."

"Wait!" said Emily. "What do you want me to do with O'Brien?"

"O'Brien?" said the voice on the phone. "What's he got to do with anything?"

Ayers nodded 'yes' and kept making the same circular motion.

"Ryan is here with me," said Emily. "He came here right after he texted Clemmie – well, you, I suppose – this address. He's worried about Clemmie. If I don't bring him, I don't know what he'll do. Something stupid, probably."

"Bring him. Get in the car. Now. We'll talk in a bit."

"Wait!" said Emily, "don't hang up!"

"Goodbye," said the voice, terminating the call.

• • •

And so I found myself heading out of Philadelphia, south on I-95, in the back seat of a black car with Pennsylvania plates that said "PI GUY", driven by a retired Philly cop named Mike; with Special Agent Ayers in the front seat, impersonating another P.I. named Frankie, and controlling, with three cellphones, four black, unmarked SUV's, a boat someplace on the River, and Matt and his helicopter, hovering somewhere and occupied by a four-man Special Weapons and Tactical Team; with Clemmie's nutty, unpredictable sister Emily sitting next to me – and not caring all that much about finding missiles and preventing terrorism, but caring very much about finding Clemmie.

ALWAYS THE RIVER
CHAPTER THIRTY-SIX

Mike concentrated on his driving – pleased to be a part of something involving the FBI. His cellphone was in his shirt pocket – on speaker mode; and he'd answered it once to have 'Bama tell us to get ourselves off of I-95, over the Platt Bridge and onto PA 291 South.

'Bama terminated the call before Rizzo – working from the FBI's Philadelphia headquarters – could further refine 'Bama's location. "Still this side of Chester, north of Paulsboro," he said, over one of Ayers's phones.

"Paulsboro's in New Jersey," said Ayers.

"Right," said Rizzo. "You've got to keep him talking."

Ayers juggled her Rizzo connection with multiple contacts including Matt and his 'copter, with someone named Dan – out on the River on a boat with two Agents; and with three cars which were following us in intricate patterns – ahead, behind, parked, opposite direction – supposedly guaranteed to avoid detection. She was the focus of the operation. She was good.

Emily sat, silent, next to me.

I felt like a middle-school kid on a bus to his first day at the new school where there were big kids. I needed to talk, or listen. Anything to take my mind off of Clemmie and what might be happening to her.

"What's 'Bama's real name," I asked Emily.

Emily looked up at me. Not wanting to break Ayers's concentration, or not wanting Ayers to hear her, she whispered, "Alphonse Rosewater."

"You made that up."

"Nope. Honest. He wouldn't tell me for days. He thought I'd make fun of him."

"Did you?"

"Of course."

"No wonder he uses 'Bama," I said.

"Yep, but Ryan O'Brien probably shouldn't make fun of another guy's name."

"What was the 'project' 'Bama and you've been working on for so long," I asked.

Emily opted for a rapid-fire whisper. "There's not time to explain it all. It's complicated. But what we started doing was all good stuff – environmental activism, saving the planet – you know. I met 'Bama at a cleanup of Little Tinicum Island. I'd just been divorced and was looking for something to do that day besides ride my motorcycle; and I was one of thirty or forty people ferried out to the Island to pick up trash and get it into dumpsters – at your boat club, actually. 'Bama was the biggest, coolest, hardest-working guy there. He seemed to really care about what he was doing; and afterwards he mentioned a meeting of the Riverkeepers that night; and I agreed to go with him. He seemed to know everything relating to the Delaware River's ecology; and he preached to me about coal ash pollution, the Army Corps of Engineers plans to dredge the channel, the Constitution Pipeline, the evils of fracking, the Greenspring Pipeline Expansion and the refinery expansion in Delaware City. He knew everything about the River – it's the last free-flowing river in the East, flows for three-hundred and thirty miles, it's got wetlands, floodplains, you name it. He told me he was planning to actually do something about keeping the River safe – really do something. Then, after I'd had a few drinks, he asked me if I wanted to help him – and I said yes. I said yes to a lot of other things, too."

Ayers interrupted. "Emily. We need the subject to stay connected longer on the next call. Get into a debate with him, if you can, about how the Emily for Clemmie exchange goes. Argue for something safe for Clemmie. Contemporaneous exchange at two different locations. Keep it complicated. Okay? Bring up Ryan's name – that seems to unsettle 'Bama."

"Got it," said Emily.

Mike's phone jingled. He answered it with a "yes".

"Are you past the airport yet?" said 'Bama.

"Yes – but just," said Mike.

"Turn left – that's south – on Bartram Avenue Road, then a quick right on Tinicum Island Road."

"Where does Bartram come in?" said Mike, doing his part for the stall.

"You can't miss it. Big intersection. Make sure you turn left."

"Wait!" called Emily. "Don't hang up. How do I know you'll release Clemmie?"

"You don't. But I will."

"That's not good enough," said Emily. "I don't trust you. I'm not going to give myself over to you without some reasonable plan to exchange Clemmie at the same time."

"You'll have to trust me."

"Sorry 'Bama. I don't trust you. Figure out a way to leave Clemmie somewhere while you pick me up. You trust me."

Ayers gave the circle sign to keep it going. And then she pointed at me.

"Maybe Ryan can pick up Emily at the same time you get me – at a different location. Cellphone confirmed. What do you think? Come on 'Bama – do it."

"Let me think about that. I'll be back to you."

"Wait!" said Emily. But 'Bama was gone.

"Rizzo," said Ayers into one of her phones, "any help?"

Rizzo's voice came over the cellphone speaker, tinny: "Yes. We've got it. According to the map, he's on I-95. Right on the Interstate. Stopped – south of the PA 420 exit. Northbound side. He's not moving, either."

"Matt," said Ayers. "Check that out. Cars two and three get there – without flashers."

Matt was the first to get there – 140 MPH as the crow flies will do that – and he checked in: "Nothing. No cars on the shoulder between the Stewart Avenue and 420 exits. Almost no cars driving either – mostly trucks."

"You're sure?" asked Ayers. "Make another pass – don't hover."

"This is car two – we confirm eggbeater's visual. Nothing here."

"Rizzo," said Ayers. "Are you sure of yourself on this? We've got nothing."

"Positive," said Rizzo. "Subject must be using a relay. I'll reconfirm on next talkie-talk."

"Roger," said Ayers. "Cars two and three – make passes every few minutes. Space yourselves. Get off and on at Stewart Avenue and 420. Got it?"

Two quick "rogers" and Ayers was turning around to talk to Emily when Mike's phone rang. Mike answered with a "Mike here" and then handed the phone to Emily.

"Where are you?" said a woman's voice.

"Who's this?" asked Emily. "Clemmie?"

"Not Clemmie," said the voice. "And it doesn't matter who I am. Where are you?"

"I'm not exactly sure," said Emily. "I think we are in Essington on East 2nd Street. Is that right, Mike?"

"Yup," said Mike.

"When you get to West 2nd Street – slow down and look for a park – on your left. Governor Printz Park. Turn around and park on the shoulder of the road. Wait for my next call."

"Wait," said Emily. "What about Clemmie?"

"Who's Clemmie?" said the voice, before it hung up.

The quality of the speaker on Mike's cellphone wasn't great. It had given us a tinny sounding female voice. Something about the voice sounded familiar to me, though – pace, inflection or intonation maybe – but damn if I could name the speaker. Anyway, I was too busy thinking that I knew how 'Bama's call was coming from an empty highway – and it wasn't scientific magic.

Ayers asked Rizzo if he'd gotten a fix on the call. Rizzo was positive it was not from the same location – it was from somewhere east of the previous ones. She ordered Matt to do inconspicuous flyovers, and to use all his gadgets – night vision, infrared, everything – to find whoever was behind the last call.

When we got to the Park, Mike passed it, did a U-turn and parked on the grassy shoulder. We waited five minutes before another call came from the same familiar female voice. "Okay," it said, "send Emily out towards the River – alone. O'Brien – stay in the car and wait for another call."

Ayers was shaking her head NO at Emily; and Emily took the phone and said, "I don't get out of the car until I know where Clemmie is. I have to know she's safe. Have 'Bama call me – now!"

"I don't think that's part of the plan, missy," said the voice.

"If you want me out of the car, contact 'Bama now and tell him what I said."

"I don't think he'll be happy with this."

"Just do it and see what he says."

Ayers immediately talked to Rizzo; and just as he confirmed

that the last call had come from somewhere nearby, 'Bama called. "Why make this so complicated, Emily? Just walk towards the River like you were told. I'll release Clemmie somewhere O'Brien can find her."

"And where will that be?" asked Emily.

"Put O'Brien on the phone. And turn off the speaker feature."

Emily handed the phone to me. "Ryan?" said 'Bama. "I owe you one – but that'll have to wait. Clemmie's on Little Tinicum Island. She's safe. Her feet are wet, but she's safe. How soon can you get to her?"

"Where is she on the Island?" I asked.

"Downriver end. West end. There's a little beach there. How soon?"

Figuring five minutes to get to *Larke*, a minute or two to get her started and cast off and ten minutes to get to the Island, I answered: "twenty-five minutes, tops."

"Okay," said 'Bama. "You're on the clock. Go. And Ryan?"

"Yes?"

"If you or anyone else tries to pick up Clemmie before I snatch Emily, I'll shoot her. Got that?"

"You're with her, then?"

"As good as. Bye."

"Did you get that, Rizzo? Where was he calling from?"

"I confirm the same I-95 location," he said.

"The same location where he is not," said Ayers. "I've got a helicopter and two cars telling me he is not there. Anyone see something I don't?"

I did. But I decided to keep my opinion to myself. I was worried that too much focus was on apprehending 'Bama, and not enough concern was being given to getting Clemmie back alive. I was pretty sure I knew where 'Bama was; and it wasn't anything other than common sense that I was using.

"Why don't we just use the boat you've got to collect Clemmie and keep Emily," I said to Ayers.

"Because then we've got nothing, no 'Bama, no mystery woman, no missiles, nothing."

"But you'll have two sisters safe and sound. And Emily knows what 'Bama's up to. Right Emily?"

"Not really," said Emily. "I guess I mean – not exactly. Anyway, 'Bama's got a lot of options. Agent Ayers is right."

"So how do we get you to your boat?" asked Ayers.

• • •

The West End Boat Club is only a quarter mile from where we were parked, and I had us through the security gate and out to the marina parking area in under five minutes. "How about a gun?" I said to Ayers as I got out of the car. "You've got firepower up the yin-yang. I've got nothing, 'Bama hates me, and we don't know where he is."

Ayers thought about it for a nanosecond. "Officially – I can't arm a civilian. I can look the other way while Mike thinks about this."

Mike said only "no round in the chamber" and handed me his gun, across Ayers and out the window. It was a Springfield Professional .45. It was close enough to the Colt I'd carried in Afghanistan. It was a beast that made great big holes in whatever it hit.

"I did not see that," said Ayers.

"See what?" said Mike.

"Thanks," I said to the front seat; and I stuck the .45 in my waistband – backside, hoping I wouldn't literally shoot my ass off – and turned and jogged out "B" Dock to *Larke*. Ayers, Emily and Mike watched me for about thirty seconds, then turned the car around and left the Club – back to the shoulder of West 2nd Street, to wait.

When I got to *Larke*, I operated on the autopilot that most sailors have when they're getting ready to sail a boat they've sailed hundreds of times – from the same slip, same dock, same river: tilt motor into water, hit choke, dial up on gas switch and pull. She started on the second yank. Not only was *Larke's* hull black, but her mast and the motor were too. Without running lights she was pretty close to invisible at night; and I left the running lights off as I cast off and we eased out past the floating dock and into the flow of the River. I aimed *Larke* downriver into the incoming tide, and when we'd passed Darby Creek and the Boeing building, I pressed the red kill button on the motor, silencing it. The tide had us in a minute or two, and we began a slow drift upriver. My phone rang. I turned it off without looking at it, and rummaged in the cluttered cabin for the paddle I'd put there once and never used. It was under fishing gear, cans of gas and life jackets.

I had three or four minutes to finish deciding what to do; and so I sat there drifting and thinking, adding up what I knew for sure, what I thought was likely, and what could be a longshot-possibility. I knew what I wanted most. Then I got the paddle out and quietly aimed *Larke*, my silent conspirator – beautiful *Larke*, invisible *Larke*, black-hulled and black-masted, with no running-lights – away from Little Tinicum Island and towards 'Bama.

LITTLE TINICUM ISLAND
CHAPTER THIRTY-SEVEN

The waters of the River are a comfortless black at night. But they conjure mirrored reflections from passing ships and planes, from industrial floodlights, from marina dock lights and from the stars and moon; and these faltering incandescences provide light enough to aim a small sailboat – operating without a motor, running lights or depth sounder – in the direction of the mouth of Darby Creek and the railroad bridge that spans that Creek.

Once the tide pushed us into the Creek proper, most of the reflections vanished; and the high, shrubby banks absorbed whatever light remained. It was close to bat-cave dark. I turned *Larke* with the single paddle so that we floated stern-first, and peered into the shrouded darkness as we drifted up the Creek – up a creek with one paddle, I thought. From a hundred yards away, I saw the blinking green lights. They alternated – left, then right, and I knew they were spaced about ten yards apart. The bridge was open – as usual. I'd never seen a train on it.

We drifted on the incoming tide towards the first of the double railroad bridges that crossed Darby Creek. The bridges were identical, but only the first was operational. The second was in a permanent up position, and led only to a parking lot on the east side of the Creek from the back of a razor-wired fence on the west side. But the first bridge, the one I needed to find in the dark and climb, was operational but seldom in use. I knew from daytime fishing nearby that they were bascule bridges, and from a know-it-all codger at the boat club, that they were more accurately called Chicago fixed-trunnion bascule bridges, and that the section that moved was constructed of pony through/plate girders. The most noticeable feature of the bridges were their enormous cast concrete counterweights – weights that were stained with the rust of the steel reinforcing rods that had held them together for almost a hundred years.

The three-knot current moved us steadily toward the first bridge. I aimed us towards the western bank, away from the counterbalance; and when I felt we were within thirty yards, I moved to *Larke's* bow and eased her anchor overboard into eight feet of water. The anchor held, and I began playing out line, backing *Larke's* stern into the bridge's superstructure – worn wood, steel and concrete. When we were within two feet of the bridge, I tied off the anchor line and returned to the stern and looked up at where I had to go. It was about eight feet up to the first horizontal girder; and I knew that if I could get myself there, the rest would be a piece of cake.

I scrambled back to *Larke's* bow and let out another six feet of anchor line. Now *Larke* was partway under the bridge, and I could shinny up her mast and grab the girder. Standing on the cabin, I made sure that Mike's .45 would stay with me for the climb, by looping a nylon line through the trigger guard, tying it around my neck and tucking it in my shirt. I'd climbed the first third of *Larke's* mast before – usually to tinker with a spreader or untangle a halyard – and I felt the usual cleats rub the usual places on the inside of my legs as I hoisted myself up the mast. When I was eye-level with the girder, I reached over with one arm, then the other, and found myself clutching a rusting and scaled girder, only one perfect pull-up away from where I wanted to be.

If Sergeant Johnson had been with me, I would have sent him up first; and by the time I'd managed the pull-up, he'd have been out along the bridge, found the perfect spot for what I wanted to do and been all set up. Hell, if he wanted, he'd have had a tent pitched, a communications center established, hot coffee waiting, and a revised and better plan than the one I had in mind. I missed him, and reminded myself that- whatever happened in this morning's darkness – I was meeting his plane in six days.

After I'd climbed to the top of the bridge, to the railroad tracks themselves, I crawled slowly out to the end of the tracks and looked down at the Creek. 'Bama would have to navigate through the gap between the bridge sections; and that gap was about twelve feet wide. I figured he'd take the gap right in the middle, he'd have a spotlight on, and be moving slowly; and so I found a steel plate to lie down behind. And I waited, thinking about what I would do next, and considering the plan I'd made up on the fly.

I was close to one-hundred percent certain that 'Bama was currently under the I-95 bridge. It made so much sense to me, I couldn't think of alternatives. Rizzo's GPS tracking of 'Bama's cellphone calls had placed him there; but even Agent Ayers hadn't realized that there was an under to the Interstate at that spot. From there, 'Bama could get to Little Tinicum Island in about five minutes – assuming he had a fast powerboat. He could hide under the bridge indefinitely. So the first leg of my plan assumed 'Bama was about five-hundred yards away from me, anchored under I-95 and waiting to make a move.

As I lay, thinking about the next step of my operational plan – OPLAN in military speak – I recalled that Emily said 'Bama's name was really Alphonse; and I decided to remember that, and to try to think of him as an Alphonse, not a 'Bama. Somehow,

Alphonse seemed less threatening; and besides, since he did not use the name, he must not like it. Anything to piss him off. I assumed that Clemmie was either with 'Bama – I mean Alphonse – on his boat, or on Little Tinicum Island, as he'd said; or, she was somewhere else entirely, and he'd lied to Emily and me. Under any of the options relating to Clemmie's whereabouts, I planned to disable Alphonse's boat by shooting his outboard motor. After that I'd either rescue Clemmie from the boat or recover her from the Island. If she was on the Island, as promised, I'd call Ayers and tell her where to find 'Bama/Alphonse. If Clemmie was not on the Island, I'd come back and beat her location out of the man himself, without the complication of FBI involvement. So that was my plan: do this, do that, if this – then that, contingencies all considered, wait, wait some more, and don't fuck it up.

I looked at my watch, the black plastic Timex, and considered that something should happen fairly soon. I'd said I could get to the Island in twenty-five minutes; and that was twenty minutes ago. I chambered a round into Mike's .45, and sighted down through an opening between two girders. Just as I began to wonder if the primary assumption I'd made about Alphonse's next move was wrong – invalidating everything I'd planned to do – I heard the quiet hum of a large four-stroke outboard engine. A spotlight shone on the water, playing back and forth from one bank of the Creek to the other. When the boat was about thirty yards away, the spotlight moved along the bridge, twice, left to right and back again. I held very still; and when the spotlight moved on to the dark waters past the bridge, I peeked over the edge of the girder, aimed the .45 with both hands and waited, motionless, until the gun's muzzle-flash wouldn't be seen.

. . .

"BLAM!" One shot. I'd forgotten how loud .45s were. I knew

I'd hit the motor. It went silent. The boat drifted forward a little from its momentum, then it was stopped by the incoming tide. I lay still and quiet, as the boat drifted back under the bridge.

"What the fuck!" said 'Bama. He was bent over the motor with a flashlight; and I realized that he did not know it had been shot.

"Fucking twelve-thousand dollar motor explodes on me! God-fucking-damn-it!"

Then he used his phone, and even though he was drifting away, I could hear every word, in the absolute silence of perfect Creek-bank and waveless-water acoustics. "Max. Listen. This is 'Bama. I can't get there. My motor's exploded or something. You'll have to deal with O'Brien yourself. Okay?"

Then he said something that confirmed that Clemmie was on the Island and not on the boat. "How's the girl holding up?"

As the boat drifted away, I considered calling Ayers. She could deal with Alphonse while I retrieved Clemmie. But my phone was off, and by the time I'd turned it on and gotten a signal, I changed my mind. Better to see Clemmie – alive and well – before blowing the whistle on Alphonse. I could always call Ayers, I couldn't uncall her.

When 'Bama/Alphonse's boat drifted out of hearing and sight, I climbed down into *Larke*. Since my four-horsepower motor is a noisy old two-stroke model, I waited for five minutes and considered how to best deal with Max. I recalled that he didn't seem terribly bright, that I'd tricked him once, and that he believed he owed me one. Then I pulled on the starter cord, left the motor running in slow forward, retrieved and stowed the anchor, put on my running lights and depth sounder and headed for Little Tinicum Island.

• • •

We were about a mile away from the Island and moving at

something just under four knots, so I had about fifteen minutes to decide exactly what to do about Max. I chose the only thing I could think of – something uncomplicated and violent. I fastened a flashlight to the main halyard, facing forward, with enough play in the line to give it the appearance of something hand-held. Next I trailed a safety line from a stern cleat out into the dark water. I'd used the line only twice before, once when I sailed solo all the way down the River to the Bay, to the edge of the Atlantic, and once again on a solitary three-day sail halfway down the Chesapeake Bay in windy weather. It trailed behind *Larke*, fifty feet or so and theoretically could give me a chance to grab hold in case I fell overboard. In this case I wouldn't be falling overboard.

Little Tinicum Island is about two miles long and only two hundred yards wide. It is visible from the air, and stretches up and down the river, nearest the Pennsylvania side. Folks with window seats, landing and taking off from Philly International, get a clear view of its empty, wooded terrain. The banks facing the River channel are made of sandy silt, a proximate beach; and driftwood lies everywhere in fantastic heaps. All tidal islands tend to shoal near their ends, from the relentless two-a-day push-pull of the tides and the ever-present silt; and Little Tinicum is no exception. To get to the channel side of the Island – the beach – I had to swing *Larke* well around the shallow downriver end of the Island, out into deeper water and only then approach the Island, Clemmie – and Max. We would be seen and heard from hundreds of yards away.

Once around the downriver end of the Island, I edged *Larke* shoreward; and then ran upriver, parallel to the white ribbon of beach and sixty or seventy yards offshore, in eight feet of water. I aimed the flashlight at the beach, knowing that Max was there, likely armed with the same weapon of choice he'd had when I sucker-punched him – a suppressed M4 carbine. It was a weapon fully capable of ruining *Larke* and killing me from this distance, but I felt I had at least two advantages over him. First, Max would have been instructed not to kill me until I'd confirmed to Emily that Clemmie was on the Island; and second, he did not know that I knew he was hiding there.

As I played the beam of the flashlight along the beach, I looked for Clemmie; and I reminded myself that if I saw her, I'd not stop the light, focus on her and acknowledge that I'd sighted her. It was important that it appear to Max that I'd missed her in my first pass along the beach. So when I saw a slim figure, standing and waving at me – an impersonal, perfunctory wave – arm up, arm down, I kept the beam moving. I thought about that spiritless, mechanical wave from Clemmie; and I realized that something was wrong. I couldn't remember the position of her head from the brief sighting, but it seemed to me that it was down, looking at the ground.

When *Larke* and I had moved upriver far enough, I turned her around and started back, retracing our course. The island was now on our starboard side. A hundred yards shy of where I'd sighted Clemmie, I aimed *Larke* diagonally at the shore, allowed for the incoming tide, and slipped off the stern, .45 around my neck, safety line in my left hand. When I'd let the fifty feet of line slip through my hand, I held on while *Larke* aimed herself at Clemmie; and when I could feel the river bottom, I let go.

I waded and swam ashore, while *Larke* and her noisy motor and flashlight aimed at Clemmie and Max. When I reached the beach, I ducked into the shrubby growth just behind the high-tide line and scrambled to my left, over piles of driftwood and through heavy vegetation. There was no need to be particularly quiet, as the noise of *Larke's* motor covered the sound of my movement. Off to my left, I could see *Larke* grounded, her full keel touching down on soft bottom in two feet of water. Even though it was dark, the dancing beam of the flashlight displayed beach, shrubs, driftwood and trees. Then the beam steadied – on Clemmie.

Clemmie was still doing her rhythmic wave, head down. She said nothing; and only her arm moved – up, down. I was certain that something was very wrong; and I increased my pace along the shore, hoping that Max was occupied watching *Larke* and the beam of the flashlight – expecting me to step ashore. I'd been very lucky to have the flashlight end up shining directly on Clemmie; and when I crawled the last twenty yards, .45 in right hand, I saw Max. He was sitting behind the tree Clemmie was tied to, pulling on the line that moved Clemmie's arm, and clutching his rifle in the other.

Ten yards from Max, I lay down and spoke. "Don't move. You are covered. This is a gun that makes very big holes."

"O'Brien? Where are you?"

"I said don't move. That means stop pulling on that fucking line that moves Clemmie's arm. Drop your rifle! And Clemmie had better be okay!"

Max faced in my direction now and stopped moving. "How do I know you are armed?"

"Easy," I said. "Listen." I fired off three rounds into the air, the signal for distress. Maybe Ayers would hear it. Damn – Mike's gun was loud.

"Okay," said Max. "You win. Don't shoot. I'm putting my rifle down. See."

He stood, began to place the rifle down and then stood and began shooting in my direction – the same silenced phut, phut, phut I'd heard on Chester Island where all this had started for me. I did the only thing I could think of – I shot him.

FREE TO GO
CHAPTER THIRTY-EIGHT

I hoped I'd shot him. The flashlight beam had danced off Max as he reached for his rifle, and all I'd seen was muzzle-flash. I'd cranked off three quick rounds, rolled left and waited, listening. No sound. It was eerie-quiet after the blasts of the .45; and I crouched in that noiseless, black limbo until *Larke* again bounced the flashlight beam off the awful tableau. I stood, and walked toward Max, with the .45 aimed down at him. He was stretched out on his side, unmoving. I flipped his rifle away from him with my foot. Then I looked up at Clemmie. Marine Corps training and day-to-day life in Iraq and Afghanistan had prepared me to never panic – under any circumstances. But the sight of Clemmie, tied to a tree, arms hanging limply at her sides, chin on her chest, prompted a frenzy in me; and I wished there'd been someone left to kill.

I moved to her, whispering – praying: "Be alive. Be alive. Please be alive." I touched her face, then her neck; and I felt a weak pulse – a tentative and insecure beating. When the beam of the flashlight moved off again, into the tangle of trees, I ran to *Larke*, pulled the anchor line off her bow and tied it onto a driftwood log. I silenced her motor; and then I retrieved the flashlight and ran back to Clemmie.

I talked to her as I untied her. She'd been tethered to the small tree with one long nylon rope, winding up from her knees to her breasts. The sick fuck who'd concocted the arm-waving idea had used thin nylon line on Clemmie; and her left wrist was abraded and bleeding. Once untied, she fell into my arms, cold and senseless; and I carried her away from the tree and lay her on the beach on her back. She was barefoot, dressed in her black restaurant pants and a thin cotton T-shirt. I removed my jacket and covered her from the waist up.

I called Ayers, and she picked up at half-ring. "Ayers. This is Ryan!"

"I know. Where are you?"

"I'm on Little Tinicum Island. Downriver end. I need a boat. Better yet – a helicopter. Clemmie's here and unconscious."

"Do you have a flashlight?"

"Yes. And Ayers?"

"Yes O'Brien?"

"I shot Max. He's probably dead."

"If he's alive, try to keep him that way. We need to talk to him."

"Okay."

"Anything else?"

"Yes. 'Bama is under the I-95 bridge that spans Darby Creek."

"How do you know that?"

"Long story. I'll tell you about it later. Send the boat. Now – please."

"I need the boat to get to 'Bama. You're getting Matt and his helicopter."

"Have him hurry. Please."

"He's already on the way. Can he set down anywhere?"

"I'll find a place. I'll wave my flashlight around."

"Right. Later. And, Ryan?"

"Yup."

"I need to talk to you. Don't disappear on me."

"Right."

• • •

I knew I'd soon hear the helicopter, and I looked for a place Matt could land. There was a flat, treeless spot near the very end of the Island, about thirty yards away that would work; and I decided to move Clemmie there. Just before I picked her up, I checked on Max. He was alive, but was unconscious and very bloody. There were wounds all over his face and hands – wounds that couldn't have been made by the .45. .45's only make big holes. These wounds looked like they'd been caused by buckshot; and I realized that one of my shots had hit the M4 and blown metal and plastic pieces of the gun up into Max's face. I felt around under his jacket and found blood on his far right side. I decided that one of my shots had grazed him there and that he'd probably live.

I carried Clemmie to the place I'd chosen for the helicopter to land; and just as we got there, I heard the thwop-thwop of the 'copter and I lay Clemmie down and signaled with the flashlight. Suddenly, the whole place was lit with the blazing incandescence of whirlybird floodlights; and a loudspeaker asked: "Is that you, Ryan? If so, wave your flashlight in circles where you want me to land."

Just before the 'copter touched down, a black-clad FBI agent dropped out, hit the ground and began gesturing to Matt. A second agent joined the first, and called to me. "You O'Brien?"

"Yes. Here's Clemmie. She's unconscious. Help me with her, will you?"

We carried Clemmie to the helicopter, and an agent inside helped secure her. There was only room for one more in the helicopter; and I had Max and *Larke* to deal with, so one agent stayed with me while the other climbed into Matt's whirlybird.

"Take her to H.U.P.," I yelled into the cabin; and the 'copter took off, heading for the city.

· · ·

I was left with an FBI agent, Max and *Larke*. The name tag on the agent's jacket said "NARKIN", so I thought it appropriate to stick out my hand and say: "O'Brien".

"I know who you are," said Narkin. "Ayers told me a few things about you."

Narkin was about my size and age. He looked fit. He gave me the impression of competence – without a sense of humor. "You're here to help me with Max, right?"

Narkin smiled and held up a small olive green kit, with a red cross on it. "Indeedy. Where is he?"

"Over this way." Narkin stayed a cautious four steps behind me as I led him to Max.

Max was now whimpering, and the blood on his face and hands were smeared. He'd rubbed at his eyes and made everything look worse than it was.

"Can you hear me, Max?" I said.

"Yes," came a whispered reply.

"This is Narkin. He can save your life if he wants to. It's up to him. Me – I'd leave you here."

Narkin took over. "Here's the deal," he said. "You're going to tell me where the missiles are, and then and only then are we going to give you first aid and get you out of here."

I could barely hear him when he said, "stop my bleeding first. Look at my ribs, man. Here on the right side."

Narkin and I opened Max's jacket and cut away his T-shirt. It was a flesh wound, a graze; and it had almost stopped bleeding. I'd had injured ribs before, knew they hurt like hell – beyond all reason; and Agent Narkin tried a slightly different approach to Max.

"You're going to bleed out – if we don't do anything," he said.

"So fix me. Please."

"Talk first. Where are the missiles?"

"Please. It hurts so much."

Narkin got out a large bandage, a roll of tape and a tube of antiseptic – and held them up in front of Max, shining his flashlight on his handful. "This goes on as soon as you talk," he said, "otherwise we leave you here and you bleed out. They say it's not a bad way to die. It's like going to sleep." He waved his hand in front of Max's eyes again.

"Okay. What do you want?"

"Where are the missiles? The two Anzas. The Mk-1's. Where are they?"

"I don't know," said Max, through his bloody lips and gritted teeth.

"If you don't know anything, then you're not worth anything to us," said Narkin. "Think hard. Where are the missiles? Have you seen them?"

"Yes. I saw them on Chester Island. I helped dig them up there."

"Have you seen them since?"

"Yes. But I don't know where I was. 'Bama blindfolded me the only time I was there. Please – treat me now."

"What is 'Bama going to use them for?"

"I don't know. He said we'd be rich, though."

Narkin and I looked at each other. "Ayers will get it out of him," he said. "Let's clean him up."

I helped apply the bandage, ointment and tape to Max's right side; and then we worked on his face. "Weapon explode on him?" Narkin said.

"I got lucky and hit the M4. It's over there." I picked up the ruined carbine. It had pieces of metal and plastic missing from its stock.

"Nice shooting," said Narkin.

"I missed. I was trying to kill him."

"Let's get him to the 'copter site."

"Then what?"

"We put him in the chopper and you go talk to Ayers."

"You're really here to babysit me, aren't you?"

"I am here to make sure you go see Ayers. Isn't that what you were going to do anyway?"

"I've got to get my sailboat off this island. She can't stay here in the dark."

"Fine. No problem. I'll go with you."

"Ayers doesn't trust me – does she?"

"Look O'Brien. I'm just doing my job. I don't know what Ayers thinks about you. If I had to guess, though, you're so pissed off about your girlfriend that you might do anything. Hell I'd feel the same way. You look to be capable of acting on impulse – doing something unpredictable. But your girlfriend is safe. Now we need to worry about two missing Pakistani surface-to-air missiles. Ayers calls the shots. Agreed?"

"Agreed," I said.

So we loaded Max into the helicopter when it returned; and we told the agents inside the 'copter that Max did not absolutely need to go directly to a hospital. Then I showed Narkin how to stay out of my way while we motored *Larke* back to the Boat Club. While I steered, Narkin talked to Ayers on a cellphone that looked a lot like mine, but likely had a lot of fancy Bureau security apps loaded on it.

"Ayers wants to meet us," said Narkin. "How does she get through the Club security gate?"

"There's a five-digit code," I said. "It's the last four digits of my social security number and a zero. Ask her if that will do."

"She says she'll see us shortly."

• • •

By the time I'd docked *Larke*, tied her up and walked off "B" Dock with Narkin to the Club's parking lot, two black SUV's were parked next to each other headlights shining out into the River; and Ayers was sitting in the front seat of one of them next to Mike, talking into a cellphone. Narkin gave Ayers a thumbs-up and climbed into the second SUV. I walked to Mike's side of the car, reached into the back of my waistband and handed him his .45, butt-first.

"Thanks," I said.

He sniffed the barrel. "You used it."

"I owe you six – no, seven – rounds. I'm sure the gun saved my life. It's not a cherry, is it?"

"Nope," said Mike, smiling. "It's had some use. Glad to lend it to you. Glad to have it back. Did it kill anyone?"

"No. It tried, though. Have you got a business card?" I asked.

"Yup. Here."

"When all this is over with, I'd like to buy you a drink – or something. Thanks again."

"No problem. It's been a very interesting night – I mean morning."

Then Mike went quiet; and I heard Ayers say, into a phone: "That's too bad. Keep at it." She turned to me and gestured towards the back seat, as in "get in O'Brien."

When I was settled, Ayers got out of the car and climbed in next to me. She sat there for a minute, without saying anything; and I found the quiet and her proximity a little unsettling. Then she spoke. "O'Brien. Ryan. I've got a lot of balls in the air right now; and I'm doing it on not much sleep. I need to know exactly what you've been up to since you got out of this car. Everything. No bullshit. No omissions. And I need to hear it right now.

She pointed a finger at me. "I don't have time to sort through half-truths or any coulda-woulda-shouldas. So. Go."

"Okay," I said. "But first – can you tell me anything about Clemmie?"

Ayers sighed. "Yes. She's at the H.U.P. E.R. She's still unconscious. There's a female agent with her. She's likely been drugged. She should be okay. That's all I know. Now – go."

I told her everything as best I could remember it. She slowed me down at places in the narrative, and asked a question or two; but mostly, she let me talk. She didn't smile when I called 'Bama 'Alphonse'. When I'd finished, she thanked me, and asked: "When did you realize 'Bama was under the I-95 bridge?"

This was the only question I'd worried about on the way to the dock; and I gave her an answer I considered not quite dishonest. "By the time I pulled away from the dock – heading out to the Island – I'd figured it out. It seemed like I could likely get to him faster than anyone else. So – like I said – I hid on the railroad bridge and shot his motor.

"I'd turned my phone off so he wouldn't hear it, and I was so charged up when I overheard his phone call to Max that I didn't think of anything except getting to Clemmie and staying alive while I did. Did I screw up?"

Ayers looked at me with a look that was, at best, ambiguous, and at worst, was an estranged and skeptical look, a disbelieving countenance, an expression that implied the imminent use of handcuffs or at a minimum, the loss of the companionable we're-all-on-the-same-team camaraderie that I'd likely only imagined anyway; and when she finally spoke she did the Sherlock thing, enumerating her hypotheses with respect to my actions – and she was right on.

"Here's what I think. I think you realized 'Bama was under the bridge when you were in the back seat of this car. I think you didn't tell me because you put together a contingency plan that was concerned only – only – with Clemmie. In that regard, it was a pretty good plan. As far as capturing 'Bama – I mean Alphonse – or finding the missing missiles, it was a bust. And it's really my fault. One of the four-hundred thousand rules we have at the Bureau is not to involve people with emotional connections in our ops. I shouldn't have used you the way I did. It's all on me."

"Does that mean you didn't find 'Bama where I said he'd be?"

"We didn't find him at all. We did find a boat with a motor that'd been shot by a .45. It'd drifted up the Creek and into the mud in the Tinicum Wildlife Preserve. No sign of 'Bama. We're towing the boat. We'll examine it for evidence when it's light out."

"Is there anything I can do?"

"What would you do next if I said no?"

"I'd get myself to the hospital to see how Clemmie is doing."

"And that is exactly why there's nothing more you can do for me. You've got Clemmie on your mind. Good for you. Bad for me. I hope some guy gets Ayers on his brain someday like you've got Clemmie on yours. In the meantime, unless you might know where Emily is – you're free to go."

"Emily's gone?"

"Yes. She got out of this car, walked towards the River and disappeared."

"Did someone pick her up?"

"No. There was absolutely no chance of that. We had Matt overhead, a boat in the water and two cars monitoring. I don't know where the hell she went. Any ideas?"

"I've never gotten on Emily's wavelength. No, no ideas."

"You're free to go then. Mike here will take you to the hospital if that's where you want to go."

"It is. Thanks. I'm sorry if I screwed anything up."

"Don't disappear. If I call you – answer."

As she got out of the car, Ayers punched me lightly on my shoulder and looked at me meaningfully. I guess, if anything, she looked disappointed in me, like my Pops did a few times during my high school career. I hated that look. I climbed into the front seat with Mike. I was free to go.

NEMO ME IMPUNE LACESSIT
CHAPTER THIRTY-NINE

It was 4:45 a.m. when Mike, his SUV and I watched the Club's chain-link security gate rattle open to let us out. By habit, I glanced over to where *Larke's* trailer was parked.

"Wait here a minute," I said to Mike. I jogged over to the trailer and lifted the tarp on Emily's motorcycle. It was still there, handsome as ever – a gleaming drop-in from the past. I suppose it was as much Emily's time machine as *Larke* was mine. Looking at the Royal Enfield gave me a just-in-case idea; and I jogged back to Mike.

"Got a pen and a piece of paper I could use?"

"Glove box for the pen," said Mike. Then, "write on this." It was the blank side of one of his time and expense sheets.

I block-printed a note to Emily. My cursive is close to illegible, even to me. It read:

EMILY: CLEMMIE AT HUP, DRUGGED & UNCONSIOUS BUT MAYBE OKAY. MY CELL: 610-555-1212. AYERS LOOKING FOR YOU.

SAFE HOUSE IF NEEDED (SAY YOU'RE CLEMMIE'S
SISTER, MY FRIEND). ASK FOR SISTER ALBERTA OR
REVEREND JONES.

Then I drew a crappy little map – more a sketch – to the
Church of Jesus Christ is Lord; and I placed the note in the
Enfield's pannier, alongside the key and replaced the tarp.

"What's that about," asked Mike, when I was back in the car
and we were through the gate and heading toward the City.

"Note to the Dockmaster," I said, acknowledging to myself
that I was lying, but rationalizing that it was for Mike's own good.
"I want my trailer moved to a different spot when he gets a
chance."

"Where to now," asked Mike.

"The hospital."

"Right."

And in twenty minutes, I was at the H.U.P. E.R., and a petite
FBI Agent block-lettered BRIGGS was politely telling me that
Clemmie was still unconscious, that she was being admitted to the
hospital soon, that a battery of bloodwork had been started to
determine how to treat her and that I had zero chance of seeing
her. I gave Briggs my cellphone number; and she promised to call
me – contingent on Ayers's blessing – if anything changed.

"Where to?" asked Mike, when I got back to the SUV – which
had been idling in the empty "Ambulance Only" lane.

"I guess I'll collect my dog and call it a night – I mean
morning."

"I'm beat," said Mike. "My partner's pissed that she missed all
the fun. I'll take her to breakfast and spend an hour swearing her
to secrecy and then tell her all about it."

We drove back to the Delancey Street condo where much of the
excitement had started. Smokey did her happy-to-see-me thing;

and I decided to walk her the seven blocks back to our apartment. Mike and I said our goodbyes and promised to stay in touch. The sun was on the verge of climbing over the buildings to the east, and the city was starting to stir. Lights were on, and people were up and getting ready to go to work.

Work. Today was to be my first day at Howell & Barrett. I was due there in two impossible hours. I was pretty sure that Sam didn't want me there in the condition I was in and I texted him a quickie:

> All-nighter with FBI
> Should sleep – not work
> Details later – Ryan

Just as Smokey and I started up the exterior stone steps to our apartment, my phone rang. It was up-and-at-'em Sam.

"What are you allowed to tell me?" he said.

"Ayers told me to keep it close, but you're 'close', right?"

"Your call."

"Okay. Clemmie was abducted by 'Bama. He's the guy with the missiles. He wanted to trade her for Emily. Emily's in the wind. 'Bama got away. We got Clemmie back. She's unconscious from being drugged. If you have any pull at H.U.P., use it for her please. I shot someone. He's alive. I'm very tired. I shouldn't work today. Okay?"

"Certainly. Thanks for sharing. You've been very concise, very – succinct. Anything else?"

"One thing. The guy I shot said that they'd be rich because of whatever they were going to do with the missiles. If you can figure that out what that means, you'll be six steps ahead of me – and a few ahead of the FBI. It was 'Bama – whose name is actually Alphonse Rosewater, by the way – who told him that. He didn't know what it meant. He was out of it when he told me that. He'd had a carbine explode in his face."

"I'll think about that. 'Alphonse Rosewater'. Okay Ryan. I've got friends at the hospital. I'll check on Clemmie for you. Call me at three o'clock."

"Right. Thanks. I'm sorry I'm not going to be at work where I'm supposed to be."

"I'm not sure you're supposed to be there, Ryan. That's for you to figure out. Bye."

• • •

After five hours of sleep, a fast, inadequate breakfast of toast, cold cereal and juice and a quick dog-walk, Smokey and I drove to the hospital, circled University City blocks on annoying one-way streets in an ever-widening gyre and finally parked in an alley eight blocks west of the hospital in the student ghetto. I cracked the car windows, told Smokey I'd be back soon and ran to the hospital. It was one staircase, two long corridors, two elevators and three double swinging doors before I got to the nurses' station on the floor where Clemmie was supposed to be. I felt like Hansel without the bread crumbs I'd need to find my way out of the place. Now where was Gretel?

"Sir," said a nurse behind an elbow-high counter topped with computer monitors and assorted electronic gizmos. "Sir, you can't go in there."

"I'm looking for Clemmie Olsen. I'm Ryan O'Brien, her boyfriend. These are visiting hours. Right?"

"I'll get someone to talk to you," said the nurse, making a brief phone call before disappearing.

The big difference between the FBI agent that appeared at my elbow and all the others I'd seen in the last twenty-four hours was that this agent was not armed, or wearing black cargo pants, boots and a jacket that said "FBI". She was wearing civvies and a white lab coat that said "FBI". She introduced herself as Doctor Nagano when she looked up at me and shook my hand with a firm, one-two, up-and-down and done, no-smile, I'm-all-business attitude.

"Agent Ayers told me to expect you," she said, with the specificity, inflection and literalness that sometimes indicated English-as-a-learned-in-school language – learned perfectly, of course.

"How's Clemmie? Can I see her?"

"I am afraid not, Mister O'Brien. She is likely going to be fine, but she is still unconscious. The hospital is still running toxicity tests to determine exactly what drug or drugs were given to her. Her vital signs are all good, she is breathing without assistance, and she seems comfortable. She is essentially – asleep."

"What is your role in her care, Doctor Nagano?"

"I am only monitoring her condition. We – that is the FBI – believe she likely has information that will be valuable to us in the ongoing investigation."

"So you are basically waiting for her to wake up so you can question her."

"Yes, but it will all be under the supervision of the hospital; and I must say, that in my professional opinion, doctors here are providing very attentive care to Ms. Olsen. Is she a celebrity of some sort?"

I thought of Sam, and declined to answer the question. I asked another: "Is there progress in the investigation?"

"I do not know. I am only involved in this aspect of it. Agent Ayers has asked me to request that you call her when we are finished here. Perhaps she has information she will share."

"So there's no chance I can look in on Clemmie?"

"Not and have me keep my job. I value my job very much."

"Alright. I'll call Agent Ayers from outside – where I'm allowed to use my cellphone."

• • •

I had just retreated through the first set of double doors, when I was tapped on the shoulder. "Ryan O'Brien?" It was another white lab coat, this time with "H.U.P." in blue block letters and "R.L. Stevenson, M.D." embroidered in fancy red cursive. It belonged to one of the taller men I'd seen this side of a basketball court.

"Yes," I said, looking up.

"Great," he said, enfolding my right hand in his and smiling. "I'm Richard Stevenson, friend of Sam Barrett. I think the world of Sam. He apparently thinks the world of you. He told me to keep an eye out for you."

"So Sam really does know everyone in the City," I said. This seemed like good news to me. Maybe I'd learn something about Clemmie. "I didn't learn much from Doctor Nagano – I mean Agent Doctor Nagano."

"She was just doing her job as she was instructed but I don't have the same constraints as she does. Let's sit for a few minutes. This is not exactly my department – I'm a cardiologist – but I've been keeping up with the Chief Toxicologist on this. He's been instructed by the FBI to keep his findings quiet, but I have not been so instructed. I hitchhiked onto this case because occasionally there are heart-related issues."

We sat in the only two chairs in the dead-end of a corridor, next to two elevators; and between the occasional arrivals and departures of nurses, doctors, staff, patients and visitors, we talked. Or rather he talked and I listened – hearing many words I'd never heard before.

"Your girlfriend has been drugged with one of the flunitrazepams, probably Rohypnol – called 'Roofies' on the street. It's likely been administered orally – she has no evidence of needles or suppositories. It is illegal in the United States, although sold by prescription in many countries. Organized crime is the major supplier here. It causes what we call anterograde amnesia – she won't remember what she's experienced while under the influence. It one of several 'date-rape' drugs, but expensive enough to be rarely used for that. She does not appear to have been sexually abused."

"When will she regain consciousness?" I asked.

"She should have begun to awaken already. Flunitrazepam has a half-life of eighteen to twenty-six hours. According to the FBI, she was delivering cogent text messages as late as 12:30 a.m. this morning and was found unconscious at about 2:30 a.m. So that makes the time of drug-administration – let's see, over twelve hours now. She should be showing signs of awakening. However, she is not. H.U.P. doctors have taken a great interest in this case. There are three current operative hypotheses: 1 – that there is some time-release aspect to this that we haven't found, 2 – the drug has been combined with some other drug – of unknown pharmacology – that induces a longer-term coma-like state."

"You mentioned three hypotheses."

"Yes. Well. The third is simply one of those 'other' categories. Such as the drug is having an unusual effect on this subject – I mean this person, your girlfriend, Clemmie Olsen – because of some personal reaction to it. Perhaps there's something in her individual chemistry that has caused this – something unique to her."

"Thank you for all this information. I guess I'll just have to sit tight. I'm not very good at that. In fact, I am terrible at 'sitting tight'."

"I understand. I wouldn't be either if I were you – if it was my wife or daughter in there. I will promise to call you if we learn anything. Your cell?"

After I gave him my cell number, I warned him the FBI was likely monitoring it. Then I asked the question I often ask doctors, company commanders, favorite uncles and parents when I'm in a jam: "What would you do if you were me?"

Dick Stevenson, M.D., so far merely precise and factual – the epitome of medical objectivity – stunned me. He stood, towered over me and spoke, blue eyes blazing. "The Stevenson Clan motto is no help on this one – it is 'Heaven, not Earth' – whatever that means. Fuck that. Better the broader Scottish slogan – which is really more of a promise. It is 'nemo me impune lacessit' and it means 'no one assails me with impunity', or maybe 'who dare meddle with me' or simply I'll get even. I'd find the bastard or bastards who did this and kill them."

"I already know who did this," I said.

"Well then. You're halfway home. Sam told me a few things about you. And don't worry. I won't give you such advice over your phone."

• • •

I retrieved Smokey from the car and walked her the six blocks to the heart of the Penn campus. The bench in front of Ben Franklin was occupied, so I shoed three pigeons off Ben, he winked at me in thanks and I followed Smokey up Locust Walk, opting for a sunny, unoccupied bench at the intersection of Locust Walk and Woodland Walk. Smokey ignored the rampant squirrels and tolerated the female freshmen who missed their own dogs and insisted on loving her. I called Ayers.

"O'Brien."

"Agent Ayers. I'm checking in as instructed."

"How is Clemmie?"

It might have been the lack of eight hours of sleep, worry about Clemmie or just a bad mood on my part, but the question pissed me off. "You already know how Clemmie is, Agent Ayers. You have Agent Doctor Nagano reporting to you and ready to begin questioning her the minute she wakes up. What you really want to know is – how I'm doing. You wish to know if I am likely to do anything stupid. You euphemistically term it 'unpredictable'. Too bad for me, I can't think of anything satisfying to do, so I'm sitting here on a bench on the Penn campus, in the sun, on a beautiful early fall day feeling helpless. For all I know, you know exactly where I am and what I'm doing anyway. If you would give me something useful to do – I would go do it."

Ayers laughed at me. That's right – she actually laughed at me. Then she apologized. "I'm sorry Ryan. It's very unprofessional of me to laugh at a time like this. It's just that something in me likes you – in a big-sisterly way probably; and you are truly so very, very unpredictable. There isn't much you can do that will give you what you need – the chance to shoot someone else or exhaust yourself climbing a railroad bridge in the dark. If you are willing, however, you could go to your boat club and meet the agents who have been looking for traces of 'Bama – I mean Alphonse. Apparently you are as familiar as anyone with Darby Creek and the channels, bridges and possible escape routes he might have taken. The agents are due back at your club in about an hour. Watch for their boat. They have maps, charts, a special Bureau version of Google Maps on a big screen and even dogs available – but so far they've found nothing."

"I'll do it," I said. "I'll leave for the Club as soon as I get back to my car. But you probably already know where it's parked and how long it will take me to get to it, how the traffic is running, and what I've had for breakfast."

"Ha."

"You don't deny it, do you Sis?"

"I promise to call you if I think there is any information I can share with you. And don't call me 'Sis' in front of anyone in the Bureau."

"How carefully worded. Bye."

• • •

I sat for a minute, almost calling Sam on my cellphone. But then I thought better of it; and I borrowed one from Smokey's current admirer – a pert brunette freshman who was happy to let Smokey's owner use her phone for a brief local call.

"Who's this?"

"It's me, Sam – Ryan. My cellphone is being monitored. Thanks for Doctor Stevenson. He was very helpful. He told me everything the FBI wouldn't and gave me interesting advice. Clemmie's still out of it. I'm going to the West End to assist the FBI. I'm not sure this task is anything other than Ayers giving me make-work to keep me out of trouble."

"Likely. Listen, I've been looking into the money aspect of this. We've found an extraordinary accumulation of short interest in two of the companies located along the River. We're just beginning to examine that in greater detail. I'll let you know if it means anything."

"Right boss."

"Boss. Does that mean you'll be coming to work soon?"

"Probably not this week. Is that alright?"

"I don't want you here with your mind elsewhere. Oh – before I forget. General Christmas called me this morning. He confirmed Sergeant Johnson's flight arrival Sunday. Sergeant Johnson has lost his left arm just below the elbow. Other than that he is physically alright. In the sense that he should be dead, he's lucky. In the sense that he's lost his hand, he's likely to need a friend."

"I'll be there. Let me think about what you've just told me. I suppose it's better news than I should have expected. But somehow it seems awful. Thanks for following up on this."

"No problem. Call me if you need anything. Bye."

DOGS
CHAPTER FORTY

How does a good dog know when a human is distraught, to discipline herself to be solemn – to leave off snuffling at trash, attending to squirrels or even walking in other than proximate and earnest fellowship with the creature she possesses; and he pondering, confused by darkling winks of half-thoughts flitting overhead like bats streaming from a cave at dusk – of Sergeant Johnson without a left wrist for his Suunto, of Clemmie Olsen slumbering in a hospital bed, of her nutty sister AWOL, of a scarred and vengeful Max and of someone worthy of killing named Alphonse Rosewater?

And how does a good dog know that a gentle chin placed on the right shoulder of the unleashed and distracted person she owns, while he drives, inattentive, the car knowing the way, that that warm chin will bring a right-hand caress and a change of attention to people, things and dogs warranting affection or respect: Agent Ayers, Uncle Ryan, Sam Barrett, Sam Smyrl, Sister Alberta, Jameson Jones, Nashir, *Larke*, Clemmie, and of course, Smokey herself – the all-knowing, resurrected totem of innocence, loyalty and wisdom?

And so I arrived at the West End Boat Club less likely to risk everything to accomplish an obligatory killing of someone, and more willing to consider the sum of all that had happened since Smokey and I made our thoughtless night-time reconnaissance of Chester Island. Uncle Ryan always counseled me to consider "the big enchilada" – even though he himself did not always do so. I remember he laughed at me when I called his advice a manifesto – and I knew I both owed him a call and wanted to hear his voice before the day was over. So occupied, I did not look for Emily's Royal Enfield upon entering the Club grounds, but drove straightaway to the dock area and looked for FBI agents.

I didn't recognize the boat – up on a flatbed, ready to be moved – but the Yamaha 225hp motor with a big hole in it was familiar. No one was around, so I figured the Bureau had finished with forensics; and I hopped up on the flatbed to look at the damage Mike's .45 had caused. It was impressive. The round had hit the top of the motor; and there was only an inward .45 caliber pucker there – but the bullet had hit something inside, turned to shrapnel and exited out the motor's port side, leaving a hole big enough for two of my fists. I reminded myself to avoid getting shot by .45s.

The only person around seemed to be a Club member laboring over the Club's ancient pile driver, so I left Smokey outside on the Club patio and went inside and asked the barmaid, Dee, about the FBI. She pointed to the pool room. It was there I found Rizzo, an assistant, and a bank of computers and screens.

Rizzo seemed happy to see me. "Ryan. I was told to expect you."

"Agent Rizzo. You're practically a member here now."

"After this is all over and if I ever get a day off, I'd like to go for a sail, have a drink at the bar, and shoot the shit with the constituents here. Seems like a friendly place."

"I'd be happy to make that happen. Please don't use the word 'constituent', when you're busy shit-shooting, though. What's going on here? Am I allowed to know?"

"Absolutely. Agent Ayers said you were part of the team – that you had valuable knowledge of the search area. Here's where our boat is now." He pointed to the largest screen, where a small icon on a Bureau version of Google Earth moved imperceptibly riverward in Darby Creek. It was set on satellite view; and the clarity of the screen was exceptional. There were add-ons to the program that enabled a nearly-infinite zoom. Humans could clearly be seen repairing the PA 291 bridge over the Creek – in real time, and in impressive detail. I could plainly see one laborer working with a shovel, while five others stood and watched.

Rizzo showed me how to move the view around the landscape and zoom in and out; and I spent the next half hour imagining where Alphonse might have abandoned his boat and escaped. I started by having Rizzo indicate where the boat had been found – stuck in the mud of what was officially called the John Heinz National Wildlife Refuge at Tinicum, and almost two miles from the railroad bridge. Allowing for a two-knot current and assuming that Alphonse had abandoned ship soon after losing his motor, I decided that he must have bailed out between the PA 291 bridge and the small marina that featured a waterfront restaurant with the upbeat name of "A Taste of Key West". The marina and restaurant would have been closed when Alphonse came ashore; and I placed my bet on the marina boat ramp, an easy place for a fully-clothed, wet swimmer to get out of the water in the dark, and I mentioned this to Rizzo. Then I occupied myself by looking at some of the places I'd fished; and I recollected an eight-pound channel catfish here, a tiny first-year striper there and a lure-caught yellow perch by the marina docks.

I noted that the icon representing the FBI boat was approaching the outer docks at the Club, and so I went to meet the boat. I caught the dock line thrown by one of the three agents in the boat and secured it to a cleat. The division of labor on the boat looked like: one skipper, one dog-handler, one supervisor and one dog. The dog was a friendly, calm blond lab named Dora. She was an explosives detection dog – the only kind of dogs the FBI has – and not a tracking dog. But she was what the Philadelphia office had available, and they'd been up and down the banks of the Creek with her, after giving her the opportunity to smell a jacket found on Alphonse's boat. I was invited to go back out with the team, to offer opinions on-site; and they had no objections to Smokey's tagging along.

• • •

The two dogs greeted each other like Rotary Club members; and since they hadn't hands to shake, they settled for a couple of sniffs, a lick or two and got down to business. Dora called dibs on explosives detection and Smokey claimed all-around responsibility for Ryan O'Brien. They sat next to each other in the stern of the boat, facing forward, eyes half-closed against the temporary wind produced by the zoom of the boat – back out into the River and then up the Creek. It was too noisy to talk until we reached the railroad bridges and needed to do the slow-no-wake thing.

"We've already been all over these banks and found nothing," said Supervisor Sid. "What would you suggest?"

"How much time do we have?" I asked.

"The official answer to that is – however long you need. The unofficial answer is that we've been at this since sunup, and gotten nowhere. My suggestion is that instead of some orderly, sequenced approach, you give us your very best one-shot idea. We try that. Maybe we get lucky. Maybe we quit afterwards. Okay?"

"Sure. In that case, head under the I-95 Bridge, stay close to the port bank and slow down near the boat ramp."

Nearing the ramp, we looked up at the surroundings. We saw boats on trailers, chain link fencing, a parking lot with several cars in it, a restaurant and an old-fashioned phone booth. "If I had to make one, and only one, guess, I'd go with the hunch that Alphonse exited the water up that ramp, saw the phone booth, called and had someone pick him up – over by that gate. If he did, maybe the phone company can find out who he called."

"It's worth a shot," said Sid. "We know about when the call would have taken place."

So we tied up on the dock next to the ramp. A still-spry Dora leapt up on to the dock, while Smokey dropped off into the water – any excuse for a swim. We humans followed the dogs and saw Dora declare the area free of explosives and Smokey bring me a stick. Neither dog showed an interest in the phone booth when Sid walked to it, opened the folding door and wrote down the phone number. He took a couple of photos with his phone – of the booth, the roads, and the rest of the marina; and he sent them to Ayers with a text suggesting she have someone check with the phone company. He likely called it a long-shot.

On the way out of the Creek, before we reached zoom speed, Sid answered his phone. I could only hear his half of the conversation.

"Yes. He's still here. On the boat. So's his dog. It was his idea. Same number? Tell him? Are you sure? Okay. Out.

"Agent Ayers says that your idea was a very good one. There was one phone call made at 2:17 a.m. The call was made to the same number we traced to the female who called us when we were sitting in Mike's car – planning to trade Emily for Clemmie. The phone was a prepaid burner, so we didn't learn much there; but we placed 'Bama – I mean Alphonse – at that marina and connected him to an accomplice. Ayers says 'good work'. She says that if you think of anything else, tell me."

• • •

I basked in Ayers-praise for a nanosecond, and then decided to clean up *Larke*. She was still muddy from the morning's doings on Little Tinicum. After the hosedown, I sat on *Larke's* cabin top and looked out at the River, while Smokey chewed on the stick she'd taken from the marina. Watching the river always soothed me in a way I could not explain, even to myself. The River was always there, a constant, always doing the very same thing. The tide was almost dead low, and would soon be incoming. Tidal rivers are eccentric; and if I threw Smokey's stick into the River and prevented her from retrieving it, the stick would float upriver for the next five and a half hours, then downriver for seven. The progress the stick would make to the Atlantic Ocean would be slow, ten miles a day, maximum, and take a month or so to complete the journey. The two steps forward, one step back nature of the tidal River reminded me of my own life.

Just as I was about to solve the riddle of being human, Jack Walker wandered out to *Larke* and told me I had a phone call. He handed me his own cellphone, saying that the caller had called the Club's land line, asked for me, asked about the FBI; and, at Jack's suggestion, redialed Jack with the promise he'd hand me his phone – away from the noisy bar and the FBI. "It's a guy," said Jack, turning away to give me some privacy.

"Hello?"

"Pilgrim?"

There was no mistaking the voice. "Jameson!"

"Yes. Sorry for the secrecy, but there's someone here at the Church. Says she knows you. Says she's Clemmie's sister. Says she's 'Emily'. Says you gave her my name and this address. Came on a noisy motorcycle. Got the kids all excited. Emily – if that is her name – asked me to call you. Told me not to use your cellphone. Does any of this make sense?"

"Yes. May I talk to her?"

"She'd like to see you, if that's possible."

"I'd be happy to drive on down. I owe Nashir some reading anyway."

"She says not to drive here. She's afraid you'd be followed. She's pretty insistent."

"She's always insistent. I think I'm sorry I gave her your address."

"Nevertheless. Here we are talking."

"How am I supposed to get there if I'm not allowed to drive? I've got Smokey with me."

"I suppose you might prevail upon the only pastor you know in the City of Chester to pick you up."

"Would you do that?"

"Yep. Sister says I owe you for getting that citation fixed. Maybe she's right. I'll pick you up in front of that park in Tinicum. What's its name?"

"Governor Printz Park."

"Twenty minutes."

"Right."

I wasn't at all sure it was a good idea to get involved with Emily; and I considered calling Ayers. But I knew Ayers wouldn't let me do anything meaningful, and the thought of Clemmie in a hospital bed vetoed that idea. It was a five minute walk to the Park, so I invested the next ten minutes in checking in with Rizzo, asking about Clemmie, about Max and acting like I was ready for assignment.

"I'm not in the Clemmie loop," said Rizzo, "so I don't know how she's doing. Max is going to be fine. Ayers confirmed that he is an idiot and likely knows nothing much about what Alphonse has planned. Apparently Max has been blindfolded whenever Alphonse took him anywhere important. There's nothing much for you to do here."

"I'm going to walk my dog, then," I said.

Outside the Club, on the way to the Park, I called Doc Stevenson, to get a Clemmie-update. I guess I won the talk-to-a-busy-doctor lottery, since he answered my call.

"O'Brien. I'm glad you called. There's nothing at all new on Clemmie Olsen, but I wanted to talk to you anyway."

"Sure. What about?"

"I'm a little concerned that I might have been wrong when I encouraged you to murder someone. That was highly unprofessional of me."

"I appreciated your thoughts. Whatever I do, it's on me, not you, Doc."

"Good. Now I want to rephrase what I said to you anyway. Since we're having such a hard time figuring out what Ms. Olsen was given to induce her coma, I would not kill her abductor – at least not right away."

"Why's that?"

"Because I'd want to know what drugs he used. So I'd get that information out of him, then I might kill him."

"Remind me not to get on your bad side, Doc."

"Little chance of that, Ryan. By the way, Sam wants you to call him when you get a chance. He says to use his work land-line. Ask for his secretary – Sue."

"Thanks much. Please call me if there's any change in Clemmie."

"Will do."

I decided to wait and use the phone at the Church of Jesus Christ is Lord to call Sam. Smokey and I walked to the Park; and Smokey engaged me in a stick-throwing game to keep my mind from wandering off into its darkest corners. When Jameson flashed his headlights at us and pulled over, she herded me into the shotgun seat before laboring into the back seat. She made herself comfortable, decided she'd accomplished all she could with me for the day, wondered if she was getting old, promptly fell asleep, and dreamed of something or other requiring intermittent yips, whines, and leg twitches.

"I'M COMING"
CHAPTER FORTY-ONE

Jameson's faded blue and rust '94 Buick Century 4-door wagon had an automatic transmission, loosey-goosey steering, a noisy V-6 engine and a crack in the passenger-side windshield. I looked over at the odometer – eighty-six thousand and something.

"What? You think I'm dumb enough to own a car someone would steal? With no garage? In Chester?"

"No comment. I'm just grateful for the ride. Thanks for picking me up."

"That odometer's been around at least once that I know of. I'm fond of this car. I can get most of the choir in it. Anyway, you're driving a six-year-old Subaru full of boat stuff, with dents from pulling your trailer."

"Guilty as charged. I am fond of my Forester – she's right after my boat and my dog. And Clemmie, of course."

"How is Clemmie?"

"Not good. Unconscious. Confusing the good doctors at Penn. She should be awake by now – but she isn't."

"How are you?"

"Physically fine – mentally confused. I'm back and forth between letting the FBI handle everything and doing something myself."

"Like what?"

"I don't know. Find Alphonse, I guess. Beat the name of the drugs he's given Clemmie out of him. Turn him over to the FBI before he blows something up. Happily ever after."

"Alphonse is also 'Bama, I take it?"

"Yep. His real name is Alphonse Rosewater."

"No wonder he uses 'Bama. Oh – by the way. Thanks so much for telling Nashir I'd explain that paragraph in the MacDonald book to him – the one about racial equality, the struggle and fifteen percent of Negro America being ready for the Now. In case you don't recognize sarcasm – that was my best effort."

"I didn't know what else to do. I've read MacDonald for years – for the pure fun of it. I have no idea what he was trying to say in that paragraph. I figured you'd screw it up less than I would. What did you tell him?"

"I don't remember. Something about how it had all happened a long time ago. That none of it applied to him anyway. I did end up reading the book, though. Pretty good. In fact, very good. Travis McGee would know where to find 'Bama – I mean Alphonse. He'd know what to do to him, too."

"Yep. Where is he when you need him?"

And so for the twenty minute drive to the Church, we enjoyed each other's company, in that way folks have who like each other – a liking incidental to age or race. It was a different kind of chat I had with Emily after we arrived.

• • •

In the quiet of the warm Church kitchen, Emily thanked me for coming, asked for and got a medical update on Clemmie, hoped I'd not mentioned anything to the FBI, and began to ask me to help her do something about Alphonse.

"The FBI only cares about the missiles," she said. "I understand that. They've got their job to do. But they've got it backwards. They only care about Clemmie as a source for information about 'Bama. They want her out of her coma so she can talk to them – maybe tell them where he is. I want 'Bama so I can get Clemmie awake and back to being Clemmie. How can I convince you to help me?"

"Talk to me, I guess. I'm already half-convinced that I need to do something independent of the FBI – if I can figure out how that would help Clemmie. I spent most of the last week falling in love with her. And I listened to people I respect tell me that they'd give anything for the chance to be involved with something that matters. Well this matters. I've got the rest of my life to sit around and be bored. So I'm already convinced. But I don't know what I can do. I don't know where Alphonse is. And I'm calling him 'Alphonse' because I know he wouldn't like it.

"Most of all, I have no idea if I can trust you. Why should I? I haven't seen you do anything that makes the slightest bit of sense yet. So: talk to me."

I didn't know what I expected Emily to do – maybe look hurt, cry and tell me why I should trust her, or go the other direction and get angry with me and start yelling. But she surprised me. She simply looked at me and said, "I don't expect you to trust me. I wouldn't trust me either, if I were you and you'd seen me pretend to shoot 'Bama, drive my motorcycle a hundred miles an hour and run from the FBI. Frankly, I've been borderline crazy ever since my marriage to Timmy Putnam went south. But it's Clemmie we're talking about here; and she's the reason you should at least listen to me. I love her too. She deserves a lot better than for the two of us to fail to help her because we can't get along.

"And by the way – you're as crazy as I am. I saw you almost get killed over that wristwatch you're wearing. That's truly whacked. Most important: I might know where 'Bama – I mean Alphonse – is.

"He took me to where he's got the missiles stored – only once. I remember where we started, but he made me put a blindfold on in his pickup truck five minutes before we went somewhere by a boat he had waiting for him. I timed all the turns, the boat ride and everything, but it would take someone familiar with Jersey back roads and the River to figure it out – and they'd likely need charts, or satellite-imaging or something."

"In other words, the FBI could probably figure this out pretty fast. Right?"

"Yes. And the FBI will go there and secure the missiles at any cost. Alphonse will not surrender, he'll be killed, and we'll never know what drugs he gave Clemmie."

"Devil's advocate here. If we get both get killed doing something without the FBI's knowledge, then Alphonse shoots off the missiles and Clemmie's no better off. We all lose. We need a backup plan. Someone has to know where we went – and that's if we can figure out where we need to go."

"Any ideas about how we can do that?"

"Yes. That's something we can do. We'll need to go back to the West End, look at their enhanced Google Earth, you need to tell me about the blindfolded turns; and we need to make a bunch of assumptions and try to figure out where you were."

"Will Agent Ayers be there? I bailed on her."

"No. That's why I think we might be able to finesse this. One more thing, though. We'll need a gun. My nearest weapon is back at my apartment. That adds an hour to our timing. I'm not going to ask Jameson for a gun. I don't doubt that he has one, but the Church needs to stay out of this."

"I've got a gun in my motorcycle. The pannier has a false bottom."

"Of course you do. Of course it does. What is it?'

"I don't know – but it's new. Alphonse gave it to me. I'm sure you'll know how to use it. So if we can figure out where he took me, and if we can figure out how to get there, and if we have a way to involve the FBI if we fail – then it's a go. Right?"

"Right. What are the odds? Do the math. Clemmie says you're a genius."

"Clemmie's got all the people skills. It's the thing I'm most jealous of. I've got useless math smarts. That used to annoy Clemmie. Damn it. I just said 'used to' – as in past tense. I mean still annoys her – in her sleep, I suppose."

"Okay. Let's suppose it's fifty-fifty that we can work out where you were with Alphonse. Assume it's fifty-fifty that we can figure out how to get there, fifty-fifty that we don't get shot once we're there, and fifty-fifty that we get the FBI lined up in some contingent way that makes sense. What are the overall odds?"

"None of the odds are really fifty-fifty. But if they were, the quick answer would be – six and a quarter percent."

"In horse racing terms?"

"Approximately sixteen-to-one. But that's very simplistic. Some of the planned actions negate others. If we can't figure out where I was, for example, everything after that doesn't matter. So it's much more complicated than that. I've had courses in logic and statistics that could use this as a case study for decision tree analysis. They'd use words like 'event outcomes', 'hyperplanes', 'lattice-points', 'polytopes' and 'nearest-neighbor-queries'. At the end of the day, we'd still be stuck with what it is we want to do. I'm hoping you trust me enough to at least take the next step."

"I don't trust you, but I want to take the next step anyway."

"Fair enough. Thanks Ryan. I thought you'd be a pain in the ass about this. I thought you'd look at this in some weird way that went with your haircut."

"My haircut?"

"You know – military: Inflexible. Sexist."

"Oh. That. I forgot. You signed up with Alphonse to be a tree-hugger. You believe in global warming, windmills and solar panels. You likely hate the military – the military that you know nothing about. Let's see if Jameson can drive us back to the Club."

· · ·

Jameson could drive us, and he did; and he also agreed to be a small part of our contingency plan. If I failed to call him by midnight, he was to call Sam Barrett. Sam would then call the West End, and ask for me. He would then have the bartender read the message we'd left at the bar for him and then call Agent Ayers and tell her what we'd done. It was a little too complicated, but it wouldn't matter to us by then, since we'd be in serious trouble – maybe dead. I did not tell Jameson anything other than to call Sam, because I wanted the Church of Jesus Christ is Lord insulated from the FBI. We stopped at a pay phone in Essington, and I called Sam and told him what we were up to. I suggested that he not mention to the FBI that he'd known about any of this ahead of time; he agreed. He had some additional news about his research, but said it could wait – that he didn't want to clutter my mind with data. I wondered what that meant.

When we got to the Club, Emily and I walked directly to the room where Rizzo was watching computer screens, monitoring communications and wondering where I was.

"Helluva dog walk," he said.

"I needed to think through some things. This is Emily – Clemmie's sister. She's wondering if there's any news about her condition."

"I'm out of that loop. I'll call Agent Ayers for you if you want."

"No. Don't bother her. Mind if I show Emily the Google Maps? It'll take her mind off her sister."

"No problem."

We sat in front of the giant satellite shot of the area, and I zoomed out, until I had an area about thirty square miles showing – with Chester Island smack in the middle. We laughed a little and tried to act casual for Rizzo's benefit. Emily had a pad of paper and a pen.

"What's the last thing you saw – before the blindfold?' I asked.

"We were in New Jersey, headed north on US 322, until we passed over I-295. That's where he made me put the blindfold on. We soon made a right hand turn, drove for about four minutes and turned left. We weren't going very fast – maybe twenty-five. Then we got on bumpy roads and went even slower."

I zoomed in on the area Emily mentioned and made some guesses as to where she'd been. She had a good memory, and was concentrating hard when I realized I knew where she'd been – at the boat ramp off the Old Canal, the very place where Uncle Ryan and I'd set the camera on the power line tower.

"Okay. Stop. I know where you got on the boat. I've been there. Was Alphonse skippering the boat, or was it someone else?"

"Someone else. A woman. I've never seen her, but I think it was the same woman Agent Ayers put on the speaker phone when we were trying to trade me for Clemmie."

"How long was the boat ride?"

"No more than fifteen minutes. And the last few minutes we were going slow."

"Was the motor loud or quiet?"

"Quiet."

"Okay. An electric motor. Not fast. You're doing great." I zoomed in again, where the Old Canal ran into the River, southwest of Chester Island. "When did he take the blindfold off you?"

"When we were inside a much bigger boat."

"What was it like?"

"It wasn't like any boat I've ever been on. More like a ship. After we went down some steps, it was mostly open space inside. Lots of open space. Steel walls or bulkheads or whatever you call them. Alphonse had it all fitted out with lights, weapons and security gear. And the missiles were there."

"Were they in boxes?"

"No. They were on sawhorses, with lights over them, like someone had been working on them."

"How long did you stay there?"

"About an hour. Then we did the whole thing in reverse. Any ideas?"

I zoomed in on the barge impoundment area just upriver from the Commodore Barry Bridge, on the New Jersey side. It had been dredged out of the River many years before, when environmental regulations hadn't existed. Since then, vegetation in the form of small trees, shrubs and grass had grown on it. Rock piles had been added for stabilization. It was approximately square, with a downriver opening for access. The barges were inside. There were four of them, rafted together with a tender in the middle. They were dredge barges, used to take the spoils away from areas being dredged. The Google scale indicated that they were almost a football field in length. One of the barges had a planked deck over the cargo area. I figured that's where Emily had been taken. I noted the coordinates: 39.82 degrees north, 75.36 degrees west on a napkin, left the curser on the barge and stood up.

"We'll be out there," I said to Rizzo, nodding towards the bar. Emily and I pushed through the poolroom doors and sat at a corner of the bar. I had some things to fight with her about.

• • •

I asked Emily to write the note that we'd leave with the bartender, since her handwriting was much better than mine.

When she'd finished, I looked at it. It was clearly written and succinct. The FBI would be able to follow us with it. Then I began the argument. "I don't think you should come with me."

"What! What are you talking about! I'm coming!"

"Relax. I agree in advance that it's your decision – but hear me out first."

"I don't need to hear it. I'm coming. Clemmie's my sister. You've only know her for a week."

"Just hear me out. Okay?"

"I knew this was too good to be true. You arrogant shit!"

A couple of West-Enders looked in our direction. Most of them smiled. Statements like Emily's were not uncommon in the neighborhood.

"Emily. Please listen. I told you – if after you've heard what I've got to say you still want to come – then I agree."

"I'll listen – but it's only to shut you up so we can get started. Okay. Talk."

"There are three reasons you shouldn't be part of this. First – you'll likely jeopardize the mission. It will be very difficult physically. There's a half mile of rocks and trees, a swim and then a hard climb. Second – if you stay here, we eliminate Jameson's and Sam's involvement, and we make sure the FBI knows exactly where I went. Third – if we both get killed, that leaves Clemmie without a sister or a boyfriend."

"I don't care about any of that. I'm coming. I owe 'Bama personally. Here's a newsflash that no one knows but you – not even Clemmie. I married the asshole – and I'm coming. When are we leaving?"

I looked at her in disbelief. She married the guy. No wonder she was so pissed at him – she was really pissed at herself. "We need to leave as soon as it's full dark. In about forty-five minutes. I'm disappointed, Emily. In your own words, you've been borderline crazy for months. Here's a chance to be a grown-up, to be sane, to do the right thing for both Clemmie and yourself. I hope you reconsider."

"Fuck you, Ryan. I'm coming."

NIGHT RIVER
CHAPTER FORTY-TWO

We left the Club through the side door and the small foyer where smokers were still permitted to fire up cigarettes. We moved Emily's Enfield away from floodlights and she opened the false bottom of one of the two panniers. The gun was a Sig Sauer .40.

She handed it to me, handle first. "Is this an okay gun?"

"This is a very fine weapon," I said. "It's a thousand dollar gun. I'm comfortable with it. Any bullets?"

She reached back into the pannier and found two magazines, each holding ten rounds; and I placed them with the gun, in a large plastic baggie I'd got at the bar. Then the package went into my jacket pocket, zipped shut. Then Emily, Smokey and I walked out to *Larke*, in the thickening dusk. When we got to *Larke's* slip, B-27, Emily and I sat on the finger pier with Smokey between us; and we reviewed what we had planned for the next few hours of our lives.

By the time we finished talking, it was dark. Time to go. I stepped carefully onto *Larke*, pulled the starter cord on the motor. "Cast off those three lines – the two bow lines and the one spring line, then step aboard," I said to Emily over the noise of the motor.

Emily looked at me and decided to argue. "No way. Once I cast off, you'll leave without me. You think I'm stupid?"

"I think you're anything but stupid, but that was not my plan. I gave you my word you could come. You can come."

Emily stood there on the finger pier. "Nevertheless," she said.

I stepped off onto the finger pier. "Okay. I'll cast off those lines. You get aboard and do those other two."

Emily just stood there. "You really didn't plan to leave me behind, did you? You didn't even think of it."

"I'm thinking of it now."

"What about Smokey?" she said.

"What about her?"

"She's not coming with us, is she?"

"Nope. I almost got her killed once. Remember?"

"So she stays here on the dock?"

"Until we get back."

"What if we don't get back?"

"Then someone from the West End will end up with her. Maybe Clemmie will figure it out. Come on. Time to go."

"I think we should leave a note about Smokey. In case."

"Okay. You take a note up to the bar and give it to the bartender."

"You'd leave without me."

"I confess. I would – now that you've helped me think of it. Come on. Get aboard."

Emily uncleated three lines, coiled them carefully on the dock and sat down beside Smokey. She placed an arm over the dog's shoulders. "I'm not coming. You were right all along. Someone needs to stay here. I'll call Jameson and Sam and tell them their part in this is off."

"I'm proud of you," I said, and I meant it. "If something bad happens, take care of Clemmie. Don't let her forget me for at least a week or two."

"I will. Good luck," she said, and I think she meant it.

• • •

The Night River and I were becoming intimate, almost amigos, I thought, as I aimed *Larke* downriver and diagonally out toward the shipping channel. The usual lightshow reflected off the River's dark waters; and after I made sure *Larke's* running lights were working and nothing dreadful and big was headed my way, we crossed the channel and aimed for New Jersey. Once we were in ten feet of water, thirty yards off New Jersey, I switched off the running lights, slowed *Larke* and let the outgoing tide do most of the work. I felt my phone vibrate in my pocket and reached for it, supposing it to be Emily with another mind-change. It was Smyrl. I'd always take a call from him.

"Smyrl! Long time no hear."

"O'Brien. I need to mention a couple of things to you."

"Okay. Shoot."

"You know the video cameras you and your Uncle Ryan set up?"

"Sure. What about them?"

"Have you checked them at all lately?"

"No. Too much other stuff going on."

"Well, we've been monitoring them periodically, and we came up with something today. The one you put on the power line tower showed a boat and three people coming and going."

"When was that?"

"Four days ago."

I realized it must have been Emily, Alphonse and the other woman Emily mentioned. "What do you make of it? Recognize anyone?"

"Well yes. The woman driving the boat is our very own officer

Bardeaux. She's been on sick leave for a week now. No one's heard from her."

"You should tell this to Agent Ayers. She'd want to know."

"I already did. Ayers said to ask you if you could guess who the others were. Can you?"

"When did you call Ayers?"

"Ten minutes ago."

"She told you to call me?"

"That's what I just said. She said you'd be at your boat club and available. Are you?"

I dissembled. "I am available. In fact, I am always available for you, Smyrl. The other two people in the boat were Emily – Clemmie's sister and one Alphonse Rosewater, a.k.a. 'Bama. Exactly what they were up to four days ago, I don't know. I'm fairly certain that Bardeaux was on the phone to Ayers, attempting a kidnapping exchange – early Monday morning."

Smyrl sighed into the phone. "So Bardeaux has gone dark side on us. Too bad."

"I never trusted her, especially since Smokey growled at her. Remember?"

"Yes, O'Brien. I remember. I'd better call Agent Ayers and tell her what you've confirmed. Anything else you can think of I should know?"

"Not right now. I'll stay up late, though."

"Me too. Bye."

I hated to be anything less than honest with Smyrl. I recollected him galoshing to the site of a murder on Chester Island, with me behind him in handcuffs. He'd kept me out of jail on that, and gone out of his way to do so. If I lived through the night, I'd buy him lunch at Walt's.

I knew that Smyrl would call Ayers, Ayers would call me, and I might have to lie to her. Lying to Sherlock was much more difficult than taradiddling to Smyrl. Ayers would ask me, specifically, if I was still at the West End, ask to speak to Rizzo, then ask to speak to Emily, then to me again – and tell me not to move until she got there. I thought that this was likely the most significant hitch in the giddy-up that was my plan of action.

• • •

Then – just then – the whole downriver sky blossomed a bright yellow-orange, backlighting the Commodore Barry Bridge. I automatically counted one-one-thousand, two-one-thousand as I'd been trained to do; and I got to about thirty seconds, before I heard the explosion. The sound was a slow-motion roar, echoing on for about fifteen seconds. Then it went dark – that dark that comes after brightness as ultimate as what I'd just witnessed. Something very big had exploded, five or six miles away, on the Pennsylvania side of the River. I thought of the little river town of Marcus Hook, and wondered if it was still there – and I wondered if Alphonse Rosewater had anything to do with what I'd just seen and heard.

I shut down the motor, let my eyes readjust to the night, and continued to drift downriver. I got the paddle out, to do some steering. After five minutes or so, my phone vibrated again; and I looked at the caller, prepared to ignore Agent Ayers. It was Sam Barrett – another person whose call I'd always answer.

"Sam. What's up?"

"Alphonse just blew up the Marcellus shale processing plant in Marcus Hook. Did you see it?"

"Yes. But how do you know it was Alphonse?"

"One of the two firms we found which had unusual levels of shorted stock – and significant short-term put options to boot – was the company that partnered with Sunoco on the converting the old refinery to a natural gas-processing plant. We did as much looking around as we could, and found a Rosa Wasserman Trust was behind the short sales. Get it? 'Rosa Wasserman' – 'Rosewater man' in German."

"Holy shit! He blew up a natural gas plant with a missile?"

"Looks like. The plant liquefies natural gas so it can be shipped. That's why the bang was so big. I'm looking at it now on TV. It's on every channel. What a mess. Environmentalists have hated the whole idea of the plant for years. So does much of our domestic chemical industry. They want to keep the price of natural gas low. You've probably read about it."

"No, but I did watch the explosion from the River. Bigger than anything I saw in Iraq or Afghanistan."

"Ryan. I've got to call Agent Ayers on this. She's got to know about this."

"Can it wait a couple of hours?"

"No. It can't."

"Why not? Just a couple of hours."

"Remember when I mentioned that there were two companies we'd uncovered with short interest and unusual put option activity?"

"Yes. So what?"

"The other company owns the casino and racetrack across the River from Chester Island. There's usually a thousand people there. That's why."

"Uh oh. Okay. Do what's right. Tell me later what Ayers said. You might have trouble reaching her. She's probably in a helicopter right now. Call Agent Rizzo at the West End if you can't reach her."

"Right. Be safe. You work for me next week, remember?'

"I remember."

• • •

I'd never had more food for thought, as *Larke* and I drifted down the narrow channel that runs behind Chester Island and along the New Jersey shoreline. My recollection of the missile specs was that they were infra-red and heat-seeking, really intended for surface-to-air combat and had a range of a couple of miles. I could see how they might work for a gas plant – with ambient heat and elevated stacks – but not for a casino. Maybe Alphonse had converted them somehow. I recalled that they were about six feet long, weighed about thirty pounds including the launcher. It seemed unlikely that one small boat would carry and launch two of the missiles at the same time. In fact, I wondered if Alphonse and Bardeaux had survived the gas explosion. If they'd fired the missile from across the River, they'd have been about a mile away from the explosion. Whatever the case, even if most of the blast was vertical, it must have given them quite a thrill. Maybe their adrenalin rush would make them less careful the rest of the night.

Larke and I drifted past the southeast side of Chester Island and were approaching the mouth of the Old Canal, when the current began to take us out into the River. I steered and paddled, and managed to reach the impoundment bank, well away from the barges and near some tall trees overhanging the River. I anchored close to shore, where the trees would hide *Larke's* mast; and I waded with a stern line, tying it to one of the trees. Then I muddied up my face and hands, double-knotted my shoelaces, put my cellphone in plastic with the Sig Sauer, clipped a small penlight to my sleeve for use later and began to move along the impoundment. It was about a half mile to where the barges were anchored.

Rocks, scrub trees and briars made for slow going, but provided some cover. I hoped they'd not repaired the mobile radar unit I'd damaged way back at the beginning of everything. I stopped every two minutes or so to look and listen, but I saw nothing of significance and heard only the night noises that belonged to the River. I glanced at Johnson's Suunto – a talisman offering me luck and maybe some of the courage I needed – and noted that it was 3:17 a.m. in Kandahar.

After forty-five careful minutes, I reached the first of the barges. It appeared gigantic in the semi-dark, and I wondered how I could possibly get aboard – it had a freeboard of over ten feet from waterline to top and was sheer and without any obvious handholds. I waited five minutes before edging along the bank until I was adjacent to the next barge in the rafting, and waited, listened and watched for another five minutes. Then I moved along until I was adjacent to the tender; and I saw how I could get aboard the barges, by swimming to the tender, climbing its anchor line and walking across the tethered barges.

Seeing and hearing nothing, I slipped into the water and swam to the tender's anchor line. I was happy Emily had chosen not to come with me, as I looked up at the heavy line arcing up to the bow of the tender. I wrapped my legs around the line from beneath it, slung my wet jacket pocket with the Sig Sauer and cellphone onto my chest and began a slow shinny up, hanging from underneath. It wasn't too difficult at first, where the line was mostly horizontal to the water, but progress was harder as I reached the section that was nearly vertical. It reminded me of a section of the double obstacle course at The Basic School in Quantico, absent the soft mulch underneath to catch me if I fell, and without wise-cracking Marine 2nd Lieutenants competing with me.

I bumped the back of my head on the steel bow of the barge tender, and managed to inch a little higher, retrieve the Sig Sauer and cellphone from my pocket and slide the plastic pack containing them through the opening in the gunwale into which the anchor line disappeared. Free from worrying about losing the gun into the water, I muscled myself onto the deck and lay there, listening. More quiet.

AN UNEXPECTED PLEASURE
CHAPTER FORTY-THREE

Retrieving the gun, ammo and cellphone, I made my way amidships of the tender, and stepped over into the barge I suspected held the second missile. I crept along the deck to the stern, where I found a padlocked steel hatch – no one home, and no obvious way to enter. I moved to the bow and tried to lift one of the deck planks. It was about twenty feet long, four or five inches thick and ten inches wide; and all I managed to do was get splinters in my hands. It had likely been put in place with a hoist of some kind. There were half-inch gaps between each plank, though, and I wondered if I had something to use as a crowbar I might move enough planks to gain access. I was not much concerned with making noise at this point – no one could have padlocked themselves into the barge; and so I walked back to the tender, looking for a lever of some kind. I rejected the aluminum boathook that was clipped to a bulkhead, and found a six foot length of angle iron and some wooden chock blocks.

I manically worried away at the plank decking, moving one plank at a time, using the chock blocks as a lever and working down the whole length of each one before pausing to listen to the quiet. It was noisy, hard work, and by the time I'd moved twenty planks I was drenched in sweat. I shone the penlight's narrow beam down into the dark. The deck of the barge looked to be about twelve feet below me, but it sloped up at a forty-five degree angle where it reached the side – there it was about eight feet below me. I lowered myself through the narrow opening near the side, hung from a plank, and dropped, hitting the steel deck and rolling down the incline. I'd made a lot of noise; and I lay still, listening.

I heard nothing, stood, aimed the narrow beam of the penlight aft into the black void of the barge's deep hull and saw nothing. I walked aft, to where I thought the hatch access would be, and found Alphonse's empty lair. There were three cots, sleeping bags, the remains of take-out food and other detritus. On a sawhorse, with tools scattered around it, was a missile. One missile.

On the steel deck, next to one of the cots were three prescription containers and a syringe. I gave myself a mental high-five, thinking that Clemmie had slept on that cot and been given those drugs. The first container I picked up was a two-year old prescription for Rohypnol – for Alphonse Rosewater, issued from a CVS in Mobile, Alabama. It was empty. The label on the second container read: Depo/methotrexate and had no date of issue or other information. It was half full of a liquid. The third container was for 0.00l mg pellets that said "21-day release"; and it was written by a veterinarian, also from Mobile.

A fucking veterinarian! Alphonse had used time-release capsules meant for animals on Clemmie. I guessed he'd filled them with the syringe with whatever the liquid was and mixed it with the powdered roofies Doctor Stevenson had told me about. On one hand I was terminally pissed at Alphonse for what he'd done, but on the other hand, I'd found what I'd come for and had no reason to stick around. I was free to call the good doctor with the information, Agent Ayers with my location and then scram.

I listened carefully – again to nothing – before getting my cellphone from the plastic baggie in my jacket pocket. The "no service" message appeared after I turned it on, so I moved around inside the barge's hull, looking for a signal. No luck. The barge's steel hull was likely the problem. I returned to the bow, thinking to climb out and make the call from the deck, when I realized that getting out of the barge might be difficult. I couldn't reach the opening in the planks I'd made from standing anywhere, and jumping left me a foot or so short. I secured the phone in a pocket, ran across the deck, up the sloped section and jumped, reaching up with my right hand. I managed to grab the edge of a plank, got a handful of splinters for my effort, dropped to the deck and decided to rethink things.

I came up with the idea of a cot, leaning against the bulkhead under the opening; and I went to get one. Before carrying it to the opening, I scanned the area one more time; and I saw the missile lying there, content with itself in its impersonal mechanical lethality, smug and silver shiny next to its olive-green launcher and bedecked with symbols decaled on in Pakistan, serene in the knowledge that its brother had likely blown up a small Pennsylvania river town, and looking forward – at last – to sending hundreds of grey-haired, slot-machine-playing Americans to Hell. And so I decided to sabotage it.

It would be easy to wreck the launcher – it had a trigger mechanism, moveable sights and bolts holding two tubular sections together. But I reasoned that Alphonse and Bardeaux might still have the launcher from the first missile; and besides, the launcher was just an inanimate object, a tool. The missile was the damnable creature of malevolent intent; and it was what needed to be ruined – and it would be best if the damage I intended to do it wasn't visible.

I looked it over carefully, and felt its smooth, uninterrupted surface. Only its base had possibilities for access, as it had three recessed screws that secured the round base plate. The screws were unlike anything I'd ever seen – each one had three radial slots, each in the shape of a small wing, together forming a triangle. I shone the penlight around on the deck, looking for the tool that might drive the screws. The tiny beam of the penlight covered such a small area, that it took me five minutes to find the drive that I was close to stepping on.

I carefully removed the screws. They were about an inch and a half long. I put them in my pocket and jiggered off the base plate itself, holding it carefully a half inch away from the missile. My light revealed that the plate had three wires – a red, green and black – soldered to it, and that the wires disappeared into the next stage of the missile. Hoping that I was not about to blow myself up, I clipped each of the wires, placed the plate on the deck and looked inside the missile. The other end of the wires ran through a round bulkhead; and I thought that further disassembly might be dangerous. So I replaced the base plate and screws. I put the tools back approximately where I found them, gave the missile a middle finger salute and prepared to leave.

Since I'd sabotaged the missile in a way that might not be noticed, I decided to attempt an invisible exit from the barge – one without moving a cot. This time, I gave the run up the incline and jump my best shot, and managed to grab a plank with both hands. Pulling myself through the narrow opening between deck planks was difficult and noisy, but I managed. I sat on the plank, legs dangling into the dark hold below and congratulated myself for everything I'd managed to accomplish. I was kind of a Travis McGee, wasn't I, reincarnated or stepping out from the pages of MacDonald's last, unpublished novel – incorporating a color into the title, of course. Most of the good colors had already been used in the twenty-one books; and I sat there catching my breath and came up with 'magenta' – a striking color not used; and as I tried to think of the rest of the title – it would be alliterative and clever – I was blinded by a flashlight. It was aimed at my face from about ten feet away; and as I shielded my eyes from the light, I counted four legs and feet.

• • •

"O'Brien," said a familiar voice. Alphonse. "Look who's invited himself to the party Bardeaux. An unexpected pleasure. What are you doing here?"

"Looking for you," I said. "Trying to find out what drugs you gave Clemmie."

"Who knows you're here?"

"Emily, of course. She told me where you were."

"Who else?"

"No one yet." I raised my hands over my head and stood up.

"What do you mean by 'yet'?"

I looked at my watch – the Suunto. "I mean that if I don't call her in an hour and ten minutes," she's to inform the FBI of my whereabouts."

Alphonse and Bardeaux whispered to each other for a few seconds before deciding to kill me.

"Here's what's going to happen, O'Brien. We're going to shoot you, right here. We'll stuff your body back into that hole you just crawled out of. Then we're going to go below, grab the remaining missile and shoot a casino with it. We will then disappear. We can manage all that in about forty-five minutes."

"It's heat-seeking, isn't it," I asked. "How will you hit the casino with it?"

"Taken care of," said Bardeaux, deciding to contribute a little gloating of her own. "I planted three simple infra-red lights on the outside walls of the casino. They're battery-powered and – ta da – on as we speak."

I couldn't think of much to say, but wanted to stay alive as long as possible. Funny how that works – the desire to put off an ugly inevitability. I decided to give talking about something I had in common with each of them; and I tried Bardeaux first.

"I suppose you'd like to know how I disappeared that night in the conference room before you shoot me," I said to her.

"Feel free," she said. "I know it wasn't whatever you called it – 'absentials' as I recall – or you'd be doing it right now. Go on, give me some classic O'Brian mullarky."

"You're too smart for me, Bardeaux. It was indeed bullshit. I simply hid in the drop ceiling that night. Pretty uncomfortable sleep. What were you really going to do to me?"

"You were going to be killed escaping. I was going to tell Smyrl you'd confessed to Marvin's murder."

"He wouldn't have bought it."

"He'd always wonder about me, I suppose. But he couldn't ever prove anything."

I decided to try Alphonse. "I suppose that you want your watch back. Right?"

"Why not," he said, taking one step in my direction and holding out his hand.

I slowly lowered my arms and slipped the Suunto off my wrist. I held it out to him; and he lowered his M4 and stepped between Bardeaux and me. He reached for the bright, shiny object – like a kid having a nickel found in his ear by his grandfather; and I grabbed his jacket front and pulled us both over the side of the barge and into the dark waters below.

• • •

We fell together, me backwards, Alphonse on top; and when we reached the water, I grabbed for his carbine, but he'd lost it in the fall, so I kicked away from him and looked up. Bardeaux was aiming her pistol at me, then Alphonse. She couldn't tell who was who.

"'Bama!" she yelled. "Raise your right arm, so I know who to shoot."

We raised our arms simultaneously. "You bastard Ryan!" I yelled at Alphonse. Then I pointed at him and screamed. "Shoot him! Shoot him!"

Alphonse pointed at me and screamed, "No! I'm 'Bama. Shoot him!"

I knew Bardeaux would soon pick the right one of us to kill, so I made a decision. I dove underwater as if to swim away from Alphonse; and then I reversed direction and swam under him and towards the bow of the barge. I swam as deep as I could and held my breath until even the feeling of ghost bullets in my back was overwhelmed by the need to breathe. I managed to surface quietly, just around the bow from where we'd fallen into the water together. The noise of Alphonse and Bardeaux calling to each other diminished as they worked their way aft in the opposite direction I'd taken. I assumed that a small boat was tied up there and that they were anxious to reach it before I did. If they were going to shoot a missile at a casino, they needed to be quick about it and were not going to waste time looking for me.

The tide had slacked and was just changing to incoming; and I moved along the bow of the barge, to the tender, to the next barge and then swam across to the bank of the impoundment, scrabbled up into the trees and rested. I pulled the Suunto out of my jacket pocket and replaced it on my wrist. It was the bright shiny bauble that had saved my hide; and I looked forward to telling Sergeant Johnson about it.

Then I dug the Sig Sauer out of my pocket, just in case, and powered up the cellphone. My first call was to Doc Stevenson, and I juggled the penlight, the phone and the prescription containers. He answered on the second ring.

"O'Brien. What can I do for you?"

"I know what drugs were given to Clemmie," I said, and I read the labels to him, and told him of my theory of how they'd been administered to her. "Will that help?"

"I'm sure it will," he said. "I'm still at the hospital, and I'll take care of it right away. Did you kill anyone tonight?"

"Nope. I almost got killed myself. I fucked things up pretty good for bad guys, though."

"Well that's good enough, I suppose," he said, before hanging up.

My next call was to Emily, care of the Club bar. The bartender everyone called Stoney answered at a very noisy bar, and he couldn't hear me very well, until I yelled into the phone, told him it was me, Ryan O'Brien, and that I had to talk to the pretty brunette named Emily sitting at the corner of the bar. "Have her come behind the bar and talk to me," I said.

"Emily," I said.

"Ryan. Wait a minute, I can't hear a thing." Then I heard her best drill sergeant voice scream something like: "Everyone shut up! This is an emergency! No shit – a real emergency. I'm sorry to be yelling in your bar – but shut . . . up! I'll buy a round later. Okay?"

"Now I can hear you," she said. "I'm glad you're alive. How did it go?"

"Good. I just talked to Doc Stevenson with the prescriptions Alphonse gave Clemmie. I disabled the missile while Alphonse and Bardeaux were elsewhere. They're going to try to hit the casino with it, but I don't think it will launch. I think they're headed for Chester Island – that was where they intended to take the missile all along. It's directly across the River from the casino. Go tell Rizzo everything I just told you – and show him on the screen where I went. I'd call Ayers directly, but I'm sure she's off looking at the gas plant."

"Will do. Smokey misses you. We're glad you're alive."

"Thanks. Me too."

I sat still for a minute and heard the purr of an electric motor. The sound came from off to my left and seemed to be heading upriver – toward Chester Island and away from me. They'd given up on me; and the sound faded to the normal quiet of the Night River.

I decided I owed Smyrl a call, but he didn't answer; and so I left him a voicemail summarizing things. Since he was officially still on the hook for solving Marvin's murder, I told him that Alphonse was in the general vicinity of Chester Island, in a small boat with an electric motor, Officer Bardeaux and a missile that I'd sabotaged. Then I ran out of people to call and things to do; and I decided to sit still, be safe and watch the show.

I Am A Dreamer
Chapter Forty-Four

I expected that the show would be something fast, competent and loud, maybe with bright lights, helicopters and boats; and I looked forward to being nothing more than a spectator. When it was over, I'd take *Larke* back to her berth at the West End, give Smokey a hug and take Emily to see her sister. The sound of a helicopter from over my left shoulder, downriver, would likely be the start of it. My phone vibrated.

"Agent Ayers."

"Ryan. Where are you?"

"Safe. Technically I guess this is New Jersey. I can make out Chester Island from here. I think I see your lights. That is you in the helicopter. Right?"

"Yes. Tell me about the missile. I don't like the Ryan to Emily to Rizzo to Ayers whisper-down-the-lane. So, from the horse's mouth: where is the missile and what did you do to it?"

"It's an Anza Mk-1, it's probably already on Chester Island, taken there by Alphonse and Bardeaux in a small boat. I sabotaged it."

"What did you do to it? Exactly what did you do to it?"

"I took the base plate off and cut three wires – a red, a black and a white. Then I put the plate back on."

"Anything else?"

"Not missile related. Is there anything you want me to do?"

"No. Absolutely not. Do not do anything. Stay wherever you are until I call you. Got it?"

"I do. Staying put. Spectating. Hope to enjoy the show."

"This isn't a show Ryan. In case you've forgotten, Anzas are surface to air missiles and I'm in the air and Alphonse is on the surface; and I'm relying on a grunt just out of the Marine Corps to have sabotaged an old model Pakistani missile. In fact, I'm about to bet my life on it, and the lives of four other Agents. I'm concerned. Bye."

Ayers had made it clear that I was not part of anything operational, that I was to stand or sit by and do nothing; and so I watched the helicopter's flashing lights move toward the Island. I wished it was daylight so I had a better view of events. The chopper and its blinking lights crisscrossed the Island in a search pattern, and then hovered near the edge facing the main River, and the casino – not far from where I'd started the swim on the night that started everything for me.

I wondered what the FBI tactical approach would be; and I wished I could see in the dark. Even though the missile itself was buggered, Alphonse and Bardeaux still had other weapons – a carbine and a pistol; and I strategized a chopper landing away from the missile, then a tactical surrounding of the site. Then the helicopter's brilliant floodlights beamed straight down at the grassy Island. Abruptly they were extinguished; and a momentary dazzling white light, followed by a loud boom brought me to my feet.

• • •

Good Lord. The missile had fired. I hadn't sabotaged it. Alphonse had blown up the helicopter with it. Ayers! She'd bet her life on my handiwork and lost it. I took off, scrabbling through the rocks and brush, to *Larke*, my promise to Ayers to stay put no longer mattered. I decided to follow my instincts, to the Island; and I had *Larke* under way in a wet, panicky flurry of line-untying and anchor pulling.

Heading toward the Island, I remembered that the tide was incoming, but low – and that the shallows my side of the Island would cause *Larke* to run aground fifty yards or so from shore. I also realized that my motor was making its usual noise, and could be heard from the Island. I shut it down, listened and drifted toward the shallows on Chester Island's south side. Just then, I heard the quiet purr of an electric motor, headed my way; and I got out the Sig Sauer and chambered a round.

Larke's running lights were off, and I knew that her black hull would be close to invisible. I inched forward and lay prone on her deck and listened to the boat approach us, my pistol extended and resting on the deck, under the bow rail. The boat was almost on us, when I heard Alphonse call out in surprise – "holy shit" – as he veered to avoid ramming us. I fired at the boat, at Alphonse, at the electric motor; and I used all ten rounds from the magazine and ejected it.

As I rolled on my back to access my jacket pocket and the other clip, Alphonse returned fire; and I heard the unmistakable phut-phut-phut of a silenced carbine. This was very bad, in that I was outgunned, but good, in that the muzzle flashes gave me a target. We fired at each other across the dark waters for a minute. I counted nine rounds from my pistol, and kept one in reserve. I decided to scrabble back down into *Larke's* cockpit; and as I scrambled over her cabin top, Alphonse shot me.

I fell into the cockpit in pain and the beginning of shock. I was hit somewhere in my left side, under my armpit. It hurt like hell, and when I felt the wound, my right hand came away bloody. I lay still, trying to think of what to do, my brain foggy with the intense pain. Then I felt a slight nudge at *Larke's* port side and a gentle rocking, as Alphonse reached a hand over the coaming – he was coming to finish the job.

"O'Brien," he whispered, "where are you? I'm sure I shot you. Are you already dead? I need to borrow your boat. You ruined mine."

• • •

I lay still, Sig Sauer aimed with two shaking hands at the empty space above Alphonse's hand. I was heading for a dream state from pain and loss of blood; and knew that if he waited me out, I'd soon be dead. But he couldn't wait, didn't wait, and surged up over *Larke's* port side, screaming. He held the carbine in his right hand, and it saved me, because as he swung it around to shoot in my direction, I shot him – in the face; and he collapsed on top of me in a bloody mess.

The horror of his mutilated face gave me the adrenaline I needed to get myself out from under him and the insight to know I was going to bleed to death next to his corpse if I didn't do something. I felt my left side and the sticky blood welling from the wound there. I managed to get my jacket off, wad it into a ball and press it against the wound with my left arm. It seemed to help, but I knew I'd soon pass out, and so I stretched a bungee cord around my chest and left arm – jamming the arm and jacket tight against the wound. Then I fumbled for the air horn, the small canister of noise that every boater is required to carry; and I sent three loud blasts out into the dark and passed out.

• • •

I am a dreamer. Not in the abstract sense of imagining alternative realities while awake; but literally, in sleeping visualization, usually of people, places and events that connect only through me – the dreamer, and the actor, author and critic. My dreams include people that will never met, at places they'll never be, doing something they'd often never do; and on the occasions when I remember them, the dreams are comfort to me. I don't know about the whole window-into-the-soul thing, or openings into the primeval cosmic night; but I don't discount much when it comes to dreams.

I am a dreamer. I dreamed of Smyrl, without his galoshes, wondering what I was doing wherever it was we were and telling me to get up, that I was late for something or other and that it was important that I listen to him for a change; and I dreamed of Ayers seeming both angry with me, glad to see me and sad about something, all at once, her telling me that it was time to go from wherever it was we were and that she would see me soon; and I dreamed of Matt the helicopter pilot, flying his chopper in Afghanistan on the outskirts of Kandahar with me as the only passenger, and him motoring away on Emily's noisy Royal Enfield when we landed, and me worrying about IEDs; and of Doc Stevenson, looming over me and congratulating me for killing someone named Alphonse; and I dreamed of Sam Barrett meeting Sergeant Johnson for me and handing him the Suunto, saying that Lieutenant O'Brien had been wounded in action, but was recovering; and I dreamed of my dog, Smokey, waiting on the dock for me at the West End Boat Club, with Emily's arm around her; and I dreamed of *Larke*, with carbine bullet holes in her hull, needing some attention from her neglectful owner; and I dreamed of Uncle Ryan and me, out in a line squall at night, looking for and seeing each other only intermittently, when lightning lit the sky, and me seeing Devlin Meyer and calling to him, naming him

"Travis" as he laughed at me, gave me a thumbs-up and disappeared; and I dreamed of Nashir as an adult, being sworn in at some important ceremony or other, one hand raised un the air and the other hand on *Darker Than Amber* and the Reverend Jameson Jones, Sister Alberta and choir members beaming with pride.

• • •

But I did not dream of Clemmie. As soon as my dream-self understood that she was missing, I woke up – heart-sick and panicky. I was in a hospital room, by myself. I pushed what I thought was the nurses' call button, and a nurse with a nametag stating she was "Blanche" came into the room. She took my vitals, while I thought I'd never met anyone named Blanche before.

"We've been wondering when you'd wake up."

"Where am I?"

"At the Hospital of the University of Pennsylvania – H.U.P."

"How long have I been here?"

"Let me check your chart. Hmm. A day and a half."

"What day is it?"

"Thursday."

I felt around and realized I was hooked up to a bunch of things: an intravenous drip, a morphine pump, a catheter and a heart monitor. "When can I get up? There's someone here I need to see."

"How's your pain level?" she asked, after taking the thermometer out of my mouth.

"No pain. I need to find out about another patient."

"Sit up."

I pushed down on the hospital bed with my hands and sat up – to a horrible shooting pain in my left side. I managed not to scream or whimper, but my face gave me away.

"That bad, huh? I'm not surprised. You're missing a piece of rib. It's going to hurt for awhile."

"How soon can I get disconnected from this stuff?"

"Catheter now, if you want to deal with the pain of moving around. The other stuff – doctor's orders. But you're not leaving anytime soon. You lost gallons of blood."

"Is Doctor Stevenson one of my doctors?"

"Yes he is. He stopped in an hour ago. You were still out. You have a visitor outside waiting to see you."

"Who?"

"Her name is Emily."

Visitors
Chapter Forty-Five

Emily was the first of many visitors I had over the next four days. She told me that Clemmie had just awakened – perhaps at the very same time I had – but was confused and suffering from a young person's version of something called post-coma cognitive dysfunction. Clemmie remembered nothing of the incidents that put her in a coma; she recognized Emily as her sister, but not much else. Emily was visiting frequently, taking care of Smokey and auditing Clemmie's classes for her. The FBI was not charging Emily; and Emily was committed to becoming a responsible grownup.

Smyrl visited and told me he'd been the first to reach me, thanks to Uncle Ryan's video camera, my voicemail to him and the noisy blasts of air horn. He'd had people monitoring the Chester Island camera and saw the explosion and had been on his way by boat to the Island when he'd heard the horn. He believed I would have bled out, if not for Ayers and her helicopter. He declined to say what had happened on the Island, telling me that Agent Ayers should be the one to talk to me about that.

Agent Ayer's visit was one-third pissed-off interrogation, one-third friendly chat, and one-third distracted talking on her cellphone about the goddamn paperwork the FBI mandated to lay the whole affair to rest. She was angry with me about getting myself shot, but happy that I'd managed to prevent Alphonse from getting away. She told me that she'd witnessed Bardeaux aiming the missile at the helicopter and saw it blow up in her face. Apparently I'd only half-sabotaged the missile. Bardeaux died instantly in the explosion; and Alphonse high-tailed it back to his runabout. Nineteen people died in the gas processing plant explosion, and there were over eight-hundred people in the casino at the time it all went down. Casino management wanted to thank me in person when I was feeling up to it. Pilot Matt had asked for me, and wanted me to mention him to Emily, whose motorcycle he coveted.

Doc Stevenson visited me twice, once to congratulate me on killing Alphonse and to report that Clemmie was making enough progress for me to visit in a day or so. His second visit was to remove all the heart-monitors and to introduce me to the surgeon who'd removed splinters of rib from my wound.

Sam Barrett visited every day, laughing as he accused me of doing almost anything, including getting myself killed, to avoid coming to work at Howell & Barrett. He told me that he was rethinking my job there, and had an idea about a more "outside" position for me when I recovered. Howell & Barrett was working with the FBI to unravel the ownership of the Rosa Wasserman Trust and determine what should be done with the profits it had made from blowing up the gas plant. Alphonse had parlayed about six million dollars in margined short sales and put options into thirty-one million dollars; and everyone was trying to figure out who it belonged to and what to do with it. I told him that Emily had married Alphonse; and Sam laughed and said he'd crank that into the equation. He agreed to carry my Suunto to Sergeant

Johnson, just as I'd dreamed it; but he did something even better. He met Johnson's flight at Dover on Sunday, and brought him to see me. Seeing the Sergeant's empty left sleeve brought tears to my eyes, but hearing his deep wisecracking voice, telling me to get the hell out of the sack made me hoot with laughter – until Nurse Blanche shooed them out of my room.

Several West Enders visited in an awkward, blue-collar group, and told me they'd salvaged *Larke* and were repairing her – requiring new members to put in their allotted hours doing the dirtiest of the work. They told me that they missed the excitement of having the FBI around in the pool room, and hoped I'd be back around the Club soon, even if I was a blowboater.

The Reverend Jameson Jones had crammed Sister Alberta, Nashir and half the church choir into his old Buick and they'd visited. The kids were quiet, shy and subdued until I asked them to sing about the tree being planted by the water; and they quietly sang a shortened hospital version of I Shall Not Be Moved. After that, they wanted to hear all about what had happened to me. Jameson had purchased *The Deep Blue Goodbye* for Nashir, telling me that he might as well start at the beginning of it all; and before they left, Nashir read the opening lines to me, while I shut my eyes and listened to familiar words:

> *IT WAS TO HAVE BEEN a quiet evening at home.*
> *Home is the Busted Flush, 52-foot barge-type*
> *houseboat, Slip F-18, Bahia Mar, Lauderdale.*

I called Uncle Ryan and told him about everything that had happened and that his cameras had saved my life. I also told him that I'd dreamed of Devlin Meyer while I was out of it; and that Devlin had been right all along – it was always all about the money. Uncle Ryan prescribed fishing in warm waters, with him, as the very next thing on my non-bucket list; and he agreed to talk to Mom and Pops for me, minimizing my injuries – until I felt up to going home and talking to them myself. I told him that the FBI was considering giving me Alphonse's little runabout; and that if they did, I'd name it the *Munequita*.

I was finally allowed to visit Clemmie. We were shy with each other; and I could tell that she didn't remember much about us. She was as beautiful as ever, and I think I saw a flicker of happy recollection dance out of her eyes when I promised her ice cream for breakfast when we were discharged.

ACKNOWLEDGMENTS

Night River is a work of fiction, and characters, events and incidents are either products of the author's imagination or used fictitiously. The places in *Night River* are almost all real, however, and the Delaware River, Chester Island, Little Tinicum Island, Darby Creek, Aunt Deb's Ditch and the Old Canal, for example, comprise most of the setting of *Night River*.

Three real people have graciously allowed the use of their names: Phil Sheridan, a former Philadelphia Inquirer sports writer who now blogs and tweets about the Philadelphia Eagles for ESPN; Lieutenant General George "Ron" Christmas, USMC (Ret.); and Major Don Davis, USMC (Ret.)

The Pub & Kitchen is a fine restaurant in Philadelphia; and Walt's is a cheese steak mecca and Delaware County, Pennsylvania institution since 1939.

The statue of Benjamin Franklin that sits in front of College Hall at the University of Pennsylvania is inspirational to students and alumni in many ways; and our protagonist is no exception. Ben offers good advice in the Chapter titled SINE MORIBUS VANAE as well as reveals the true motto of the University.

Delaware Valley Orienteering Association, DVOA, is comprised of a few hundred orienteering devotees, bright and enthusiastic folks who have been promoting the sport, making maps and hosting events since 1967. The Sandy, Ed and Mary mentioned are real first names. The author has experienced every travail mentioned by Ryan O'Brien in the Chapter titled *One Bird, One Stone.*

The West End Boat Club, WEBC, is my boat club and where I begin many days of sailing and fishing. On the Delaware River for 120 years, WEBC's membership is made up of 300 or so power boaters, sailors, fishermen (and women), drinkers and some of the most opinionated, argumentative, eccentric and wonderful characters to be found this side of fiction. The membership roundly endorses this book and promises to cooperate with the making of the eventual movie – which they earnestly hope is directed by Clint Eastwood.

Finally, I thank family and friends for their nomination of *Night River* for the Kindle Scout contest, especially daughter Ann and son Hugh. Without Ann's relentless social media campaign, *Night River* might not have garnered enough nominations to be a book, and her careful reading of the book produced a number of important improvements. Without Hugh's proofreading, *Night River* would include numerous typographical errors, and without his careful attention to format and typesetting, *Night River* wouldn't look much like a book.

Made in the USA
Middletown, DE
26 June 2015